Endless Knight

ALSO IN THE ARCANA CHRONICLES

Poison Princess

KRESLEY COLE

ENDLESS KNIGHT

The Arcana Chronicles

SIMON & SCHUSTER BFYR

NEW YORK LONDON TORONTO SYDNEY NEW DELHI

SIMON & SCHUSTER BFYR

. An imprint of Simon & Schuster Children's Publishing Division
1230 Avenue of the Americas, New York, New York 10020

This book is a work of fiction. Any references to historical events, real people, or real places are used fictitiously. Other names, characters, places, and events are products of the author's imagination, and any resemblance to actual events or places or persons, living or dead, is entirely coincidental.

Text copyright © 2013 by Kresley Cole
Cover photo-illustration copyright © 2013 by Aaron Goodman
Photograph of field copyright © 2013 by Blackbeck/Vetta/Getty Images
All rights reserved, including the right of reproduction in whole or in part in any form.
SIMON & SCHUSTER BFYR is a trademark of Simon & Schuster, Inc.
For information about special discounts for bulk purchases, please contact Simon & Schuster Special Sales at 1-866-506-1949 or business@simonandschuster.com.
The Simon & Schuster Speakers Bureau can bring authors to your live event.
For more information or to book an event, contact the Simon & Schuster Speakers Bureau at 1-866-248-3049 or visit our website at www.simonspeakers.com.
Also available in a SIMON & SCHUSTER BFYR hardcover edition
Book design by Krista Vossen
The text for this book is set in Bulmer MT.
Manufactured in the United States of America
This SIMON & SCHUSTER BFYR paperback edition October 2013
2 4 6 8 10 9 7 5 3 1
The Library of Congress has cataloged the hardcover edition as follows:
Cole, Kresley.
Endless knight / Kresley Cole.
pages cm. — (The Arcana chronicles ; [2])
Summary: "Evie has fully come into her powers as the tarot Empress. As one of twenty-two teens given powers following the apocalypse, she knows a war is brewing, and it's kill or be killed"—Provided by publisher.
ISBN 978-1-4424-3667-1 (hardback) — ISBN 978-1-4424-3669-5 (eBook)
[1. Supernatural—Fiction. 2. Ability—Fiction. 3. Prophecies—Fiction. 4. Tarot—Fiction.] I. Title.
PZ7.C673494End 2013
[Fic]—dc23
2013023627
ISBN 978-1-4814-0503-4 (Walmart proprietary edition)

DEDICATED WITH MUCH LOVE
TO MY FAMILY. I'M SO LUCKY
TO HAVE YOU ALL.

ACKNOWLEDGMENTS

Thank you so much to Ralph Miller for all your help with research and for being a dear friend. Many thanks to Jonah T. for saving the day once again with your all-things-Cajun expertise.

And *tusen tack* to Swede, for encouraging me to swing for the fences with this one. . . .

THE FIELD OF BATTLE

During the Flash, a global cataclysmic flare, the surface of the earth was scorched to ash and bodies of water flash-evaporated. All plant life was killed, most animals as well. The vast majority of humans perished, with women hardest hit. Rain has not fallen in eight months.

OBSTACLES

Militias and slavers unify, consolidating power, all bent on capturing females. Plague spreads; cannibals flourish. The Bagmen, contagious zombies created by the Flash, roam the night, thirsting for moisture in any form, even blood.

FOES

The Arcana. Into every dark age, twenty-two kids are born with supernatural powers and destined to fight in a life-or-death game. Our stories are depicted on the Major Arcana cards of a Tarot deck. I'm the Empress; we play again *now*. Death, the reigning victor, won't stop until my blood bathes his sword.

ARSENAL

To defeat him and the others, I'll have to draw on my Empress powers: enhanced healing, the ability to control anything that roots or blooms, thorn tornadoes—and poison. Because I'm the princess of it. . . .

Endless Knight

1

This is what I truly am. . . .

Jackson stumbled back from me, making the sign of the cross. Just as I once predicted.

With that one gesture, he has broken my heart utterly.

—And yet I could not be prouder, Empress— seductive Death whispered in my mind.

I heard him so clearly; he must be close. I had nothing left to lose, no reason to live in fear of him. *Watch your six, Reaper, I'm on the hunt.*

A rasping chuckle. *—Your Death awaits.—*

I started laughing, and I couldn't stop.

Jackson paled even more. I hoped he would desert me now and take the other three with him, out of my reach.

Because otherwise, the Empress might just kill them all—

Moisture tracked down my face. A tear?

Rain.

As Jackson and I stared at each other, drops began to fall between us.

My laughter died when I saw him clutching my hair ribbon so tightly that his battered knuckles were white—as if by holding on to it, he could hold on to the sweet girl he thought he'd known.

She was gone, replaced by the Empress, still tensed to fight, standing in a puddle of the Alchemist's remains. As my reddened hair streamed over my cheeks, I felt my face twisting into an expression I'd never made before. One of menace.

I was half-surprised Jackson hadn't drawn on me, but his deadly crossbow was still slung over his shoulder.

Along with the ominous drizzle, fog began rolling into this ghost town, obscuring everything, but I spied movement out of the corner of my eye. I dragged my gaze away from Jackson to the rest of our ragtag group, three other Arcana like myself.

Selena, Matthew, and Finn.

It was Selena I focused on. She'd removed her bow from her back and was now slipping an arrow from her thigh quiver.

I raised my brows with surprise. I supposed the Archer had finally gotten tired of waiting to kill us.

When she nocked that arrow, the whirling thorn tornado above me tightened. The little vine by my face straightened in her direction, a viper poised to strike.

"So that's how it's going to be, Archer?" My voice was raw from screaming in pain. I sounded like a movie villainess. I felt like one too. *There's a heat in battle—* just as Matthew had told me. "Do we do this now?" Exhaustion was setting in as my body regenerated. Though the Alchemist's acid grenades had eaten away part of my clothes—and skin—I still had some fight left in me.

But for how long?

"Whoa, ladies, what's going down here?" Finn asked in his SoCal surfer accent. "Selena, why in the hell are you drawing on Evie?"

Matthew murmured, "The Moon rises. The Moon sets."

Selena ignored both boys. "I don't want to hurt you, Evie," she said, even as she aimed at me. Her flawless skin glowed, tinged with red like a hunter's moon. Her long hair streamed around her face, silvery blond, the color of moonlight. "But I will protect myself until you rein this back in."

"I've remembered what we're meant to do, Selena." Kill each other. "Give me one reason why I shouldn't end you right now." I waved to the two huge oaks I'd revived earlier. Behind her, the ground rumbled as their roots snaked closer, readying to drag her into the earth.

My soldiers awaiting my order. It would be a horrific way to go.

"You need me," she said. "You and I—along with some other cards—will ally to kill Death. He's too strong for any one of us to take out alone. We work together until we defeat him. Then all bets are off."

"And if I say no?"

She drew back on her bowstring.

The glyphs winding along my skin burned brighter with aggression. "Shoot me, Selena. I *want* you to. I'll just regenerate, and I'll bury you." Big talk, considering I was weakening by the second. My soldiers as well.

Selena chanced a glance over her shoulder. "We don't have time for this right now! Bagmen are coming, more than I've ever seen together." No night after the apocalypse was complete without those bloodthirsty zombies. "But J.D."—she jerked her chin at Jackson—"and I only have a few arrows between us. We had to steal a jeep from that militia to get here. Let's just say they didn't give it up easily."

I could hear the Bagmen's bloodcurdling wails somewhere out in the night. Like counting seconds between a lightning strike and thunder, I figured they were some distance away.

But it also sounded like tons of them.

"On top of that, other cards have been on our trail for a day," Selena continued. "By now they know you offed an Arcana—the Alchemist's death will draw them here. Soon."

Jackson gazed back and forth between me and

Selena. Fifteen minutes ago, he'd thought we were two somewhat normal girls—or as normal as we could be A.F., after the Flash.

Now we were talking about killing each other, killing a card named *Death*. While a thorn tornado swirled above us. Not to mention that Jackson had seen the Alchemist's remains, and knew I'd ripped a teenager to pieces.

Selena eased up a fraction on her bowstring. "We need to call a truce for the night and get as far away as possible."

"A truce—there we go, good idea!" Finn said. "Let's get on the road and talk this out. Evie, tell me you have my truck."

"Out of gas."

"Shit. Ours, too. Looks like we're on foot."

No reaction from Jackson. He looked both stunned and whipped with fatigue. Eyes bloodshot. Stubble covering his rugged jaw.

The heat of battle was ebbing; I no longer had to stifle the overwhelming urge to annihilate the other Arcana. Maybe it had flared hotter because I'd denied my Empress nature for so long.

Selena *would* be an idiot to take me out while Death lived. Was an alliance possible? I needed time to think about everything, to consider my options. "Truce," I agreed. "For tonight."

She popped her arrow off the string, sliding it into

her quiver with one fluid movement. I couldn't help but roll my eyes. Such a show-off.

Without that threat, I began reining in my powers. As my claws morphed into regular pink nails, I directed my tornado of thorns to drop to the street. The barbs plummeted like a swarm of bees dying in unison. On my left forearm, a skin glyph of three thorns shimmered from gold to green before dimming.

I pressed a farewell kiss to the caressing vine. When its length seeped into the skin of my right arm as if submerging underwater, a winding vine glyph glowed, then faded. My red, leaf-strewn hair lightened back to blond. I knew my eyes were changing from green to my normal blue.

Jackson, ever watchful, studied my movements, my reactions. Warily, as he might a wild animal. I didn't blame him. I would be losing my mind to see this stuff for the first time.

And actually, I *had* lost my mind when I'd first seen these things through Matthew's visions.

Tonight Jackson had learned the world wasn't at all what he'd thought it was. Right now, he looked like he wanted to be anywhere but here.

But if he feared me—or us—then why hadn't he left?

I was about to ask him when a wave of dizziness and chills hit me, regeneration sapping the last of my strength. The drops of rain were sparse but enough to dampen my hair and uncovered skin. As I limped to go find my jacket, I wondered if I would have time to harvest the life out of the oaks.

I could sink my claws into their bark and suck them dry, like mainlining energy. But it took time. One bad thing about using trees as weapons? After the Flash, I had to load them with my own life force, my blood.

Another bad thing? You couldn't take them with you.

The others followed me inside, skirting the puddle of remains. *Not really "inside,"* I thought, gazing at the surreal scene.

Though the house was split in two, its exterior walls and roof collapsed, parts of the parlor were untouched. Doilies clung to tables. The fire lingered in the standing hearth.

This house was like me. We'd started out the day one way, and now we were both damaged beyond repair. *But a part of me remains the same. I hope.*

Jackson's gaze flickered over the dribbled burn marks on the floor. Acid had eaten away areas in the same scatter-patter array that marked my blistered legs. The wood was pocked around two perfect footprints, like twin islands.

When he looked at my healing skin, I knew he was putting together what had happened to me here. Surely he'd understand why I'd had to do what I did.

My eyes fell on Arthur's recorder, still sitting atop an end table, now dotted with raindrops. A tape of my life's story lay within. It'd clicked off just before he'd threatened to carve up my face with a scalpel. . . .

Matthew crossed to me, grinning down at me from his towering height, big brown eyes so trusting. "I missed Evie. The Empress is my friend."

The flare of aggression I'd felt while in full Empress mode had faded almost to nothing. Had I really believed that I might harm the others? I was ashamed of my thoughts.

Of course I'd never hurt Matthew. Which meant I'd never play this game.

He raised his ruddy face to the sky, catching drizzle. We'd gone eight months without rain; Matthew had predicted all bad things would come with it.

One threat at a time. "We need to find shelter, sweetheart. Preferably one with a standing roof and no body parts scattered around." Wincing at the pain in my legs, I asked, "Do I have enough time to drain energy from the oaks?"

Just as Matthew answered, "No," Finn yelled, "Bagmen!"

2

The five of us ran to the porch. From the shadows, dozens of Baggers skulked toward the front yard. Their leathery, Flash-burned skin excreted reeking slime.

"How'd they get here so quick?" Finn cried. "They sounded miles off."

"The fog's playing tricks on us." *The fog lies, Evie—* my grandmother's words from long ago.

The closest Baggers were three tall males, wearing matching black Adidas suits. A zombie track team? Behind them, a bony female in a bra and Spanx lurched forward, one spongy pink curler bobbing in her stringy hair.

Scores more shuffled down the street. A doctor in her tattered scrubs. An old guy in plaid pajamas. A cop with his gun belt dangling from his gaunt waist.

There was no thought in their pale, runny eyes.

Since their creation in the Flash, Bagmen had obeyed only their thirst.

Selena aimed her bow, backing closer to me. "Won't the rain tide them over now?"

They surged forward. "Guess not! Evie, attack with your trees!" She turned to me, scowling at whatever she saw. "Your glyphs got way dimmer. Damn it, try anyway."

Dim? I'd learned that meant the reserve of my powers was depleted, my Empress fuel gauge on empty. Still, I waved my arm, commanding the two colossal oaks to sweep their limbs across the yard. They groaned in protest, slow to obey—like overworked muscles. "Come on, come on!"

They managed to hit a line of Bagmen, bowling pins sent airborne.

"Holy shit!" Finn yelled. "I knew you could make 'em dance, but to *see* it!"

"*Mère de Dieu,*" I heard Jackson rasp. Mother of God. First time he'd spoken.

Before I could strike again, more Baggers had flooded into the yard. I'd never seen so many, not even at Matthew's place when we rescued him.

Though I struggled to control the trees, they were as weak and clumsy as I was. They swayed gently, nothing like the angry hydras they'd resembled before.

The Baggers attacked the trees like jackals seizing injured game, chewing at the limbs; I could feel every bite. Finally, my soldiers just . . . gave out. When they went limp, I tottered, Matthew catching me against him.

Selena cursed me. "Way to use up all your juice, idiot."

I gasped out, "You're saying that with one arrow left in your quiver?"

"Ladies," Finn cried, "time to RUN!"

He and Selena sprinted past me toward the back of the house. As Jackson followed, he snatched his crossbow off his back and fired three shots. The trio of track teamers dropped, arrows jutting from their skulls, but Jackson held off firing his remaining ammo.

When he reached me, he barely slowed. After all the time I'd spent with him, I half-expected him to grab my arm and yell, "Move your ass, *bébé*!" With a dark glance, he might have hesitated a split second, indicating that I should run in front of him.

Grabbing Matthew's hand, I did, limping as fast as I could to the back.

Over his shoulder, Finn said, "They're out this way too!"

Selena dropped into position on the back porch, her moonbeam hair streaming, bow aimed. But she'd never use that last arrow. "Evie, you got anything else in your bag of tricks?"

My other powers sucked against zombies. Poison only worked on living things. A thorn tornado would flay their skin, but couldn't kill them. Maybe it could slow the Bagmen down. Though my thorn glyph was dark, I raised my hands to call on the barbs once more. I sensed them vibrating on the pavement . . . bees struggling back to life . . . then nothing.

"T-tapped out." I told Finn, "Create an illusion, make it look like we're running the other way."

"I'm almost tapped out too! I disguised our jeep for forty-eight hours. A *moving* jeep, without letting the Cajun driver in on the secret. But I'll try." He began to whisper his mysterious Magician language, the air around him heating.

Soon we were rendered invisible, while five illusions of us appeared to run down the front porch steps and beyond. The closest Bagmen followed them. For now.

Unfortunately, Finn couldn't disguise our scent.

Jackson did a double-take at the illusions. "More Baggers are coming! The house'll be surrounded in seconds."

My gaze was drawn to the right, toward the basement steps.

Jackson followed my gaze and started for them. Selena hurried after him, motioning for me to stay close. I followed them, Matthew and Finn right behind me. But at the threshold, I resisted returning to that lab.

Finn reached past Matthew to give me a little shove. "Come on, Eves!"

I swung around on him. "The last boy who pushed me down these steps became a *smear*."

Finn held his hands up, eyes wide. "No problem, chica. 'S'cool." He created another illusion, this one of a lantern to light the way. "Everything's better with a little light, yeah?"

Farther down, Jackson scowled at the magic. So tonight was the first time he'd witnessed it? We'd agreed to keep our powers secret from non-Arcana.

Secret? Guess I blew this bitch wide open.

He and Matthew both had to duck under the doorframe. After we all filed inside, Jackson eased the basement door closed, then slid a metal table in front of it.

We backed away, deeper into the lab, closer to the blood-spattered plastic drapes separating the dungeon. The others peered around, their gazes flickering over the Bunsen burners atop a long steel counter, the shelves of jarred body parts. Left over from my battle with the Alchemist, broken glass and spilled serums covered the packed earth floor.

Finn said, "It's official—this is the creepiest place I've ever been. Some mad scientist just called, wants his lab back."

You haven't seen the worst.

Once the rancid smell from the dungeon hit them, Finn covered his mouth. "What the hell's back there?"

"A corpse," I answered tonelessly. "It's . . . decomposing." My shivers started anew.

When Matthew put his arm around my shoulders, I pressed my face against his damp shirt.

As if they couldn't help themselves, one by one, Jackson, Selena, and Finn slipped past those spattered curtains.

Matthew led me to the back wall, using his battered tennis shoes to shuffle glass from a spot on the floor.

When we sat on the chilly ground, I said, "You already know what's back there, don't you?"

"A butcher's block. Drain fields. Bone saws and cleavers. Rusted shackles dangling from the wall." He shrugged. "I see far." He'd shown me visions of the past, present, and future—of Arcana and even non-Arcana.

But he'd once told me the future flowed like waves— or eddies—and that it was difficult to read. "Did you know I was going to defeat the Alchemist?"

He shook his head. He seemed less confused than usual. "I see far, not all." He grasped my right hand, tapping the new marking. "I bet on you to take his icon."

I supposed those symbols were a way to keep score in this sick game.

I thought I heard a gasp from the dungeon, and tried to imagine that space through their eyes. Would seeing the chained-up corpse make them understand what I'd faced?

If I'd gotten to Arthur's earlier, maybe I could've saved that girl. I tipped my head back and stared at the low ceiling. How many others were out there in chains, waiting to be freed. . . ?

3

Finn stumbled out of the dungeon first, hand over his mouth. "About to Technicolor yawn." He retched but kept it down.

Selena's expression was blank when she exited. Without a word, she took a seat atop one of the counters.

When Jackson emerged, he looked like he was struggling to control his rage. For a boy who so often resorted to his fists, he despised violence against women.

He crossed to the table blocking the door, then sank down on the ground to sit against one of the table legs. To reinforce his blockade? Or because it was the spot in the room farthest away from me?

He seemed to be thrumming with frustrated energy, like a tiger prowling a cage. And like a trapped animal, Jackson now had nowhere to go.

I tried to put myself in his shoes. What would I do if I thought he was one way and he turned out to be something supernaturally different? I knew well what I looked like in the throes of my powers—I'd been horrified to see a past Empress in my nightmares.

If I'd been revolted, how could he not be?

Skittering sounded from above us, then a *boom!* as if furniture had been upended. "They're back," I whispered. Bagmen on our trail.

We all gazed up at the ceiling, Jackson and Selena raising their bows. How many were there? Would the decomposing body down here camouflage our scent?

After several heartbeats passed, they roved on. Selena and Jackson gradually lowered their weapons.

With a sigh of relief, Finn took a seat right beside Selena, clearly still infatuated; she glared.

"I'm guessing we'll be here awhile," he began, "and I need some questions answered. Like why you two were acting like you wanted to kill each other. Some of the last hot chicks on earth, I might add."

"Tell them, Selena," I bit out. I was still regenerating, which meant pain was radiating throughout my body. "Tell them everything you know about the game—everything you've hidden from us all along."

"Oh, you're one to talk!" Selena gripped the bow in her lap as if she was longing to fire on me.

"What do you mean by *game*?" Finn asked. "Strip poker's a game. Quarters is a game. Games are fun."

As though the words were dragged from her, Selena said, "Every few centuries, a contest begins, pitting twenty-two kids against each other in a life-or-death conflict. We're called Arcana, and we have special powers, the same in each game."

Finn held up his hand. "Whoa, you said before that you didn't know why we had powers."

"I lied," she said without an ounce of shame. "The last one standing gets to live until the next contest, as an immortal. Our histories were recorded—on Tarot cards."

I glanced over at Jackson to see how he was taking all these revelations. His eyes were narrowed, the wheels turning. *Yes, Cajun, we all hid secrets from you, me most of all. Yes, we're not totally, well, human. And,* oui, *you're stuck in a cellar with the freaks.*

Selena continued, "Some families keep logs of the players and battles, detailed chronicles. My family did. Evie's as well. Her grandmother's a wisewoman of the Tarot, a Tarasova. Yet for some reason, Evie says she's forgotten everything about the game."

"I forgot because I was young!" I snapped, though this was far from the whole truth. No need to confide to her that I'd been "deprogrammed" at CLC, an Atlanta loony bin. "I was eight the last time I saw her."

Selena pointed to my hand. "Now Evie's entered the game for real. She made a kill."

Finn asked me, "So the guy out in the yard—the mad

scientist—was an Arcana? How did you find him?"

"I heard his call, and I followed it."

Selena explained to Jackson, "All Arcana have a catchphrase, like a signature about their character. We can hear each other's. It's how we communicate, I guess. How we can tell who's getting closer."

To find the Alchemist, I'd learned how to block out some calls and home in on others, like dialing in a station on an antique radio. Even when I wasn't tuned in to the Arcana Channel, the broadcast would still play for others. "That's right, Selena," I said. "And yet you told us that you'd never heard voices, called us crazy." Finn gave me a *damn straight!* look.

As if I hadn't spoken, she told Jackson, "We can even hear some thoughts if they're accompanied by sharp emotions."

Right now the Arcana were abuzz, and we were all hearing it:

—*Empress made her first kill!*—

—*Alchemist no more!*—

—*She's worth two icons now.*—

The others fell silent when Death spoke: —*The Empress's blood is* mine *to spill. Govern your game accordingly.*—

Having been threatened by him for months, I wasn't even fazed by his words. Death wanted to gank me? Must be Tuesday.

Finn asked, "How come Death gets to talk to everybody?"

Like Matthew, Death could mentally communicate with all of us. But especially with me.

"He's won the last three games," Selena said. "He's over two thousand years old. I'm sure he's figured out some tricks."

I supposed as the last victor, he was king of the airwaves or something. Did that explain how he could read my thoughts?

If Selena expected Jackson to enter the dialogue, she was disappointed. He didn't reply, didn't ask a question. Why? He was a puzzle-solver, and if there were ever a puzzle to be solved . . .

"The guy you offed was the Alchemist, huh?" Finn asked me. "What? No *Serial Killer Card*? Or *The Deranged Murderer*?"

I shook my head. "Also known as the Hermit Card. He had healing serums and potions to give him superhuman strength, but he didn't even know about the game. He told me he was archiving folks' stories of the apocalypse and promised me a meal if I let him tape mine." A total ruse. "I noticed that he'd drugged my drink, so I played along, acting out-of-it, because I thought I'd heard someone in the basement." My eyes darted to the dungeon. "He had four girls chained in there, experimenting on them. One hadn't survived it.

I freed the others." I turned to Matthew. "Will they be safe tonight?"

"The girls are fleeing Requiem. Two will live. Third wouldn't in any scenario."

My heart sank.

Selena said, "So you made the Alchemist pay."

Seriously? "I didn't want to hurt him, never wanted to kill anyone. Part of me refused to believe that only one of us was getting out of here alive. Not until he told me to dig my new collar out of those remains and put it around my neck!"

"Duuude," Finn murmured, the word imbued with sympathy. "Looks like the Alchemist dicked with the wrong chick."

I didn't deny that, because, well, he had.

"Now I get why Matthew keeps talking about killing bad cards," Finn said. "Are most of them homicidal? Are those freaks going to be coming after us for that immortality prize? And hey, why were you two talking about killing *each other*?"

Matthew stage-whispered, "Kill the bad cards."

When he'd first said that a few days ago, I'd thought he meant a battle between good and evil. How naïve of me. In a way, we'd all been born to do evil.

"*Bad* cards, Matto." Finn raked his fingers through his sun-bleached hair. "We're not bad. So nobody's offing anybody. We're all friends. Right, Selena? I mean, yeah, I broke apart our new little fam unit with my ill-timed illusion," he said, his dudebrah accent thick. "But I'm hereby saying I'm sorry. I screwed up—my bad. Guys, I didn't mean anything by it."

Ill-timed illusion? Had he used his powers to make himself look like Jackson, then kissed Selena? I'd begun to suspect as much—or rather, to hope. "Finn, that was you, with . . . her?"

Finn gave a pained nod; Selena stared daggers at him.

I recalled that same night when Finn had asked me how to win her over. He'd told me he would "devise something." God, had he ever.

Then where had Jackson been? We met gazes. He lifted his chin as if to say, *You had me* all *wrong.*

How did I feel about him, knowing he'd never kissed her? I tried to take a mental inventory of my emotions. Everything was raw and numb. But it didn't matter how I felt about him. He'd revealed his disgust with me.

The sign of the cross, Jack? Really? Did he think I was some sort of demon to be warded off? Should he? I looked for my red ribbon. At some point he'd either tucked it into his pocket—or discarded it.

Selena told Finn, "You're lucky to be alive after what you pulled with me. See, Evie? I've already made sacrifices for this alliance. Normally I would've punished the Magician for using his powers on me. He played me—"

"For a fool," Matthew said.

Selena glared at him, then said, "But I've made allowances to keep us strong."

"Are we an alliance?" I asked. As of a few days ago, the Archer had been plotting to kill me. "Why the turnaround?"

Her eyes flitted to Matthew and back. "We're an alliance," she said in a firm tone. He must've told her something about the future.

"Punish me?" Finn snapped. "Stop talking like you're a warlord, Selena. I didn't mean to treat you like a fool. I can't control it . . . sometimes I *have* to trick people—"

More skittering upstairs. I jumped when one Bagman gave a sharp wail.

"I don't understand this," Selena whispered. "Shouldn't they be happy in the rain? Why aren't they standing there with their mouths raised to the sky?"

"Back to the subject at hand." Finn's gaze fell on Selena's bow. "Tell me you hadn't ever planned to kill *us* in this game."

"Of course she had," I said in a low voice. "You heard her. First we take out Death, then all bets are off."

Gazing around wildly, Finn opened his mouth and closed it. Open, closed. "You guys are humming my balls, right?"

Everyone frowned at him.

"Gargling my marbles? Screwing with me?" His eyes looked frantic. "Tell me, Selena!"

She didn't reply. Just stared straight ahead.

"Tell me or I swear I'll yell."

Jackson raised his brows, giving the boy a *dafuq?* look. With a subtle movement, he aimed his bow, ready to shut the Magician up in case of emergency—ever the survivor, prepared to do whatever it took.

At length, Selena said, "One player gets to live. That's the rule. I was raised to play this game, but that doesn't mean I enjoy any of it."

Finn looked like something had broken in him, any yell quashed.

Jackson lowered his bow, a disturbed expression crossing his face. He and Selena might never have been involved, but I was sure he'd considered her a friend.

Not a cold-blooded murderer. This game was going to turn us all into murderers.

If we let it.

Jackson glanced at my bare legs, at the skin mending itself, then slipped his flask from his pocket for a generous slug. *Freaked out much, Cajun?* Not that he ever needed an excuse to drink.

Finn hopped down from the counter to sit by himself. "I can't believe I gave you food and shelter," he told Selena. "I even gave you my last Snickers bar! Might've been the last one on earth."

Her face was blank.

"So why have you held off?" he asked her. "From ganking us?"

Selena looked at me rather than him. "Though it galls me to say this, I need you."

I made a scoffing sound. "I'm supposed to trust the Bringer of Doubt not to slit my throat if I lower my guard for a second?" Apparently I could no longer depend on Jackson to watch over me as I slept.

Finn turned to me. "Now that you've remembered the game, are *you* gonna kill us?"

"No."

Selena whipped her head around. "Now who's the liar?"

"I don't play games where I don't make the rules," I said, sounding like a Frau Badass, like my fierce mother had been. *Finally.* And more, I believed what I was saying. "I'll take out Death. Then I'll stop."

I'd get a handle on that "heat in battle" aspect. Yes, bottling up my powers had caused me problems, but I had an ace up my sleeve. "My grandmother, *the Tarasova*, will help me. All I have to do is reach her in North Carolina." Assuming she was still alive. Which I did. I *felt* like she was.

Selena was eyeing me with new interest. "You can't just stop."

"Watch me." Maybe I didn't have to reject my abilities. I could use them outside of the game to help people, like those girls in the dungeon. If I'd been empowered to play this messed-up game, I could repurpose myself, fight freaking crime if I had to. "I want no part in this game. I'd rather die than hurt Matthew." He patted my marked hand again.

"How are you going to get past the other cards?" Selena asked. "I already sensed some not too far away. With the Alchemist's death, they'll come running for us. They could be waiting outside this basement in the morning, ready to give us a wake-up kiss."

"Then I'll have to convince them not to play." Was my voice growing fainter? "I'll start a different kind of alliance."

"We go up against the wrong cards and you'll never get a word out."

Despite the threat of more Arcana, I leaned against Matthew as another wave of dizziness hit. "I'll take my chances," I said, barely keeping my eyes open.

Finn considered all this, then asked me, "What's so important about this Death dude? Why's he the only one you'll fight?"

"Because he's a psychopath, who won't stop until I'm dead."

Poor Matthew's stomach was growling. Even as exhaustion dragged me down, I asked, "Anybody got any food for Matthew?"

Finn raised his brows at Jackson. "*Somebody* didn't give us a lot of time to provision for the *gotta-save-Evie* trip." To me, he said, "We abandoned my copious stores. Glad we got here in time to save you, by the way."

I turned to Jackson.

He held up one empty hand and his crossbow. In a curt tone, he said, "I got nothing for *coo-yôn*." Cajun for *fool*. "My bag's in the truck."

What had he been thinking to leave his bug-out bag? He considered separation from one's survival gear to be a cardinal sin, like suicide, had dog-cussed me whenever I'd stepped even five feet from mine. "You doan have this bag?" he'd said, shoving it into my arms. "Then you're done. You hear me? DONE."

I'd managed to hold on to mine until I'd been kidnapped by that militia group. Jackson had saved me from those men, proving himself a hero.

Had that only been three days ago?

Now he was right here with me. And he'd never been with Selena. I wanted his strong arms around me. I wanted him murmuring Cajun French to me in that rumbling voice of his, the words I alone understood. But he felt a thousand miles distant.

I couldn't stop myself from asking him, "You're not going to say anything about all this?"

He gave me a cruel smirk, a flash of his white teeth. "This ain't my party, now is it?" Anger gleamed in his gray eyes.

"No. It isn't."

Everyone fell silent.

Despite the tension thick in the air, my lids grew heavier. Sleep was about to overwhelm me, but I feared Selena.

Matthew whispered in my mind —*She'll protect you with her life, until Death is done. If Death is done. She knows you're his sole weakness.*—

And me? Will I hurt them? By accidentally unleashing poisonous spores and such.

—*Safe. You have control now.*—

At that, I closed my eyes. I could feel Jackson's gaze on me, even before Matthew said —*He stares. He stares. He hungers to know what's behind your false face. The curiosity burns him.*—

I turned in to Matthew, wanting to hear more. *False face? Is that why he looks like he hates me?*

—*Loathe/love. Hurting/hating.*—

I don't understand.

Matthew didn't reply. Probably staring at his hand, which always meant: subject closed. And I didn't have the energy left to press.

Finn cleared his throat. "So this Death dude, he wouldn't, like, trouble himself to come after a second-stringer like me?"

Just as I slipped off to sleep and into dreams, Matthew murmured woefully, "Death comes for us all. . . ."

I've lost too much blood; it streams from a wound in my side, dripping to the desert sands.

My enemies have closed in on me. We've collected in this place like leaves on a whirlpool. Their calls sound even louder in my head. I've already killed four of their strongest, but am now drained of power, injured.

I have no thorns, no vines, no trees to aid me. Nothing grows in this wasted land. No water in any direction, just canyon wall after wall.

And I have no idea how to navigate the terrain, no horse to carry me. As I stumble through a maze of interconnecting gorges, my feet sink into the sand. Going in circles?

There, ahead . . . I see my own blood trail. I have been walking in circles! I lean back against a rock. Why couldn't I have been gifted with the Mistress of Fauna's senses?

Hoofbeats begin to echo through the canyon, what sounds like a massive steed. Death? Has he found me at last? I somehow manage to increase my pace, a shuffling run. Sweat pours. Blood pours—

I stumble to a stop. I've reached a dead end. Trapped. I spin around as the Reaper comes into view.

He is alone, astride a white stallion with red eyes. He wears black armor, a helmet covering his face. Two swords hang from his belt. A polished scythe juts from a saddle holster. "Empress," he intones.

"Death," I bite out, trying to disguise the severity of my wound.

"I watched you battle the others today," he says, his voice deep and raspy. "Your powers are monstrous, creature."

"And yours are not?" He can kill just by touching another's skin. Other Arcana whisper that he prefers to kill with his touch.

But I want to live! I have only eighteen springs, am far from ready to leave this world.

Death tilts his helmeted head. "Your flesh repairs itself. I wonder if the others could even kill you at all."

"They cannot," I lie. "Nor can you. So leave me."

As if I haven't spoken, he removes his helmet, revealing a shocking sight: his face.

He is . . . beautiful.

His masculine features are even and bold, with a proud brow and nose. His tanned skin and light blond hair make his amber eyes stand out. I guess his age to be no more than seventeen.

He dismounts with a lethal grace. As he stalks closer, I have to crane my head up and up to hold his gaze. He must be over six feet tall. His bearing bespeaks arrogance. Obviously highborn.

His gaze falls on the bloody hand I use to clutch my side. "So many icons. Soon to be mine."

If he murders me, those images will appear on his hand, my kills becoming his own. Whichever Arcana has all the marks at the end, the last one standing, wins.

Lions roar in the distance. Fauna with her beasts.

Where are my allies? Fool, have you forsaken me?

When Death draws a sword, I spit blood at his face and run to the right; he cuts me off with unnatural *speed. I run to the left, the same. I splay my fingers and slash at his armor, expecting to furrow the metal with my indestructible thorn claws.*

Sparks flicker, but my claws dull, leaving nary a scratch.

Gasping for breath, I shake my head wildly, thrashing my reddened hair. No poison whispers from my tresses. I raise my free hand and call upon my lotus to appear. Nothing. I press my lips together, licking them. They are numb, cracked. No toxin covers them for a fatal kiss.

I've used up my powers earning the four icons on my hand, my glyphs gone dim in this hated desert.

"Beg me for your life."

I jut my chin, even as my lungs struggle for air. "I am the great Empress . . . the May Queen, a killer of the first order. . . . I will never beg."

He gives me a grudging nod, as if he respects me for this. "You've earned an honorable death, creature." He meets my gaze; his eyes begin to glow, as if filled with stars. I can't look away. "This will not hurt for long."

Without a sound, he thrusts his sword, stabbing me through. I shriek in pain, clutching the blade that pins me to the rock. My screams die when I begin to choke on blood.

There is no sympathy in Death's starry eyes, nothing but resolve as he secures my wrists, pinning them with one gloved hand. He raises the other to his mouth, using his teeth to tug off the gauntlet.

To touch me.

And it is then that I know: this boy will win the entire game. . . .

4

—I'm coming for you, Empress.—

I woke, shooting upright. Death was in my dreams and in my mind. It was as if I could sense his presence in my head, a heavy feeling.

Like being possessed.

That dream with him had been so vivid, I pressed my hands to my stomach, expecting to feel a sword.

The details of his handsome face floated at the edges of my memory. He'd looked younger in the dream than he was now, and his black armor had been different, appearing ancient. Was this some kind of vision from another, even earlier game?

Just as Death's presence faded, a draft ghosted over me. I raised my head, gazing around with unease. I was alone in the lab? With the moldering corpse? Were my surroundings or my nightmare to blame for this ominous feeling I had—

"Get dressed, Evie," Selena yelled as she bounded down the cellar steps, lobbing a waterproof pack to land right at my feet. "Quickly!"

"What's going on?" I knelt beside the pack, digging in to find a navy parka, jeans, thick socks, T-shirts, even a supply of undergarments. Leather lace-up boots too. They looked to be about my size.

Under the clothes were Mayday bars, MREs, and energy gel packs—an apocalyptic lunchbox.

As I yanked off my ragged shirt, Selena filled me in. "Baggers are gone for the day, but Matthew foresaw Arcana company approaching. Cards following a kill, as I predicted," she added in a superior tone.

"Which ones?"

"The Tower, Judgment, and the World."

I'd seen the first two in battle in a vision Matthew had shown me. Even if I were eager to play the game, I wouldn't want to tangle with them, especially when I was still so weakened from yesterday. "Have you heard their calls?" Had I slept right through them?

"Not yet. Think they're still too far away. We were ransacking the Alchemist's supplies—bastard had everything—when Matt started muttering about jamming the frequencies. Does that mean anything to you?"

I shook my head.

"He said these cards are coming in fast, that we have less than an hour."

"So we can slip away?" I wondered if I would have time to drain the oaks, or would they be my parting gift to Requiem? At Selena's nod, I said, "Why are you so keen to avoid a fight?"

She stared me down. "Because today we'd lose."

Good reason.

She held up a laminated map of the Southeast, dappled with burnout holes. "I'm going to plan our exit out of this valley." Like a gazelle, she bounded back up the steps.

I drew off what was left of my pants, relieved to see my skin had healed. After I yanked on the new jeans—too long in the legs, too tight in the ass: story o' my life—I laced up the boots. At least those fit.

With one last glance around, I shouldered the pack and hurried upstairs. Even in the midst of this crisis, I realized I was nervous about seeing Jackson, wondering how he would act today. I wished I'd dreamed of him instead of Death.

In the morning's dim light, the house looked even stranger, with Bagman slime everywhere and furniture tossed. Drizzle misted my hair through the gaping roof. Wispy clouds sped across the muted sun. After months of either blue skies or brutal dust storms, this gray haze was freaky.

Not to mention Matthew's prediction that we'd be weak in the rain while our enemies grew stronger.

As Selena pored over the map, Finn helped Matthew

stuff supplies into a pack. I noticed Matthew had on a new coat. A relief—he'd been in sore need of something warm to wear. Like most clothing we'd been seeing A.F., it had dark-ringed bullet holes in it, from the previous owner's demise.

I suspected Finn had sourced it for him. Was the Magician being helpful to make up for his trick? Though pissed at him for his illusion, I did think the boy had a decent heart.

But where was Jackson? I had a moment of panic, wondering if he'd bailed. Surely, he wouldn't leave me without a word. Not after all we'd been through. *It's you for me, peekôn.*

Still, I was about to ask when Selena announced, "We're in a valley with mountains on three sides. Two sides are too high to scale. The third leads to cannibal country."

Finn swallowed hard. He'd seen the cannibals when he'd crossed the mountains in the past.

Sensing Finn's distress, Matthew patted him on his head. "There, there."

Selena continued, "The only road out of here is a bottleneck. If we can squeeze out before the other Arcana show, I say we head south back to Finn's cabin. Lure Death to our foxhole, fight him on our home turf. Evie's powers work best when she can dig in and prepare."

Finn wiped mist from his face. "You assume I'm

inviting you back to my pad, Selena? I'm not leaving this town with you. We'll be fine on our own."

She shoved the map into her pack. "Listen, you deceptive little shit, Evie's the linchpin. I go where she goes—"

"The linchpin's still going to find her grandmother," I interrupted. "Like I said, I'm heading to the Outer Banks." I gazed around. "Where's Jackson?"

Finn zipped Matthew's pack closed. "Um, Jack bugged out before we woke up," he said, his demeanor guilty. "He's gone, Evie."

"Not a card," Matthew said. He'd never felt comfortable with Jackson, a non-Arcana, around.

"*Gone* gone?" No, I refused to believe he would abandon me without so much as a look back. *Like you abandoned him?* my conscience whispered.

Selena rolled her eyes. "What'd you expect? J.D. witnessed you go full-on Empress, all *Little Shop of Horrors*. I think he got the message: we're—not—human. Not to mention what he heard in the cellar, about us being in Death's crosshairs. If I were him, I'd be sprinting away from us as fast as I could."

That was . . . fair. "I'm surprised you didn't chase after him."

"If he'd liked me back, I might've asked him to run with me," Selena admitted. "Even though I've accepted that an alliance with you is the single thing that might keep me alive."

I asked Matthew, "I don't suppose he's coming back?"

Matthew gazed at the cloudy sky. "He should've said good-bye."

I surveyed the yard, seeing the Bagmen bodies from the night before. Jackson had collected his arrows from those corpses—on his way out. *Ever practical, Cajun.*

My eyes watered, but I forced a blank expression on my face. "It's for the best anyway." I hated that he'd left! "He didn't belong with us." He belonged with me.

Never to see him again? The idea hurt me worse than a sword to the stomach. I asked Matthew, "If Jack is still nearby, will he be safe from other cards?"

Matthew nodded. "Not Arcana."

Yet we were, which meant we were all in danger. I couldn't afford to think about Jack right now—I needed to figure out how to survive the next hour!

"All right, Evie, what do we do?" Finn checked a new watch. "We've got company in less than forty-five minutes." He looked at me like I was his leader, like he'd listen to whatever a girl like me had to say.

In the past, no one had consulted me about anything. And I'd been okay with that.

"We run out of the valley, threading the needle," I said. "But if you want to go with me, then we make a pact not to harm each other, and we make it fast."

Selena and Finn scowled at each other.

"What are our options?" I demanded. "Say we

go back to Finn's, and Death comes. Say we somehow defeat him. Do we even take a fiver to celebrate our team's victory—or do we start wiping each other out directly?"

When they remained unconvinced, I said, "Matthew showed me a vision of another alliance of three. They fought Death. They were organized, skilled, and committed. They never would've hurt each other, which means they had to be planning an exit from the game." I turned to Matthew. "Right?"

He didn't deny it, just said, "System the game, game the system. There's a heat in battle."

"There is," I said. "We might need to fight, but that doesn't mean we have to kill each other. If we all commit to this, then we don't have to become murderers. Your hands are clean." Unlike my marked one.

Finn asked Selena, "Think a pact's even doable for you?"

"If we can come up with a viable way to get out of this game, then I won't hurt any of you," she said. "Otherwise, we're back to the take-out-Death alliance."

I shared a look with Finn. *Best we're gonna get.*

He tapped his watch. "We're getting close on time."

Which meant I'd be leaving my trees. *You're welcome, Requiem!* "All right. First order of alliance business: run."

They both grabbed their packs, like I'd given marching orders.

Grasping Matthew's hand, I hurried toward the

yard. "Can you see how far away the other cards are?" We crossed over the front porch—the place where I'd finished the Alchemist. There was no sign of his blood. Baggers must've licked the boards clean.

"You need to stay here and fight, Empress."

The mere idea made me queasy, my legs feeling rubbery. "We're taking off, honey. It'll be safer for you."

His big brown eyes were solemn as he said, "I hope you are terrified and angry and sad for as long as it rains."

"Matthew! Why would you say that?" I cast him a hurt look. "Never mind, we'll talk about this later."

"Death watches. Strike first, or be first-struck."

He kept saying that, but even if I unleashed my full arsenal, I didn't know if I could kill Death. He would slice through my barriers and vines with his swords. His armor would protect him from my thorns and claws. Just like in my dream. Now that I wasn't all roided out on Empress juice, I didn't have high hopes for my chances. "One threat at a time, okay?"

We hadn't made it out of the yard when everyone froze midstep; Arcana calls sounded.

—*Eyes to the skies, lads, I strike from above!*—

—*I watch you like a hawk.*—

I'd heard these before, had seen their owners in Matthew's shared visions. The first call belonged to the Tower Card, Joules. The second was from Gabriel, the Judgment Card, a winged boy.

Shit, this was happening! "Matthew, you told us we had an hour!"

"Less than. This is less than."

"They're already in the valley." Selena scowled. "And if we heard their calls, you better believe they heard ours. We can't get past them now. The bottleneck's too narrow."

Just as Finn said, "The four of us can handle a pair, right?" we heard another call:

—*Trapped in the palm of my hand.*—

I'd never heard that one before. "Who's that?"

Matthew answered, "Tess Quinn, the World Card, one of the elementals. Quintessence dances across the world."

What I wouldn't give for a decoder ring! "What are Tess's powers?"

"Intangibility, levitation, time manipulation, teleportation, astral projection . . ." He took a breath to keep going.

I cut him off. "Okay, okay. What do we do?"

"This trio comes for you. Joules wants your death. To spite Death."

Just then, we heard the Reaper telling all Arcana:

—*The Empress's life is mine to take. Disobey and I won't kill you, not for ages.*—

Finn said, "Why's this Joules cat so hard up for Evie? And why does Death give a shit?"

"Matthew showed me a vision of Death killing

Calanthe, Joules's girlfriend," I quickly explained. "She was the Temperance Card. Joules was devastated. The Tower, Judgment, and Temperance were the ones in that tight alliance I mentioned."

Selena drew her bow. "If Joules wants Evie, then he's going to have a fight on his hands."

How odd that Selena was now bent on protecting me. I wondered what exactly Matthew had told her.

Finn asked me, "How's the juice? You got anything? I'm running low myself."

Selena said, "And I'm still rocking a single arrow. Maybe we can set a trap and ambush them?"

"Conserve and converge," Matthew chirped.

"Hello, listen to yourselves!" I squeezed my temples. "We're not fighting them! If we have to face them, we need to try to ally with them. Then we would be seven, united against Death. No one has cause to hate him like Joules. We can use that."

Selena looked at me like I was crazy. "Or Joules could end us all, get our icons and more power to take Death on himself. This is the Tower we're talking about, as in *a heavy hitter*."

"As much as I hate to admit it," Finn said, "Selena's got a point. If we try to recruit them when we're weak, it's just going to look like we're wheedling for our lives. We've got to lower the boom on them, then offer them mercy if they join us."

They were right. This alliance business was just like

my old cheerleading squad—it had to look like the cool kids were in it, or no one would try out.

"Matthew, we need your help. What do we do?"

"Look at my new kicks." He raised one boot. "Finn said I'm ballin' like a pimp now." Then he frowned. "Good thing?"

"Yes, yes, but—"

"He took care of me when you abandoned me."

God, the guilt. In a rush, I said, "I thought you'd be safer at Finn's than going back out on the road with me! You know how dangerous it'll be to reach the coast." But then, I'd believed that before I'd understood how lethal I could be.

"Dangerous Empress!"

"I had no idea Jackson would drag all of you up here." He'd come for me, wanting to be with me. Until he'd witnessed what I was. "Sweetheart, can you please concentrate? What should we do?"

"Fight to the death."

"Damn it, Matthew!"

Selena grabbed my upper arm. "You want me to join in this make-love-not-war bullshit? Then convince me it's even possible. You might not be able to defeat them, but you better *look* like you can. . . ."

5

"This isn't working!" Back on Arthur's front porch, I'd shed my pack and new parka, willing my claws to appear. They'd tingled but remained dormant. "Tapped out." My glyphs were dark, the fuel gauge blinking *E*. "I used everything in my arsenal last night—"

Selena's hand shot out and smacked my face.

"What the hell?" When I raised my palm to my cheek, she slapped the other one harder.

I felt my glyphs stirring.

"If you don't want these cards to die, then get to work, Evie! You need to look like the Empress of Old, slithery and creepy and sexy all at the same time."

"Touch me again, and you'll see slithery and creepy—"

With her enhanced speed, she shoved me back before I could even react. I tripped over my pack, landing on my ass. "You bitch!" I bounded up, thorn claws bared.

"That's it! *Sell* it, sister, or we are dead!"

I gazed down at my body, at my skin glowing through the fabric of my clothes. Sharp emotions like fury and utter terror always sparked my powers; Selena had pissed me off enough to give me a jump-start. I narrowed my eyes at Matthew. "This is why you want me angry, terrified, and sad for the rainy season?"

Blank smile.

Which power to choose? The flower glyph was my lotus, the barbs my tornado. The gleaming vine circling my upper arm was ready to spring to life, leaving my body to maim and kill. The dotted pattern shivering across my torso represented my poisons.

I opened my palm, peering down at the three thorns that emerged from my skin. I tossed them into the air, watching the barbs multiply in the sky, forming a tornado.

"Rad-ick-ull!" Finn cried.

You haven't seen anything. A few slashes of my claws across my forearms gave me blood to grow vines. I let it drip to my fingers, flinging drops across the ground. Greenery slithered to life. When I popped a crick in my neck, my two oaks whipped to attention.

"Now we're talking, girl." Selena strung her arrow, holding her bow at the ready. "Jungle this up!"

I surveyed my arsenal. Not as petrifying as the

one I'd conjured last night, but . . . "It is what it is."

We all took up positions on the porch. In this lull, my mind flashed to Jackson, and my chest ached. *Don't think about him, don't think about him.* He was obviously safer away from us. Right now, we were facing a possible supernatural battle.

Selena asked me, "You really think your good ole granny can help you exit the game?"

"She might be the last living chronicler." Before, I'd needed to reach her to ask about my nightmares and hallucinations, about the physical changes taking place inside me. Now I needed her to help keep me from turning into a stone-cold killer, one who'd had the impulse to murder her friends. "She'll have answers."

Yes, Gran had once told me I'd have to "kill them all," but she'd just been reciting ancient rules. The fact was that her granddaughter Empress hadn't turned out right.

This Empress wanted *nothing* to do with the game.

"How could the cards find us here and so fast?" Finn asked. "Evie just toasted one of these freaks yesterday."

Selena scanned the street. "We're drawn to each other, seeking something that will bring us into the fray. They were probably close already."

"Convergence," Matthew said.

Finn wiped his sweating palms along his jeans. "What if some player had been in the Antarctic before the Flash? It isn't like he could fly or take a boat now."

A good guess, since there were no planes. Or oceans.

"Convergence," Matthew repeated in an overly patient tone. "We are led. We lead. We follow MacGuffins! The Tower's alliance arrives in twenty . . . nineteen . . . eighteen . . ."

As he continued his hushed countdown, Finn asked, "If the Tower is a heavy hitter, what's this guy packing?"

I murmured, "Control over all electricity and straight-up lightning. He has these silver javelins that appear in his hand. Wherever he throws them, lightning strikes. Plus he can electrify his skin."

"Fourteen . . . thirteen . . ."

Selena explained, "A direct strike could fry my insides, but I might survive. Evie would be stunned, maybe long enough for him to take her head. Finn, you and Matt die instantly."

Finn scowled, wrinkling his freckled nose. "That's not fair! Why are we so lame?"

"Matt should be able to foresee a strike, and you should elude it with your magic. But he's crazy and you're weak."

"Eight . . . seven . . ."

Here we were: a mentally unstable Fool, an all but arrowless Archer, a magically challenged Magician, and me, running on fumes and anger.

What could possibly go wrong?

I reminded myself that today's encounter might be step one in bringing down this ancient contest. I imagined the game as a machine with cogs and wheels grinding to life every few centuries. I wanted to jam a stick of dynamite into the cogs and laugh as it exploded forever.

"Shh." Matthew covered his lips with his forefinger. "They're here."

When the three rounded the corner, two on foot and one in the air, my adrenaline surged. Yet then I noticed that our adversaries weren't as intimidating as I'd expected. Gabriel, for one, flew in obvious pain, blood seeping from one silky black wing, staining his old-timey gray suit. Underneath hanks of jet hair, his face was pale.

As an Arcana, I could see his *tableau*, a brief super-imposed picture, like a Tarot card. His was of an arch-angel carrying a staff and sword, flying over a mass of bodies.

Selena murmured, "He's injured."

"Death stabbed his wing," I replied. "Right before he beheaded the Temperance Card."

And the World? Tess Quinn was a chubby bru-nette with nervous eyes. She carried a battered staff. Presently she was biting the nails of her free hand to the quick. Hardly a seasoned killer.

I'd wager she had as little control over her powers as I used to. Her tableau was a bare-chested maiden with a swath of cloth around her hips, symbols of the four elements framing her.

But Joules looked malicious, his dark eyes flashing as sparks glittered over his skin. His tableau was the most terrifying—charred bodies plummeting from a lightning-struck tower.

When the three paused in front of the house, he called out, "Get a gander at all the vines! Empress must've spilled pints of blood to grow 'em!" His Irish accent was pronounced. "And the grand trees too? I'll bet you're right wasted. That tornado's fierce-looking, but Gabe can fly circles around it." He opened his right hand and a javelin appeared in it.

At this sign of aggression, my claws tingled anew, the heat rising. *Come, Tower, touch,* was on the tip of my tongue. Instead I inhaled for control and forced myself to say, "Hi, Joules, my name is Evie."

Double take from the Tower.

"And I want you to know that I'm sorry about what happened to Calanthe. She was a brave fighter. She deserved better."

In my head, Death tsked. —*You wound me, creature.*—

Ignoring him, I told Joules, "We want to join with you in an alliance to take out Death. Then we would be seven, gunning for him."

Joules twirled his javelin with ease. It was a thing of beauty, gleaming, etched with ancient symbols. "Or

I could end you all today, snag your icons and more power to take him on myself."

Out of the side of her mouth, Selena muttered, "Told you, dumb-ass."

"We don't want any trouble with you," I called.

"Too bad. 'Cause it's trouble you'll be gettin'."

"What happened to *the enemy of my enemy is my friend*?"

"Death stole my lass from me. Now I'm going to steal what he's hankerin' for most: your demise."

I was selling this as hard as I could, and it still looked like we were about to throw down. "It won't happen, Joules. Our alliance is too powerful. Already the Fool has foreseen that we would win this fight and all three of you will die." Bluffing. "We could've hidden ourselves with the Magician's illusions and ambushed you, but I wanted to offer an alliance. We're not playing this game. We refuse to kill any other player except for Death. We can make that vow to you today."

Tess's eyes widened, excitement in her expression. Hovering above us, Gabriel tilted his head, his face unreadable. Joules looked even more furious. "The vicious Empress is making promises? Problem is, you never keep them. Everybody knows you break your vows each game."

Had I? I slanted Selena a questioning glance, but she had her laser focus locked on Joules.

"Well, then, this game is different. We refuse to kill."

"Oh, is that so?" His hostility was palpable—and strengthening, for some reason.

"It is." My hopes for an alliance were circling the drain. Now I just wanted to get out of here alive. I readied my army. I could bind them with vines, giving us time to escape.

"Liar!" Joules yelled. "You think I canna see your hand, bitch? You already killed!" Without warning, he heaved his javelin straight at me.

Like a blur, Selena loosed her arrow; it struck his javelin, sending it off course. The spear hit the neighboring house. Lightning exploded it, firing debris over us.

Chunks of the house hit the closest oak like ax blows, cracking its trunk wide, sending pain ripping through me. Shingle fragments sliced into the side of my face, and blood streamed. He'd attacked? After I'd offered a truce?

He'd attacked . . . *me*? Fury filled me, and I screamed with it, my red hair whipping, my hands directing. Roots erupted from the deep, piercing the surface of the ground around him and Tess. As Joules aimed another javelin, a vine snaked around his waist and arms, slamming him to the ground.

Limbs from the remaining oak curled around him, the wood groaning as it ratcheted tighter. He thrashed to get free, but he was bound fast.

Gabriel sounded a battle call, diving to attack, but my tornado forced him back.

When vines circled Tess like serpents, she gave a nervous cry and swirled her staff in a circle above her head, as she might a lasso. Both Joules and Gabriel appeared to wait with bated breath.

Nothing happened. She was supposed to be one of the strongest? I stifled a yawn when she twirled her little stick again. Bored with the World, I launched my vines at her.

She batted them with her staff, but they kept coming. Tears streaming, she hunched down with a whimper.

Joules flailed against his bindings. "Let me go, you bitch!"

Death laughed. —*I knew this Empress of Peace act wouldn't last long. You're far too proud of your . . . craft.*—

Before I'd even made a conscious decision, I was sprinting for Joules, tree limbs parting for me. Nearly mindless with rage, I leapt atop him, perching on the limb clenched around his chest, careful to avoid his electrified skin. I could feel his currents bombarding his bindings.

"Wood," I explained. "Such a poor conductor." As he struggled, I raised my dripping claws to finish him. "Looks like you're helpless."

Death urged me —*Do it. You once told me how good it feels to sink your claws into flesh. Don't you remember?*—

Tess screamed, "Don't you hurt him! P-please, don't!"

Yelling with frustration, Gabriel tried to elude my tempest to save his friend, but he was too injured, too slow.

"*Póg mo thóin*," Joules grated. "Kiss my arse, Empress."

"Ah, Tower, you should have taken my offer." My voice was breathier, evil-sounding. "Poison is such a painful way to go."

Death whispered —*Why must you always taunt them so? Make a clean kill and be done with it.*—

Shut up!

Though Joules appeared horrified, his tone was full of bravado. "Do it, then. What I want is on the other side anyway."

I leaned my head closer to his, savoring the way my burning glyphs reflected in his terrified eyes. "Come. Touch. But you'll pay a—" The words strangled in my throat, because I'd caught sight of . . .

Jackson.

He'd come running down a nearby alley, bow at the ready, but froze upon seeing me.

My heart leapt. He hadn't left us?

He took cover behind an old shed not fifty feet away. He wore a hunter's coat, a hoodie, and fingerless gloves. The straps of his familiar bug-out bag fitted over his broad shoulders. His biker boots had been replaced with hiking boots.

He'd been resupplying before coming back for me! I should've had more faith.

Jackson's lips parted at my appearance. He'd seen the aftermath of my battle with the Alchemist—now he had a front-row seat to an execution.

Execution?

This wasn't me. I wasn't a killer. Jack hadn't left us this morning—but I knew if I did this thing now, I would lose him forever. I glanced down at Joules.

No longer did I see the malicious Tower Card. This was just a kid, sweating with fear. I shook my head hard, reining in the fury. Inhale. Exhale. Glance at Jack. Better.

To Joules, I said, "I told you I didn't want to kill. The only reason I have this marking on my hand is because I had to defend myself. I did everything I could not to harm the Alchemist."

"Just get this feckin' over wit'!"

Seeing how much rage Joules had inside him—and an apparent death wish—made me question my offer of alliance. Though I would pass on recruiting this unmerry band today, I would spare them on one condition. . . . "If I release you, will you vow not to hunt us again?"

Tess cried, "Make the vow!"

Gabriel called, "Do it, Tower."

Joules blinked at me. "You'll spare us?"

"This game is different. This time, the Empress isn't playing. I'll spare you all."

Selena, Matthew, and Finn approached, flanking

me. A unified front. "*None* of us are playing." I gazed up at Selena. "Isn't that right?"

She sighed. "Apparently, we're going to figure out a way to kill Death, then stop the game."

Joules jutted his chin. "Aye, then, I vow I'll not hunt you. But if you attack us, it's on."

Anxious to go talk to Jack, I said, "Good enough!" My barbs dropped once more to the street. My claws morphed back. My glyphs dimmed. With just a thought, I freed Tess and unraveled the Tower, offering my hand to help him up.

Joules stared at it. Muttering, "Bloody hell," he took it.

With the battle averted, Gabriel landed and gave Selena a formal bow—Archangel dug the Archer?

"Don't you need to go molt or something?" she sniffed.

In a commiserating tone, Matthew told Tess, "The World wasn't built in a day." Then he turned to Joules. Sounding more authoritative than I'd ever heard him, Matthew said, "You need to leave this valley, Tower. Before the sun sets."

Joules's gaze flickered over each of us. "Not a problem."

As soon as the Tower and his allies were out of sight, everything seemed to compete for my attention, when all I wanted to do was talk to Jackson.

Selena slapped me on the back. "If I were a nice person who didn't loathe you, I'd say you did well."

A limb from the remaining oak offered itself to my thorn claws, like an arm extended for a blood donation. Energy there for the taking.

Death had his own commentary: —*You spared the Tower, of all Arcana? Have you lost your wits, creature?*—

But I wasn't paying attention to any of them; instead I hastened toward Jackson's spot behind that shed. He'd already begun striding away.

"Jack, wait up." I trotted after him.

He kept walking toward the mountains. The ones that led to cannibal country.

Selena called after us, "J.D.!" He ignored her.

While the others held back in confusion, I followed him. "What are you doing?"

"Getting my ass out of Requiem." He tossed me my old bug-out bag, the one I'd thought was lost forever.

I gaped down at it. "How?" He must have retrieved it from the militia. I glanced inside. They'd stolen the heirloom jewelry I'd had for trading, but left some basic supplies—and my flash drive of my family's photos. "When did you get this?"

"Probably around the time you thought I was making out with Selena."

My face flamed. "You left your own bag behind last night."

"Mistake." Catching my gaze, he said, "Woan happen again." Then he kept walking.

I tried to keep up with his long-legged strides. "Where are you going?" So quickly? So away from me?

"Into the mountains."

"The ones that are teeming with cannibals?" Finn called, as he and the others snatched up the various packs and jackets and started trailing us. "That's where they live, you know, the ones who eat raw human meat, the ones I've *seen*. Does anybody listen to me?"

I did. "We're heading out the other way," I told Jack. "Through the bottleneck."

"Then you're goan to die."

"And that wouldn't bother you?"

His shoulders tensed, but he didn't slow his step. "There's a horde of zombies back there." *Bag dare.* "Bigger than last night, holed up in a warehouse about six miles down the road." He turned to address the others with a cruel look on his face. "As slow as Evie is, that ought to put y'all right in their midst by sunset."

I couldn't say anything about my slowness. Wasn't like I could back-handspring my escape.

"Mountains. Or Bagger bait," Jackson said. "That's between you and your god. Me? I'm heading away from the closest danger."

There were other things to be said, other questions to be asked—

"Have fun, *Empress*." He sneered the word.

"Why are you so angry with me?" I knew anger was his go-to emotion, but he was shaking with it.

He whipped around and stalked toward me. "You. Ain't. Right. None of you."

I gasped, rocked to the core. "I-I can't help the way I am."

"Doan mean I got to deal with it. You doan need me to babysit you anymore." He pulled up his hoodie, turned and trudged onward.

"Are you madder about what I am, or that I kept it from you?"

"Split it down the middle. Call it a day."

"You—you made a promise to my mother to get me to Gran's!"

He cast a narrow-eyed glance over his shoulder. "You're goan to pull that shit with me? Fine. Try to keep up, 'cause I'm goan that way." He pointed to the mountains, as if daring me to follow.

As if *hoping* I wouldn't.

While I stood there in shock, Matthew drew up beside me.

"Should we follow Jack?" I asked him.

"I'll lead you on the correct path. Let you know when you step off it." He trotted past me, following the Cajun.

That was the correct path? The others looked at me, again like I was their leader.

"We'll skate close to the edge," I assured Finn and

Selena. "Head south to the end of the range, then cut back for North Carolina. We won't go deep into the mountains."

"And if we lose our way?" Finn asked. "There are tons of mines up there. Each one's filled with cannibals, like ants in a hill. I told you I'd never cross the Appalachians again."

"I follow Matthew." Jackson had nothing to do with my choice. *Bullshit, Eves.*

Selena almost disguised her relief that we'd stick with Jack for now. Finn almost hid his dread. Ahead, Matthew's steps swerved as he caught rain on his tongue.

"Let's go. . . ."

For the next half hour, we meandered through the burned-out ghost town, seeing no one, expecting no one. We did pass piles of bodies left over from the Flash, though. Stripped of clothes, they looked like stacked mannequins.

I gazed up at the mountains we were heading toward. The lower parts of the rise had once been covered with forest. The Flash had scorched the trees into charred trunks, resembling power-line poles without the lines. The ground was covered with ash.

Ash. The Flash-fried remains of trees, animals, and people. I shivered, phobic about it. Since the apocalypse, it'd swirled in the windstorms and settled in drifts against the face of that incline.

A low bank of fog poured down the nearest mountain, slinking around the base of it. When it closed in on us, that ominous feeling from earlier thickened till I thought I would choke on it.

Just when I was about to tell the others that I was rethinking this plan, a Bagman wailed behind us. *Onward, Evie.*

What awaited us in those dark hills?

6

We were being watched.

After trudging uphill in the mud for what seemed like hours, we hadn't gotten anywhere near the center of this range, so it couldn't be cannibals. Nor Arcana—none of their calls sounded close by. Nor was it Bagmen; we could hear them baying in the valley below us, held in check by the diluted sun.

For now.

As the afternoon wore on, my foreboding feeling grew and grew. I was dragging ass, huffing and puffing, the acrid scent of burned wood stinging my nose. I'd trained as a dancer for years, but compared to the boys and Selena, my stamina was laughable. The ongoing drizzle provided enough moisture for the ash and mud to congeal like glue.

I'd toppled over so many times, my hands were coated with globs of it, my hair as well. Remains. In my hair.

Finn was just ahead, Matthew at my side like a pilot fish. Selena and Jackson were staggered, far in the lead as we headed for the next valley to the south. She'd mentioned seeing a town there on her map; I supposed we were heading toward it. Jackson must have been as well.

So much had happened in the last twenty-four hours, I struggled to process it all. Arthur's defeat, the return of some of my memories, the showdown with Joules, the dream of Death.

Jackson admitting what he thought of me.

Selena had been bang-on when she'd said he was disgusted. I would have given anything to talk to him, to explain that I might not be right, but it wasn't a choice I'd made to hurt him. It wasn't a choice whatsoever.

"You okay back there, Evie?" Finn asked with a worried look. "Maybe we ought to stop for a minute."

"I'm fine." *I'm dying!* "Got to keep moving." *I would chop off my right, marked hand to stop.* We'd never had to contend with mud before. I hoped it would slow down any zombies—or Arcana—who decided to pursue us.

"Okay. Cool." He carried on ahead as if I'd told him the truth or something.

I could barely talk, but questions were swirling in my head. Under my ragged breath, I said, "Matthew, last night I dreamed of a time when Death stabbed a past Empress with a sword. Did you send me that dream?"

"Yep."

"Why now? I've already learned about my abilities." I'd used most of them yesterday and today.

"Learn to defeat Death. You will fight him with your powers."

That Empress in my dream hadn't been able to *use* any powers for me to learn from. "All of those dreams have seemed familiar, but in this one, I could feel Death's sword entering my body."

"You felt it."

"Yeah, that's what I just said."

He nodded, effortlessly meandering beside me. "You felt it in a past life."

I turned on him, gritting out the words: "Past life?" He'd never told me that the nightmares I'd had were in fact about *me*. "You never said that we were reincarnates."

Of course, he'd never said we *weren't* reincarnates. Hadn't I suspected? From the visions Matthew had revealed, I'd witnessed a past Empress so horrific, I'd dubbed her the red witch.

But hadn't her deeds felt like memories?

"The Empress has a sense of humor this time," Matthew said, repeating a comment he'd made weeks ago.

This time. Because I was the same card, just a different version. Hundreds of years ago, she'd been a vicious killer.

I hadn't been anything less with Arthur.

I pressed my hand to my stomach. In a past life, I'd suffered that blow. Was that what awaited me in my present one? "The Empress from last night's dream seemed different from the one I've been seeing since before the Flash." The one who'd used sea plants to destroy whole galleons and spores to murder entire villages.

"Going back farther, farther," Matthew said. "Two games before. You were the May Queen then. Red witch was Phyta. You are Poison Princess. You are all of them: Lady Lotus, Mistress of Flora, Queen of Thorns."

He'd told me these names before, but I hadn't thought they'd referred to individual Empresses. "Why go back to another game? I've already hit my limit with dreams—with memories—of the red witch." Or Phyta, or whoever.

"*This* Death first met you then."

"You mean Death in this reincarnation?" His present life had started thousands of years ago. I might have come back as three different Empresses since then, but he'd simply endured and survived year after year, game after game. "Okay, fine, so you want me to have these memories. Then why are you piecemealing this information, Matthew? Why not just give me all the memories?"

"I did. Two games' worth. Your mind resists. Dreams relent. Safety valve."

"Wait . . ." I was struggling to keep up physically—and topic-wise. "So I have all the memories from two games, I just have to dream them? Why can't I see them all at once?"

He gave me an indulgent look. "Then you'd be like me. Crazy. You are Death's weakness."

"So you keep telling me. Does he happen to know *my* weaknesses?"

"As well as his face in the mirror. Pay attention to your dreams. I'm in his pocket, so he's in my eyes."

It wasn't the first time Matthew had told me that, but I hadn't understood him. Now I did. Death could see me through Matthew's eyes, so he always knew what was happening with me. And though I didn't understand *how*, Death could drop in on my thoughts at will. Our last exchange had been during this morning's harried climb:

—*You deserve every second of this misery and fear, creature.*—

And you know where you can shove your scythe.

It was one thing to have the others broadcasting in there, or to have silent conversations with Matthew. But Death poking around unnerved the hell out of me. "How can Death hear my thoughts?"

"Through the switchboard."

Recalling Selena's comments about Matthew jamming frequencies, I asked, "Do you consider our calls and thoughts frequencies?" I'd termed it Arcana

Radio. Maybe it was really Arcana Switchboard. With a nervous laugh, I said, "You're not the switchboard operator, are you?"

As if talking to a child, he said, "I'm the Fool."

"Then how are we connected?"

"Through me. The switchboard operator. The Fool is the Gamekeeper."

I sputtered, "But you told me that you weren't . . ." I trailed off. He hadn't actually denied it, had he? "So that's one of your abilities?" No wonder he was so often confused.

"*Respons*ibility."

"You need to disconnect this circuit, Matthew!" I'd thought mind reading was simply one of Death's powers. Then I recalled the Reaper once telling me, "Matto remembers his debts. He'll show you to me. . . ."

"Inside voices are important," Matthew insisted.

"Why would you allow him in my head?" I couldn't comprehend this. "A couple of weeks ago, he said something about you paying your debts?" Nothing. "Do you let him hear everyone's thoughts?"

"Death only wants yours. Death possessing Life. I'm in his pocket."

"So let me get this straight. You connect the Arcana calls. You let Death communicate with us all. And you allow him access to my brain alone—because of some debt?"

Matthew offered me a charred pinecone.

Patience! "You do understand that Death will always know what we're planning."

"Doesn't care about what we plan. No more than you would care what cannibal ants in mines plan. He laughs at our plans."

"I don't want a killer like him in my head!"

Matthew slowed, looking down at me with an expression that seemed far wiser than his years. "I do things for reasons."

Gaze darting, I said, "I've got to tell the others. This is a huge weakness! I can't form an alliance against an enemy when he knows all our moves in advance."

"You feel his presence. Learn when he's home. Death knew my gaze. Learn his."

"I can learn to tell when he's snooping?" When Matthew had showed me that last vision of Death battling Joules and his friends, the Reaper had sensed us. And didn't I perceive a heaviness whenever he was about? "Until then, how do I know Death won't try to prevent me from reaching Gran?" I asked, hoping that Matthew might confirm she was even alive.

"Bores Death. He doesn't believe in her as you do."

"Can you please tell me if she's safe?"

"Define *safe*," Matthew said with a look at his hand. Subject done.

She had to be alive. I had to believe Matthew cared about me enough *not* to let me go on a wild-goose chase.

"Why does Death have such an interest in me, anyway? There are other cards to terrorize."

Shrug.

"You know, but you're not telling me."

Smile. "Crazy like a fox!"

"Matthew, come on—" A branch snapped some distance to my right. I jerked around but saw nothing. A clammy feeling crawled over my nape. "Are we being watched?"

He blinked at me. "Why wouldn't we be?"

"Are we in danger?"

He chuckled, shaking his forefinger at me. "Sense of humor."

Yeah, I guessed we never got *out* of danger. I kept walking. "Is Jackson going to leave us?" As soon as I'd asked this, I regretted the expenditure of breath. I *knew* the answer to that question.

He'd been taking point, trudging onward, with his hoodie pulled up. All day his expression had varied between enraged and more enraged. Like he was getting pissed off anew every few minutes.

He wasn't talking to me, but he also ignored Selena and Finn. Yep, he'd checked out mentally. I figured he'd get ghost as soon as we made the next town.

"Should've said good-bye. Arcana and non-Arcana mix poorly." Matthew sighed. "Dee-vee-oh stares at you when you don't see. Hunter. Watching. You're the angel atop the Christmas tree that he can never reach. Gift beneath that he can't unwrap."

You'd have thought I'd be used to Matthew's ramblings. I wasn't.

"All his life, all false faces. Born of a false face. You showed him yours."

Jackson still carried the scars of his poverty-stricken childhood. His father had refused to pay support, or even to acknowledge his destitute son. His mother had been an alcoholic who'd entertained drunken lovers. Those men had abused her—and beaten Jackson, teaching him not to trust.

Teaching him to be ruthless and to communicate with his fists.

All he'd ever known was deception and violence.

How could he not see me as deceitful and violent, as more of the same? Before his eyes, I'd turned into a viney-skinned, poisonous monster—one who'd been cackling to slit some scrawny Irish kid's throat.

Matthew said, "Think less about Dee-vee-oh, more about game."

Toiling up a steep incline, I considered what I remembered about the cards. Last night, when I'd gazed at my new icon, memories of my grandmother had flooded me in a rush. They were still fragments, but growing more fully formed with each hour.

I could recall her telling me about players who

controlled animals as I did plants. I remembered cards that could manipulate the elements.

Her voice seemed to echo in my head: *"The details of the images are important. They're to be read like a map." "Study the cards. Memorize them. The symbols are all there for a reason, Evie. They tell you about the players."*

How I wished I could lay hands on a deck. I knew the cards were chock-full of dots to connect, threads in common. Some cards had animal images on them, some plants. Others had water or fire.

I recalled Gran humming as she'd shuffled her deck, preparing to quiz me. "Which cards are the best spellbinders?"

I'd chirped, "The Hierophant and the Lovers. And me!"

"The strongest in body?"

"The Devil! The Devil is so strong!"

No wonder my mom had gotten spooked.

At the top of the rise, Finn waited up for us. "Evie, I wanted to apologize again for making myself look like Jack and accidentally tricking you and making you run away and all. Forgive me?"

Was I still mad? I'd been trying to look on the bright side. Okay, yeah, I was now broken up with Jackson beyond all reconciliation, a murderer, and a fugitive from a zombie horde.

But . . . I'd remembered a lot about the Arcana game, I'd saved three—well, two—girls' lives and maybe others who would've fallen into Arthur's trap. And I'd learned to control my powers.

It was a wash. Yet then I recalled how Finn had looked out for Matthew over the last two days. "I accept your apology, Finn. Just don't pull a stunt like that again."

Farther ahead, Jackson was taking a breather, drinking from his canteen. He gazed back down the mountain. God, he was so tall and proud. So strong. His rugged features were sigh-worthy.

We were this close, and still I missed him.

Finn caught my gaze. "I know things seem rough with him right now, but he'll come around. He went nuts when you were missing."

"He has a temper." Which wasn't surprising, considering his tragic background.

"No, Evie. He was . . . frantic, out of control. I'm talking Hulk-smash on ye olde cabin. When he realized our lack of transportation was the sole thing keeping him from you, he stormed back into that militia's camp, striding into a hail of bullets. Dude didn't duck, didn't sidestep, just rolled in, killed, took that jeep."

My lips parted as I stared up at Jackson in amazement.

"He loves you," Finn insisted.

As if he could sense he was the subject of our

discussion, Jack cast me a derisive look over his shoulder, then marched on.

"Clearly."

"He does. The reason he didn't have his bug-out bag last night was because he wasn't thinking about his own survival—only yours."

I glanced at Matthew, who gave me a short nod: *That's true.*

"He just needs some time to get used to the idea of you with powers." Finn tilted his head, taking in my face—which I knew was bright red from exertion and streaked with remains. "His girlfriend went from bunny to viper. From hot piece of ass to smokin' monsteress."

I raised my brows. "Smokin'? I was repulsive."

Finn helped me over a log. "When you turned all Eviezilla, I had a boner the size of . . . well, something large and boner-shaped."

My cheeks heated even more, but I didn't put too much stock in what Finn said. He wasn't exactly discriminating with girls. "Well, Jackson didn't think so. He's written me off. He's got this intense sense of curiosity. He's wicked intelligent, and he loves to solve puzzles, to dig at secrets. Yet he hasn't asked a single question about us, about me? It's because we're not going to be a part of his life for much longer."

I paused, catching my breath somewhat. One thing I had to know . . . "What were you thinking when you deceived Selena that night? Was it worth it for one kiss?"

Finn raked his fingers through his hair. "Hell no. I was way out of bounds."

"You think? You can't treat girls that way."

"I know, I know. But sometimes I feel forced to trick others."

Matthew piped up: "In his blood."

Finn nodded eagerly. "The more I use my illusions, the more I need to. I get antsy if I don't. That was one of the reasons I was deported from SoCal to South Carolina to live with the redneck cuzzes—because of the pranks on my parents."

"Like what?"

"My mom freaked when she woke up with a pink faux-hawk the day of a society dinner. My dad, weirdly, didn't think it was funny to see a clown with a bloody ax in our pool house. They didn't know for certain that it was me, but they knew something was going on and couldn't handle it. But still, I couldn't make myself stop. It's like a compulsion."

I flashed him a startled look. "The more I use my powers . . ." I trailed off.

"The more you want to kill us," Finn finished for me.

As Matthew always did, I shrugged. But this conversation made me wonder: would Matthew gain clarity if he could wean himself from seeing visions of the future? Once things calmed down, I would ask him to try.

Conserving our powers seemed wise anyway. Our

abilities weren't infinite. Both Finn and I had tapped ourselves out, and needed to recharge. I gazed up at Selena, vaulting a gully with ease. So what happened to her if she used hers too much, other than running out of arrows? What were her weaknesses?

Changing the subject, I told Finn, "It seems like having problems with parents is an Arcana trait. Like, more than just a few spats over curfew."

Was it our curse to be misunderstood by them? My beloved mom, rest her soul, had sent me to a nuthouse. Matthew's mom had tried to drown him. Even Arthur had hinted that he'd melted his father in acid—

I heard another snapping branch, this time to my left. When I jerked my head around, I tripped but bounced upright. Ahead, Selena paused, canting her head. Sensing something too? She petted the flights of her last arrow, retrieved before we'd left Requiem. But after a moment, she continued walking.

Finn's eyes were on her as well.

"For what it's worth, I'm sorry about how it worked out with Selena," I said. "I know how much you like her."

"Past tense. It's one thing to like a girl who wants another guy. It's another to like a girl who plans to murder you at a time of her convenience."

"She said she was raised for this. I guess she can't help it." I couldn't believe I was taking up for Selena. I turned to Matthew. "What'd you tell her to get her on my side?"

"The future. If she kills you, Death stabs her in the eye with her own arrow."

"Such a lovely guy."

A raindrop pelted me in the face then. Drops began to fall more steadily, as did the temperature, our breaths smoking. "Matthew, you told me that we'd grow weaker when the rain came. You said, 'You've never known terror, not like you will when the rains come.' How? Why?"

"Sunny and green? You annihilate. Now?" He shook his head. "Powers. Stop. Start. Fits. A plant with no sun is weak. Already you feel it. Plus, obstacles get faster, stronger. Foes laugh at us."

Matthew's lessons had fallen into four categories: arsenal, foes, field of battle, and obstacles. "Which obstacles?" No answer. "At least tell me how long the rain will last."

With a decisive nod, he said, "Until the snow comes." As if that answered everything.

"When will that be?"

"The Army grinds on, a windmill spins. The one who learns most wins last."

Whatever that meant. Matthew couldn't be pumped for information and he couldn't be rushed to predict things.

When I saw that Jackson and Selena had stopped atop another rise ahead, I almost moaned with relief. The sun would set soon. Maybe there was a shelter nearby?

Once we reached them, I struggled to disguise how

exhausted I was. Judging by Jackson's rolled eyes, I fooled no one.

"I didn't . . . say a word," I gasped. "Not . . . complaining."

After a hesitation, he muttered, "No, you never do."

That had sounded almost not cruel.

From this vantage, we could see down into Requiem, all the way along the road to that warehouse. Just as Jackson had said, it was overflowing with Baggers. They were spilling out of doorways, huddled in alcoves. Some briefly braved the day, scurrying back to shelter. Like they were testing the sunlight.

"Is it just me, or do they look faster?" Selena asked.

I nodded. "What's driving them out? What's got them in such a frenzy?"

Matthew said, "Bloodlust."

Finn shook his head. "I thought they turned to blood because there was no water around."

"Rain means they're always strong enough to track blood. New battery."

"You're joking." I pinched my forehead. "They prefer blood?" The rain would just energize them. Sure enough, the obstacles would get faster, stronger. No longer would we see their crumbly bodies on the sides of the roads. "They'll follow at nightfall?"

"Loved the Alchemist's taste," Matthew answered. "Five of us for the taking. Most blood for miles and miles. The hunt is afoot."

Even with all our Arcana powers, we were at a serious disadvantage against that many Bagmen. Selena had one arrow. Finn could disguise us, but the zombies would just follow our scent. Matthew had no attack powers.

And me? I didn't fight well on the run, much less with powers that were stopping and starting in fits.

"What's the matter, Empress?" Jackson grated with a glare at my muddy right hand, at my icon. "Why you look scared, you? You can just take them all out." The *not cruel* vibe of earlier had been short-lived.

I exhaled wearily. "No. No, I can't."

"Ain't like you can die anyway."

Matthew shook his head. "She can die. Death sees to her."

—*Count on it.*— came Death's whisper. —*You'll be under my sword within the week.*—

7

"Sooo . . . anybody else have a sense of impending doom?" Finn asked around a mouthful of Mayday bar. "I mean, more so than usual. Or maybe just of being watched?"

Teeth clattering, I said, "Oh, y-yeah." I had since we'd left Requiem two days ago.

That first night we'd spent miserable, restless hours huddled in the shelter of some rocks. Tonight, after we'd plodded around nearly blind in the dark, Jack had come across a hunter's shooting house. Basically it was a metal hut about five feet tall, with peeling camouflage paint and one open end.

When we'd all piled into his "find," Jack had gazed at the sky for patience, but didn't say anything.

There was enough room inside for each of us to have a little space, if we didn't try to stand up. It allowed us to escape the drizzle and provided some protection until we could set out at dawn.

We were betting our lives that the Baggers couldn't catch up with us before then.

I squeezed out my hair, settling in. "I've g-got an ominous f-feeling."

Finn had produced another illusion lantern for us. I could swear the nights were getting longer, even as we headed into summer months, while the temperature kept dropping.

One day, would the sun forget to rise?

Despite everyone being waterlogged and freezing— except for Selena with her perfect outdoor gear—we didn't light a fire. She had dry kindling in her pack, natch, but any wet firewood would smoke like crazy, and we still had Bagmen on our tail.

All day we'd wondered if the zombies could match our hectic pace. From what I understood, they didn't heal from injuries, and most had been created the night of the Flash. At eight months old, they must have some wear and tear there.

Unless they'd been newly created by a Bagman's contagious bite.

Fifteen hours ago at dawn, Selena had run back and scouted. Her assessment? "There are *more* of them."

I'd asked her, "Where are they going to spend the day?" Though drizzly, it'd still been bright. And we hadn't passed a single house, just mile after mile of burned-out woods.

She'd hesitated, then said, "They're burrowing. Into the muck. The good news is that if any Arcana think to follow us, they'll be in for a hell of a surprise."

Like a Bagman minefield. I'd shivered at the imagery. And for the rest of the day, I'd wondered with my every step if I was going to find a *Bagmine*.

Now Selena said, "I'm getting the same feeling as you two. Like we're being stalked, as hunters do with deer." Plucking her bowstring, she admitted, "I'm not used to being on this side of things."

I gazed over at Jackson, sitting outside our circle near the open exit, on edge as well. He'd told me that nothing could get the drop on him, and for the past several weeks, nothing had.

Did he remain with us because we shared a mutual direction, or because he felt forced to keep that promise to my mother? Since he'd refused to talk to me, I couldn't imagine how he was handling everything. Matthew had said he burned with curiosity. Tonight I could almost *feel* the intensity of it.

Though Jackson hadn't asked a single question— not his party, I supposed—he was listening, learning. During the day, I'd caught him staring at me again and again, his expression ranging from enraged to . . . confused.

"Matthew, do you sense anything?"

In answer, he studied his hand. He was pensive about something too. I wished he would talk to me, even if I understood little of what he said.

I placed half of my Mayday bar in his hand, curling my gloved fingers around his until he held it on his own. Eventually he glanced down, appearing surprised to find it in his hand. But he ate it.

"Who could be watching us?" I asked.

"Not Bagmen," Selena said. "They would just attack. Cannibals?"

Finn shook his head. "They don't hunt far from home."

We were coming up on one of the charred holes in Selena's map. I almost got the sense that we were about to fall off the face of the earth, like it should read: *Here be dragons!*

But as long as we were edging away from those mines—and a horde of Bagmen—I was game to go on. "We'd hear other Arcana calls, right?"

Suddenly Finn jerked a glance over his shoulder. The rest of us tensed and stared out the open end of the hut in that same direction, all at the same time, like meerkats.

He muttered, "I wish whatever's out there would nut up or shut up."

"Hear, hear." Needing to take my mind off my jitters, I turned to Selena. "If you're so keen to be in an alliance with us, why don't you tell us what you know?"

With a condescending smile, she opened her bag—and took out a deck of Tarot cards.

"You had a deck the whole time! At moments like this, I can see the appeal of the game."

She shrugged, laying them out atop her silvery reflective heat blanket.

"If you were trying to get me into an alliance, why keep all this secret?" I persisted.

"Because of that whole I-don't-remember-the-game line you've been feeding us. I thought you were lying." She dealt the cards in a cross formation, much like Gran used to. As soon as I saw the Tarot images, memories came into focus, springing to life like poppies bursting through a layer of snow.

Trying to draw Matthew into our conversation, I said, "Look, here's Matthew's." I pointed out his card; on it, a smiling young man with an oblivious expression walked a desolate land, carrying a rucksack and a single white rose. A yapping dog nipped at his heels.

Matthew tilted his head at the likeness. "In a place where nothing grows, I carry a flower. The memory of you."

I smiled at him. "That is so sweet."

He frowned. "That literally happened."

"Oh."

Finn said, "That's just like the image I saw the first time we met. It flashed over him."

I nodded. "We all have those. They're called tableaux."

Finn held the card up next to Matthew's face, comparing the likeness. "You look stoned, Matto."

Matthew sighed with contentment. "Thank you."

I held up Selena's card. "The Moon." Hers depicted a glowing goddess of the hunt.

Finn's expression darkened. "Not interested. Next."

Selena glared at him.

I pulled another card. The lightning-struck tower. "You guys already know the Tower, that pleasant Irishman who was such a joy to meet. And here's Death." I pointed to his card. The Reaper was clad in that black armor, scythe at the ready, riding a pale horse with evil red eyes. He carried a black flag emblazoned with a white rose.

Finn muttered, "Jesus. That dude's real?" He wadded up his Mayday wrapper, tossing it into the shadows. "So what are his powers?"

Everyone looked at me for an answer. Even Matthew, as if he were quizzing me.

"He's a horseman and knight with supernatural speed and strength. He uses two swords and can strike with them so fast they're a blur. His armor is impenetrable, even to my claws. He's fearless. In one of Matthew's visions, I saw him walk into Joules's lightning shower like it was nothing." Kind of the way I imagined Jackson had walked into a hail of militia bullets. "His touch is deadly." And he'd been able to read my mind for weeks. Though not without detection; I felt him even now.

"Weaknesses?" Finn asked.

"One," Selena answered. "The Empress."

"Yeah, so I keep hearing," I said.

Finn frowned. "If he's a swordsman, what's to stop him from chopping down your trees, going all Paul Bunyan on your ass?"

Had Jackson eased closer to us? To me?

Selena said, "It must be her poison, then."

"So how do I get close enough to him to deliver a toxin without getting stabbed myself? How do I get past his armor?"

Selena pinned me with her gaze. "We'll have to figure that out if we want to live."

After a moment, I looked away. "To think I used to feel sorry for him."

—I do not want your sympathy, creature!—

You no longer have it!

—I've missed our times together. Missed touching you.—

Because he killed with his touch.

You're sick!

"Evie?" Finn snapped his fingers in front of me.

"What? What'd you say?"

"Your card." He held it up.

The Empress sat upon a throne with her arms

opened wide. In the background were rolling hills of green and red, from crops—and blood. A waterfall cascaded in the distance.

"You look scary. And sexy."

I was about to say, *Not me.* But it had been me, in a previous life.

Finn showed the card to Jackson, whose gray gaze flicked from the card to me and back.

"Okay, so you've got poison in your claws," Finn said, "and a lotus thingy that pops up from your palm to choke and paralyze people, and a tornado of thorns, and your blood revives dead plants. Oh, and wound regeneration. Did I miss anything?"

Toxic spores from my hair. I could lay waste to an entire city with them. Hearing someone else outline these things, I felt even more like a freak. I gazed at Jackson, wishing he could understand that no one wanted to be a monster, to be feared. Hell, even a fiend like Death called me *creature*.

One of the good things about going full-on Empress? When I was burning with that white-hot battle fury, there was no room for doubt.

Now, as Jackson tilted his head at me, I was awash in it.

Selena happily added, "She can also mesmerize guys." Revealed, no doubt, for Jackson's benefit.

He narrowed his eyes, his expression saying, *Son of a bitch! That explains a lot.*

Finn looked excited. "Mesmerize? Really? It goes with your eerie Arcana call." Making his voice breathy, Finn said, "'Come, touch, but you'll pay a price.'"

Jackson gave a bitter laugh.

Though the Empress's arms were welcoming on the card, her gaze was menacing—as if she was thinking her call right at that moment. But then, that was her—*my*—MO. To beckon, to allure, then to strike.

"Mesmerizing is not something I do every day," I hastily explained. "Just when I'm in full Empress mode. It doesn't always work, and not for long anyway. I went all-out against the Alchemist, and he was still keen to slice my tongue out and pickle it in a jar!"

Selena nodded. "Uh-huh, whatever you say, Evie."

I turned on her. "And what about you, *La Luna*? You have the power to seed doubt and to lure people to you with moonlight!" *Beware the lures.* "You set a trap for me at your house in Georgia, but Jack was with me so you held off attacking. You know, I'd bet that wasn't even your place—I never saw a single photo of you on the walls."

As she'd told me once before, she said, "Prove it."

Everyone fell silent.

"What are your weaknesses?" Finn finally asked me.

Again Selena was happy to answer: "When there are no plants around to feed her energy, she taps out quickly, even more so if she has to use her blood to revive or create plants. She needs the sun. Her power is collaborative—some cards are more dependent on the environment than others."

Keen to get the attention off of me, I said, "And what are your weaknesses?"

"Isn't it obvious?" Selena pointed to her thigh quiver, which held one real arrow and two makeshift ones. She'd been trying to replenish her supply, but, as she'd explained, there wasn't any green wood to carve new ones from.

I supposed I could help her with that—open a vein, coax a sapling to life—but I didn't yet trust her enough to weaken myself just to make her stronger. And it wasn't like I had a lot of juice on tap.

Just as Matthew had warned, my powers continued to deteriorate in this rain.

"Eventually, I will always run out of arrows. Then I have to depend on my enhanced speed, endurance, and grace."

Rolling my eyes, I picked up the Devil Card. "So, this is Ogen, a.k.a., El Diablo. He allies with Death. He's got horns and hooves like a goat man, but his body is all ogre—with superhuman strength. His call? *I'll make a feast of your bones.*"

"Ogen, the ogre?" Finn raised his brows. "Really?"

I shrugged. "I don't make the news, I just report it." I picked up the Judgment Card next. "You guys have met Gabriel as well. He can strike like a missile from above."

Selena added, "And he's got animal senses. That's why it's so dangerous that he's hooked up with Joules. Gabriel can scent us even through Finn's illusions, then Joules could just wait up on some vantage, pointing and shooting, picking us off."

Strengths and weaknesses. I needed to ask Matthew what could take me out, besides the Touch of Death.

Finn sniffed to Selena, "Hide *you* with my illusions?"

I'd seen *Survivor* alliances tighter than mine.

He asked me, "What happens if one of us bites it due to natural causes?"

I didn't remember the answer, so I waved to Selena.

"The Arcana closest to you gets your icon."

"What happens to the losers?"

Selena answered him, "They're reborn, with no memory of their past lives. Well, except for him." She pointed at Matthew. "The Fool sees everything. That's what makes him crazy."

Matthew nodded happily at her.

Directing a scowl her way, I shuffled through some more cards, but Finn stayed my hand over one. "Wait, I've seen this guy." His face paled.

"The Hierophant?" The image was of a robed figure giving a blessing to his kneeling followers. They all had milky white eyes. I handed Finn the card.

In a hushed tone, Matthew said, "Hierophant. He of the Dark Rites."

I remembered Gran warning me about him: *He's a*

charmer, Evie, a spellbinder. Never look him in the eyes. You are vulnerable to him. And he's not the only one. "My grandmother told me he can control your mind to make you commit monstrous acts. Once you do, you'll be enslaved forever—even after his death, you'll keep doing whatever it is he wanted from you. The monstrous acts vary each game." Having been brainwashed in a nuthouse, I had a particular dread of mind control.

Eyes locked on the image in his shaking hand, Finn said, "He was with the cannibals. I think I can guess what the monstrous act is. He's making people eat human flesh."

"No one needs to force people to eat others." Jackson was joining in the conversation? "In case you haven't noticed, there's no food in these mountains. None."

We were going on months of empty grocery stores and zero crops growing. Few animals were alive to be hunted.

His voice a whisper, Finn said, "These particular cannibals feed . . . on the living. Not just raw. *Living.* Monstrous enough for you?"

No. No way.

Finn looked at Matthew, his gaze haunted. "These Arcana are sick, and they aren't just fighting each other. What the hell is the point of our existence?"

Matthew glanced up, startled. "Point? Cachet. We are champions of the gods!"

"Gods?" I croaked, peering up at the low ceiling. "Are there, like, deities running around, controlling the game?"

"They left—"

Suddenly Jackson yanked his crossbow over his back, aiming out the hut's opening. "We got company."

Selena had already risen to one knee, her bow and arrow aimed—a little too close to my head. "It's a wolf," she said just as I spied gleaming yellow eyes in the burned woods.

Big yellow eyes.

Though Jackson relaxed his aim a fraction, Selena looked even more deadly. Before I could say a word, her arrow zoomed past my ear toward the animal.

When we heard the creature speeding away through the mud, Selena bit out a curse.

"Why would you kill it?" I demanded. "That might be the last of its kind on earth!"

Even Jackson—a seasoned hunter—was giving her a look that said, *Not cool.*

"That was no ordinary wolf." Selena looked uneasy. Selena *never* looked uneasy. "We've been scouted by the Strength Card. The Mistress of Fauna."

I remembered that card, and Gran's words: *Fauna can control animals, Evie, borrowing their senses and making them her familiars.*

"Why didn't we hear her call grow louder?" Finn said.

Selena had already strung one of her makeshift arrows. "Because she isn't near us, not yet. Only her familiars."

I scrambled out of the line of fire. "Why didn't she sic the wolf on us?"

Selena shook her head. "I don't know why, but Fauna just wanted a look-see. And I think . . ."

"What?"

"I think she wanted us to know she's watching us. That wolf has been stalking us for days, but I never caught sight of it. Now it reveals itself?"

I swallowed, and Finn said, "What do you mean, watching us? And why would the Strength Card be involved with animals?"

I remembered this one—I'd had the same question eight years ago. "People only started calling her Strength in recent times. She used to be the Fortitude Card, referring to her single-minded purpose. She thinks the way animals do, like beasts on the hunt, with a sole, blood-driven resolve."

I drew out her card, showing them a delicate girl in a white robe, holding the mouth of a ferocious lion. "Her card is one of the most literal. She can manipulate animals the same way I do plants. Like Gabriel, she has animal senses."

Selena said, "Not only that—she can *tap into* the senses of nearby creatures."

I nodded. "I remember that. If she wanted to spy on

us, she could get a crow to fly over and see us through its eyes." Even Jackson was listening intently to this. "And if she exchanges her blood with an animal, it becomes her familiar, connected to her forever. I don't know how exactly. Selena?"

"Trade secret. Sometimes we don't know all the powers. Though Matthew would."

He cast her a mulish look. "Not *your* psychic."

"Matthew, please," I murmured, "can you tell us anything?"

He gazed down at his hand. Yet now he seemed to be looking for something there.

Or maybe my paranoia was spreading like kudzu. I asked Selena, "Do you ever ally with Fauna? Does her family chronicle?"

"Not normally. Each game she's allied with different cards."

Finn stared for long moments at the image. "She's got an infinity symbol on her card. It's right above her head. Like on mine."

Those shared symbols. Death's card had a waterfall like mine and a rose upon his flag. In essence, he carried a single white rose—as the Fool did on his card. ". . . *to be read like a map.*"

Seeming to give himself an inner shake, Finn said, "So, to recap, we've got zombies on our trail and cannibal mines nearby, and now we've got another Arcana on our ass."

"Look on the bright side," I said. "How many animals can still be alive? This game, it would suck to be the Mistress of Fauna." No sooner had the words left my mouth than a wolf howled in the distance.

With plaintive calls, two more answered.

8

Blood spilling from my mouth and wound, I writhe on Death's sword.

Please. *The word is on my lips, but I am too proud to utter it.*

Though I want to live, I will never beg!

The Reaper removes his gauntlet, revealing a hand covered with icons. He must have nine kills.

Soon to harvest five more.

He reaches for me with that bared hand, a weapon in itself. I shudder with fear and agony. The more I shake, the more his sword slices at my entrails and raps against my spine. Tears blur my vision, spilling down my cheeks.

In the distance, a lion roars.

"This will hurt for nary a moment more," he promises, his eyes intent on mine.

All the things I wish I'd done. At least my family will pass on to future Empresses what knowledge I've garnered. I made sure of that.

He's so close I can perceive his breaths on my face, cooling my tears.

I am looking upon Death, as his hand inches closer. . . .

I shot awake, swiping my palm over my cheek, stunned that there weren't tears streaming down, stunned that Death wasn't right beside me. As I blinked my eyes, I probed, realizing his presence was gone.

It was dark in the hut, but my shirt was riding up, revealing a glowing glyph. It cast enough light to see Matthew's sleeping form nearby. Selena and Finn were asleep as well.

Jackson was awake, seated across from me—and staring at the glyph. It reflected in his gray gaze.

In a low tone, he said, "Can you feel them things, you?" There was no rage in his voice.

"They're like shivers." I admitted, "It's comforting to feel them." Because they represented my arsenal, and I believed that somehow, someway, they were all that stood between me and Death.

Jackson's gaze flickered over my face, studying. Always studying. "What's it feel like when you change completely?"

Amazing. No room for uncertainty, just sizzling power. "It's definitely different."

"You were like a . . . a *divinité*."

I sat up. Still his words could thrill me. Still I was one heartbeat away from telling him how much I—

"You ain't human, no?"

The thrill flared out, leaving cold ash. Though the statement was fair, it still stung. How to answer? "Both my parents were. You know my mom was." Jackson had met her the night before she died, giving her enough time to get to know him, to rest assured that he could keep me safe. "I never wanted to deceive you, Jack. I was just getting used to this stuff myself. Didn't know my way around it."

He scrubbed a hand over his tired face. "Why didn't you tell me about all this shit?"

"I was warned against confiding in others." *Arcana means secrets*, as Matthew had said.

"*Coo-yôn* must've told you that!"

Selena sighed without rousing. Finn smacked his lips and muttered, "Mom, how long I gotta stay there?"

Without a word, Jack collected his gear and stormed out into the mist, taking a seat on a nearby shelf of rock.

Though uninvited, I joined him.

"You listened to *coo-yôn*, trusting him over me?"

"Yes, Jackson, the psychic I trust with my life told me not to tell anyone. You know, the kid who predicted the end of the world and saved me from the Flash. Besides, you and I had a deal: I'd tell you my secrets once you got me to my grandmother's."

"Like you would've told me then. You wrote me a note and took off from Finn's without a word because you knew how I'd react."

"That's not true. After our fight, I decided that you deserved to know the truth, warning or no. I was coming to reveal everything when I saw you and Selena—"

"Not *me*."

"Not you," I whispered.

He fell silent. *Talk to me*, I wanted to scream. *Tell me what you're thinking.*

"You told me I quieted the voices." The Arcana calls I'd heard but hadn't understood. "Seems like you'd need to hear them now."

"For some reason, you quiet the buzz of all of them. But if one came close enough I'd still hear it, just as I did Selena's call."

"Does it scare you, knowing these people want to kill you?"

I nodded. "I've known for months that Death has some kind of sick interest in me. I don't know why, but he does." I thought of my dream. Apparently, he always had. "Matthew's shown me visions of his skill, his lack of mercy." And Death had said I wouldn't last this week. "But I try not to dwell on it, try to think about other things."

"Like what?"

Like wishing I were normal and we were back together. "I think about you a lot."

"Why's that? You doan need a protector anymore."

Debatable. And maybe we needed to protect each other. Besides . . . "That's not the reason I liked you."

"Oh, this I gotta hear." His tone was snide.

"Just forget it. It doesn't matter. Why should I explain anything to you? You're going to leave as soon as we get to the next town. That's clear."

"Is it?"

"It's for the best anyway. You'll be safer once we separate." Separate. A life without Jackson Deveaux. The mere idea sent my emotions spiraling.

My skin began to glow anew, and even through my T-shirt, the glyphs shone as they wound along my arms, across my chest. I knew my face was casting off light as well.

He stared at the changes in me.

"Look at you, Jack! You're disgusted."

"Not used to you." He got up on his knees before me, wary, like a mongoose sidling around a serpent. "Just let me do this, okay?"

As he reached for me, he yanked off his fingerless gloves, as Death had done in my dream. *Block that out.*

Jackson lifted the hem of my shirt, baring my torso to little bites of rain—and his avid gaze. With his muscles tensed as if he might have to leap away at any moment, he tentatively touched me.

I gasped at the contact.

Growing bolder, he skimmed the backs of his fingers along a glyph as it floated across my damp skin. His hooded eyes followed the path of his fingers. *"Hypnotique."* His breaths were short puffs of smoke in the cold night, his expression fascinated.

With infinite slowness, he stroked until I was panting, until I ached. I bit my bottom lip to keep from moaning out loud. I needed him to kiss me. I needed those strong arms, squeezing me to him.

"Your skin is so soft. *Satinée*," he murmured. "You goan to drive me crazy before it's all done, ain't you?"

"Jack, please."

"Please what?" He looked up, met my eyes.

Accept me, kiss me. I moistened my lips.

He noticed. Though his brows drew together as if he were pained, he didn't give me the kiss I craved from him. Yet his fingers still traced my skin, higher, higher.

When he bared my bra and grazed his knuckles over me, I couldn't stand it anymore—I scrambled to my knees, grasped his broad shoulders, and kissed him.

His muscles stiffened beneath my palms. Against his lips, I murmured, "Kiss me back?"

Heartbeats passed.

Then, with a groan, he did. Slow slants of his lips over mine grew more heated, more urgent. He leaned me down over his arm, laying his rough palm on my cheek to hold me steady for his kiss.

Groans broke from his lungs, moans from my lips. As ever, the fire between us stoked into an inferno. That combustible chemistry. He kissed me like he wanted to brand me—

Someone cleared his throat.

When Jackson released me and drew back, I saw Matthew standing awkwardly at the entrance to the hut.

As I pulled my shirt down, Jackson grated to me, "You taste like my Evie, feel like her. But you're not her." He swiped the back of his hand over his lips.

Ah, and here was the rage.

"We're out here with no protection from Baggers, no lookout, and I'm still a heartbeat from taking you! You mesmerizing me too? That's the only goddamned reason I'd still be thinking about you after all this shit. All my life, I never went looking for trouble, but it always found me! You're just the latest helping of grief."

My eyes pricked with tears. "I didn't want it to be like this."

"Then let me go! End this hold you got over me."

"I didn't mesmerize you. I wouldn't." Surely I wouldn't?

"'Come, touch, pay a price?' That's your call? Well, I *did*. I'm paying it still."

He snatched up his bow and bag and strode away into the dark, leaving me trembling, cold, adrift. I stared after him for long moments. When I pulled my knees to my chest, Matthew crossed to sit beside me. "Not Arcana."

"Can you see Jackson's future?"

"I see far." He frowned. "Not with him. Unknown. Variable. Strike from equation!"

"Would he be safer away from us?"

Matthew gave me a raised-brow *really?* look. Stupid question. Then he tilted his head. "More dreams of Death?"

I forced myself to stop staring in Jackson's direction and pay attention to Matthew, who sounded relatively coherent. "Yes. The same encounter with Death, after he's stabbed me." Again, I'd noted that he looked younger then. "If he's immortal, how does Death age?"

"Duration of the games. Game begins—he ages. Game ends—he stops."

"He doesn't look that much older now. How long do these games last?"

Matthew sighed. "This will be one of the longest."

"If I can regenerate, then is his Touch of Death the only way to kill me?" Or maybe I was like the Bagmen, taken out with a shot to the brainpan?

Shrug.

Change of tack. "Does he always kill me?"

"Not always. And Lady Lotus didn't die once."

I swallowed. "Meaning others have slain me—and I actually won a game?" I almost wished I hadn't known that. "How many did I personally take out then?"

Hesitation. "More than anyone before. Or since."

I was a record-holder. No wonder Selena worried about me getting a word out when we met new Arcana. They'd all be after my head. "Who else got me?"

Matthew studied his hand, hard, end of subject.

"At least tell me how many times Death has done it."

"*This* Death? Two out of last three." Matthew's brown eyes were so grave as he said, "Practice makes perfect."

9

"If it seems too good to be true . . ." Jackson muttered
to no one in particular.

We'd come upon an abandoned homestead, a quaint
cabin perched high on a rise, with rocking chairs on the
front porch and a nearby barn. It looked like it'd once
belonged to someone who'd smoked a corncob pipe,
wore "dungarees," and called bears "bars."

At the sight of a man-made shelter, I almost salivated.
We hadn't had a proper roof over our heads since the
hut five days ago. As usual, everyone except Selena was
soaked and freezing. My teeth were chattering again,
my stomach growling. At these higher altitudes there
was more bone-chilling fog and even frost.

But we were all wary.

"Even if it's empty, can we risk staying here?" Finn
asked, looking at the place as longingly as I was.

Zombies continued to trail us, and we still had a couple of hours before dusk. "The Baggers sh-should have trouble on that l-last rise, right?" I asked.

"Just like you, Evie!" Selena said brightly.

Bitch. There'd been a sheer rock face to scale. We'd had to use a rope! I'd never climbed a cliff in my life and had flailed like a trout on a line. I'd been as worried about Matthew as about myself, but compared to me he was a mountaineer.

Jackson didn't join in the discussion, just started toward the cabin. When we followed, he said, "I go alone."

In the past, Selena would've trotted after him anyway, but she'd been remaining close to me. Like gum on the bottom of my boot.

I told him, *"Fais gaffe à toi."* Watch out for yourself.

Jackson's gaze cut to me, and I saw some emotion flicker there before he masked it.

As I watched him stride off, crossbow ready, I wondered yet again what was going on in that head of his. We hadn't spoken since I'd kissed him. Did he still regret kissing me back?

After that night, I'd thought he was done with me, but I kept catching him staring at me. Sometimes his expression was filled with bitterness, as if I'd wronged him. But on the whole, his looks hadn't been as withering, more . . . troubled.

Like he was trying to bring to light an unsettling mystery.

On the way to the cabin, he inspected the small barn. It must've gotten the all-clear, because no one got shot. Then into the cabin . . .

Please be safe, please be safe.

Not long after, I saw smoke curling from the chimney. My knees went weak with relief—and excitement. He was safe, and we'd have a real roof, a real fire.

Finn said, "I can disguise the smoke."

Selena shook her head. "No need. We're up in the clouds. Which J.D. knows, or he wouldn't have lit it."

He emerged from inside. With a chin jerk, he indicated for us to join him.

Self-respect flew out the window, and we ran for it like it was a friendly country's border.

Though dusty inside, the snug little cabin had a bed, a wooden bathtub, and now a fire in its potbelly stove. We'd passed a full rain barrel on our way in. A dented pot hung above the stove. Cords of wood had been stacked alongside one wall by some owner who'd never returned. Put all that together . . .

Hot. Bath. I even had a travel-size bottle of shampoo and body wash.

This was such a bonanza, such a turnaround from our usual circumstances, that I was paranoid—like this cabin would slip from my grasp, running off to join the circus or something.

"Rock-paper-scissors decides who gets the first bath," I announced, but it was only between Finn, Selena, and me. Matthew was too psychic to play—he'd settled into one of the rocking chairs on the front porch—and Jackson wasn't interested.

"Goan grouse hunting," he said, setting off without another word. His tone and demeanor said, *And I'm goan by myself.*

The odds of him finding grouse were so slim I considered telling him to keep an eye out for yeti while he was at it.

Selena gazed after him with a concerned look, reminding me that Jackson might not come back at all.

For days, she'd been pining for him. It was so obvious. At first I'd been irritated, but then I'd put myself in her shoes. When Finn had tricked her, she'd thought that Jackson had chosen her. That her dream had come true. In her mind, she'd experienced his arms around her.

How strange for her, to be traveling with the boy she'd thought she'd kissed—and also with the boy who'd deceived her.

Now that everyone seemed to hate Selena, I was starting to feel sorry for her, even after the shit she'd dealt my way. Days ago, I'd realized nobody wanted to be a monster—yet that was how we were treating her.

Though she'd tried to draw Jackson into conversation again and again, he'd continued to ignore her, as if he couldn't even hear her. With his hood over his head, he'd trudged on, seeming lost in thought. He hadn't committed to anything.

I was past caring. I *was*.

Don't think about him. I planned to make the most of this windfall of water—and time—to wash the ash away. Sometimes I felt like that ash was becoming a part of me, obscuring me, just as it had overcome Haven House, my home in Louisiana.

When I won the first round with the bathtub, Selena rolled her eyes. But she did sit outside with Matthew, settling in to whittle arrows. Finn ambled toward the barn, sourcing for supplies.

I shut the door and turned to my task. How hard could it be to boil bathwater? I'd watched an episode of *Little House on the Prairie* once. Ergo: *Let's do this bitch*.

Four burn wounds and an hour later, I was lowering myself into the little tub, waist-deep water steaming around me. Bubbles from my bath wash pillowed over the surface. If my blistered feet hadn't been stinging as they regenerated, I'd have sworn I was dreaming.

And if I hadn't felt dread over Jackson's leaving.

In front of the crackling fire, I soaped and rinsed my hair, reflecting on the last week.

Each day we'd hauled ass away from the Bagmen, but were forced each night to hide out. The Baggers did just the opposite, eating up the miles every night before dawn drove them into the ground, a thought that still gave me chills.

Our stop-start race had gone on for days. We were strung out on too little sleep.

I'd been constantly wary, unable to relax for a second. And I was still weakening. Yes, my blisters were regenerating, but more slowly. I'd figured out that since my skin returned to its state prior to any injury, I would never build up calluses.

Which meant I'd always have blisters. Beauty.

I wasn't the only one who was wary. As a huntress, Selena always seemed hyper-aware, but now she was completely on edge. Each morning she would back-track to scout the Baggers behind us. Yesterday, she'd told us, "Their numbers are still growing. They must be absorbing any stragglers they come across." It was like a snowball, amassing size through contact with more snow. If that horde caught us . . .

Finn too grew antsier, but he was more like an addict coming off gear. What would happen if he *didn't* pull a trick soon?

When we'd first met, he'd been a fun-loving jokester. Now he was always nervous—insisting on checking and rechecking our map to make sure we didn't sidle too close to the mines.

He was over Selena, hadn't spoken more than a few words to her, and he seemed determined to get Jackson and me back together, as if he was the sole cause of the dissension between me and the Cajun.

Good luck. I feared this was past even the power of magic.

Matthew had grown increasingly withdrawn, often gazing at Jackson with a speculative look. I had difficulty getting the boy to eat, and he was no longer making any sense in conversations.

If I asked him if his head was hurting him, he'd answer, "Beware the Touch of Death." One night he'd torn at his hair, screaming, "Water! Water!" I'd scrambled to get him my canteen before he hurt himself, but he'd chucked it away.

Surprisingly, Jackson had been the one to calm Matthew down. As if he were talking to a spooked horse, Jackson had said, "Whoa, boy, *tracasse-toi pas. Prend-lé aisé.*" Don't you worry. Take it easy.

Whenever I could catch a couple of hours of sleep, I'd had more dreams of Death, all set in that same desert, all of that same encounter. With his hand reaching ever closer to me, I would scent the burning sands and his sweat-lathered horse. In the last dream, I'd looked up at the sky, and through my tears I'd seen the Judgment Card circling above.

Death had popped into my head less and less. I guessed he'd gotten busy or something. Right now my mind was blissfully free of him. . . .

Fauna's three wolves continued to stalk us, their eyes gleaming in the darkness, like freaking cartoon fossa. But they never moved in enough for us to get a good look at them.

Yesterday, Fauna's Arcana call—*Red of tooth and claw!*—had begun to echo louder than all others. Which meant she was finally within striking distance.

When would she make her move? Why not attack with her beasts?

My sense of foreboding grew. The stress of our situation was nearly unbearable. Wolves flanked us, Bagmen pursued, and we were skirting close to subterranean cannibals.

To top it off, the constant faint drizzle of rain was so irritating. Despite Matthew's warnings, I almost wished it would pound down from the sky. Now it was like someone was poking your arm, going, "Nyeh, nyeh, nyeh."

Jackson's behavior kept me on edge as well. He'd begun doing little things, considerate things. Like starting this fire in the stove without staying to enjoy it.

And two nights ago, in the group's makeshift shelter, he'd moved some branches from the ground by his side. So I'd sit beside him? Or just to bolster our windbreak?

Yes, he'd helped me calm down Matthew. To keep the boy quiet from Bagmen? Yesterday on the trail, I'd seen him slip Matthew half of an energy bar. When I smiled at him, Jackson had scowled as if he'd been caught doing something stupid.

This morning, he'd begun something new. Several times he'd opened his mouth as if he were about to speak, then abruptly closed it—much like he had when we'd been in school together. He'd also remained close to me throughout the day.

Maybe he was softening toward me because I hadn't gone Empress in days? Or maybe I was searching for signs that weren't there.

I missed him, my chest aching when I remembered the pair of us on the road together. How the two of us, as different as we were, had begun to grow closer.

I'd just put my head in my hands when I heard someone bounding up the porch steps.

From outside, Finn said, "Uh, Evie's in there, dude— OW! What the hell, Cajun?" Finn sounded like he was holding his nose.

Had Jackson just hit him?

"You ever make yourself look like me again," Jackson grated, "and I'll give you more than a tap next time, me. *Compris?*"

Why this sudden anger, days later?

"Yeah, cool," Finn said thickly. "Kind of been expecting this."

"Now, all of you get scarce. The barn's awaiting."

Jackson was coming in here? I'd never have time to reach my clothes. Shit! I ducked down in the tub, draping my arms over my breasts, hoping the suds covered everything lower. . . .

10

The door burst open. Jackson stood in the doorway, dripping from rain.

I was so stunned by the intent look in his eyes that it took me a second to sputter, *"O-out!* Now!"

As if I hadn't spoken, he entered, shutting the door behind him, tossing his bow and backpack on the table. He shook out his hair like an animal, sending pinpricks of cool water across my face and arms. Black locks whipped across his handsome face.

"What the hell are you doing?"

He removed his jacket and hung it on a rickety chair to dry in front of the fire. "We're goan to talk." He dragged out another chair, sinking his tall frame into it, his gaze leisurely roaming over me.

"Get—out—now!"

"You doan like me here? Then you're welcome to stand up and walk out."

I darted a glance at my clothes. I'd set out a clean outfit—jeans, a sweater, an almost-matching bra and panty set. The bra was red silk, the undies pink lace; close enough. Unfortunately, they were a good five feet away.

I cast him a baleful look, tightening my arms over my chest. "What do you want to talk about that can't wait? You haven't said more than a few words in days. Then when I'm enjoying my first hot bath in forever, you get chatty?"

"This way I know you ain't goan anywhere. And we got a lot to *chat* about, you and me." All his cockiness firmly in place, he said, "You're in love with me."

Be cool, Evie, don't let on. "Ahhh, now I see. You found crack out in the woods, didn't you? Seasoned with bath salts?"

My answer didn't appear to insult him; in fact, he seemed encouraged by it. "Nah, just some of this." He pulled a mason jar of clear liquid out of his backpack.

He'd scored moonshine? "You're like a blood-hound for liquor."

He took a sip from it, then leered over me with a drunken grin. "Um, um, *UM*, Evie."

I sank lower in the tub. Were the bubbles dissolving? "Why don't you go enjoy that someplace else?"

"Been doing a lot of thinking, figured out some stuff, but I still got questions, me."

I'd been wondering when, and *if*, this would come.

But I never would have expected it during bath time. "This can't wait?"

"We ain't leaving here till we get something settled." He shook his head hard, seeming determined to talk to me—and to keep his gaze from wandering again. "Like we should've done at Finn's before you ran out on me, stealing his truck to get away from me."

"And you know why."

"*Ouais.*" Yeah. "You thought you saw me and Selena goan at it and you couldn't handle it."

"You're not going to make me feel guilty about this. I believed my own eyes. And you'd just yelled at me: 'I am done with you!' I took your words to heart."

"I was drunk and pissed off that you wouldn't trust me enough to tell me what was goan on with you. I'm still pissed."

"And still drunk as well."

He didn't deny it.

"In any case, seeing you with Selena—"

"It wasn't me!"

"—isn't the only reason I left."

"I know your other reason. *Coo-yôn* said you were afraid you were goan to poison me or get me killed by Death, or something." He waved that away.

"Matthew told you that?"

Breezing past my question, he said, "Which just proves my point. You doan want anything to happen to me. Because you got it bad for me, *peekôn*."

My face flushed, the truth laid bare.

"You got it even worse than you let on that night at Finn's. You remember our little talk?"

"Of course I remember. *I* wasn't chugging whiskey like a marooned sailor at the island oasis." Jackson had talked about starting a life with me—on one condition. "You said I had to give up my quest to find my grandmother. When I told you I couldn't, you broke up with me."

"I didn't break up with you, no. I just shot my mouth off because I was frustrated. Never met a *fille* so frustrating as you."

How odd to be having this conversation when I was dressed in disappearing suds.

"I've been going over my options." He raised a forefinger. "Ignore my every survival instinct and stick around some kids who are out to kill each other. Some real sick ones, too." He raised a second finger. "Or leave and go after the Army of the Southeast, get my revenge."

Jack and his adopted sister Clotile had been in that army. Only one of them had made it out alive.

"What was your decision?"

"Still here, ain't I?"

"What swayed you? And why now? It isn't like you've learned something new to change your mind, not since you informed me that I'm not *right*," I said pointedly. Unless he had . . . *No*. That suspicion was too humiliating even to contemplate.

"Like I said, I figured some stuff out on my own."

"Look, Jackson, say I did have feelings for you. That was before I realized you could never accept my nature. You saw me and freaked out."

He narrowed his eyes. "I doan freak out, no. I think I've handled this pretty damn well. If you'd shown me that shit before, instead of springing it on me—"

"That *shit* saved my life."

"From what I understand, it also led you to a madman. The Alchemist, *non*?"

Touché. "You treated me like a leper when you saw my abilities."

He shot to his feet, pacing, and took another swig. "You expect me to get it right the first time every time!"

"Get what right?"

"My reactions, my words, everything. I ain't goan to. I saw something I've never seen before, and I reacted."

"With the sign of the cross? Really, Jack?"

"I'm a Catholic boy, me. And the sweet girl I knew had just slaughtered some kid and looked mighty pleased about it. It was like you were possessed by a demon or something!" He shook his head. "You expect me to be perfect."

"It hurt, Jackson. Okay?" I pulled my knees to my chest, sloshing water.

As if helpless not to, he glanced down, seeming enthralled with my movements.

But he jerked his gaze up when I cried, "It broke my

heart! I'd just gone through the most horrific event in my life. I needed you, but you were disgusted with me." My eyes pricked with tears. "I needed you!"

He pinched the bridge of his nose. "Does it count for nothing that . . . that I'm *trying* to handle all this?"

"Maybe you shouldn't have to try so hard. Come on, we have problems that extend past the game. We're always fighting, always on a different page. I can count on one hand the number of times we've had a civil conversation. Most of the time I don't know what's going on in that head of yours."

"What you want to know?" He sank down in the chair again, resting his elbows on his knees. "You want me to talk out my feelings? Goddamn it, how do I even start?"

I blinked in surprise. He wasn't being a smart-ass. He was genuinely baffled how to do this. And why shouldn't he be? Where would he have learned how to discuss his thoughts and emotions?

Not from his mother. She hadn't even been able to *feed* Jackson as a boy, much less teach him to talk about things that bothered him. From his dad? The man had washed his hands of his son.

It was a wonder Jackson was as decent as he was. I remember how he'd admitted that he didn't know how to behave with me. *You can teach me how to court you. 'Cause I doan know my way around that.*

He *was* trying. And how should I help him with this? Offer advice? *Use your words, Jack.*

"You spring this shit on me, then within days you expect me to get over the fact that my girlfriend ain't exactly human!"

I didn't know what bewildered me more—the *girlfriend* or the *human* part.

"Damn it, Evie, you been to my house, you saw how I lived. Can't you understand why I hate surprises? Why I doan like it when people live secret lives?"

Maybe we *were* too different. "Too much has happened. And you've been hideous to me for days."

"I was angry because I didn't understand any of this. I doan like things I doan understand. And that morning in Requiem, just when I was trying to come to terms with this, I returned—right as you were about to cut that Irish kid's throat."

"He attacked us, after I tried to call a truce."

"I get that people are gonna be hurt. I understand the program—hell, I wrote the program on people getting hurt, well before the Flash. But when I saw you liked it . . ."

I buried my head in my hands. "I don't want to!"

"I understand that now. Something comes over you. It's still you, but you got a problem. *Peekôn*, look at me."

I glanced up.

"If you got a problem, I can work with that."

I wasn't convinced. "Being with you hurts."

"But sometimes it's good. *Real* good between us. You thought my kiss was 'perfect.'" His gaze flicked from my lips, to my neck, to my collarbones . . .

"I never told you—" Realization dawned. "Oh, my God." My jaw dropped, my earlier suspicion confirmed. Yep, just as humiliating as I'd feared. "You took the Alchemist's recorder!" Which contained the tape of my life story.

Jackson flashed me a shameless grin. "*Ouais*. Been listening to it for days. That was one reason why I got held up that morning in Requiem. I was sourcing for some earphones, so I could listen under my hood."

"You wouldn't!"

"I played a big role in that tale, wanted to make sure you got me right."

"That's why you've been so up and down?" The angry looks, the troubled looks. The smirks?

"Some things you said pissed me off." Expression darkening, he grated, "Had to listen to you talking about your boyfriend. Bad enough the first time around."

Brand had been a good guy. Immature, maybe, but he'd had a good heart. His and Jackson's personalities had been as different as day and night. The two had hated each other.

"But then you'd turn around and say something good. Like when you were nice to Clotile. You smiled at her and waved hello, when not another person in school was kind to her."

I could've been nicer to her, wished I had been.

"Or when you described our kiss at the pool at Selena's house." Jack scrubbed a hand over his face. "I must've worn a groove in the tape listening to that over and over."

The way his lids went heavy and he shuddered, you'd think he'd had an eargasm. My breaths grew shallow in reaction. And suddenly I was very aware of my nakedness, of the cooling water. Of Jackson peering at my damp skin.

"That tape was private!"

"You'd tell this Arthur guy, a stranger, our story?"

"By that point, I was fairly sure he would never tell another soul." My skin began to glow with remembered fury, glyphs winding along my arms, across my chest. Were my eyes turning green?

Jackson stared at the changes in me. "You showing me these . . . these *glyphs* to scare me off?"

Huh. He had the lingo right.

"It woan work. That tape let me wade into this Arcana thing, let me learn about it little by little. Like you did. And I heard you say that I was your anchor."

"Yeah, so?"

"You pulled back from killing that Irish kid—once you saw *me*. Do you deny that?"

At length, I shook my head.

"You need me, and now I know it," he said. "You warned me it wasn't ever goan to be easy with you. I'm still signing on."

"Why would you? This is deadly and weird and terrifying."

"So is this whole world!" He shoved his fingers through his wet hair. "Here's how messed up in the head I am: I can accept this game better than I can your secrets. At least now I know what I'm up against."

Part of me was delighted that he wanted me. Part of me thought anything between us was doomed. "Let's just be realistic about our chances—"

"You wanna know what I'm feeling? Lemme tell you, *bébé*. Amusement. You're acting like we got some kind of choice in this matter. You're just as screwed as I am—because we're both too far gone for the other."

I bristled. "Liking me is akin to being screwed? I thought you were smoother than this, ladies' man, with all your *gaiennes*."

He shrugged. "The other night after we kissed, I told myself to just keep walking. That this shit was too heavy for me and none of my business. I told myself not to think about you."

I'd told myself the same and had just as little success.

"Hell, you expected me to desert you anyway. But I got sicker with each step, like someone had strung up my guts with barbed wire. And I realized you got me by the balls. Stupid to fight it. Doan give a damn what you are."

"Be still my heart," I said in an arch tone, but I was softening toward him, as ever.

Yet then I remembered more of what I'd said on that tape. Such as how jealous and hurt I'd been when he'd flirted with Selena. Or how I felt like I'd lost my ever-living mind when he'd kissed me.

Was that what he'd been smirking over? "I still can't believe you'd violate my privacy like that!" In school, when Jackson had wanted to see my journal, he'd stolen it. When he'd wanted to listen to my messages to my boyfriend? He'd stolen Brand's phone.

Jackson kept running roughshod over me, and I was sick of it. "You need to leave." My glyphs were so vivid, they lit the room more brightly than the fire. "I want to get dressed."

"Doan let me stop you. I ain't leaving until you admit how you feel."

"You're going to blackmail me?" Now it was a matter of principle. He'd crossed the line by listening to that tape, and now he expected me to reward him for it?

"You can always go." He propped his boots up on the table, easing back to balance his chair on two legs. With a smug grin, he put his hands behind his head.

He was so cocky, I wanted—nay, *needed*—to wipe that grin off his face. I'd reached my limit. I could die tomorrow, and I refused to spend my last night on earth getting manipulated by a moonshine-guzzling Cajun.

Besides, I wasn't too shy. I'd worn my skimpy cheer uniform to school in front of slavering teenage boys, and my best friend Melissa had pantsed me routinely. "Fine." I twisted in the tub to rise with my back to him, then stepped out and marched to my clothes—

Wham! He'd crashed back in his chair?

Stifling a grin, I wiped myself semi-dry with my old T-shirt, then pulled on the panties.

"E-Evie?" His voice sounded strangled.

I reached for my bra, might've showed side-boob, didn't care. When I had the strap fastened, I glanced over one shoulder.

Next to the overturned chair, Jackson knelt with his lips parted, breaths ragged. His high cheekbones were flushed, and his muscles were tensed—like he was about to lunge at me. "You . . . you stood up?" He swiped a shaking hand over his mouth, and again, his eyes dark with lust. "Never thought you'd stand up, *ma bonne fille*." My good girl.

With a shrug, I reached for my jeans. "If you can't take the heat, stay out of the cabin."

He swallowed audibly. *"Brûlant."* Sizzling hot. "And believe me, *cher*, I plan to *take* that heat." Then he was on his feet, coming for me, those heavy boots pounding the wood floor. His every step multiplied my anticipation. He was going to kiss me again, and just the idea filled me with energy.

No, no, no! This was wrong. I didn't want him to hit on me just because he was drunk and hard up.

Before I could put on my clothes, he'd spun me

around, looping his arm around my lower back. "You swished that pretty ass in the wrong direction, *bébé*. You should've come to me when you were all naked and wet."

"Don't you dare make moves on me! You're just going to accuse me again of mesmerizing you."

"I realized you didn't have all your powers when I first started wanting you."

"Why would you think that?"

"Because if you were mesmerizing back then, all them Sterling boys would've been panting over you instead of Clotile."

Chin raised, I said, "Hey, I didn't do too bad, Cajun."

"For true. When I saw you that day alone in the school courtyard, in your cheer skirt . . ." His expression was smoldering. "I wanted to lay you back on that table and take you right there, Evangeline."

I shivered at the way my name rolled off his tongue in that accent. Irresistible. I knew this, because I was struggling to resist.

He was right; I was gone for him. Stupid to fight it. I gazed up at him, whispering, "Just, just don't hurt me again. If I kiss you, and then you get disgusted . . ."

He gave a low laugh, moving his hips against mine. "Does it feel like I'm disgusted?"

I gasped. "Jackson!"

"You smell like honeysuckle. You likin' ole Jack now?"

"I never *stopped* liking you. Even when you were warding me away with the power of Catholicism."

"Can't help the way I was raised—anything supernatural is supposed to be either a miracle or satanic."

I rolled my eyes. "And you're still trying to figure out which I am?"

"*Non*. I'm trying to figure out if I'm still Catholic." He grinned that heart-stopping grin.

Gorgeous lips. I wanted them on mine.

Just before he kissed me, he said, "You might be different from what I thought, but I'm goan to protect you anyway. I'm goan to try to accept all this. But you got to accept me."

"Accept *you*? What are you talking about?"

"I'm a nineteen-year-old bayou boy. I got a fondness for liquor. I'm goan to say stupid shit. Doan you go getting your feelings hurt at the drop of a hat."

I laid my palm against his face. "You're going to get more than your feelings hurt if you stay with us. And it will be my fault because I don't want to separate from you. You wanted me to let you go."

"That was before I realized something this week. I wasn't goan to live a long life even before the apocalypse. Before there were Baggers, cannibals, and plague. Now I figure I'll spend my limited time left doing what I want."

"And what do you want?"

His grin deepened. "You're what I want, and I'd like

to be doing you." He leaned down, pressing his lips to mine.

At that contact, the rain began to pour down at last, pelting the cabin's tin roof. I hadn't heard that sound since the night I'd gone to Jack's home in the bayou.

He drew back. "Christ, your lips are sweet. *Douces comme du miel.*" Sweet like honey. He yanked off his shirt, revealing his damp chest, the rosary around his neck. I'd missed seeing him like this.

My fingers skimmed over the raised scar on his arm. How I loved that mark. If he hadn't been getting that wound tended to the night of the Flash, he would've died like most everyone else.

His hands landed on my ass, giving it a possessive squeeze. "*T'es pour moi*, Evie. You're mine. Every part of you." He leaned down, took my lips once more. Between kisses, he said, "I told you once and I'll tell you again: there is nothing that can happen to you that we can't get past. Just give me a chance to get to you. Promise me."

"Jack . . ."

"Promise me. You doan leave me again."

"I promise." Staring at his lips, I said, "Would you always come for me?"

He drunkenly murmured, "Chase you like a junk-yard dog."

I laughed. How could I feel this much happiness in our situation? "I'm glad I don't have to hide this any longer. No more secrets then—for either of us." Wait. Had his eyes darted? "Do you have something you want to tell me?"

"*Non, rien.*" No, nothing.

"Are you . . . are you *lying* to me? Jack, nothing is more important than trust right now. Considering this game, this whole world, we have to be able to depend on each other."

"I'm not lying. You can trust me alone, Evie," he said more firmly. "I got no secrets, *peekôn*. Except for how bad I want you."

Relieved, I gave him a shaky nod. "I believe you."

"Good." He swept me up, cradling my body against his chest to head for the bed. "That night by the pool, you would've let me have you if I'd gone slower. I'll do that now. Nice and slow, me."

"We can't be together like that. What if I hurt you with my powers?"

"What a way to go, *ma belle*."

"I'm serious."

"So am I." He strode toward the bed, dipping his mouth to mine for brief, wicked kisses, blanking my thoughts. "You love me too much to hurt me."

I didn't bother denying it.

"Now, hush. We do best when we doan talk."

Brows raised, I tilted my head. Because he had a point. I leaned up for more of his lips. Our kiss grew deeper, tongues tangling. I'd heard the phrase "drunk from his lips." I literally was from the moonshine.

There was French kissing, and then there was *Cajun* French kissing. Spicier, harder, wilder.

That's how it was with Jackson. Burning out of control. Probably just as destructive as an inferno. And I didn't care.

He drew back and tossed me on the bed—

The blanket collapsed; I was plummeting into a pit, arms flailing. At the last second, I snagged the edge with my fingertips.

Jack dove for me. He snatched my wrists just before I lost my grip. "Jesus! I've got you!"

I could barely hear him. An ear-splitting foghorn sounded from the roof of the cabin.

A signal for this . . . trap?

As Jack lifted me back into the room, I gazed below. Rusted rebar jutted from the ground at least ten feet down. He yanked me against him, cupping the back of my head protectively.

There'd been no mattress; someone had spread a thin layer of foam across a bed frame, then camouflaged it with a bright blanket and pillows.

"Dear God," I muttered when the horn died down. In my panic and confusion, I thought I heard wolves howling in the distance.

He hugged me tighter until I could feel his every shuddering breath. "I . . . I could've killed you."

Again debatable. But it definitely would've hurt.

"Wh-who would do this?" I asked, though I knew. That blaring signal had been like a quitting-time horn for a factory—or for a mine.

"Cannibals." Jack grabbed my clothes, shoved them into my arms. "If this is their trap, they're goan to come running. We got to go, *bébé*. Fast."

11

"Why do they call it a downpour," Finn mused as we climbed in the pitch dark, "as opposed to an uppour?"

The rain came down so hard it drummed our heads, had since we'd fled the cabin three nights ago.

I'd grown up in Louisiana; I knew thunderstorms. I'd never felt rain like this. Why had I wished it would pound down from the sky?

Finn swiped a muddy hand over his face. "For the record, dealing with cannibal crazies on top of Arcana crazies blows goats." He melodramatically raised his fist to the sky. "Serenity now!"

Matthew piped up. "Cannibal Arcana!"

"Yeah, yeah, thanks for reminding me that some can be both."

Though midnight had come and gone, we continued to flee, clawing our way uphill, digging into the mud, into the ash I hated. Streams of gushing water sluiced all around our ankles, threatening to trip us with every step. Tree trunks toppled over left and right, pushed down by rivers of runoff.

But now Jack was there to help me through it.

The threat of cannibals had us charging forward into the night. Even the specter of Bagmen hadn't motivated us to run like this. Yes, Matthew had told me I'd never "known terror" like I would when the rains came.

We were being hunted by people who wanted to *eat* us—it didn't get more terrifying than that.

With no stars to guide us and no sun during the day, we couldn't pinpoint our position, just kept heading south. We hoped.

After that foghorn, we'd all scrambled together outside the barn; even in the midst of our panic, the three other Arcana had noticed that Jack kept my hand clasped tight in his. With his chest bowed proudly, he'd announced, "Evie's with me now."

Matthew had tilted his head. "Not Arcana."

Finn had grinned, and Selena had looked gutted. But she hadn't said a word then or since, had seemed to stoically accept it.

Now when we came upon a rushing stream, Jack said, "Come on, you." He scooped me into his arms, hugging me against his chest as he trudged through the knee-deep water.

I was shivering, miserable, would have given anything to be warm and dry.

"We're goan to get through this, Evie. And just think, at this pace, we'll be at your grand-mère's in no time."

Now that we were officially together, Jack's attitude had changed. He was even fiercer, even more determined, as if he had something to fight for. For three days we'd been stealing kisses, whispering conversations.

In one, he'd solemnly told me, "After we bring down this game, I'm goan to rebuild Haven for you, *ma belle*. You see if I doan." In another, he'd admitted, "By the pool wasn't our first kiss. When I returned for you after the Flash and you were knocked out in your bed, I'd never seen anything like you, all soft in sleep. I stole a *bec doux*." A sweet kiss. "I was gone for you, even then."

Last night we'd camped for a few hours in the cab of an old logging truck. With Selena on watch, Jack had finally fallen asleep with me in his arms. Drifting off, he'd pressed his lips to my hair, inhaling. In French, he'd murmured, "Honeysuckle. Even now, I could die a happy man."

Whenever I was freaked out more than usual, he would tease me. Yesterday he'd trailed behind me for long moments. "I meant what I said about you not being human."

Just when I was about to flare, he'd said, "Evie, that ass of yours—um, um, UM! *C'est surhumain*." It's superhuman.

On the other side of the stream, he set me on my

feet, but lingered with his arms around me, resting his chin on my head. "We're goan to find us a place to hole up, then pick up where we left off." His voice was husky, sending shivers all over me.

Even amidst so much hardship and fear, I found myself imagining what would've happened if the cabin hadn't been a trap.

Good money said I'd no longer be a virgin. "Jack, I don't know h-how many more miles I have in me."

"Just a couple more rises. Then we'll stop for an hour or two."

"O-okay." We pressed on. . . .

The Arcana calls were always abuzz, but a pair had grown louder, even with Jack's presence.

—*Red of tooth and claw!*—

—*We go now to our bloody business.*—

We were used to Fauna's, but I didn't know who the second one belonged to. Neither did Selena. We only knew he was male. Somewhere in these forsaken mountains was a boy who might crave our deaths. Could it be the Hierophant?

I'd asked Matthew. His answer: "The water!"

I'd been hearing Death as well, feeling his presence as he spoke directly to me. Once he'd whispered about Jack: —*The mortal boy will never understand you. But then, that could be because you're soon to die.*—

Shut up! I'm sick of you!

He'd just laughed.

If Matthew had sent me those dreams of Death to teach me more about him and the game, then I knew I needed to study every detail. In that long-ago contest, other players had been close by the canyon. I recalled that Fauna had controlled lions then, but it was still unclear whether she'd been my ally or my foe. Had Judgment been gloating over my looming demise, circling like a buzzard? Or had he been preparing to attack Death from above—

A coughing fit overtook me. My breaths were heaving so hard, I'd inhaled rain.

Over the pounding shower, Jack told the others, "We need to take a break!"

Despite my dread of cannibals, by this point I thought I'd almost rather make a stand than keep running. I couldn't release poisonous spores in this kind of weather, but a tornado of thorns could do some damage. If I could manage one. "We can't run anymore."

"Figures you'd say that since you're so shitty at it!" Selena snapped.

Suddenly, Finn, Selena, Matt, and I fell silent, freezing in place. An Arcana call began boiling up in our minds. I slapped my hands over my ears, as if that would help. Then a booming: —*RED OF TOOTH AND CLAW!*—

Jack raised his bow and yanked me behind him. "What's goan on here?" His gaze darted. I grabbed Matthew, dragging him close.

"Fauna. She's coming," I answered. Would she fight us? She had to be alone—so why would she approach an alliance of four Arcana?

Just as Selena flanked me, raising her own bow, a pretty girl appeared, seeming to materialize from the rain.

She looked Eurasian, with doe-brown eyes that swept up at the corners. A baggy conductor's hat covered her black hair, and she wore a camouflage coat. Freckles dotted her pale skin. She couldn't have been more than fourteen or fifteen.

Though she sported no visible weapons, a huge hawk perched on one shoulder—and three enormous black wolves surrounded her protectively, baring their fangs.

Pet wolves in the movies were always majestic; these were the ugliest I'd ever imagined, with patches of fur missing and scars all over. Raised lines crisscrossed their snouts. One was missing an eye. Another limped.

"State your business," Jack ordered, pointing his crossbow.

Her tableau flashed over her, a girl controlling the gaping mouth of a lion. Then the image was gone.

Finn stared at her, his lips parted. All of his recent illusions began to waver over him in a rush, as if from an involuntary response to the girl. He went invisible—twice—as he mumbled to her, "We b-both have infinity symbols on our cards."

She frowned at him, then said to the group, "I'm Lark. And we're in trouble."

12

"Why shouldn't I kill you right now?" Selena demanded with her bow aimed at the girl's face. "Why should we trust anything you have to say?"

"Because I've come here as an ally," she said. "And to prove myself, I'm about to save your asses."

Selena gave a laugh and drew back farther on her bowstring.

Finn and I gaped at the Archer. "Let her talk!" he said.

"She's been following us for days? And now all of a sudden she's here to help?"

Lark nodded. "Yeah. I had to make sure you weren't psycho like other Arcana I've seen. Besides, you haven't needed my help before."

"But we do now?" Selena scoffed.

"You've got a horde of Baggers to the north and gaining fast."

"We *know* this."

"Did you know that cannibal scouts to the east spotted you and are CB-ing for reinforcements right now? Four-wheel drives and ATVs will be coming, full of them. For this many healthy people, the Teeth'll bring an army."

"The Teeth?" I asked.

Finn said, "You'll get it when you see them."

Lark cast him a surprised look. "You know them?"

He nodded. "I crossed these mountains before. Invisible. I saw . . . everything."

Selena relaxed the tension on her bow a fraction. "Baggers to the north, cannibals to the east? What about south and west?"

"One direction dead-ends in a sheer rock face," Lark explained. "The other funnels into a narrow pass that's littered with snares. Bear traps and pitfalls."

I was familiar with the latter.

"And it's rocky." Lark turned to me. "Not a lot of dead trees for you to revive, Empress."

Weird that a stranger was calling me that.

To Selena, she said, "And it'll be close quarters with no vantage points. Not favorable for an archer."

So she had recognized our tableaux and knew who we were, which meant she knew the deck, knew the game.

"Why would you guys come this way?" Lark asked.

Rain ran off the brim of her hat in sheets. "You've got the Fool with you, and he led you here? Tactically, this is about as bad as it gets."

"The better question?" Selena said. "Why would you *stay* here?"

"This is my hood. I know these brutes, know the mountains and the mines." Her accent did sound Southern. "Plus the Teeth keep the worst of the Arcana away. But now they've expanded their territory."

"Why? When?" Finn's voice scaled an octave higher. Whatever he'd seen had done a permanent number on him.

"Recently. They're starving down in the mines. For fresh meat and three breeders, the Teeth'll hunt us to the ends of the earth."

"Breeders?" I asked.

In a deadpan tone, she said, "Cannibals need love too."

I glanced at Finn. He appeared fascinated by Lark.

Selena glared at him. Was she the type of girl who wouldn't want her former admirer ever to move on?

Lark said, "The good news is that they will try to take us alive. Flesh wounds and clubbed heads."

Finn muttered, "Because they lack refrigeration." Had he sidled closer to Lark?

"Then we run." Selena finally lowered her bow. "We take our chances on that pass, *if* it's rigged as you say."

Lark scratched one wolf behind its scarred ear. "You try running that canyon in the dark, you're going to die."

"Why aren't *you* running?" Selena demanded. "You could've slipped away from all this."

"I told you—I want in on your alliance."

"Obviously you know all about this game," I said. "But our group is a little different. We're not planning to play. We don't want to kill anybody." Except for Death.

Lark's lips parted, as if this news was too good to be true. Her tough-girl façade cracked a little, and I thought her brown eyes watered. "Not to kill?" God, she looked so young. "I've been alone out here, and when I saw Gabriel and his crew closing in on the area, I freaked, thought I was done for sure."

Selena's shoulders tensed. "They were here?"

Damn it, I would've expected them to head in the opposite direction!

"So close that Gabriel almost ran into my falcon. They turned back, but I realized my cannibal cover wouldn't keep me safe much longer. Sooner or later, Arcana are going to come for the Hierophant."

"We've heard his call, then," I said. *We go now to our bloody business.* "He's near."

Lark nodded. "Figures, since he's in charge of the cannibals. His name's Guthrie. He spouts all this stuff, twisting religion. He's got them all enthralled. It's a cult, a cannibal miner cult. They file their teeth to look like him."

I hadn't thought they could get eerier in my mind. They just had.

Selena's expression was suspicious. "Why has the Hierophant never targeted you?"

"I'm pretty sure Guthrie doesn't know about the game. He hears my call and thinks an angel is chatting at him or something."

"Which force will reach us first?" Jack asked. "How long do we have?

"I'll get a real-time estimate." She murmured something to the bird on her shoulder. It unfurled its wings behind Lark's head, bouncing on its thick legs. It even had a little leather helmet.

Any chick who carried around a bird of prey with a little helmet was cool in my book. Oh, man, I really hoped she didn't intend to kill us all. "Can you see through the hawk's eyes?"

"She's a gyrfalcon. And yes." In a flash of feathers, the falcon took off from Lark's slim shoulder, soaring up into the rainy sky. The bird's size blew my mind, its wingspan at least four feet.

Lark's gaze grew blank, her eyes beginning to sparkle red—the color of an animal's gaze caught in headlights. When her head and body canted to the side, like a kid playing airplane, I realized her senses and the falcon's had married. They were changing directions in flight.

Again: *cool*.

Moments later, Lark blinked, her eyes clearing. "The Bagmen'll be here around midnight. I forecast the Teeth'll show about the same time."

"Both of them?" In four hours.

Finn crossed to the wolves. They growled, but he ignored the warning.

"Don't!" Lark cried. "They'll kill you. They're war wolves—"

After a hesitation, they began licking his outstretched hand. Lark's jaw slackened. Score one for Finn.

"These guys have seen some action, huh?" Turning to Lark, Finn said, "So our choices are either to fight a horde of zombies *and* a cult of cannibals—or to risk running a booby-trapped mountain pass in the pitch dark?"

Her tough-girl façade back in place, Lark smiled, showing sharp canines. "Bingo. There will be at least five dozen of the cannibals mobilizing. Double that in Baggers."

"Then we make a stand here," I said. I'd been ready before. Now I saw no choice.

Jack muttered to me, "A word." He squired me

some distance away. "I don't suppose you'll run with me, give that sheer rock face a try?" When my gaze fell on Matthew, Jack bit out a curse. "Always with *coo-yôn*. He could've warned us about this, could've steered us out of this valley."

"He told me he'd let us know when we stepped off the correct path."

"Does this feel correct to you?"

"I've asked him to use his powers as little as possible. I hoped it would make him clearer."

Jack motioned for Selena to join us. She did, still shaking her head. Matthew followed her. Finn made apologies to Lark, then hastened over like we were huddling up.

"Well, Matthew?" I asked. "Give us the skinny on her."

He whispered, "Basement."

Huh? "Does she mean to do us harm?"

"Good. Bad. Good. Bad. Good. Good. Bad. Bad. Good. Bad. Good—"

"I get the picture," I said, interrupting. With a sigh, I brushed his wet hair off his brow. "Thank you, sweetheart. We're going to figure this out."

Jack asked us, "You think this *fille*'s telling the truth?"

Finn glanced to Lark and back. "Totally."

"I think she's a little liar." Selena might've lowered

her bow, but she kept an arrow strung. "I don't believe a word of this."

"Yeah, but you don't trust anybody," I pointed out.

"I trust you," she said, surprising me. "I believe you will do what you say and not lie to me."

I frowned with realization. I kind of trusted her too.

Selena tilted her head at me. "Do *you* think she's telling the truth?"

I couldn't be certain. But I knew I'd have to chance it—because we needed numbers. We could turn this game, but only if we attracted more players to our movement. "I think we have to take a leap and trust her, for no other reason than to grow our alliance."

Selena rolled her eyes.

"I have to look at the big picture on this," I explained. "Plus, what she says makes sense. We know the Bagmen are closing in, and we tripped the cannibals' alarm." Everyone was listening to me again, like I was a leader. Screw it; I owned it. "If we believe these things, then we should assume there's a booby-trapped canyon. So the next step is deciding which of the options she presented is the least likely to get us killed."

Finn said, "I think we should stay and use our powers." Glancing at me, he added in as nice a way as possible, "You might, uh, have trouble getting down a rocky canyon?"

Another *dafuq?* look from Jackson. "Worry about yourself—I'll carry her ass if I have to."

I laid my hand on Jack's chest. "He's right. We should use our powers." And my MO was to lie in wait.

Or maybe I just didn't want to risk a bear trap snapping any of our leg bones in half.

"Then we're going to need Lark's wolves too," Finn said. "I say we call her over."

We all gazed at her. The falcon had just returned to land on her shoulder, shaking off its feathers. She rubbed her nose against its beak.

"You're kidding, right?" Selena looked aghast. Just as I hadn't trusted her, Selena didn't trust Lark.

But Finn had already waved the girl over.

"What did you decide?" Lark asked me.

"We're going to fight."

Jack exhaled, blowing rainwater. "Then let's be smart about this. We got two enemies. When you got a pair, best thing to do is make 'em touch gloves." I frowned. "It's what we did to break you out of the militia jail—we sicced Bagmen on them. We all know how hard Baggers are to take down. If there are twice as many Bagmen, the Teeth stand no chance. Selena, let me see that map."

She pulled it out of her pack, handing it over.

Jack slung his crossbow over his back. "Remember the last valley we passed, with the stretch of flat ground?

It's a kill zone, a tactical nightmare. Hard to get out of. If the cannibals are in trucks, they'll have to drive through there to get as close to us as possible. So we lure the Baggers to them. Selena and I can get their attention, get them to chase us."

Jack as bait? There had to be a better way.

Selena studied the area. "It's perfect, but we'd be creating more zombies." One bite was contagious, assuming the victim lived through the attack.

Jack shrugged. "Lesser of two evils. At least Baggers can't think."

"I have an idea," I said. "We should *drive* the Bagmen down there. I could make a chute of briars, corralling them."

Finn tapped a spot on the map. "I could make it look like the mountain starts here, creating a funnel into Evie's briars."

"My wolves could nip at their heels, driving them down."

Jack said, "Selena and I could be firing on them at the same time, spooking them forward."

A gauntlet of briars, snapping wolves, illusions, and arrows. "If this works, those cannibals would be dead, and the Bagmen would drink from them for days. We'd have plenty of time to escape."

Jack nodded. "How long would it take us to get ready?"

How long for me to bloodlet enough to create a plant feature like that? "Two hours?"

In French, Jack said to me, "Good. Then we have some time to talk to the girl and find out if any of this is even approaching true."

13

Crunch.

I grimaced each time Lark's giant wolves bit through a bone.

After completing our preparations, we'd found a nearby cave, unable to do anything but kick back and wait for the battle to come. Lark's falcon would keep us updated on any arrivals. Once we'd settled in, her wolves—Scarface, Cyclops, and Maneater—had disappeared for a while, coming back with old bones. Human ones.

As Lark had explained, "Wolves gotta eat. Corpses are A.F. Alpo."

To distract myself, I kept gazing out at my briar chute like a proud parent.

It was a thing of beauty, if I did say so myself. I'd seeded enough plants to make two twelve-foot-high walls, thickly tangled. Impenetrable. So glossy and green against the ashy black earth. Thorns jutted out protectively, each a few inches long.

I wanted to live among the stalks, but I doubted Jack would want to live with me there.

I was sitting with my back against his chest. Blood loss had left me freezing, but I was gradually warming up from the heat of him and from the fire we'd built. Matthew was close by, drowsy, staring at the flames, while Selena tweaked more of her makeshift arrows.

Lark sat shoulder to shoulder with Finn, with the wolves spread out behind her. We'd learned that these war wolves had heightened intelligence, ferocity—and apparently appetites.

Crunch. Crunch.

Jack seemed to be handling all this insanity well. Earlier, when I'd rolled up my coat sleeve to make the first slice of my skin, he'd been uneasy.

"Are you sure you want to see this?" I'd asked, hesitating with my claws above one wrist.

Lips thinned, he'd said, *"Ouais."*

I'd sliced. He'd winced.

"It'll heal, Jack."

"But it's still got to hurt, no?"

Bloodletting always hurt like hell. I'd gritted my teeth, white-knuckling through the pain as I sliced my arms up and down. As my skin had healed, he'd watched, riveted. I was dizzy and chilled through by the time it was done.

He'd rubbed my shoulders for warmth. "So *that* is how you were making food for your *mère*."

While we'd worked on the chute, Selena had been scouting the area for any holes to be plugged. Matthew had rested under a nearby overhang, almost obscured by a thick veil of water. Not far away, Finn had been practicing his illusions, with a wide-eyed Lark at his side.

I'd heard some of their conversation and had been delighted that he'd recovered his beautiful bullshit. "I'm not perfect, Lark," he'd told her gravely. "Due to some self-esteem issues, I always put out on the first date. Working through that, though. Help me?"

She'd laughed, clearly liking him too. Maybe they did have some kind of infinity-symbol connection. It gave me a tendril of hope. If they fell in love, we'd have another pair of Arcana who would never hurt the other. One more stick of dynamite in the machine.

Normally I wouldn't be thinking about hookups at a time like this. But these mini-alliances were critical.

Now Selena asked her, "What do you know about the game, Lark?"

"You want to talk about the specifics in front of a Muggle?" She hiked her thumb at Jack.

"He knows everything," I assured her. "What can you tell us?"

"My family chronicled," she said, buffing her claws. They weren't like my thorn ones. Hers were narrower and curling, talonlike. Plus, hers never disappeared completely.

Selena gave a laugh. "Oh, really? See, I heard you got capped first in the previous game. Numero uno. When would you have had time to set up a centuries-old paper trail for your family's descendants?"

Finn glowered. "Ease off, Selena."

"No, it's okay," the girl said. "Granted, I know more about the *current* game, like what the big dogs are up to."

"Big dogs?" I asked.

"The players with the most bite, like you and Selena. Like Death and Tess."

"We met her. What do you know about her?"

Matthew muttered, "Bad cards."

"She's the World Card," Lark said. "The fifth element. She was with Joules and Gabriel a week ago. They must've taken her on as an ally. Smart move on their part, since she can pretty much control space and time. One problem: the chronicler of her line dropped the ball, so she doesn't understand why she levitates every time she sneezes. If she gets turned on, time races and stuff."

Finn looked captivated with Lark, resting his chin on his hand as he gazed at her. "How's that work?"

"Don't ask me. I'm not a doctor *or* a quantum physicist."

He and Lark laughed, but then her smile faded. "I

shouldn't poke fun. She looked like a sweet girl. Cried a lot though, and bit her nails till they bled. Not understanding your powers must be a bitch."

It was. I remembered when I'd been in the same boat, wondering why plants responded to me. I felt for Tess, wanting to help her.

"But I'm sure Joules and Gabriel will get her up to speed about the game, if they haven't already." Lark pointed to Matthew. "The Fool's got a big target on his back too. He knows everyone's weaknesses and powers."

Matthew blinked at her. "Arsenals."

"And Evie?" Jack asked.

Lark turned to me. "The ones who understand the game want to keep you alive so you can take out Death. But there are some who don't know better. And now that you're worth a pair of icons . . ." She trailed off, eyeing my hand. "Well, it's tempting."

Two icons, mine and the Alchemist's.

Jack covered my hand with his own. "It might be tempting—but it ain't happening."

She gave him a *duh* look. "Hello, we're allies now." Reaching into her coat pocket, she pulled out a laminated scroll, handing it to me.

I unfurled it, finding archaic writing on yellowed parchment, with grease-pencil notes.

"It's a list of players with their formal titles," she said. "I've written in the current names that I know and updated the losers."

— The Players —

The Fool, Gamekeeper of Old (Matthew)
The Magician, Master of Illusions (Finneas)
The High Priestess, Ruler of the Deep
The Empress, Our Lady of Thorns (Evie)
The Emperor, Stone Overlord
The Hierophant, He of the Dark Rites (Guthrie)
The Lovers, Duke & Duchess Most Perverse
The Chariot, Wicked Champion
Strength, Mistress of Fauna (LARK!)
~~The Hermit, Master of Alchemy~~
Wheel of Fortune, Lady of Fate
~~Justice, She Who Harrows~~ (Spite)
The Hanged Man, Our Lord Uncanny
Death, The Endless Knight
~~Temperance, Collectress of Sins~~ (Calanthe)
The Devil, Foul Desecrator (Ogen)
The Tower, Lord of Lightning (Joules)
The Star, Arcane Navigator
The Moon, Bringer of Doubt (Selena)
The Sun, Hail the Glorious Illuminator
Judgment, The Archangel (Gabriel)
The World, This Unearthly One

"Where did you get this?" I asked.

"Off my fridge door. Kidding. Like I said, my family chronicled. I wager more players have died, but I only scratch off those I can confirm through the calls.

I heard others clamoring when Spite got offed. It was early on. Don't know who did it though."

"The Alchemist"—I cleared my throat—"was named Arthur."

She tilted her head at me. "Okay. I'll update it." Her eyes began to glow red. "Hold on, we pause for this public service announcement. . . . We've got about two more hours till showtime."

Showtime. It sank in that we might all die tonight. Hell, Death had given me a week, and I was about at the end of it. If I only had a few more hours, I wanted to spend some time alone with Jack—and I wanted it badly enough to leave our cozy fire and head back out into the storm.

I mentally asked Matthew, *Will you be okay with Finn for a bit?*

—*Empress is my friend. Finn is my friend.*—

Yes, we are. I'll be back soon. I'm going to talk to Jackson.

—*He won't like that.*—

I begged to differ. I rose, offering Jack my hand as I murmured, "You and I should recheck the perimeters. Just to be sure there aren't any early birds."

He shot to his feet in an instant, grabbing my hand and his gear, announcing, "Perimeters are important."

I tried not to notice when Selena glanced away, her expression stricken.

"Finn, you'll stay with Matthew?"

"Matto and I are inseparable. Haven't you heard?"

Matthew said, "Peas. Pod."

At that, Jack hastily squired me outside, as if he thought I'd change my mind.

I could hear Finn chuckling. "Checking perimeters? Is that what the Louisiana kids are calling it these days? Hey, Lark, can I check your perimeter?"

Jack was already dragging me out into the night. I'd been dizzy, cold, and weak just moments ago, but as I gazed at him, excitement filled me.

I felt *alive.* . . .

14

He led me past one of the briar walls to the overhang where Matthew had sheltered earlier, and we leapt through that veil of water. Inside, it was like being cocooned from the world.

He shook his hair out in that way I loved.

"Aren't you glad you stayed with us?" I asked him in a wry tone.

"It's never dull." He pulled me close, nuzzling my ear. "Miss you, *peekôn*. Been with you the entire day, so how does that work?"

God, I'd missed him more.

"I doan know about the new girl though. All I been hearing is how these players are supposed to kill you. But I bet you're still thinking new friend, new ally, *non*?"

"Me? I'm not thinking new friend." Okay, I *might* have been thinking new friend. She was funny. I liked her attitude.

"Hell, Selena was ready to off you without blinking an eye. You kept telling me you didn't trust her. Now I know why."

I frowned. "But she's changed. She's made up her mind to keep me alive."

"Look, all we know for certain about Lark is that she's got monster wolves to do her bidding. I doan trust her. Just keep it close to the vest, Evie. No need to tell her anything about us. You're the best secret keeper I know."

"Okay, I'll try to learn more from her than I reveal."

He nodded. "If this thing goes sideways tonight, I want you to run."

I stroked the backs of my fingers along his jaw. "I'd never leave you in danger."

"You mean that, doan you?"

"Yes. But if anything happens to me, I need you to take care of Matthew."

"Doan you dare talk like that, *bébé*." He gripped my nape, a move that was at once protective and possessive. "I'm not goan to let anything happen to you, no."

"Well, don't go leaping in front of bullets or anything. Remember, I regenerate."

"What if you got shot in the head, like Bagmen?"

"I've wondered the same. But I think the Touch of Death is what I need to be looking out for."

"He's not goan to hurt you either. Not while I've got a breath in my body."

When I shivered, Jack said, "I'll start a fire." He gathered some dry branches and kindling, arranging them near a shelf of raised ground in the back. With efficient moves, he struck his hunting knife against a flint, coaxing a fire to life. As it grew, he collected his sleeping bag from his pack, laying it atop that shelf.

Shadows danced, the air soon heating. We sat side by side, warming our hands.

The setting, the fire, the rushing water outside, the looming danger . . . everything was intense, *primal*. And at that moment, I felt as if I had been destined to end up in this place with this boy.

We felt fated.

He gazed down at me. "You know what we used to say about girls like you?"

I shook my head.

"You fall in love with your first."

"Ah." I bumped my shoulder into his. "Now I see why you pushed so hard to score with me that night by the pool. All becomes clear."

His expression was serious. "I wanted you. Christ, I wanted you. But for a lot longer than a night. In my mind, if we slept together, we'd stay together. I needed that. I need that now."

Sometimes it was so apparent that he'd been raised in a different culture, one in which a boy carried a girl's things to signal possession to other beaux. "What gives you that idea about me?"

"Deny it, then."

I'd never had a first, much less stayed with him. But if Jack was mine, I thought his theory would prove to be correct.

He raked his fingers through his hair. "Made me crazed when I heard your message to Brandon. That you were goan to let him have you."

Little had I known that Jackson had stolen Brandon's phone, had listened to my message.

"That was one of the reasons I was so angry when you came to my house that night," Jack explained. "I figured you were already lost to me, but after what you saw there, I knew you were out of my reach. I didn't act right."

"That's past. I'm here with you now." I placed my hand on his knee. "Like you said, we can pick up where we left off."

His body shot tight with tension.

I bit my lip. "Just in case we somehow live past tonight, do you, uh, have protection?"

"*Ouais*, and it's from this century," he teased, referencing our first ill-fated make-out session. "You sure about this? Last time . . ."

I cupped his face. "We could die tonight."

Jack grinned down at me. "Now, hold on, Evie. You doan have to pull the last-night-on-earth con with me. I'm a sure thing."

I grinned back. "So am I."

I loved the flash of disbelief on his face, and the bob of his Adam's apple as he registered this was going to happen.

Every reason I'd held back from having sex before had been eliminated. I was in a relationship with Jack, and I trusted him, so I knew I wouldn't get nailed and bailed. Before Jack, I'd felt no curiosity about it or passion. Now I could barely wait to take this step. An added bonus: I loved the boy. Which he already knew.

So I daubed my tongue to my bottom lip, and he took the hint.

Light grazes of his mouth over mine turned to deep kissing. Without breaking lip contact, we yanked off our coats, fumbled off our boots, peeled off our wet jeans. He drew back only to grab the hem of my shirt and pull it over my head.

Once he'd removed his own, I gazed at his rosary. It was like Jack's own emblem, his own symbol. Then I frowned at the tiny details around the cross, spying an engraved rose in the center.

Rosary. Rose-ary. Jack carried a rose as well. Again, that fated feeling swept me up.

When he laid me back, my hands flew to his chest. With utter delight, I began learning that damp skin, those rippling muscles, loving the way they leapt to my touch.

As I explored him, he stared down at me in my underwear, rapt. My glyphs were shimmering across my skin. "Mercy me, Evie." He leaned in to kiss the one winding across my chest, following it with his lips. "These spooked me before," he rasped against my skin. "But now I think they're sexy. Everything about you is sexy." He gave it a lick that made my toes curl.

"Hey, I-I'm sure you're just mesmerized." I wanted the rest of my clothes off, felt confined by damp lace.

"Does it matter if I am? *Non*, not if I like it," he said, shucking off his boxers.

I caught a peek at him and gasped, my breaths shallowing.

He was still smiling when he kissed me again. Soon I was so mindless, I scarcely noticed that he'd stripped off my bra—until his warm, rigid chest pressed against my bare breasts. He shuddered at the contact, groaning into our kiss. The weight of his body atop me was divine, welcome. Our hips began rocking, grinding, seeking.

Then his forefingers hooked the edges of my panties. "Up you go, *bébé*."

When I lifted my hips, he tugged off the last barrier between us. Well, almost the last. From his jeans pocket, he took a condom pack, tearing the corner with his teeth. As he began rolling it on, I was transfixed. Utter lust.

Seeming unaware of my gawking, he moved between my legs. His outer thighs brushed my inner ones, and then I felt him hard against me. My cheeks heated, my body softening for him.

But as soon as he stretched over me, that pressure in my head increased. —*The mortal is not for you!*—

I jerked in Jack's arms.

"What? Too fast?" He raised up above me. "You can tell me to stop if you want, Evie. Anytime you want me to."

—*You cannot know him this way.*—

"No, I don't want to stop. It's one of the voices. Death's. It's like he's in my head!"

—*He's not for you, creature!*— Death repeated.

Why are you doing this to me? Are you such a hard-ass that you won't allow the girl you plan on murdering some enjoyment in her final days?

—*You deserve nothing but* misery!—

Jack clenched his fists, the muscles in his arms corded with strain. "I'm goan to kill that son of a bitch, just for this."

Get in line. *How in the hell is this your business?*

—*Your death is mine, which means your* life *is mine.*—

You're insane! Never had I heard Death like this. Before, he'd always been smoothly mocking, taunting me with my upcoming demise.

Now his words were seething. —*I am owed, Empress! Do this, and you will pay.*—

"Evie?"

"I want this, Jack! Kiss me."

He did, briefly muting the Reaper, rekindling my excitement.

But Death was *yelling*. —*NEVER, CREATURE!*—

This place was perfect, a moment in time; it should be just me and Jack. Now Death was ruining it. "It's no use. He doesn't want us to do this. And I don't understand why."

"Look at me, Evie. Stay with me."

I gazed up at Jack, peering into his eyes. They were stormy gray, filled with desire, yearning. Even vulnerability. "He doan get a goddamned say, now, does he?"

When Jack held my gaze, Death was quieted, the heavy weight of his presence ebbing. —*Sievā, do not do this. . . .*—

See-whatta? Then he faded.

Faded to nothing.

"His voice is quiet. This is working!"

"Then I'm goan to be looking into your eyes when I take you. You hear me?"

I nodded, wanting this more than I'd ever imagined I could.

He traced his hand between us, lower, lower, dipping his fingers. "So hot," he groaned. "So perfect. You want this too." It wasn't a question.

He began touching me as I needed him to, petting me. Whatever he was doing made me crazed for more. I rocked my hips to his caressing fingers, lids growing heavy, but I kept my gaze pinned to his.

His hips rocked too, wedging his hardness against me. My eyes went wide when he started to press inside. My glyphs ghosted over me faster.

"Doan be scared, *bébé*," he rasped with a brief kiss to my lips. "I'm goan to take care of you." Staring down into my eyes, he began prodding deeper. "I've wanted you for so long." And deeper. "My God, woman!" When he was all the way in, a strangled groan burst from his chest.

Pain. I just stifled a wince, far from enamored with this.

Voice gone hoarse, he said, "You're mine now, Evangeline. No one else's."

He must be right—because Death's presence had disappeared completely.

Jack held himself still, murmuring, "Doan hurt, doan hurt."

"It's getting better."

"Ready for more?"

I nodded. Then regretted it. *Pain.*

Between gritted teeth, he said, "Evie, I got to touch you, got to kiss you. Or you woan like this." A bead of sweat dropped from his forehead onto my neck, tickling its way down to my collarbone.

"O-okay."

Still inside me, he raised himself up on his knees, his damp chest flexing. His hands covered me, cupped, kneaded, his thumbs rubbing. When I started arching my back for more, his body moved. And it was . . .

Rapture.

"Jack! Yes!"

In a strained tone, he said, "God almighty—I am home, Evangeline." Another thrust had me soaring. "*Finally* found the place . . . I'm supposed to be."

He leaned down, delivering scorching kisses up my neck and down to my breasts, bringing me closer and closer to a just-out-of-reach peak.

Each time he rocked over me, I sensed a barely harnessed aggression in him. Between panting breaths, I said, "Don't hold back! You don't have to with me." I lightly grazed my nails over his back, spurring him until he was taking me with all his might—growling with need as I moaned.

Pleasure built and built . . . broke free . . . wicked bliss seized me, seized him.

As I cried out uncontrollably, he yelled, "*À moi, Evangeline!*" Mine.

"Yes, Jack, *yes*. . . ."

Then after-shudders. A final moan. A last groan.

As his weight sank heavily over me, I ran my hands up and down his back, wanting him to know how much I loved that.

How much I loved him.

He raised himself up on his forearms, cheeks flushed, lids heavy with satisfaction. "I knew it would be like this." His voice was even more hoarse. "I knew from the first moment I saw you." Stroking my hair, he started kissing my face, pressing his lips to my jaw, my forehead, the tip of my nose. "I am home, Evie Greene," he repeated between kisses.

I never wanted him to stop. He'd been an amazing lover, but his afterplay? He was adoring.

"The first priest I find, I'm goan to marry you. I'm all in, *peekôn*." His kisses grew more and more heated. Against my lips, he rasped, "How come I can't ever get enough of you?"

Just as that rush returned and I knew we were about to get another round of this, I heard panting—comprehended that it wasn't my own. I broke away. "Jack?"

We both turned to find a wolf nosing through the waterfall, its head halfway in. It blinked at us, then howled.

Not a second later, Lark called, "Hey, guys! You in there? I told the others I'd find you. We're heading out. It won't be long now."

Jack rested his forehead against my own. "We're goan to pick this up later."

"Even more incentive to live through the night?" To Lark, I called, "Be right there."

With one last lingering kiss, Jack helped me to my feet, collecting our clothes. As we dressed, I caught him grinning at me, knew I was giving him goofy smiles. I'd played my V card, and had zero regrets.

Hand in hand, I walked with Jack up to our pre-planned vantage point. Death's presence was a memory. *Good riddance. . . .*

Jack squeezed my hand and gazed down at me. "*À moi*, Evangeline."

I promised him: "Always."

15

"So three Bagmen and a slaver go into a bar . . ." Finn began as the wails grew closer.

We were lying in wait on a cliff high above the chute. And we were invisible.

Selena whipped her head around, hissing, "Are you serious, Magician? They're almost here."

The horde was like one giant, wailing beast scrabbling up the mountain. Though the night was dark, we could see their creamy, pale eyes as if they glowed.

Selena and Jack aimed their bows. Matthew and Jack lay on either side of me, Finn beside Lark. She was spaced out, monitoring the approach of the cannibals through her falcon.

Her wolves crouched behind Finn's illusion, ready to attack the horde from behind.

"What?" Finn whispered. "Just because we're

about to be swarmed by bloodthirsty zombies doesn't mean we can't have a laugh."

Matthew made a *eureka!* hand gesture. "Zomedy!"

"Damn straight, Matto." Finn always seemed a little surprised by how much he liked the boy.

I'd wanted to ask Matthew about my latest interaction with Death, but he'd seemed preoccupied before. Now it was too late.

When the horde began funneling into the chute like a rolling wave, doubt over my plan racked me. What if this didn't work? Our sole escape hatch was that booby-trapped canyon. If the cannibals prevailed and pursued, we'd have to hit it faster than we'd ever imagined, at night, in the pouring rain. . . .

The bad part about having ideas that people listened to? The responsibility.

The Baggers lurched closer, their path decided for them. I held my breath as they approached our cliff. *Keep it moving. Nothing to see here.*

Yet when they were directly beneath us, they stopped, scenting the air—

They'd detected us this high up! Even over their own stench?

More wails sounded; they began attacking the barrier to reach us. With vicious strength, they tore at the briars, biting them, uncaring as the barbs ripped their slimy skin. I felt every blow, every bite.

Jack snapped, "Fire, Selena!"

They began shooting, dropping Bagmen, but more replaced them.

I gritted my teeth, sweating, getting my ass kicked by proxy. My hair turned red, my glyphs burning bright.

Jack reloaded. "Evie, hang on!"

"I've got this." But power was draining from me in this damn rain. Pain reverberated throughout my body like the tolling of a bell. We had to make them *want* to run. I gazed over at Lark. "H-hurry with the wolves!"

"Not yet!" Her red eyes were narrowed, her claws digging into the rock, her canines lengthening. "The Teeth are just hitting the valley now. Buy us five minutes!"

I grated to Finn, "Make your mountain move!"

"I'll try!"

I'd only been in battle with one opponent before. Now enemies teemed. Just when Jack and Selena had both run out of arrows, we heard a welcome sound.

Howls.

The Bagger tide swept forward, driven by the snapping beasts. Screams of pain sounded. Some zombies stumbled a retreat, now missing hands and feet.

Red of tooth and claw, Lark's wolves snatched out throats by the dozens. By the time the Bagmen started descending into the valley, the beasts' fangs dripped, their sable coats soaked with rancid slime. It oozed off them in the rain, like thick paint.

Dizziness as I'd never known seized me. I sucked in ragged breaths.

"Evie!" Jack lunged toward me, pulling me against him.

Finn collapsed to his back, muttering, "I can't believe I used to think creating illusions was better than sex."

The cannibals arrived in the valley, only to be greeted by hell.

Jack helped me to my feet. From our spot, we surveyed the scene as the Bagmen charged the Teeth. We heard men yelling orders. Shots fired. Chaos. Muzzle flashes lit up the night, but there were too many Baggers.

Just a matter of time.

Selena said, "Holy shit, they ran right for the Teeth!"

Despite my exhaustion, I couldn't stop smiling. "It worked!" I turned to hug Matthew. "We did it!"

He blinked. "Did we?"

Face beaming, Finn turned to Lark, words leaving his mouth in a rush: "I'm hooked on you like phonics."

She gave him a startled half-smile.

When Finn stared at her smile, she grew flustered, closing her mouth to cover her fangs. Embarrassed in front of the cute boy.

She cast him a woebegone look, but he grinned. "Let your freak flag fly, hotness."

As if she couldn't help herself, she grinned back, flashing fang.

As I gazed over our alliance, pride surged through me. We'd combined our powers and had created a perfect storm of badassery. I felt in my bones that we could defeat Death.

Because we were unstoppable. With wonderment, I thought, *We can do anything!*

I realized I'd spoken aloud when everyone turned to me.

Jack, the boy I loved, pulled me closer, resting his chin on my head. Lark grinned, giving me a gang sign of respect. Finn put his arm around her. Even Selena's shoulders jutted back.

That was when we heard the first cannon.

16

"What the hell?" Selena cried as more booms shook the night.

Then what sounded like machine guns on steroids began blasting.

"I know that sound." Jack's expression was grim. "It's artillery. Just like the Army of the Southeast had." No longer were men screaming—they were yelling with pleasure, mowing down the zombies.

From the backs of newly arrived pickup trucks, they aimed huge guns, their bullets cutting through the Bagmen, scythes through hay.

Selena narrowed her eyes at Lark. "You couldn't see that they were sporting that kind of weaponry?" She strapped her bow over her chest, preparing to run.

"I said they had trucks. I didn't know what was in them!"

"'This is my hood,'" Selena said, imitating Lark's

voice. "'I know the Teeth up and down.' How could you miss that they're armed like the national guard?"

"They'll be coming for us." Jack grabbed my arm and started down the rise.

My legs were already like jelly. I reached for Matthew to hold my hand. The others followed.

As we ran, Lark said, "They must've found an arms depot in the last week or something." By the time we'd reached the ground, her wolves had caught up, flanking her as we wound around charred tree trunks.

Selena snapped, "Or maybe you didn't miss it—how do we know you're not working with the Hierophant?"

"Don't know if you've noticed this, Archer, but my happy ass is running right alongside yours, straight into that canyon. And I've got twelve paws to be concerned about down there."

The tree trunks thinned out, the ground turning gravelly. In the distance, gunshots grew sporadic. Truck engines revved as the Teeth began rolling out.

Finn jerked his head around. "They're coming!" I'd never seen him look so terrified.

"Through there," Lark called, pointing to the looming canyon.

The rock walls were sheer, about four stories high, the width between them no more than a two-lane highway.

Jack stopped at the entrance, cupping my face. "Stick to me like a shadow, you." How many times had he told me that?

"I regenerate. I need to go first!"

Dafuq. "You're goan to stay behind me and step where I step. Same for you, *coo-yôn*. This ain't up for discussion!"

"The wolves can go first," Lark said, concern in her eyes. "They should take the lead."

Jack raised his brows. *"Mais yeah!"* For sure. "Send 'em through!"

The trio started forward swiftly. They were difficult to see, blending with the dark. Jack rushed to catch up with them, dragging me behind him, while I yanked on Matthew.

Within the walls, it was even darker. Sound was amplified, the rainfall deafening. I could barely hear the others trailing behind us.

Ten minutes passed, twenty. How much farther could it be? *Terror in the rain, Matto?* When would it end?

"Hang on, *bébé*. Not too much longer—"

A scream sounded over the din.

"Ahhh, my leg!"

We whirled around, saw Finn collapsing to his back, a bear trap biting into his right calf. Blood poured.

"Finn!"

As he screamed, his illusions began to flash erratically all around us—day to night, the mountainside he'd created.

Jack rushed back, dropping to his knees, grappling

with the metal jaws. The muscles in his neck bulged as he wedged the rusted jaws a couple of inches wider, but they slammed back shut.

Finn screamed again, his eyes rolling back in his head as he passed out.

"I can cut through it!" I called.

"You and *coo-yôn* doan move a goddamned inch! Look at that boulder, Evie!" He jerked his chin at a nearby rock.

I could see where that trap was attached by a chain to an anchored bolt. I could also see several other bolts and disguised chains leading to still-hidden traps.

We were surrounded by them. Selena, Lark, and Matthew froze. I started sweating in the rain.

Jack used his crossbow to wedge open the jaws, freeing Finn at last. Then he reeled in the chain of the trap, throwing it like a lasso onto the ground between me and him. One trap snapped, leaping off the ground. Another.

He turned behind him, doing the same for Lark and Selena. "There could still be more," he said as he hefted Finn over his shoulder. "And watch your six for Teeth!"

We'd just started forward when bullets began to rain down.

Lark cried, "They're above us on the canyon walls!"

"Move your ass, Evie!" Jack yelled as he came storming toward me, Finn secured in a fireman's carry. The wolves waited until we'd started moving once more.

Bullets pelted the ground around us, but the men were careful not to hit us—

One of the wolves stumbled. Immediately, I heard a thick whizzing sound. A tree trunk hurtled through the air, a battle ram swinging from a height right toward the wolves. Jack lobbed Finn at me, knocking me and Matthew over like dominos—just as the trunk hit a wolf.

Impact. The creature came flying back at us, its great body colliding with *Jack.* They were both hurled into the air, careening over where we lay. I screamed as they landed, twisting over on my stomach to keep him in sight.

The wolf scrambled up, unharmed, revealing Jack's limp body, his head bashed against a rock. He was unconscious, blood streaming.

As bullets continued to ping, I untangled myself from Finn and Matthew and crawled to Jack. "Please wake up. Oh, God, please, Jack!"

Behind me, Matthew sat rocking, muttering incoherently. "The three, the three. . . ."

Selena sprinted for me, Lark behind her. "The Teeth are coming down the canyon behind us!"

Fangs bared, Lark's wolves charged back to attack. Machine-gun fire rang out. Whimpers, howls. Then the wolves went quiet.

The last one limped back to its mistress, falling dead

at Lark's feet, twitching. She stared down with parted lips. Shock.

Selena grabbed my arm. "We need to run, Evie!"

Run? Jack and Finn were unconscious. "Never! I'm not leaving them."

"You're going to get them killed! We run and draw the fire." Though the bastards weren't aiming at us, bullets were ricocheting right above our heads. "We can break the guys out later, just like J.D. and I did with the militia."

What she said made sense, but I couldn't bring myself to leave Jack. "Wake up, Jack! Please wake up!"

Spotlights flared down, blinding us. By the time my eyes adjusted, we were surrounded, armed cannibals spilling out of a nearby trap door in the ground.

Like ants.

17

Hell was a cannibal mine, and its entrance was just as we expected—torchlit, foggy, littered with bones.

Ten guards surrounded us, forcing us closer. They had spiky teeth and sickly skin. Their bodies were gaunt, starving.

Each had milky white, clouded eyes, a sign of the Hierophant's enthrallment.

Seven of the men leveled rifles at Selena, Lark, Matthew, and me, even though we were bound, stripped of gear and weapons.

Neither Jack nor Finn had awakened, filling me with even more panic. One guard dragged Finn by an ankle. Two more hauled Jack by his arms. Matthew seemed not to register any of this, just kept murmuring, "The three. Water. The three."

With dread, I realized the Hierophant's call was getting louder. "He's down there," I whispered to Selena.

She nodded, her eyes a little wild. "Just stay calm. Your glyphs are dark. Every second we can survive, you recharge from the Bagger attack."

"Recharge? In a mine?" My stomach roiled, my steps halting. I glanced over my shoulder, saw Lark's eyes fill with tears. She was too young for this. We were *all* too young. She'd lost her beloved wolves, and we'd still been captured.

At the threshold, the lead guard collected a torch. His filed teeth were blackened. Like the others, his eyes were clouded. Sores bubbled around his lips, pus glistening in the firelight. His mouth looked like one you'd see on a meth addict's mug shot. Meth-mouth.

On the long and jarring truck ride here, he'd lamented that he and his men couldn't eat one of our "boys" for the road; they were starving, you see. But they obeyed the boss absolutely.

As we stepped into their underground lair, panic took root. Only my concern for the others kept me from resisting. My empty claws ached to sink into flesh.

Our captors forced us to descend deeper. Human bones and skulls were strewn throughout the mine. Rainwater seeped from the rock walls, gathering in streams at the sides of the shaft; it frothed over those bones, snagging them, tumbling them ever lower.

Oh, God, the stench was unimaginable—rot, mold, decomposition. I couldn't get enough air, as if my lungs were constricting.

Selena said, "Easy, girl, we'll get out of this." But with every step deeper, she started to look as freaked out as I was.

Farther in, men were digging ditches to divert the water. From what?

Meth-mouth informed us, "Your arrival came at a perfect time. We were gettin' mighty low on stores." *On bodies.* "Just been nibbling here and there."

Nibbling? I shuddered.

"We've about done starved, you see. Been conserving—but no longer! Tonight we're gonna celebrate our catch with a feast from the pantry."

Pantry?

"Why don't you eat your own fallen?" Selena said with hardly a tremble.

"We'd never eat one of our own," he said, adding ruefully, "no tougher meat than a cannibal's."

They all laughed like this was one of those everyday, regrettable truths, as if he'd just said, "Toast always lands butter-side down."

When he saw me staring at his filed teeth, he snapped them at me. "The better to eat you with, my pretty."

Their cackles echoed off the walls.

I tasted blood, realized I'd been biting the inside of my cheek. I was almost glad Jack was knocked out rather than have him witness this.

We entered what looked like their central gathering

hub, a cavern that split into more shafts, like the spokes of a wheel. Too few wall torches fought with the dark. Dirty faces peered out from the shadows. Some smiled with excitement, flashing those eerie teeth.

The area was shaped like an amphitheater. The highest level was a raised dais, with a thronelike chair and a bloodstained dining table. A second level had tables and benches, the ground littered with more bones. In the center of the cavern was a depression that looked as if it were filled with oil. But when I saw meat hooks dangling from the high ceiling, I realized the oil was . . . blood.

I gazed around at the people impatiently waiting for a body to be hung there. *They don't even grill.* My skin crawled, the hair on my nape standing up.

We passed a dug-out room filled with piles of clothes and packs. No, not piles, *hills*. The Teeth must've captured an entire town's worth of people. Two of the guards chucked our things—bug-out bags, weapons, coats—in there as well.

Selena was gazing longingly at her beloved bow when I muttered, "Be on the watch for the Hierophant. And be careful not to look him in the eye, or you'll end up like these people."

She nodded.

The guards steered us into one of those split-off shafts, a murkier corridor. The ceiling was lower, the air colder and more ominous.

The end of the shaft had been remodeled as a jail with iron bars—and plenty of shackles, just like in Arthur's dungeon. A single torch burned outside, casting flickering shadows over the occupants within.

"Welcome to the pantry," Meth-mouth said as he and his men forced us inside.

Six prisoners were already fettered, all in various stages of starvation—and mutilation. They were "the stores" the Teeth had been conserving, the ones they'd been nibbling on.

The guards began chaining us throughout the cell, wherever there was a free set of shackles.

I wanted to fight. Needed to. *There's a heat in battle.* The Empress didn't get chained!

As if Selena could tell what I was thinking, she muttered, "This isn't the time, Evie."

She was right. There were too many people in this small area. Even if I could disperse spores, I might kill everyone. If I slashed at the guards with my empty claws, the other men would sound the alarm before I could stop them. Jack and Finn remained unconscious, unable to run—Finn couldn't even if he woke up.

For these reasons, I would wait, but also because my overarching strategy had just changed. In this game, I planned to kill Death—*and* the Hierophant. My claws tingled at the thought, my poison beginning to renew. I just needed to find him.

I had a feeling he'd soon come to see his catch, but not until we were contained.

Meth-mouth shackled Selena himself, saying, "Prettiest breeders I ever did see." Spittle bubbled up on his blistered lips. "Don't you worry—you won't go on the hooks for a long, long time."

Matthew stared blankly as he was chained. He'd checked out, and considering our circumstances, I didn't blame him.

Jack roused just as his wrist cuffs clicked shut. Blood streaming down his face, he lunged for the guard, who laughed.

When Jack and I shared a look, I tried not to reveal how on edge I was.

The men must've considered Lark and me to be minimal threats; we were the only ones with a single ankle cuff.

They think we're helpless girls. I might've laughed. *Worst mistake of their lives.*

As the guards filed out, Meth-mouth pointed to the prisoner closest to me. "You're on the hooks as soon as we gather the flock."

The prisoner whimpered at this news. Dressed in rags, he had no limbs, just cauterized, oozing stumps where his legs and arms should be.

"See you in ten." As they returned to their hub, the guards' laughter echoed down the mine.

I almost vomited, but choked it back.

The doomed man was in shock, feverish, his eyes glassy. Between chapped lips, he rasped, "T-ten minutes, then."

The other captives murmured phrases of sympathy to him—because he was about to be eaten. They called him Tad.

Jack grated, "Evie, did they hurt you?"

I shook my head. "Finn's the worst off." The wide, bloody holes on his pants leg revealed gouged-out skin. But I didn't think the bone had snapped. Surely he'd wake soon.

"We're goan to get out of here. Doan you worry."

Tad turned those desperate eyes—to me. "Please, h-help me. Can you reach me? They don't waste a bullet first."

Finn had said that the cannibals fed on the living. I don't think I'd quite believed it until tonight. I'd once seen a deer being cleaned, the gutting. For Tad to go through that while conscious . . .

But how could I help him? "We're going to escape. Just hang on." *Hang on?* I bit my lip. *Stupid Evie, he doesn't have arms!*

Selena rolled her eyes at me, and I deserved worse.

"Finn, wake up!" With his illusions we could escape. He would make us invisible. The guards would open the cell door, see no one inside, then dash off to recapture us. I would use my claws to sever the chains. We'd stroll out of here.

Finn didn't stir.

"There's no escape," one of the other prisoners said, the sole woman, a middle-aged lady with sunken eyes, clad in a tattered sack dress. A square chunk of skin was missing from each of her thighs.

Tad begged me, "Kill me. Smother me."

"Evie, you stay put!" Jack ordered. "You can't help him."

Was I going to sit back and let a man be butchered alive? In Arthur's basement, I'd realized that I had power to fight back against evil, that I could help others. All I had to do was repurpose myself. I'd wondered how many were chained out in the world.

With that thought in mind, I reached for my cuff and used a claw to jimmy it open, earning a stern: "Damn it, *fille*."

The lock popped open with a click, spooking the other prisoners. "Stop this, girl!" "They'll come quicker, and there's no fighting them." "Tad's gone anyway." "They'll whip us for this!"

Selena snapped, "They're going to kill every single one of us—or worse—and you're worried about a whipping? You might be resigned to your fate down here, but I'm not!" To me she said, "Carry the hell on, Evie. Your glyphs are getting brighter. Free us all, and we fight."

Jack shook his head. "You doan listen to her. Sit your ass back down and act chained. We doan make a move without Finn, and he should wake soon. If those guards come back and see you freed, they might take you instead!"

I wavered.

"*Bébé*, we can't help everyone. Be smart about this." In French, he added, "That man will never survive, even if we freed him."

In a desolate voice, Tad said, "The others are r-right. There's no fighting the Teeth. Not that I would be a help anyway. They bring even more guards when they harvest. More than a dozen of them."

God, I *wanted* to fight.

Tad was now crying. "But could you . . . would you put your hand . . . over my mouth and nose? Please. I can't hurt you, can't stop you. It'd be a mercy."

I glanced at Jack. He shook his head firmly. "You need to look like you're chained." Whatever he saw in my expression made him bite out a curse, then mutter, "Hurry."

Lark said, "I can let you know when they're coming."

"How?"

Her eyes began to sparkle red. "They have a couple of rats that survived down here. I've moved them into the central area now."

I crossed to Tad, lifting his head into my lap, shocked by how little he weighed. "I'll make this better." I sounded so assured, while inside I was horrified, had no idea how I was going to do this.

Tears welled as my glyphs began to brighten and

swirl, my emotions fueling my arsenal. Others in the cell gasped in shock, but Tad gazed up at me with a dazed stare, as if I were a savior.

Just before I leaned down, I murmured, "A kiss good-bye, then?"

"B-bless you," the man whispered, closing his eyes. "Angel."

My tears hit his face as our lips met. My poison seeped into him.

Without even a twitch, he stopped breathing forever. Awash with grief, I straightened, a nebulous idea forming.

Jack's brows were drawn. "Get back, now!"

I nodded, yet that idea kept insisting I acknowledge it. *What an evil plan*, I thought, embarrassed even to consider it.

But how better to deal with evil people?

"I have an idea." My hair was changing colors, my claws sharpening. The prisoners fell into stunned silence.

Matthew finally spoke. "Arsenal." He was telling me to use it.

Jack looked alarmed. "What are you thinking? Talk to me!"

I raised my dripping claws.

Lark's expression flashed with comprehension. "Poison."

Selena nodded slowly, admiration in her gaze. "Fuckin' A. Do it!"

Jack repeated, *"Hurry!"*

"I'm so sorry," I said as I sank my claws into Tad's side. Like a snake, I injected my venom into his chest muscles, his neck, what was left of his shoulders. To disguise the marks, I connected them until they looked like solid gashes.

Silence fell over the cell. No one dared speak. The prisoners were terrified of me. Nothing new there.

Lark said, "And now?"

I'd injected so much, I was weakened to the point of exhaustion. My fingers felt like they'd been asleep for years. Vision blurring, I whispered, "Now we wait." I'd desecrated a body and couldn't tell if I was ashamed. Or proud.

Standing up was beyond me, so I began crawling back to my chain.

"They're coming, Evie!" Lark hissed. "And they're bringing *him.* . . ."

18

—WE GO NOW TO OUR BLOODY BUSINESS.—

I'd just clasped my ankle cuff back together, pressing the seam against the ground, when the gate groaned open.

They did bring back a dozen guards—and also the Hierophant.

He stood silhouetted in torchlight. He had thick gold rings on each of his fingers but no icons on his hands. He wore a black rain poncho. With the hood down, it resembled a robe. Looking to be no more than eighteen or nineteen, he was dark-haired with a bloated face, eyes like beads, and red, feverish cheeks.

His tableau flashed over him, an image of a robed male holding his right hand high, two fingers raised, blessing his followers.

The Hierophant cast the older prisoners a

grandfatherly smile—with hideous jagged teeth—then did a double take at me.

At my tableau. His eyes met mine. "What a little beauty." His voice was even-toned, pleasant. Unlike his men, he had no discernible accent. "I can see that the spirits surround you too."

Don't look at him, don't look at him. "You're sick. All of this is sick."

"I'm quite hale, thank you," he said, purposely misunderstanding me.

Don't look. But whenever he spoke, he compelled my gaze toward him, no matter how hard I resisted. I peeked up, saw he'd started perspiring. He was trying to mesmerize me, and as with most Arcana, using his power was taxing.

"My name is Guthrie, and these are my people. You and I must've been destined to meet, for I've heard your voice in my visions."

My Arcana call.

"Would you like to break bread with us, child? Commune with us?"

I had to think about his question before I could sputter, "N-never!"

If I mesmerized someone, it might buy me a second to use some element of my arsenal. Yet this man's spell-binding gaze would take hold like a disease, never ending until his death.

Unless he made me eat.

If I "broke bread" with him, if I committed that monstrous act, then I'd be doomed forever. His control would last even after he died—

"What's your name?"

Say nothing! "Evie," I answered, frowning at myself. He was so much stronger than me! Even as I ordered myself not to look, even as I heard Selena and Jack urging me not to, I glanced up again.

Guthrie's beady eyes had turned a filmy white. Because he was using his power?

Such intriguing eyes. I couldn't seem to break his stare.

"I sense strength in you," he told me. "And uniqueness. Yet there's no need for individuality here. In our commune, we're all the same."

"Individuality isn't bad," I said, but it sounded like a question.

He smiled. "It's unnecessary. But we'll take care of that for you, little one. When you get hungry, I want you to call for my guards." Maybe I *should* call for them when I got hungry. "They'll bring you to my table, to sit at my right hand." At Guthrie's right hand. "We have quail, pork, and beef—more food than you've seen in days, by the look of you. It's a fine setting, like a mead hall of old, full of good cheer. All you have to do is make the choice to come to me. And then choose to eat."

"Choose to eat," I repeated.

"Evangeline!" Jack grated. "Snap out of this!"

"Out of what?" All I was going to do was call the guards when I got hungry. I wasn't hungry now, though. My stomach was in knots.

"Why are her eyes clouding?" Jack demanded, his words panicked.

The Hierophant smiled down at me. "Evie, you're going to like it here." I just knew that I would. "Eventually, your friends will too. After I've dined and rested up, we'll come back to convert them as well. We're each surrounded by spirits."

He was so sure about this, it must be true.

"Be calm, relax. And know that all good things are coming to you." With a wink, the Hierophant left.

I sank back against the wall, confused as to why I'd been so bent on escaping.

Meth-mouth scowled in Tad's direction. "He died? Son of a bitch! I knew he didn't have long." He snapped his fingers, and one of the guards hefted Tad under his arm, carrying him like a suitcase. "Hurry before the flesh cools. Come on, be quick about it."

On his way out, the last guard hit Jack with the end of a rifle. "It's impolite to interrupt the boss."

Jack collapsed back, head lolling, as if he saw the ceiling spinning. But, to be fair, he shouldn't have interrupted the Hierophant.

Matthew began squirming, trying to hit his fists against his head.

I turned to him. "Relax, sweetheart. All good things are coming our way."

"Water!" he yelled. "Water water WATER!"

"Okay, honey. I'll bring you some as soon as I get out of here. Just have to get hungry first."

With effort, Jack reached his leg over and kicked Matthew's. "Easy, *coo-yôn*," he said weakly. "We need you focused."

To my amazement, Matthew calmed.

His outburst had roused Finn. By degrees, the boy opened his eyes and sat up, cringing at the damage to his leg. "I take it they've got us?"

"About time you came to." Lark's face was stamped with relief.

Finn gazed around the cell. "Jesus. How long was I out?" he asked, sounding like a condemned man.

I didn't understand his alarm. We were all going to like it here.

"Couple of hours," Lark said. "We're working on an escape. One little glitch: the sole person who could free us from these shackles looks like a contented flower child over there. Pun intended."

I waved at them. When would I get hungry?

"Her eyes are clouded?" Finn asked.

Selena nodded. "If he makes her eat, she'll be like that forever. Even if we take him out, there'll be no saving her from this."

As if that was a bad thing?

Finn said, "Escapes are my specialty. Just give me a chance to shake off this pain so I can concentrate. Damn, is it me, or is the cell spinning?"

Jack muttered, "It ain't just you. . . ."

Time passed. Everyone was too frightened to talk, not relaxing as they ought to. Finally I felt the first twinge of hunger. "Guards," I called with excitement. "I'm hungry." I started braiding my damp hair, wanting to look halfway presentable for a big dinner. "Guards!"

Jack was cursing, telling me in French to shut my trap.

I pursed my lips. "You're supposed to relax, Jack."

Meth-mouth slunk back to the pantry, his chin bloody for some reason. He was picking at his sharp teeth with a pinkie nail.

Jack was tensed against his shackles, muscles tight beneath his shirt. "You hurt her, and I'll kill you!" Blood poured from his wrists. "I swear to Christ, I'll gut you!"

Meth-mouth ignored him and reached down to release my ankle cuff.

I admitted, "I used my claws to break it open. Sorry."

He just rolled his eyes: yeah, right. With a harsh grip on my arm, he escorted me out. As he locked the gate behind us, Jack continued to bellow, thrashing against those chains.

Once we reached the cavern, I blinked at how different everything seemed now. The area looked exactly as

Guthrie had described it: a mead hall of old. Boisterous men and women drank from tankards and ate heartily of the beef, pork, and quail. Guthrie ate alone on a dais above all the others. And he wanted me to join him in that place of honor.

Meth-mouth led me up the steps, bones crunching beneath my feet—probably leftovers tossed to the dogs, like the Vikings used to do.

Guthrie welcomed me, offering the chair beside his. When I sat, he blinked at me. "You smell like flowers."

"I get that a lot. It's because I'm the Empress."

He looked charmed. "Oh? Of what?"

"Of Tarot cards."

His amiable expression faltered. "You sound over-tired. You should eat. What would you like first?"

"Quail." Was there blood on the table? No, no. Mead halls didn't have bloody tables. As I waited to be served, Guthrie kissed my hand suavely; Jack yelled in the distance, "Damn you, girl, doan eat ANYTHING!" He must be jealous that I was about to get a full meal.

But when Meth-mouth returned with a metal camping plate filled with gore, I frowned. He grinned at me, cracking his lip blisters open. Pus ran down his bloody chin, dripping onto the plate.

I was no longer hungry.

"Is the leg of quail not to your liking?" Guthrie was looking at me intently. "You're so hungry."

I was starving! Like I'd give up a free meal?

Finding no silverware, I picked up the quail. It wasn't very hot, and felt spongier than any I'd ever eaten. Still, I leaned in to take a bite—

Suddenly I heard Death's coaxing voice: —*Ask her about the game, Guthrie.*—

When Guthrie saw me stiffen, he said, "You heard that too? His voice often fills my mind—has for months! Is he the devil?"

I huffed with irritation, tossing down my quail, making the plate rattle. "No, that's a totally different card. You're hearing Death. Because he always butts in when I'm enjoying myself. Earlier today, I was with Jack in a cave, and—"

"Who is Death?" Guthrie interrupted. "Why can I hear him? What is this game he speaks of? Answer me!"

I looked longingly at my quail, but obeyed Guthrie's order. "Death is one of the Arcana, a group of twenty-two kids who've been chosen to play in a life-or-death game, all with special powers. We're commemorated on Tarot cards, yadda, yadda. You're one of us—the Hierophant. You can brainwash people." I lowered my voice to a confidential tone. "I know you think you see spirits, but it's really the images of our cards flashing over us. You hear our calls when we get near."

"Why should I believe this?"

"You heard a boy murmuring *Crazy like a fox*, didn't you? And a girl saying *Behold the Bringer of Doubt*."

His lips parted. His were cracked almost as bad as Meth-mouth's. "How could you know these things?"

"You might want to rework some of our commune's beliefs. A tweak here and there?" I grimaced as I asked, "I just overstepped, didn't I?" *Way to insult your leader, Eves.*

"I-I don't understand." For the first time I heard uncertainty in Guthrie's melodic voice. "Who started the game? Why was I chosen?"

I put my elbow on the wet table—had someone spilled ketchup or something?—and settled in to dish. "Oh, Guthrie. Where do I even start?"

"At the beginning. But first, I want you to have a bite." He flashed his pointy smile.

Death whispered in our minds: —*Don't you want to know who she slaughtered last week? This creature cut a man in two.*—

Guthrie scowled, but couldn't resist saying, "What is he speaking of? Someone like you could never harm another in such a manner."

As I put down my supper yet again, I mentally yelled at Death: *Leave us the hell alone!* Struggling for composure, I said, "It's an awful story, but if you really want to know . . ." Then I proceeded to tell him about Arthur. Throughout the tale, Guthrie's skin grew paler, and his face started dripping with sweat.

I'd had no idea I was such a compelling storyteller!

A vague recollection tugged at the edges of my

attention, of some wrong I might have done him, but I was too caught up answering his questions to pin-point it.

Suddenly he clutched the table, nails digging in, and gave a long groan of pain. I heard more groans from the lower tables, then frenzied cries. Throughout the cavern, people started dropping to the floor, convulsing, clawing at their throats as if they couldn't get enough air.

Guthrie shot to his feet, teetering as he swung his gaze on me. "What have you . . . wrought?"

My eyes went wide. "Oh, God, my poison! I didn't know you then! Had no idea what you would come to mean to me!"

With a strangled gasp, he collapsed to his back, as if his legs had been taken out from under him. I rushed to kneel at his side, filled with guilt. Below, chairs clattered, tables overturning. Grown men screamed.

Over the pandemonium, I could hear Jack bellowing my name to the sound of rattling shackles.

"There are . . . more of us," Guthrie grated to me. "Whole clans. Scouts, followers . . . throughout this range. They'll feel my death . . . will follow my last order."

"You can't die!"

The chaos was already beginning to fade, the death throes below growing quieter and quieter.

With his eyes clouded like those of his followers,

Guthrie yelled, "Avenge me! Kill this girl! She is everything that is foul, all that is unclean!" His words boomed across the cavern.

I was foul? If Guthrie said it, then it must be true. Hadn't I known I was a monster? Jack hadn't been able to accept me until he'd heard all about my trials and my fears, until he'd thought he could help me with my problem.

As life left Guthrie's body, the echoes subsided. His last words to me: "You'll . . . rot . . . in hell . . . for this."

"Wait, I'm so—" I fell back on my ass, jolted out of my panic.

Exactly why was I apologizing to a murderous cannibal? I scrambled to my feet, gaze locked on my plate, on the "quail" in the center. Human flesh had been cut in a square like a serving of lasagna, only the layers were striations of skin, fat, muscle.

I'd been inches from putting that in my mouth! Because I'd been . . . brainwashed? Again, to have another control my thoughts! I'd nearly eaten part of Tad. I'd nearly become a slave to the Hierophant. Fury boiled up inside me.

"What have I wrought, Guthrie?" I surveyed the amphitheater full of bodies. "I've wrought your doom."

The back of my hand tingled as a marking appeared. Beside the Alchemist's icon was a tiny likeness of two raised fingers. The Hierophant's symbol.

I'd destroyed him, and I was glad. *Kill them all.*

Heat in battle. As I grinned down at my pair of icons, I craved more. There were four other Arcana in this mine, chained and helpless.

No! *Rein it in, Evie!* That wasn't how this night would end. My next move was getting everyone free. On unsteady feet, I hurried toward the pantry, speeding down the stairs, winding around contorted bodies—

A hand shot out to seize my ankle. Meth-mouth. He was still holding a chunk of flesh in his other hand. "You're unclean. Must die!" he choked out just before his body relaxed, his bladder emptying.

I peeled his fingers off me, then ran all-out for the cell. At the gate, I found Jack still straining against his chains. When he saw me, he rasped, "Evangeline, you . . . back?"

"I'm back." I used my claws to break the gate lock, then freed Jack. He yanked me into his arms, squeezing till it hurt.

"You bagged the Hierophant!" Selena looked jubilant. "You took him out, Empress." Possibly the first time she'd ever addressed me as that. "Now, let's get out of here."

"Are you okay, Jack?" I reached up to gingerly touch his head. "Goose egg, huh? Isn't that supposed to be a good sign?"

"You're worried about my head? I didn't know what the hell they were doing to you out there!" Jack was growing more and more alert. "Free the others, *fille.*

Patrols might return soon. Just because Guthrie's dead doan mean the others' eyes will clear. They're bound to him even after death, right?"

"Yes." Meth-mouth's eyes had still been cloudy, Guthrie's last order foremost in his thoughts. . . .

Once I'd popped everyone's cuffs, I helped the other prisoners to their feet, while Selena and Lark lifted Finn between them. Wide-eyed, Matthew scuffed close to me, but he was holding steady.

We moved out as a large group, Jack in the lead. "We need to lay hands on our gear, our bows. Do you know where they stashed them?"

I nodded. "Just ahead, there's a hub. You'll see piles of supplies."

When we reached the central cavern, everyone froze in place at the carnage: Tad's grisly remains and my poison's work. Corpses with unseeing eyes, faces frozen in agony. Meth-mouth with bloody flesh clutched in his hand.

Jack drew back, yanking me into his chest. "Doan look, *bébé*. I'm goan to get our things. Get your warm coat. Everything's goan to be okay, just keep your back to this place." He took me by the shoulders and turned me around like I was a little girl.

I understood his concern. Now that the heat had passed, I didn't want to see. But I comprehended that I'd killed dozens. I told myself they were murderers who would never have returned to normal.

Maybe it helped.

"Selena, a hand," Jack said, loping off to reclaim our things. She and Lark propped Finn against a wall; then Selena ran after Jack.

"Look for the littlest camo jacket," Lark called, "that's mine!"

The other prisoners murmured to each other, seeming equally uncomfortable with the prospect of leaving our protection—and standing near me.

Jack and Selena returned shortly after to distribute a pile of our gear. They'd also scored two flashlights, arrows, a torch, and some clean-looking material for a bandage.

As Lark wrapped Finn's calf, Jack helped me into my coat, strapping my pack over my shoulders, warming my arms. But he made sure to keep me facing away from the main cavern. "Now, which way do we go? I got no idea where we are."

Lark knotted Finn's bandage tight, wincing when he did. "We go through the mountain." She shrugged into her camouflage coat, checking the pockets for her things.

"That's not the way," the woman prisoner said, limping forward. "We know these mines, have lived near here all our lives."

"If you go out the front entrance, you run the risk of more Teeth," Lark said. To us, she explained, "My way takes us to the other side of the mountain in hours.

You were heading south? This will save you days of climbing."

Climbing?

"Finn could never make it in his condition," she added, pretty much cementing my decision. Her two rats scurried to her then, startling the prisoners.

Even I got weirded out when the rodents climbed her like a jungle gym, clinging to the back of her coat with their tiny paws, baby-possum style.

Finn cracked a smile, as if he thought that was adorable.

At that, the locals started heading out, but the woman lingered to say, "We're going to resupply, then make our way out the front. If you go deeper into the mine, you're going the wrong way." She followed the others.

I turned to Matthew, reaching up to brush hair from his forehead. "What do you think, sweetheart?"

His brows drew together, his eyes glinting. His pupils looked dilated from shock. "There's one, there's two, there's three."

"I don't understand. Do you mean three directions?" I asked, but he just blinked at me.

As Selena looped one of Finn's arms across her shoulders, he said, "Let's do this—Lark'll lead the way."

Selena glared at him. "Why not follow the locals?"

"I know this place," Lark insisted. "I'm saving us days."

I turned to Jack. If we trusted her now and she didn't betray us, we'd be locking down our alliance. Without a strong alliance, we were dead anyway.

In French, he grudgingly said, "Separating from those people is probably for the best."

For better or worse, we followed Lark.

19

At the start of an offshoot shaft, Jack had tried to hand Lark his torch, but she'd said, "Night vision, dude." Then she'd set off farther into the mountain, with those two rats clinging to her back.

If she was distraught over the deaths of her wolves or her missing falcon, she had a hell of a poker face. Were we seeing the Strength Card's *single-minded purpose*?

Jack, Matthew, and I were right behind her, Selena helping Finn along behind us.

Lark seemed to know where she was going. In short succession, she'd made several turns, confusing me. But she appeared confident.

Even this far underground, water sprinkled down from the ceilings, making Jack's torch hiss. As usual, we were soaked, freezing. I remained exhausted from expending so much poison, leaning against Jack for support.

I worried about his head, Finn's leg, and Matthew's

haunted gaze. The boy was squeezing my hand so hard I thought the bones might break. Yet I didn't say a word to stop him.

Whatever he needed to get through this night.

"Get your flashlight ready," Jack grated to Selena. His torch was dwindling. It wouldn't be long now before it guttered out altogether. And Finn was much too weak to conjure a lantern.

Lark might be able to see in the dark, but none of us could. And down here, dark would be pitch black.

"Finn, you doing okay?" I called over my shoulder.

"My leg hurts like hell, but I'll live. By the way, I hate that dick! Guthrie puts the *cult* in *difficult*, huh?"

Selena said, "Past tense."

"Yeah, waking up in his cell was like getting a glass of cold piss in the face. Thanks for offing him, Eves."

"Uh, sure."

We'd just made yet another turn when I thought I felt the ground moving beneath my feet. "Did you feel that?"

Jack shook his head. But to Lark, he demanded, "How much longer?" I knew this had to be freaking him out as much as it was me. We were both born and raised in Louisiana—there weren't exactly a lot of mines in cane country. We might as well be atop the Alps. Or on the moon.

"Not long now," she answered. Was one of the rats on her back peeking at me? Creepy. "We're going to hit a low spot, then we'll start ascending. We'll see light soon after."

When another quake trembled, I murmured, "Jack . . ."

He exhaled a gust of breath. "I felt it."

Just then the entire shaft rocked. We had to sidestep to keep our balance. Pebbles, sand, and water rained over us.

Once Jack's torch hissed its death, he and Selena scrambled to turn on their flashlights, the beams reflecting off a pool of water ahead.

We'd come upon the low spot. One problem: it was covered with water.

And it was rising fast, sloshing like rapids.

"This is new," Lark said in a casual tone. "We'll have to cross it. How deep do you figure it is?"

Jack handed me his flashlight, gave my shoulder a squeeze, then strode toward the edge. Without hesitation, he waded out into the water, knee-high, then waist-high; he abruptly sank beneath the surface. Just when I was about to run for him, he bobbed up and swam back toward us.

In the weak beams from the flashlights, his normally-tanned face looked pale, his limbs stiff as he strode out. How cold was it in there?

"It drops off. And it's deep. We'd have to swim it."

At his words, Matthew grew wild-eyed, crushing my hand. "WATER!"

Of course he was terrified after nearly drowning in his basement. That was why Matthew had been so pensive—he'd known this was in our future. So why not give us a heads-up? "Swim it, Jack? What about Matthew and Finn? Maybe we can go back the way we came?"

"If we do that, we'll run out of light," he said. The flashlights were already flickering. "And we're getting close. Feel that air breezing?" He pointed toward the black expanse in front of us. "We've got to be near the end."

Finn said, "Don't stop on my account. I'd rather swim for a stretch than climb."

Another shaft-shuddering quake. What sounded like larger boulders dropped in the distance, exploding against the ground.

"I can help Finn across," Selena said, "but we need to push on. Any more quakes and we're going to get trapped down here. Look at the roof trusses." She tilted her light up.

Massive lengths of wood bowed under the weight of boulders, curving like the ribs on a ship. Ominous splintering sounds echoed.

In a rush, the water started rising even faster. To navigate that in the dark?

"WATER. WATER!" Matthew was hysterical. I was getting there myself, my heart thundering.

Jack brushed his knuckles along my cheek. His skin was shockingly cold. "Listen to me, *bébé*, it's just like a swimming pool. You were a terror in the pool, *non*? As soon as you're across, *coo-yôn* will be clamoring to follow you."

Matthew had been traumatized just weeks ago. Now we were expecting him to swim in a dark mine with rising water?

Lark said, "Look, I'll go first." She bounded into the water, diving in an arc like a porpoise. Her rats were dislodged, paddling in her wake. When she surfaced some distance away, I saw her cutting through the water—until she disappeared into the murk.

Moments later, she called, "I'm here. On the other side. Yawning." Even her echoing voice conveyed her impatience. She'd made it look so easy.

I turned to Matthew, peeling my hand from his. "I'm going to follow Lark. And then you and Jack will swim after me."

"NOOOO!" he howled, the sound paining my ears.

"*Coo-yôn*, listen to me. It's not far. How about I swim with Evie, then come right back for you? I'll be beside you the whole way."

Matthew seized my shoulders. "Dying! Dying! Death!"

With a muttered, "Screw this," Selena eased Finn down to a sitting position, then jogged off to scout the way back.

Jack tried to pull Matthew off me. "We're running out of time, kid!"

"Nooo, Empress!" Matthew thrashed, accidentally clocking me in the face.

My jaw sang. I reeled, dizziness and another tremor almost sending me onto my ass. "It's o-okay, honey, just calm down."

Selena returned. "We're blocked. Trusses fell, tangling up like pick-up sticks. There's only one way to go."

"Calm yourself, *coo-yôn*!"

Matthew's long arms connected with Jack, battering him. He was like a drowning man on land.

"Sorry 'bout this, boy." Jack drew back his fist and popped Matthew in the face.

Matthew lurched, flashed a wounded expression, then went limp.

"Jack!"

He caught Matthew, laying him on the ground. "We doan have time! I'm going with you first."

"No, you have to stay with Matthew! Make sure he gets across. I'll be fine—just like you said, I'm a t-terror in the pool."

"No way, Evie." He curled his finger under my chin, lifting my face up.

"Stay with him, Jack. Please!"

"We'll swim together, Matthew in tow." He pressed a brief kiss to my lips, then reached for my pack.

I shimmied away. "I can handle it. You've got enough to carry."

After a pause, he nodded. "Then in you go, *bébé*. You can do this." He turned to Selena. "You got Finn?"

She helped him to stand. "We're right behind you, J.D."

I hurried in, the shock of the cold water hitting me like a blizzard's blast. At the drop-off, I treaded water, startled by how much my clothes and pack weighed me down.

I aimed my light back at the shore, saw Jack dragging Matthew's lanky frame into the water. After maneuvering the boy onto his back, Jack looped one arm around Matthew's chest and started after me. "Doan look back and doan wait for me! Just get to the other side."

Teeth clattering, I started across, holding the light with one hand. Farther out, the water was rougher, waves battering me. The chill temperature numbed my limbs, but I was able to make headway.

Jack was determinedly following.

The quakes continued, rocks falling. A softball-size one struck me square on the head. Pain erupted, faintness almost overwhelming me. *I'll heal, keep swimming!* I breathed in water, coughing on it.

The mine rocked harder than ever before. Boulders began plummeting from the ceiling, roof trusses stabbing down into the water. "Jack!" I shrieked.

"Keep on, Evie—"

An entire shelf of rock landed behind me with so much force, the percussion was a punch to my stomach. A wave surged, whipping me up and toward the opposite shore. I felt weightless for a brief moment. . . .

"Ahhh!" I slammed into the shallowing water, the force flinging me forward, far into the shaft. The ground was a washboard of grit and rock scouring my face.

Over my heaving breaths and coughs, I heard Jack yelling from what sounded like miles away. The wave must've hurled him and Matthew in the other direction. The quakes kept rumbling. So dizzy. Wait, where was Lark?

—I'LL MAKE A FEAST OF YOUR BONES!—

Ogen's call. Close. Panicked, I scrambled up; my arm bent at a weird angle. Broken? I collapsed right onto my wasted face.

Selena screamed, "Evie, they're here! Watch your six!" To Finn, she snapped, "Light it up *now*, Magician, or she's done!"

With a yell, Finn threw a beam of light from the opposite shore, illuminating the shaft in front of me. . . .

Death.

He was just there, terrifying in full black armor. I shrank back from him, knowing these were my last moments alive. His tableau—the mounted Reaper wielding a scythe—looked less horrific than his actual appearance.

Selena launched a volley of arrows, one after the other, what must have been an entire quiver.

He batted them away like flies. "Come with me, Empress, if you want them to live," he said, his starry eyes aglow behind his visor. "Ogen's striking the mountain, you see." The Devil was causing the quakes? "If I do not stay him, this mine will collapse."

I gazed over my shoulder. Jack had just caught sight of Death through the falling debris and spraying water.

"Nooo!" he bellowed, desperately trying to reach me while keeping Matthew's head above water.

In a bored tone, Death said, "Sooner or later, the mortal will leave the Fool to drown. Anything to save you."

I choked out, "What d-do you want?" Behind Death, I could see a cloudy dawn light streaming into the shaft. We'd been so close. Had he already murdered Lark?

"Come with me." He offered his gloved hand. "And my allies and I will leave your . . . friends to their fates. Take my hand, and I vow they won't be killed."

Jack was getting closer. "Evie, goddamn it, *doan you dare!*"

I gazed into Jack's tormented eyes. Rocks struck like missiles all around him. He was still swimming, but had to realize he'd never get to me in time. When a boulder nearly took him and Matthew both down into the depths, I knew I had to end this.

Even if it meant ending myself.

"Make the choice," Death said. "Bend your will to

mine. What wouldn't you sacrifice for them to live?"

My right arm was broken. I had no poison, no arsenal. Didn't matter. With my good arm, I reached for Death.

Even over the rumble of the quakes, I thought I heard Jack rasp, *"Bébé?"* Then louder: "Doan you do this!"

I gasped out, "T-take care of him, Jack—"

Death yanked me to him, sweeping me up in his arms. I fought him with any strength I had left, hyperventilating, dulling my claws on his armor, not even scratching it.

Death just laughed. When he turned to stride toward the light, Jack gave an agonized yell. Selena's last arrow struck Death square in the back of his armor, shattering into splinters.

"Evie! *EVIE!*" Jack's bellows grew fainter as the light brightened. "I'm comin' for you! You know I will!"

We exited the mountain into pouring rain. Even the stormy day blinded me.

Nausea churned as Death carried me to his pale, red-eyed steed. I was shivering uncontrollably even before I saw the Reaper's fearsome scythe in a saddle holster.

With me secured in his arms, he mounted. Why not just kill me?

"Wh-what did you do to Lark . . . ?" I trailed off, blinking in disbelief.

Lark, that bitch, was on a horse beside Death's. And she was all smiles.

I cried, "H-how could you?"

"You're too damn trusting, Evie." The girl adjusted her conductor's hat. "And now you're looking at me like it's my fault that I'm taking advantage of your failing?" Her falcon had returned to her; it perched on her shoulder, dining on one of the rats.

Her same three wolves surrounded her. Back from the dead? *Familiars.*

Off to the side stood monstrous Ogen, his body gigantic, over a dozen feet tall. His mottled torso was bared. Huge tattered pants were cinched at his waist.

Like Death, his tableau—a goat-man ogre leading tethered slaves—was *less* terrifying than his actual appearance.

His uneven horns twisted up from his misshapen head. What should have been the whites of his eyes were red and webbed with thick greenish-yellow veins, his black pupils slitted. With a grotesque smile, he pounded his meaty fists even harder against the mountain, rocking it.

"No!" I screamed, striking Death's armor. Ogen would level the entire mine! "You swore you'd leave them alone! You *swore.*"

Death reined his mount around. "I'll keep my vows to you as well as you did to me."

"Wh-what does that mean?" My voice sounded so

distant. Exhaustion was overwhelming me, but I struggled to remain conscious.

"Doesn't this feel familiar, creature? You, injured in my arms, as I ride. Our history repeats itself." When he removed his spiked glove, tears welled, then streamed from my eyes.

I tried to break free, the effort sending me closer to blacking out. "Don't touch me!"

His fingers brushed along my cheek, his skin burning hot against mine. He shuddered from the slight touch; I braced for pain. This was it, then.

My eyes rolled back in my head.

Death's hand inches ever closer to my face. Closer . . .

Contact. This is my end. His skin is surprisingly hot. My lids slide shut. Scarcely conscious, I await more grueling pain.

Heartbeat, heartbeat, heartbeat.

I crack open my eyes.

I feel nothing but the continued agony of his sword. Brows drawn, he yanks off his other glove, laying both hands against my face, then running his palms down my arms.

His starry eyes glow brighter; as if in response, my glyphs shiver, awakening.

Voice gone hoarse, he says, "None of the others survived my touch. No one." He strokes my cheeks, my neck, my lips.

When was the last time he held a living person this long?

I sense something wicked beginning to seethe inside him. With a lustful gaze, he leans in to press his lips to my bloody ones. I am too stunned to react. His kiss is ardent but unsure, as if he's never done it before.

Once he draws back, he licks the blood from his lips and groans, "So sweet."

"I-I don't understand." Am I immune to him?

"I am Death—and you are Life. You were made for me alone." He grips the hilt of his sword, yanking it free from my body. As I scream with pain, he catches me with his other arm. "You will heal." Under his breath, he says, "You must."

Cradling me to his chest, he mounts his steed. "I will protect you, and you will forgive me this. I will see you well."

"L-let me go."

"Never, creature." He gazes down at me. The most beautiful male I've ever seen. "I will never let you go."

"Where are you taking me?"

He frowns, as if the answer should be obvious. "To my bed, Empress . . ."

20

When I woke, I was still on a horse, still held by Death. As in my dream/memory.

But this time, I was astride the saddle, with my back to his front, my cheek resting against his armor. Instead of sizzling desert sands, we rode through pouring rain.

How long had I been out? My broken arm was healed?

That dream of Death merged into my present reality. He could touch my skin! I was the only one he could touch without killing.

And he'd been attracted to me.

Not this time around. My wrists were so securely cuffed together even I couldn't slice my way out. At some point he must have peeled off my parka and pack, leaving me in jeans and a short-sleeved shirt. To keep me cold and weak?

"She wakes," Death intoned from behind me.

I stiffened, sitting up in the saddle. His voice brought other memories rushing into my consciousness. *Oh, God.* Ogen had battered the side of the mountain with even more force after we'd emerged. We'd been seconds from dying down there before—how could Jack and Matthew have lived through another wave of quakes? If the mine had collapsed . . .

Matthew, please answer me!

Nothing. Maybe they were trapped. Or just asleep.

Sweetheart, I need to know you're okay! PLEASE TALK TO ME!

Silence answered. And emptiness—as if the comforting presence I'd felt since before the Flash had been uprooted from me. Even Death's presence in my head was utterly gone.

Because the switchboard was no more? If Matthew had . . . died, then Jack would have as well. Selena and Finn too? "Y-you killed them."

"As I always do," Death said in an amused tone. "Ogen flattened that mountain like a sandcastle."

Grief engulfing me, I stared down at Death's spiked gloves. In a voice I barely recognized, I said, "You wear their icons?"

"Apparently I was closest to them. Earning icons that way isn't as satisfying as a direct kill, but we do what we can."

Fury began overwhelming my grief. With each of his taunting words, it burned hotter, breath on an ember.

My claws began to sharpen. I would slice Death's marked skin right off his hands—or slay him and earn them.

Death murmured, "Try to tap your powers"—cold steel made contact with my neck—"and I will shove this blade into your temple. I'll keep you like that, brain-dead, unable to move. Or to die."

"Sink the blade!" Ogen hissed from our left. Though in a more human form, he still sported those monstrous features. His cloven feet plodded through mud; one of his black horns jutted higher than the other. When he skirted a rising retention pond with a wary expression, he looked younger. Maybe fifteen.

On our right side, Lark spurred her horse to match our pace. "You should make this last, boss," she told Death. "Torment her a little. You're gonna have to wait centuries for the next opportunity to cap her ass." Even in this weather, Lark looked snug and comfortable in her camo coat. "Making her suffer will be *so much better*— trust me."

I glared at the little bitch, promising vengeance. I blamed her as much as these other two. More even.

In a thick voice, I asked Death, "Why not kill me now?"

He whispered in my ear, "Because a part of you wants me to."

Chills broke out over my drenched skin. I wanted to deny his words, but didn't know if I could. In the last

nine months, I'd lost everyone. My high school boyfriend, my best friend Mel. My mother. Now four more
people had entered my life for such a short time and
had perished much too soon. The boy I loved . . . gone.

"Kill her NOW!" Ogen's fangs dripped slime, his
veiny eyes crazed. "A feast of her bones! Now, now!"

Death snapped something to the Devil in a foreign
language, and Ogen quieted like an obedient dog.

The raw winds buffeted us, driving the rain sideways, but I was too dazed to perceive it. Hypothermia?
My thoughts were as numb as my body.

My friends are dead. Jack is dead. What did I have
to live for?

Revenge.

When we reached a hill that was covered with banks
of sliding mud, Death sheathed his blade, wrapped one
arm around me, and spurred his mount. The stallion
seemed to gallop in place until it got purchase, finally
vaulting over the edge onto a paved street. Ogen and
Lark followed.

Once we were on flat ground, I told Death, "Let me
off this horse." My teeth were clattering.

"Silence."

"Let me off! Let me off!" I thrashed against him,
spooking his mount. "LET ME OFF!" I shrieked.

"I can be obliging." Death plucked me up and discarded me over the side of his stallion. My legs must
have fallen asleep in the saddle; they couldn't support

me. I staggered for a few feet before collapsing into the gutter. Unable to catch myself quickly enough with my bound hands, I smashed my forehead on the edge of the curb.

Pain seared along my split skin. Blood coursed down my face, dripping off my chin and jaw. Just as it had in the barn when I'd first discovered I could bring plants to life.

Ogen laughed at my fall. Lark muttered, "Dumb-ass."

Drip, drip, drip.

Too weak to move, I stayed in that position, on my knees in the gutter, face-planted, as if the curb were my pillow. With my back to the three, I watched runoff race around me, draining into a nearby opening.

"Get up," Lark said. "Stop dicking around."

Hadn't we passed a retention pond just moments ago? One with charred trees and dead reeds all around it? My blood was probably rushing toward that pond even now.

"More cannibals are coming, Evie." Lark huffed with impatience. "They're hot on our trail, because you're 'unclean' or something. Surely we're better than they were."

No. No, you're not. At least the cannibals were loyal to their own. Lark was a two-faced betrayer. Because of her, my Jack and my Matthew had died horribly.

That ember of fury was flaring into a wildfire, so hot I almost missed a telltale electric tingle pricking my skin. Something nearby was coming to life, unfurling for me. Rising from the dead. Seconds later, I detected tree trunks fattening with life, new limbs splaying.

Bleeding, kneeling like a victim, I smiled. Because I was about to kill this trio. My army was silently stretching to the sky, slithering along that muddy slope, sneaking up behind these Arcana. I'd show them *unclean.*

There was no reason to quell the heat of battle now. I would give myself up to it.

To fight, I needed to get free. The cuffs around my wrists were welded together, preventing me from reaching a claw down to slice the metal open. If I could just work one hand through the tight circle . . .

I strained to twist my smaller left hand free, but my thumb got in the way. The heat of battle was like a growing thing within me. I knew what the red witch would do in this situation. Hatred scalding me inside, I gazed down at my thumb.

Pitilessly.

I couldn't reach the metal, but I could reach my own flesh. Didn't know how long it'd take me to regenerate, didn't care.

With an undertone of disquiet in his voice, Death ordered, "Empress, rise."

Oh, I'm about to. The Empress didn't get caged or collared—or captured.

Biting the inside of my cheek, I used the claw of my right forefinger to slice halfway through my left thumb.

A nerve there sang, the pain dizzying, but rage blunted the shock of what I was doing. Blood spurted into the rushing water. More fuel for my growing fire.

Death's stallion stamped its sharpened hooves on the street, sensing the building threat. Lark's wolves growled and raised their snouts to sniff the air. They'd scent nothing out of the ordinary.

Death commanded, "Rise, Empress, or Fauna will send her familiars in for a bite." I heard him dismount, his spurs spinning.

With another swipe and a stifled scream, I severed my thumb. Out of the corner of my eye I watched the water sweep it away. My mutilated left hand slipped through the cuff with ease. The right cuff was no match for my claws.

Freed.

I was a marionette, and hatred pulled the strings. Finally, I was ready to rise.

21

I turned to them, my face a mask of blood, my reddening hair whipping in the wind.

Death's eyes glowed behind his helmet grille just before he twisted around, drawing his swords.

A wall of murderous green towered above him like a tidal wave. He craned his head up and up.

I commanded the swell to break over this embankment, to swamp them all. With a yell, Death flashed out his swords. But he was not yet my focus—I had a plan for him. I tried to ignore the pain as he slashed through my battalion.

Lark sicced her wolves on me. If they caught me, they'd rip me to shreds, as they had those Bagmen. It would be *my* legs cracking beneath their fangs. Before they could reach me, vines snatched their paws, trapping the beasts upside down. Whimpers, howls. They couldn't be killed until I took out Lark.

All in good time.

Ogen bellowed, leaping for me; a cypress crashed down on him. Pinned, he punched the trunk with fists like anvils. Agony racked my body. So I punished him with a larger toppling tree. His yell was cut short. Another tree, and another. To combat his strength, I sent poisoned thorn stalks to bind and kill him. Just to be safe, I ordered roots to suck him into the earth, wrenching him down.

Other plants were at work on a more insidious task. . . .

Eyes wide with horror, Lark abandoned her wolves, sprinting a retreat. My vines seized her, suspending her upside down as well, like the Hanging Man. As she dangled and screeched, I waved for her to be brought closer, until our faces were inches apart. "You're worse than they are," I murmured, canting my head at her. "We trusted you."

"Wait, Evie! Please!" Her eyes were terrified. As Joules's had been.

I enjoyed it just as much. "You're going to die extra bad."

I sensed there was little of that retention pond left, the surface replaced with a bed of writhing plants. Vines and slimy water strands. I waved my hand, and Lark was sent airborne, screaming as she sailed directly into that squirming green morass.

Trapped there. A nest of serpents. A nightmare.

One vine reared above her like a viper, plummeting down to gore her. She twisted and rolled, dodging it. Again the vine struck. She eluded it, but she was getting slower.

"There is no shame in surrender," I told her, as a past Empress had once assured her victims.

Death had cut through the battalion I'd sent his way, and now was coming for me. All according to plan.

I watched him nearing, readying to take my head. Hatred, hatred, *boiling*. In the midst of this frenzy, another memory of my grandmother's voice floated into my head: *You take after Demeter, a goddess who was not to be crossed. When someone stole her daughter, she was so enraged, she refused to let crops grow, starving the entire world. Evie, there's a viciousness in you that I must nurture. . . .*

Flanked by protective thorns, I screamed with a godlike rage, and the whole world seemed to tremble.

I screamed for Jack and Matthew. For Finn, and even Selena. I screamed for my family and friends I'd lost. For this entire ruined planet.

I screamed because I was about to embrace the red witch once again.

I am *the red witch!* Would a future Empress see an image of this grisly scene and recoil? *No. Because I'm going to win the entire game!*

Kill them all? With pleasure.

When my scream ebbed, I motioned Death closer

with both hands, nine wriggling fingers. He couldn't know that my soldiers had bored out the side of this hill and the underpinning of the asphalt that stretched between him and me. A few steps closer, and he would plummet, hurtling through a chute to be trapped below with Lark.

"Afraid to strike? Come to me, Death. *Touch* me again."

He approached as if in a trance. "Ease your wrath, and I won't kill you today."

I laughed, a throaty sound.

He reached my trap. The roadway crumbled; before he could escape, he dropped. At the last second, he stabbed one sword into the asphalt. He clung to his anchor as vines snaked up his body, curling around his shoulders and neck to drag him down. One of them struck his helmet free, revealing his perfect face, his grimly determined features. He showed no panic, not even when vines tangled over his head, across his mouth.

I stared into his glowing eyes. In a rush of dizziness, I remembered a time when they were bright in the night, looking down on me like stars. Just before his lips met mine—

Wham! Ogen tackled me with the force of a freight train. *How?!*

We crashed into the ground, with me breaking his fall. Ribs snapped. My head was flung back, cracking my skull. My vision wavered, my army stunned.

How had he escaped my poison and the pressure of those trees?

With the last of my strength, I sank my claws into the tough hide of his neck, injecting him with toxin until my fingers went numb.

He wrapped a hand around my throat, squeezing harder and harder. The Devil's strength wasn't fading?

As I stabbed Ogen frantically, I glimpsed Death with a blade between his teeth, climbing up from my trap.

Victorious.

Now it was Death's turn to laugh. "Ogen is one of two players immune to your poisons. Come, Empress, ask yourself: why else would someone like me ally with someone like him?"

Under Ogen's grip, something deep in my neck popped. My arms fell limp beside me. I couldn't feel them. As my lids slid shut and consciousness faded once more, I heard Death grate words to Ogen in that foreign language.

What was the Reaper saying . . . ?

"To match your eyes."

I gaze at the gift Death presents: a golden collar studded with emeralds. My sworn enemy is trying to woo me, has already declared his intention to take me to his bed.

I've been with him for four days, recuperating from his sword blow.

He sits next to me on my pallet in the tent we share. "Do you like it?" he asks, reaching forward to stroke my hair from my forehead. At the contact, his amber irises lighten, beginning to glow.

Death touches me at any chance, will shudder with want just from brushing his thumb over my bottom lip. He seems to relish baring his hands around me, snatching off his hated gloves the second he enters our dwelling.

"It's beautiful," I answer with honesty. He must have purchased the piece at the bazaar we passed earlier. I wish I could touch the gold, but my arms are bound behind me. Death wants me, but he does not yet trust me.

Though I am almost healed, I haven't determined my strategy with him. I know I must escape him, but he has met up with his ally, the Devil. That brute guards the tent whenever Death leaves.

"The gift is very kind."

"Kindness has nothing to do with it." His lids grow heavy as he grazes the backs of his fingers along my jawline, then across my collarbone. "You are mine, Empress. You deserve fine things."

His. Death's. He intends to take me to his home far in the frozen north, far from my home of winter grasses and endless fields. As alien as this desert.

"Allow me." He moves to put the collar around my neck, lifting up the length of my hair. Once he fastens the clasp, he presses a lingering kiss to my nape.

When I shiver, he groans against my skin, "You like my touch."

Gods help me, I do. The hands that deliver death with such ease are beyond tender to me.

He moves closer, facing me. "Ah, creature, for that reaction, I shall buy you jewels every day."

How different this must be for a boy who has killed everything else he touched. How many new experiences he can enjoy with me alone. I've caught myself wondering what it would be like to be possessed by him.

Still, when I am completely healed, I will strike.

Only one can win.

I woke to the sound of metal being pounded and the smell of wet dog. It was nighttime, and I was tied up once more, lying on a dry sleeping bag.

Direct from another disturbing dream.

One of Lark's wolves lay before me, its snout inches from my face, eyes gazing into mine with that unnatural intelligence. Or rather, its *eye*, singular. Hello, Cyclops. Probably the mangiest of the three.

The other Arcana had made camp beneath a bridge and lit a fire, seeming to dare anyone to attack.

In addition to posting the guard wolf, they'd bound my elbows tightly behind my back, making it impossible for my claws to reach the rope. I still had difficulty moving in general, but at least feeling had returned to my limbs. Unfortunately, that meant I experienced every second of regeneration as bones reset and regrew, as skin fashioned itself anew. My thumb was a fleshy nub.

I tried to call on my powers—like the Empress in my dream, I was ready to strike—but they were tapped out. Damn this rain! Even if I could manage spores, they probably wouldn't be strong enough to kill this trio.

I gazed past Cyclops to find Ogen and Death beside the blazing fire. The two horses rested nearby. No sign of Lark or the other wolves.

Ogen squatted next to the flames. In the firelight, his eyes were even more revolting. Around his diamond-shaped pupils, those greenish-yellow veins bulged. They were the color of sickness, of infection. Uneven before, his horns were now the same length. I squinted. There were two raised scars across his back. As if something had been cut from him.

Without hesitation, he placed his arms directly in the fire to stir the logs. Immune to fire *and* poison? Would've been good to know.

I'd failed to defeat them today, with my full arsenal and a devious plan. Against me, they were invincible together, as Death must know.

Unless I could get him out of his armor.

Tonight he'd shed his helmet and breastplate. As I watched, he used his sword blade to carve a line of metal from the side of the latter. He handed that metal strip over to Ogen, who plunged it into the flames with his bare hands. The Devil blew on the fire till it climbed high.

Why hadn't Death let Ogen kill me? What plans did he have for me? Obviously not the same ones as he'd had in a past life.

Lark reappeared, briefly parting the curtain of water running off the sides of the bridge. Her arms were full of wet firewood, and her other two wolves each carried a log in their jaws, dropping them at Ogen's feet. She told Death, "The falcon can scout for another couple of hours, but then she's got to sleep."

A weakness. Her animals could only go so long. Yet another Arcana who needed to conserve.

"Very well." Death couldn't have sounded less interested.

Lark tugged down her poncho hood as the wolves shook out their sodden fur. "You almost done?" she asked him.

Ignoring her, he began tinkering with his breastplate, tightening screws on the sides of it. Had I somehow pierced the armor? Maybe they were repairing it.

When that strip of metal glowed red, Ogen removed it from the fire. Placing it on a nearby boulder, he hammered the piece with his fist, flattening it.

Leaving Ogen to his work, Death put his breastplate back on, then leaned against the embankment. His helmet was close at hand. I watched as he sharpened one of his swords, running a stone over the edge again and again. He seemed soothed by this repetition.

Lark sat nearby. When I caught her gaze, she flashed me a wounded look—as if *I* had betrayed *her*—then turned away in a huff.

I worked myself into a sitting position, tilting my head to study Death. How different he was now from the boy I'd dreamed of. He looked about six or seven years older and much harder, even more ruthless.

Death lifted his sword and eyed the edge in the firelight. "What are you looking at, creature?"

"A stone-cold killer."

"Shouldn't be such a new sight." He lifted his other sword to sharpen. "I'm sure you pass a mirror every now and again."

"Where are you taking me?"

"To my stronghold. If you survive the next week."

"Where is it?"

He didn't deign to answer.

Okay, so if his lair was a week's journey away from the Hierophant's, that could mean Virginia, West Virginia, Kentucky, either of the Carolinas.

"What are you planning to do with me?" What was *I* planning to do with me? If I could escape, I supposed I'd start for the Outer Banks once more. Give myself the time I needed to grieve all I'd lost, and fulfill my promise to my mother. I'd sworn I would get to my grandmother, find out why the earth had failed, find out if I could help it.

For all I knew, Death might be taking me in the right direction.

To carry on my mission without Jack and Matthew? The idea sent anguish ripping through me, worse than any physical pain I'd ever known.

The Reaper finally faced me, resting his weapon across his lap. "I plan to make you suffer, up until the moment I decide to cut off your head."

His confidence was disturbing. I decided then that I would do anything to deprive him of that pleasure— and of my icons. I'd rather Joules have them. "And when will that decision be?"

"Every morning when I wake, I'll ask myself, 'Is this the day I decapitate the creature?' If you retain your worthless life by that night, then you'll know my answer. And so it will be every day."

I narrowed my gritty eyes. "Why do you hate me so much?" I noticed Lark was listening intently, acting like she was absorbed with rearranging her pack.

"Because I *know* what you are." He clasped the hilt of his sword as if he could barely refrain from attacking me. "You have others fooled, but I know you better than you know yourself."

"Then tell me what I'm really like."

"You're selfish, weak, cowardly, and disloyal. You blame Fauna for her duplicity when you are no better, a seductress who lures men to their doom."

I strained against my bindings, wishing I had power

left. "Was I weak when my vines were dragging you down to a hellish end? Was I cowardly and disloyal when I fought to avenge my friends?"

"Your friends—or the mortal you professed to love?"

"Both."

Death's lips curled. "Deveaux wouldn't have wanted you if he'd known what you were truly like. He wouldn't have bedded you, and he certainly wouldn't have given his life for you. Yet another you doomed."

I'll spend my limited time left doing what I want . . . Jack's voice, his grin as he said it . . .

Limited. He'd died three nights later.

All my fault. I should have sent him away. Because I hadn't, a strong, proud man was gone.

Death was right. I *was* weak and selfish.

I turned away, lying with my back to him, casting my mind back to the last moments I'd seen Jack. As if I were in that mine, I could feel the rocks hitting the water, punches to my stomach. Boulders had plummeted—well before Ogen intensified his attack.

Flattened like a sandcastle.

Had Jack even made it to shore with Matthew? My bottom lip trembled. *Maybe Matthew never woke up before he drowned.*

Through watering eyes, I stared out at the veil of water, like the one at the cave entrance where Jack and I had been together.

That perfect moment in time.

Tears began to spill, and I couldn't stop them. All but sobbing, I tried to muffle the sound. As much as I hated Death, I hated myself for crying.

"Ah, the sound of that." When Death chuckled, I glared over my shoulder.

"You were right, Fauna." With a smirk, he reclined, hands tucked behind his head, eyes glowing in the night. "This is *much* better."

22

"I can feel your eyes on my ass, perv," I said over my shoulder. For the past six days, whenever Death's helmet was off, I would catch glimpses of an unnerving hunger in his expression. How could he be so disgusted with me—and struggling against attraction?

I twisted around to find him comfortably riding his horse, an ill-humored stallion he called Thanatos. He was flanked by Ogen on foot and Lark on horseback.

Sure enough, Death's molten gaze was locked on my backside as I trudged shoeless and parka-less over a stony flat. My bare feet were sliced. Yet if my blood revived plants, they yellowed and withered, because I was still flagging.

All this abuse he'd dealt my way ensured that my body was constantly playing catch-up to regenerate. I'd already fallen twice this morning. Again, Death had tied my elbows together so I couldn't break my falls.

My shoulders were numb, and I felt like I hadn't caught my breath for the better part of the last week.

Death raised his brows, unashamed to be caught ogling. "Just because you're a gutless harlot doesn't mean I won't find your . . . attributes attractive. I might be immortal, but I'm still a red-blooded male."

Attributes? Was that why he'd kept me alive? Each morning, I had asked him, "Have you decided whether you're going to kill me today?"

He'd always answer, "Not yet, creature." Each night by the fire, Death used the tip of one sword to carve barbs in that flattened metal strip from his armor. Though I had no idea why, he seemed very pleased with himself, would gaze at me as he worked. Was his attraction intensifying . . . ?

"Harlot? Who talks like that? Father Time, meet the Flintstones."

"You are bold, considering you were roundly defeated and all your people were lost."

I gritted my teeth against a scream. The idea that he bore my friends' icons burned inside me like the Alchemist's acid. Death always wore those gloves, so I hadn't seen the markings. But I knew he had to have them because Lark's and Ogen's hands were clean.

"I have suffered loss," I told him. "But at least I know what it's like to have had those relationships. I had trust and caring." Love and passion with Jackson. I would hold those memories of him close for the rest of my life, short as that might prove. "And you—you've got Ogen."

Hearing his name, the Devil lumbered closer to me. If Death looked at me like he wanted to sleep with me, Ogen looked like he couldn't decide if he wanted to sleep with me—or suck the marrow from my bones. His foul appearance was equaled only by his stench.

"You believe you had trust?" Death scoffed. "Arcana rule number one: trust no one."

I stopped to face him with a look of realization. "No wonder you're so good at this game. It's all you'll ever really have."

"You know nothing about me. Take care that you don't provoke *my* wrath." With a last sneer, he rode forward.

Death would soon regret his decision to spare me so far. For the last several months, I'd wanted to kill him because he was so bent on killing me. Now I craved a bloody revenge, one that would make the red witch proud.

If I couldn't take out this trio by myself, I figured I had two options.

Catch Death without his armor, which wasn't likely.

Or get help. In that case, my first step was escape. I might have worried that Death would just read my thoughts and foil any attempt. But I believed the link between us had been broken. Severed with Matthew's passing. *Don't cry. Don't give him the satisfaction. . . .*

So far there'd been no opportunity to get away. It wasn't like I ever had privacy. Lark accompanied me each morning to wash off, her wolves trailing us like chain-gang guards. When I was alone with her, she always looked like she wanted to tell me something. Information there for the taking? But I hadn't yet been able to bite back bile and cozy up to her.

"Yo, boss," Lark said, her eyes going red. Falcon-cam. "We got a pretty big river ahead."

The fog began to thicken. Soon I could hear the sound of rushing water. With each step closer to this unseen river, Ogen grew antsier. I'd learned the Devil was more afraid of bodies of water than Matthew had been. I doubted the beast could swim.

Fifteen minutes later, we reached the edge of the rapids; all four of us came to a halt, staring at the sur-real scene. The violent currents carted along pieces of houses, a huge satellite dish, and a . . . car. A red Volkswagen rocketed past us, the steering wheel spin-ning as wreckage hit the tires.

Taking Ogen's temperature, I said, "Right on. I vote we swim it."

He whimpered. "No swim—NO SWIM!"

Death commanded him in that foreign tongue, and he shut up.

"Well, aren't you a good wittle doggie, Ogen?" I said. "You know how to sit, stay, and hush even better than Lark's wolves."

He stared, disbelieving that I'd just insulted him like that. "I am the DESECRATOR! I sit upon Lucifer's knee!"

"That makes total sense, Scooby."

With a puzzled expression, Death said, "You taunt him at your peril."

"What's he going to do? Kill me?" Over my shoulder I told Ogen, "Get in line, dick."

Ignoring both of us, Death said, "We cross there."

I followed his gaze to a suspension bridge above, so high it was nearly cloaked in clouds. Connecting two canyon walls, it looked charred and rickety, as if those support cables could snap at any second.

Lark nodded eagerly. "Good idea, boss."

"Ass kisser," I said, earning a flash of her fangs.

Up the muddy trail, she and Death rode their horses. I had to climb, my feet getting sucked down in the calf-deep muck.

Maybe when we got up on the bridge I'd jump, *Last of the Mohicans* their asses!

I'd thought that half in jest, but the idea wouldn't go away. I didn't know if I had the guts to leap from that height, but strategically it made sense. The water would carry me away faster than their horses could follow in this terrain. The three would relax their guard up there, because no one in her right mind would dare that jump.

Ogen would be too phobic to follow me, Lark too

spineless in general. Death couldn't without removing his armor first.

My lips curled. If he did shuck his armor and follow? Win-win. Either I escaped, or I'd face him with his defenses lowered.

What would Jack do in this situation? He was always practical. Except at the end of his life when he'd known better than to stay with me, but did it anyway. *Don't think about that!* Not now, not yet . . .

Would I survive the drop? Would the water be deep enough? Knowing my luck, I'd probably bean another car.

As I climbed, I recalled a long-ago conversation with my grandmother. She'd been explaining my weaknesses; I'd just wanted to play with my dolls. Losing interest, I'd absently asked, "De-cappa-what?"

I knew Gran had revealed at least one other way I could die, but I couldn't remember. Today, I'd be betting my life that she *hadn't* said: "You can drown."

Once we reached the beginning of the bridge, I gasped, "I need to rest."

Lark slowed her horse. "No can do, Empress. I got the falcon scouting the entire county, and we've got Teeth all around us."

Even better. I'd float right past them! "I can't walk any farther. My feet are about to fall off."

Death said, "Carry on, or I can drag you behind my horse."

"Too tired," I wheezed.

Studying my face, Death narrowed his gaze. "Have you a plan, creature?"

"Can't read my thoughts anymore?"

"Perhaps not. But I can tell you are malingering."

"Malingering? I don't speak S.A.T." The fog was so thick I couldn't see the middle of the bridge. Would I even know where to jump? I might leap right onto the exposed edge of the riverbed. After my experience in the mines, the last place I wanted to be was in the water. Could I make myself do this?

"You act exhausted," Death said. "But you've fight left in you yet." He sounded approving.

"I do. And I'm going to fight my way. On my time."

His eyes widened with realization. "Stem your idiocy—"

I was already running, sprinting as far along the bridge as I dared before veering toward the railing. Death spurred his mount, Ogen on his heels. Right before they reached me, I clambered atop the concrete railing. "No closer!" Unable to use my arms to steady myself, I tottered. The railing was the width of a balance beam. I'd trained on a beam—I could do a backflip on this if I needed to, I assured myself.

I chanced a look down and gulped. Not even a glimpse of the water. Which meant I couldn't time my jump around a passing car or a piece of house. I'd have to fall blindly into that thick bank of fog.

Behind me, Death dismounted with a curse of frustration. "Do not do this thing." Over my shoulder, I watched him ease closer, just as he had in one of my visions. A sense of déjà vu racked me as I recalled him at the edge of the cane field, stretching his arm toward me. I shook my head hard, almost pitching off the rail.

"If you jump, you'll die, Empress." Debatable. "As I'm closest to you, I'll harvest your icons. You'd give them to me so easily?" Death tsked. "Our game's no fun if you're weak."

"I've got your weak." I took a deep breath. I closed my eyes.

Stepped off.

He bellowed curses as I plummeted. Rushing air whipped my hair above my head like the tail of a comet. My stomach dropped. I fell, and fell, and fell—

Water! Freezing!

The impact wrenched the breath from my lungs, the cold stunning my muscles. Rapids tossed me as I struggled to stay above the surface using only my legs. I sputtered, choking for air as debris battered me. Boards with nails, a piece of corrugated tin. Gouge. Slice. I felt the pressure of the wounds—and the odd warmth of my blood in the water around me—but not pain. Numb.

The foggy shore slid by so quickly. Racing. Like the road had when I'd been on the back of Jack's motorcycle.

Over all the sounds, one roar grew louder. Was I moving faster? Drop-off ahead? I couldn't wipe my eyes to see. . . .

"*Ahhh!*" I plunged dozens of feet. The pressure of the falls shoved me into the deep, but I bobbed up like a cork. Just as quickly I was sucked down again. A vortex?

Only this time, instead of surfacing, I felt my arms yanked behind me. The rope was caught on something! I strained to see in the churning water.

Eerie shapes and muted sounds all around me. A watery grave. *No—not yet!*

Behind me were huge blocks of cement, spiked with twisted rebar rods. I must be caught on one. If I could get lower, I could unhook my arms. But the water kept whooshing me higher like a geyser.

I struggled to swim down against that vertical current. Weakening.

I was caught fast, couldn't find the edge of the concrete. I used my claws to slice behind me at anything I came in contact with. Cement, metal . . . running out of air . . . *Fight, Evie!*

My lungs screamed, my eyes bulging. Trapped. My mind was still working, my will to live clamoring—but my body . . . stopped.

Arms limp, legs dangling.

Maybe I'd be seeing my family soon, my friends.

Jack. Maybe Arcana didn't get to dream about heaven—

Though I fought as hard as I could not to, I inhaled water. The end, then. My eyelids slid shut.

A watery grave.

23

I sat on a tree trunk on the riverbank, watching without emotion as Death carried my corpse to the shore.

Out-of-body experience? Didn't know. I felt aloof, as if I could be eating popcorn as I watched the scene play out. Maybe this was what peace felt like. I wondered if my mom had encountered it when she'd been fading away.

Why was there no bright light calling me home? Oh, yeah: no heaven for Arcana.

As Death laid my body on the sand, I saw I was in seriously bad shape. My bluish lips were parted, yet no breaths passed them. My skin was fish-belly white, my hair tangled all over my face. My arms were still bound behind my back.

With a roll of my eyes, I realized my Death-defying bid for freedom had lasted a nanosecond; I hadn't gotten more than a couple hundred feet down the river. The bridge loomed, seeming to taunt me.

Death stood and paced, dressed only in his pants. No armor, his defenses down. What a missed opportunity.

Wait, he had markings on his skin? Across his chest were black tattoos of weird-looking runes, jagged designs that seemed to scream *blade*. With reluctance, I admitted that they didn't detract from his perfection. His body was still magnificent to look at.

He ran his hand over his wet face, glancing down at me, his eyes burning with emotion. Death was disgusted with me? Shocking. But then I thought I made out something more. Something . . . inexplicable.

The sound of pounding hooves neared. Lark leapt from her galloping horse, rushing up to Death. "Resuscitate her!"

He ignored the girl, continuing to pace.

"If you let her die, then she stole from you—her death is yours to deliver, not hers to take whenever she freaking feels like it!"

Ogen lurched into view, howling to the rainy sky, "I feast, I feast!"

Lark kept badgering Death. "Boss, you said you enjoyed her suffering, that it was much better. Are you gonna let her cut your enjoyment short?"

Whatta bitch, I thought without real anger. This was popcorn watching, after all.

"I FEAST! Let me desecrate her—"

"Silence, both of you!" Death yelled, thunder

rumbling behind him. He muttered something in that foreign language, then fell to his knees beside my body, blocking my view. All I could see was his broad back heaving in a breath as he leaned down to deliver it to me—

His lips. I somehow felt them on mine. Warm air from his lungs flowed into my starving ones. He repeated this. And again.

Suddenly I was zooming toward my body, *into* my body—which was racked with the need to breathe. Panic seized my deadened muscles.

When Death drew back for another breath, my eyes shot open, caught his—

I rolled to my side and retched up water.

Once I'd coughed it all up, I awkwardly eased myself into a sitting position. He'd risen up on his haunches, tension emanating from him.

"Boss, you saved her," Lark said in an awed tone. "You . . . you breathed *life* into her."

Before I came to my senses, I had the insane impulse to thank him. He must have thought I was about to, because he tilted his head, his blond brows drawn tight.

I glanced down. Saw his hand. His bared hand. He had only two icons: Calanthe's and another one I didn't recognize.

None of my friends' markings. Which meant they'd all survived. Which meant Jack likely had too. *Jack, you cheated Death.*

I gave the Reaper a triumphant look.

"Always thinking of them. I should have left you to drown."

In a rough voice, I said, "Without a doubt."

His hand shot out to my neck, beginning to squeeze. "You think I won't remedy my mistake?"

—*Eyes to the skies, lads!*—

—*I watch you like a hawk.*—

—*Trapped in the palm of my hand.*—

"Arcana!" Ogen bounded over with Death's swords and armor. "Power!"

Joules's alliance was closing in? "No time to suit up, Death?" Without that protection, he was no longer invincible.

He rose, shooting me a scathing look. "And now someone must die because of your folly."

Would the Tower honor his promise to me—

A silvery javelin landed beside me, exploding into a bolt of lightning.

24

Son of a bitch! The Lord of Lightning was up on the suspension bridge, his vantage making us fish in a barrel.

Ogen's body began to swell into his horrendous ogre form. He swung his horned head up at Joules, then sped off toward the bridge so quickly he sprayed rocks in his wake.

I scrambled up as fast as I could, dodging another javelin, almost barreling over Lark as she fled. I headed for a patch of burned-out woods, running parallel to her.

Javelins landed at my heels again and again, propelling me faster. I chanced a glance over my shoulder—

Plowed into a boulder. Blundered over it like a clipped running back.

I ignored my new medley of wounds and curled up behind the stone. The javelins . . . stopped? Sucking in wet breaths, I peeked around the rock, blinking against the rain.

Joules yelled, "Oi! Keep cover, you daft tart!"

The Tower had been aiding me? Pushing me to run? Yes, he could've hit me at any time—just as he could have in my vision of him at Haven, when I'd sprinted along the river's edge.

I had to get free, to help him take advantage of Death's weakness. I needed my hands! I couldn't reach the rope that bound my elbows, but I could work it over something sharp. I slashed my claws behind me, gouging out a shelf from the boulder. With panting breaths, I started sawing the rope across the edge.

Joules had turned his focus on his true enemy: Death.

Near the river, the Reaper waited without his armor, as if challenging Joules to strike. His muscles were tensed with readiness. Lightning rained down. Death's swords flashed out, a blur of movement as he deflected each bolt.

From beneath a nearby cliff, Lark screamed at Joules, "The Teeth are on their way here, idiot!"

Joules replied, "Well aware, you shifty bitch—I told them to follow the explosions. They ought to be up on that canyon rise in a couple of minutes."

Without taking his gaze from Joules, Death commanded Lark, "Call on every creature still living—stall those mortals, or they mow us all down."

"Got it, boss!" She ran off with her wolves.

Joules was using the Teeth? Clever boy. But now it sucked to be me. As I sawed faster against the rock edge, I scanned for Tess. No sign. I could hear Gabriel's rocketlike approach, but couldn't see him above the fog.

The last time Gabriel had attacked Death like this, the Reaper had winged him, sending him hurtling. Surely they wouldn't try the same plan twice. As Joules's attack intensified, the high-pitched whine grew deafening. Closer, closer.

I'd witnessed an Arcana battle through Matthew's vision. But this was visceral chaos—the bellows, the earth seeming to shake, the blinding bolts.

A clattering sound above us. That *whine* . . . When Death raised his swords to the sky to strike at Gabriel, a metal net descended over him.

They *had* changed their plan!

The net must be weighted; it made even Death collapse to his knees. With an enraged bellow, he slashed with his swords, but couldn't cut the metal. The more he struggled, the more he ensnared himself.

All Joules had to do was aim one javelin. But Ogen was almost on him, bounding across the bridge, forcing Joules to retreat. The Devil chased the Tower, just as he had in their last battle. Could Joules escape him again?

And where was Tess, the third piece of this puzzle?

Through breaks in the fog, I made out Joules's

sparking skin. "Feck you, beast! That all you got?" As Ogen's hoofs pounded, what sounded like a giant whip cracked. Then again.

The suspension cables were snapping!

Neither Joules nor Ogen seemed to notice that the bridge was rippling like a wave. Joules kept lobbing javelins to explode at the Devil's feet, taking out chunks of concrete. But the lightning didn't faze Ogen—only enraged him.

He drummed his fists across his chest, then tore off for Joules. More concrete dropped.

So *now* what was their plan?

"Tess, take out Death!" Joules yelled over his shoulder. "Ogen's on me tail!"

Movement caught my eye. Tess.

She stood a few dozen feet away between scorched trunks, shaking, a dagger in her hand. Was their backup plan to stab Death? I could almost hear their reasoning: if the World Card couldn't control her powers, she should at least be able to plunge a knife.

But this girl was terrified, watery eyes wide in her face. The knife trembled. Though she didn't seem aware of it, her feet . . . weren't touching the ground.

Heaving breaths, Death rolled to his back to kick against the edges of the net. He would be free by the time Tess reached him. Just in time for him to stab her.

"Strike, Tess!" Joules sounded even farther away.

When she looked at me with terrified brown eyes, I shook my head in warning. "Not enough time. Free me, and I'll help you!" I blinked. Were her clothes growing baggier on her body, right in front of me?

"I-I'm so sorry," she cried, and fled in Joules's direction.

The Tower must have realized she wasn't following orders. He yelled, "Gabe, take the Reaper out!"

From somewhere above the fog, Gabriel answered, "It's done." A shrill whistle sounded as he began to dive.

Death met my gaze, his eyes promising revenge.

I narrowed my own. "I told you to watch your six, Reaper."

Yet just before Gabriel attacked, I heard another explosion.

Then: "NO SWIIIIIMMMM!"

Ogen was plummeting—along with the entire bridge. Joules went careening down one edge, scrabbling for a handhold. At the last second, he snagged one of those suspension cables.

How long could he hold on to slick metal? He couldn't regenerate, wouldn't survive that fall.

When a flailing Ogen sped past the shore, helpless in the water, I raised my face. "Gabriel, save Joules!"

At once, that whine changed trajectory.

Too late. The Tower fell.

"Oh, God. . . ."

Just before Joules crashed onto the jagged rocks below, Gabriel scooped him up, rocketing back up into the clouds.

From a distance, Joules yelled, "Not how this was supposed to go down, Empress! Teeth're coming, leaving you a wee bit fecked."

Right on cue, the first vehicle in the Teeth convoy appeared at the top of the rise, another rumbling up behind it—at least ten armored vehicles moving in. A cloudy-eyed man thundered orders from the gun turret of a Humvee, and the other men gave battle cries, beginning to fire down on us.

All to avenge a male who had enslaved their minds. "Kill the unclean one!"

Being called that was really getting old. Like it'd been funny the first two times . . .

Those battle cries faded when Cyclops launched himself at the driver of one jeep. As blood splattered the windshield, the vehicle never braked. At the edge of the canyon, Cyclops leapt to safety, but the jeep rolled onward over the precipice, carrying its screaming occupants to their deaths.

The other two wolves joined the fray, snatching out throats as bullets sprayed them—and the opposite shore. *Bam bam bam.* Grit kicked up in a line along the edge of Death's net. He growled with fury when one bullet caught him. Then another.

Somehow, Death rose up, freed at last, setting off for

cover. Though he was pouring blood from his left shoulder and his right side, he didn't quicken his pace as bullets plugged the ground just inches from his feet.

He reached another boulder not twenty feet from me and dropped behind it, long legs stretched out in front of him. His head fell back against it, and he squeezed his eyes to the sky.

The sight sent me adrift, my mind recalling another time when he'd lain like that, his face raised to the sun. He'd been petting my hair as I rested my head on his lap. . . .

Now he was shot. Trapped. When I felt a pang of what might have been pity, I gave myself an inner shake. This situation was what I'd dreamed of: Death without his armor, multiple Arcana gunning for his head.

My pity was unfounded. With a bellow, Death shot up from his cover and launched one of his swords overhead. The blade flew like a throwing dagger—tip over hilt across the width of the river—to skewer the Teeth's leader through the throat.

Yet there were scores more, gearing up their larger guns. Another male took up the charge: "Kill her!"

With a black look, Death returned to his cover, gripping his remaining sword.

He and I were both screwed. If I ran, they'd gun me down, assuming Death didn't get me first. If I remained, the Teeth would capture me and do . . . worse.

Blinding streams of silver began descending on

the convoy. The first speared the hood of the largest vehicle; lightning erupted, exploding the truck high up into the air. It plummeted, spinning like a dropped pinwheel, ejecting charred bodies with each rotation.

Bodies falling. Just like Joules's Tower Card.

More javelins rained down, obliterating the vehicles one by one. Destroyed. Wolves scavenged any screaming survivors.

A dripping, enraged Ogen appeared on the opposite shore. With a hair-raising yowl, he stomped off in Joules's direction once more.

Joules called out, "Farewell, Empress. We canna kill the Reaper—it's all on you!" As he, Gabriel, and Tess fled the scene, their calls grew fainter, replaced by Ogen's yell of frustration. . . .

When Ogen eventually skulked back to Death, shoulders low with defeat, I couldn't keep myself from grinning. *Got away from you, did they?* Just as my allies had escaped Death's reach. Reminded of his lack of icons, my smile widened.

"Ah, creature, it seems you're now a beacon of hope." Death levered himself to his feet, unable to stifle a grimace of pain. "Well, you heard the Tower—it's all on you. Come end this."

"That'd be really fair, *boss*. With both hands tied behind my back? Free me and let the cards fall where they may."

"Speaking of which . . ." He whistled for his horse,

and the red-eyed mount trotted to him. From his saddlebag, Death took out that strip of metal harvested from his black armor.

Only now it looked like a barbed cuff.

"My strategy for the game has changed." As he strode toward me with a menacing expression, he said, "It will be best if you don't struggle."

25

Death freaking neutered me.

As we rode, he had his right arm slung around my neck, resting over my collarbones, his hand gripping my shoulder.

And I was powerless to do anything about it.

The metal device he'd been fashioning had a name: a cilice, an armband with spikes that dug into my skin. And when this cilice was made of the same metal as his armor, it neutralized my powers. Death weakening life, or whatever.

As the Reaper had put it earlier today: "Aside from some superficial glowing and your customary rapid healing, you're just a normal girl now. The only way for you to remove it would be to excise your bicep muscle, as you did your thumb. But you won't be alone for long enough to perform that procedure."

That bastard had painstakingly carved every single barb, knowing what it would do to me, knowing he would shove it up my arm and make Ogen squeeze it tight.

I had screamed with pain. In the hours since then, my skin had regenerated around the barbs, but they were still agonizing. No need to tie me up anymore, now that I was helpless.

Today's count: Powers defused? All. Attempts to kill Death? Several. Successful attempts? None-point-none. The Arcana were gloating:

—*Failed attempt on Death!*—

—*Empress is still his prisoner.*—

—*Until he slits her throat.*—

Despair settled over me, as bitter as the cold. We'd failed. And we'd never get a chance like that again. Even my earlier joy at finding Death's hand clear of those icons had faded. If my friends lived, then why hadn't Matthew contacted me?

What if they were still trapped in the mine?

I tried to console myself with the knowledge that I'd gained new players for our alliance, but the worry was sharp. Until I managed to escape, I couldn't do anything to help them. Unless I got this cuff off me.

I told Death, "I will get freed of this thing."

"Though you're probably vicious enough to chew your own arm off—I put nothing past you—your odds of shedding the cilice are long."

My teeth had started chattering. As usual, he'd denied me my coat, my boots. But he'd insisted on me riding with him, to make up time. We must be closing in on his home. "If you believe in this cuff thing, then why are you keeping me cold? Why not give me back my coat?"

"You thought that was to weaken you?"

"Wasn't it?"

"No, that was for our enjoyment."

Asshole!

"You should be grateful for the cilice," he said. "With it, there's no need to bind your arms."

"Then why do this now? Why not put it on me from the very beginning?"

"My armor has served me well—I preferred it unaltered. Plus, I never expected you to live this long."

"You *would* put a lot of store in that armor. In your first fight without it, you got plugged—twice—by cannibals. I bet you're still bleeding under all that metal. Which is a definite mood brightener."

"I'll heal from these as I have from all my other wounds."

I frowned. "Do you regenerate like I do?"

I heard him exhale heavily. "You truly remember nothing about me?" He sounded almost . . . troubled by this.

Matthew had told me he'd given me memories of

past games, along with some kind of safety valve to keep me from accessing them all at once. Or else I could go crazy like him. So I hedged: "I thought we weren't supposed to remember, that only the Fool and the current winner know about the past games."

"And I thought our struggles would prove unforgettable."

"Anything I recall is because Matthew showed snippets to me. Besides, why should I tell you how much I remember?"

"Why should I reveal how quickly I heal?"

Touché. "Fine. You first."

"I heal quickly, but not like you. And I retain my scars to remind me of my victories."

So he had strength, speed, skill, *and* enhanced healing? "I remember you stabbing me in a desert," I admitted. "I remember how badly I wanted to live, but you didn't care. Not until you realized you could touch my skin. You said you'd see me well."

"The Fool showed you nothing else?"

"Before you tried to kill him? No."

"If I'd wanted him dead, he would be so."

"Sure thing, *boss*."

"You think I couldn't have gotten your mortal to drop the Fool's unconscious body into the deep? The boy was already frenzied to save the female he . . . sleeps with. All it would've taken was a few cuts across your pretty flesh, or maybe a jostle of your broken arm. He would have dropped the Fool to rush headlong to you. Then I would have gutted him without even setting you down." In an absent tone, he said, "I regret not gutting him."

"Jack's smarter than you give him credit for."

"I think he's sly, like an animal, but you have him under your spell. He, at least, believed that what you gave him that night was worth dying for."

"You're disgusting."

"Merely stating fact."

"What Jack and I share is more than a single night. That was just the icing on the cake."

Death's grip on me tightened, as if he were jealous. Which made no sense. I could accept his attraction—since I was the only girl he could touch—but I couldn't accept his jealousy. Not when I knew how much he hated me.

"Everyone thinks of you as some kind of earth mother," he said. "They have no idea you're a femme fatale, more Aphrodite than Demeter."

Gran had mentioned Demeter as well.

"You used the mortal to keep you safe, until you came into your powers. Now he is obsolete."

"I didn't use Jack. And we *will* be reunited. We're fated—"

Death's arm squeezed even harder. "Do not talk to me of fate."

"I don't have to talk to you about anything," I told him, resolved to say nothing else.

Dusk came and went, the rain pouring with abandon. Late into the night, we rode.

I hadn't been on a horse for this long a span since riding my old nag Allegra. Jack and I had freed her before we'd burned down Haven, before the arrival of the Army of the Southeast. Would they have captured her? Eaten her?

Eventually I started nodding off, catching myself dozing against Death's armored chest. Each time I would pinch my arms, biting the inside of my cheek to shake my drowsiness. No use. Finally I went out like a light, didn't know for how long.

I only jerked awake when my ears began popping. Sure enough, I was relaxed back against him. I sat up, scooting forward in the saddle.

As if in reflex, Death's arm tightened around me, the four-inch long spikes of his glove hovering near my neck.

"Watch the gloves, Reaper."

"They're called *gauntlets*." When he released me, he accidentally(?) brushed my new cuff, sending pain shooting down my arm.

I hissed in a breath, eyes watering. But knowing how much he enjoyed my suffering, I refused to let him see any more of it.

I tried to get my bearings as we wound along a narrow rocky trail, but the rain and fog were thick. All I could determine was that we were already above the tree line—or what used to be the tree line—and still ascending. Up here, it was barren. I'd wager no plants had grown in this dismal terrain even before the Flash.

The higher we climbed, the more Death seemed to relax, while I grew colder and colder. Just when I decided this was the highest mountain I'd ever been on, the path widened to a gravel drive, fronted with an enormous gate. A stone wall towered over us.

"And now we arrive."

His lair was atop a mountain? Ogen lumbered ahead to open the gate, and we rode through. The horses' hooves—and Ogen's—clacked on a brick courtyard. A jaw-dropping mansion, almost a castle, came into view. Through the fog, I spied several stories and two sprawling wings.

Death lifted me from the saddle and plopped me on the ground, then dismounted. Lark did as well, and Ogen led the horses away.

"Come," Death commanded, and I had no choice but to follow.

At first I was impressed with this stronghold. Yet as we neared and details came into focus, I thought, *No, Finn, this is officially the creepiest place.*

If someone had asked me to sketch my idea of the world's eeriest mansion, I couldn't have imagined the scene before me. Death's home was so . . . Death.

Dwarfing Haven House, it was built of gray stone. Courtesy of the Flash, the walls were slashed with charred black. The slate roof had dozens of different pitches and turrets, with one looming above them all.

Chimneys climbed into the night sky. Rusted weather vanes squeaked. An unseen shutter thumped, like a spirit banging on a coffin lid. Fog seemed to be trapped in place, choking the courtyard, clinging to the walls.

As we approached, I detected animal calls growing louder and louder. Even some exotic ones. I jumped when I heard a lion's roar. Somewhere on this mountain, creatures teemed. With that many to control, Lark might prove unstoppable.

How close was this menagerie? *The fog lies.*

I glanced up, caught Death studying my reaction. Did he actually care what I thought of his home?

Lark saw my look of horror. "Hotel California, Evie. You can check out, but you can never leave."

"She's right," Death said. "You will never leave this mountaintop alive."

I waved that away. "I thought your lair was gleaming black, with ruins from all different ages."

"Ruins?"

"It looked like you, I don't know, collected them," I said as we climbed a few steps toward the huge copper-plated front doors.

"Then you saw inside my mind. I wonder why the Fool would give you access to me."

Aghast, I said, "That's what it looks like in your head?"

"Explain to me why it should look any different." He sneered, "Do you really think Death should dream in color?"

"I doubt you have dreams."

"Would it shock you to know I once did?" he asked in a strange tone—as if he were accusing me.

Before I could ask about this, we passed through the front doors into an opulent foyer, with a chandelier dangling above. He dialed on a wall switch, and the foyer went ablaze, crystals projecting prisms, lighting a grand staircase. If the exterior had been forbidding, the interior was quite the opposite.

I'd grown up in a stately southern mansion. As we walked deeper into this palatial building, I realized Haven would look quaint in comparison.

When the corridor intersected with one leading to another wing, Lark veered off. "See you in the morning, boss. Night, Evie."

I glared. "I hope you die before you wake, Lark."

She cast me a fake wince. "Ooh, burn." She trotted off, leaving me alone with Death.

"Follow me." The corridor wound seemingly forever. At last he stopped to unlock an oak door. Behind it lay a curving stairwell.

We climbed so many steps that I knew he had to be leading me to that soaring tower. The walls of the stairwell were cold, weeping moisture. I could only imagine what my cell would be like.

"Try to keep up, creature."

"I have a name."

"As you always do."

"And what's yours?" I asked. "Ogen and Lark have given names—don't you?"

"Call me Death. That's all I'll ever be to you."

The double meaning didn't escape me.

At the top of the stairs was a stone landing with a single door. He unlocked and opened it, ushering me inside.

The room was . . . lovely.

The lofty ceiling and exposed beams were painted stark white, stretching to a tented point above. The queen-size bed had a costly crimson spread on it. Rich drapes in the same material bordered panoramic windows. Up this high, the wind gusted, pelting the glass with raindrops, but the lavish room was snug and dry. A plush rug covered the stone floor, and the grand fireplace had logs already set up for a fire.

Again Death studied my reaction. I scuffed over to a cedar wardrobe. Scores of clothes filled the closet? Most looked like they would fit me.

In an adjoining modern bathroom, I found fresh towels and toiletries. Unable to curb my curiosity, I turned on the shower's hot water spigot. Almost immediately, the water began steaming.

A hot shower? I hadn't had one since we left Selena's house. When I experienced a little thrill, I went awash in guilt. My friends might be trapped in an icy mine, but I was looking forward to a shower?

And more, I didn't trust Death's motives for providing all this. "Why these kindnesses?"

"To keep you on edge. You'll pine for these indulgences all the more when I deprive you of them."

"You think I can't escape? I could jump."

"If you somehow made it past the outer walls of the compound and didn't get swallowed up on the mountainside, you'd face the world with no abilities, at the mercy of any you stumbled upon. Besides, the glass here is fortified, unbreakable for one with such minuscule strength. Even Judgment would find it difficult to break you out."

"Are you expecting Gabriel to try?"

"I *hope* he does."

My heart was sinking even before he said, "In any case, you will have a guard." He thinned his lips and gave a piercing whistle. Giant paws padded up the stairs.

You again, Cyclops? I'd noted earlier that he must've gotten zinged by one of Joules's javelins; the wolf's fur was now permed like a poodle's.

"Try to escape the grounds, and the beast will make a meal of you." Death's eyes glittered, as if he'd be happy for me to try.

Enough. "Why do you have such a burning hatred for me? That night you murdered Calanthe—"

"Murdered? That's rich. They ambushed us in an open field, with no cover from javelins—or from a winged soldier like Judgment."

"Anyway," I continued as if he hadn't spoken, "when you beheaded Calanthe, you appeared weary, as if it was an unavoidable chore."

"Perhaps it was."

"But not with me."

"No," he said gravely. "Not with you."

How had we gone from *To my bed, Empress* to this? "Will you ever tell me why?"

He turned to leave. "You'll be dead before the impulse strikes me." The door locked behind him, the sound panicking me.

No escape. A gilded cage. Like a haunted madhouse.

I'd been locked up for months at CLC. Now my freedom had been taken from me once again. At least at the center, I'd had a roommate and visits from my mom. Here?

A wolf that was looking at my legs like he wanted to gnaw on them.

26

—Crazy like a fox!—

I jerked up from my pillow, waking from my first night at Death's. My eyes were gritty from holding back tears, my muscles sore with tension. I glared to find Cyclops beside me atop the bed, his weight straining the wooden frame. He blinked his eye, giving me a *whatcha gonna do?* look.

Had I heard Matthew, or dreamed I had? Barely daring to hope, I tentatively called, *Matthew?*

—You sound scared, Empress.—

I leapt to my feet. *Matthew, is that you?!*

—Why shouting? Inside voice . . .—

Tears leaked out of the corners of my eyes. *Why haven't you answered me?*

—Hurt my head. Just wanted to sleep and sleep and sleep.—

Oh, God, are you going to be okay?

—*Jack said I have a* tête dure. *Hard head. Said the boulder got hurt worse than I did.*—

My mouth went dry. *Is he okay?*

—*Everyone's happy I'm awake. And frantic all the time. Jack thinks I'll lead him to you.*—

Tell me what happened.

In his confusing, stilted way, Matthew relayed the mine collapse. He described having to swim under fallen beams while dodging boulders. Having to dig to get at a shaft of light, before the water rose and cut off their air. Clawing at rock till they could see the bones of their fingertips.

I was horrified by what they'd been through, but so freaking proud of them for surviving. *How are they doing?*

—*Finn. Leg healing. Heart broken. Lark tricked the trickster. The Moon sets. She failed to protect you; isn't used to failing at anything.*—

Matthew, if you knew this was in our future, why allow it to happen?

—*Not all bad is bad. Endgame, endgame. We live. Hierophant dies. You are where you're supposed to be.*—

Go through hardship to get to the ultimate goal? That had been some serious hardship. *And why am I supposed to be here? Death keeps threatening to kill me. Hey, he can't hear my thoughts anymore, can he?*

—*I broke ranks! Renegade! Eyes empty of him.*—

What about your past deal? Your debts?

—*Jack is bellowing at me to tell him where you are. He is swearing to Christ a lot. I stare at my hand.*—

Have you told him I'm okay?

— *Told Jack you're* alive. *Okay in lair of Death?*—

True. But, sweetheart, maybe you could fib and tell him I'm completely safe?

—*He wants to come for you.*—

So Death could "gut" Jack? *You have to keep him out of the Reaper's way! You can't ever show Jack how to reach this place. Lead him on wild-goose chases, anything to keep him from this man. Taking Death down is all on me.*

—*Always was.*—

Then tell me how. With poison?

—*Passion.*—

That's disgusting! In the words of Finn, are you humming my balls?

—*You can't fight Death with force.*—

Um, that's kind of the definition of fight. But, Matthew, he put a cilice on me. I can't use any of my abilities.

—*If he bound your powers, then your powers are already working.*—

I don't understand.

—*He gave you that cilice because part of him thinks*

to keep *you. You are the card that Death covets.—*

The room seemed to spin. So that was what these new Empress dreams were supposed to teach me! The earlier dreams had instructed me how to use my arsenal; this one was to teach me how to use Death's one weakness against him.

His attraction to me.

Matthew had said I would fight Death with my powers. I'd thought he meant some kind of attack. But the Empress also had the power to beckon and allure. *You and all the other Arcana expect me to seduce him.* I gave a bitter laugh. *To win his trust. Was that how past Empresses got him out of his armor?*

—You fight him with your powers.—

And now Matthew believed Death had already changed his course with me, planning some kind of sick captor/hostage future. A plan I would have to capitalize on?

At least up to a point.

Two problems. Death still hated me. And even if I could turn off my own aversion to him, I was in love with someone else. How could I flirt believably with someone I was plotting to take down?

If I win him over, the first piece of armor I'm getting him to shed is this cuff around my arm. It continued to pain me, as I was sure he'd intended. *Matthew, Death despises me. What happened in our past lives?*

—You both have waterfalls on your cards.—

What does that mean?! You haven't seen him with me. He is cruel and merciless.

—The Reaper thinks about touching you. All the time.—

GROSS! I'm not talking about this with you.

—You will not leave Death's home until he trusts you. Proximity. Seduction. Freedom. It's in your nature.—

Matthew faded from my mind, leaving me more confused than ever.

In my nature? No wonder Death had called me a femme fatale. Because I'd been one! Had I coaxed him out of his armor, then tried to sink my claws into him? That would certainly give him reason to hate me above all other Arcana.

I couldn't decide what was more disturbing: how diabolical I'd been in past lives, or that I was even considering repeating history in this one. I gazed out the turret window at the dark sky and recognized the truth. I would do anything to get back to my friends. To get back to Jack.

Even seduce a knight named Death.

I now had a mission, and failure was not an option.

27

"So is this going to be my last meal?" I asked Lark as we descended the turret steps. She'd just unlocked me and Cyclops from my cell for breakfast.

When she pulled her silky black hair over one shoulder, a gecko peeked out from her purple turtleneck. "If it is, I'm not aware of the plan." Lark looked me over. "You don't seem crushed by all this."

Now that I knew my friends were alive, I'd allowed myself to enjoy the shower and the clothes. Tops, jeans, shoes, underwear, and nightgowns—all in my size. I'd dressed in a white cashmere sweater, warm slacks, and boots of butter-soft leather. Even with only a couple of hours of fitful sleep, I felt almost human again.

"You've heard from Matthew, haven't you?"

In a confused tone, I said, "And why would I tell you that, Judas?"

She just shook her head like I was being

unreasonable. "No one got their icons. Which means we left them alive."

"How do you know they're not still trapped there?" I asked, hoping she roiled with guilt. "Or that they didn't die horribly over the last week?"

Had she paled?

Once we'd arrived on the main floor, Cyclops trailing along, my attention was less on her and more on my sumptuous surroundings. I tried not to gawk as we passed a library filled with books, a media room with thousands of DVDs, a billiard room, and a well-equipped gym. But when food scents reached us, my mouth watered. "Bacon?"

"If you give this place half a chance, you'll really like it here," Lark said, leading me into a dining room.

Inside, Death sat at the head of a long table, drinking coffee, reading a faded newspaper.

No armor! He was dressed all in black—button-down, leather pants, and boots. No helmet covered his blond hair; it was longish, grazing his jawline, creating a perfect frame for his chiseled features.

Naturally *he* could pull off leather pants and long hair. He looked like a normal gorgeous young man, who was at home here amidst all this wealth. Like the heir to a fortune. Highborn.

And still, my first impulse was to stab him with a table knife. But I knew he was too fast for me to ever get the drop on him.

Without looking up, he said, "I go without armor in my own home, creature. Especially since there are no threats to contend with." Arrogance rolled off him in waves, nettling me. He was the hostage-taker. The jailor. The reigning victor over a defeated foe.

At the very least, I needed to slap him, my mission seeming farther and farther away. Ignoring me, he turned the page. Why would he be interested in old news?

"Reading an outdated newspaper, Death? How expectedly retro of you."

Lark said, "He reads anything and everything. He's already memorized all the books here . . ." She trailed off at his glower.

I noted this chilly exchange. Information *was* there for the taking. It was time to bite back bile and cozy up to Lark.

When she padded over to a sideboard topped with silver warming pans, I followed to find scrambled eggs, french toast, and, yes, bacon. I picked up the pitcher beside the coffee pot. Fresh cream. They had a dairy cow? "This is quite a spread."

"We're not without resources here," Death said from behind his paper. "We have luxuries—and the means to protect them."

"Does Ogen do the cooking?" I grabbed a plate. Fine china. Only the best.

Lark speared french toast with a serving fork. "Not

quite. We have a human servant. You'll never see him if you don't go looking for him."

I turned to Death. "Then where is El Diablo? If he sits upon Lucifer's knee, shouldn't he be at Death's right hand?"

"He lives in the guardhouse," Lark muttered. "Not allowed in the manor."

I gave Death a sympathetic look. "Housebreaking ogres is such a bitch, am I right?"

Finally he glanced up, pinning me with his uncanny amber gaze. "By your demeanor, I can assume you've been contacted by the Fool. Perhaps all in your alliance survived?"

"Every last one."

Lark's plate dropped, shattering. Cyclops lunged forward to scarf up the food—and the pieces of china. *Crunch, crunch.*

"Sorry, boss," Lark said. "Still tired from the trip."

This was interesting. "Finn lived," I said analyzing her expression. "His leg's healing."

She shrugged, but I could see her relief. So the feelings *had* gone both ways. Then why would Lark betray the boy she cared for? Maybe Death was coercing her.

I turned back to the food. In the last serving dish was fruit: melon, pineapple, strawberries. When I sensed the energy and potential in those tiny seeds, my head swung around to Death. "These are fresh."

"As I said, we have luxuries. My home shames any other."

God, the smugness! "Gas generators for lights? Running water? Big deal. Selena's house had more electricity than Joules—*and* a swimming pool. I don't suppose you have one?"

He waved a negligent hand. "Fauna will show it to you later."

They had a freaking pool. "How are you growing food? Where's the garden? It can't be outside." I narrowed my eyes. "Are you using indoor sunlamps?" I'd bet a sunlamp could give me the strength I needed to "chew off my own arm." Which would be preferable to seducing this conceited man.

"Suffice it to say that we don't use Empress blood."

"Show me the garden."

He gave me an incredulous look. "Never. All you need to know is that we're equipped to pass a comfortable apocalypse."

"Until you kill us all."

He inclined his head. "As I always do."

I gazed at Lark. She was cool with this? Without a word, she headed to the opposite end of the table. She stared at her plate.

Testing Matthew's theory—*proximity, seduction, freedom*—I sat directly beside the Reaper. He lowered his paper to frown at me.

When we'd been out on the road, he'd smelled of

rain and steel. Now I perceived his innate scent: masculine, underscored with hints of sandalwood and pine.

Which was heavenly to a girl like me.

"What do you want?"

At his question, I blinked to attention, remembering why I was here, remembering that I *hated* this man. "Whose icon is that?" I pointed to the small markings on his right hand. The image beside Calanthe's looked like miniature scales. "Who else did you kill? I'm guessing it must be Spite."

"You don't recognize it? You remember even less than I thought."

"Wouldn't you know exactly what I remembered since you were able to read my mind for weeks?"

"I could. However, that did not mean I wanted to be in your thoughts every second of the day. I had a game to play, and I could endure only so many banal and tedious musings."

I didn't know why, but that insult piqued me worse than any of his others. Trading barbs about murdering each other was one thing, but this . . .

An obviously intelligent immortal had been inside my head and found me lacking.

Then I reminded myself that I didn't give a damn what a serial killer thought of me. "So how does this supermax work? My incarceration?"

"During the day, you'll have free range of the compound—with your guard, of course. Certain areas of the manor are off-limits to you. Fauna will point those out to you. You will respect my privacy."

"Privacy? Or is it caution? Your request has nothing to do with the fact that I almost spanked your entire alliance out on the road?" When I bit into a perfectly crisp piece of bacon and couldn't stifle a moan, he gazed at me with a peculiar expression.

A forkful of eggs confirmed they were fresh as well. So in addition to a dairy cow and pigs, they had chickens too?

"That cuff has made you a non-threat, the weakest of the Arcana," he pointed out. "Further, I don't make *requests*. I give orders. If you follow them, you might keep your head a little longer."

"No ganking me today?"

He stowed his paper, surveying me. "Not yet, creature."

"Not that I'm complaining, but why are you holding off?"

"At present, I don't have enough information to make that decision."

My mom used to say that, refusing to be pushed into any decision she wasn't prepared for. *No one can make you choose anything before you're ready. No one, Evie.*

I supposed Death's decision was whether to "keep me."

"And of course," he continued, "I enjoy tormenting you with your upcoming execution."

Or not. "How about you stop killing altogether? If you free me now, I might consider allowing you to enter the truce."

"Which involves trust. Understand me, Empress, I *listen* to your call. I know you don't say those words lightly."

"Your loss." I noshed another slice of bacon.

"You truly believe your plan will work? Strange, you weren't willfully naïve in any of your other lives."

"My truce has already proven itself. Joules and his crew could've killed me, but they looked out for me instead."

He gave a mocking laugh. "You and that boy allying? Did you know that one of the first Tower cards had an image of lightning striking *a tree*? Not a castle tower. Hmm, why do you think that might be?"

I hadn't known that. "Fascinating. But if Joules and I had grief in the past, it's ended. You said history repeats itself—I don't believe it has to."

Another puzzled look. "Does it not?"

"Nope. Which means I have a solid alliance of seven Arcana, all bent on taking you out."

He exhaled. "Your 'solid alliance' will devolve as soon as the necessity of allying wears off. They always do."

"I told you—there won't be a necessity. Because I'm going to stop the game. I never agreed to it. Want no part of killing."

Death gazed at me with that unnerving intensity. "Did you decide this before or after the Alchemist? Perhaps after you poisoned the cannibals' limbless captive? Tell me, did you already know you were going to envenom his corpse when you volunteered to murder him?"

I set down my fork, tossing my napkin on my plate. "His name was Tad. And no, I'd never thought to use him after his death. I just wanted to end his suffering."

"Don't tell me you possess empathy this time around." He sounded amused. "Do you think other cards are of like mind? Do you believe, for instance, that the Lovers will honor your truce?"

Their powers were temptation and mind control, among others. What had Gran said? *The Duke and Duchess can control any who love, warping them, perverting them. Pain becomes pleasure. . . .*

Okay, we might have to take the Lovers out too.

"They have an army," Death continued, "larger than any in all the history of the game. Exponentially larger than the Hierophant's miners. They drive north toward us now."

"Great. Then all signs point to you finally losing. Even you couldn't defeat an army, huh?" Then I frowned. "Which army?"

"One you're familiar with. The Army of the Southeast."

My mouth went dry. Vincent and Violet, the twin

children of General Milovníci, were the Duke and Duchess Most Perverse?

"The twins will not be brought to heel as easily as you think," Death said. "They marched thousands of men on your home just to capture you."

The Army grinds on, a windmill spins—Matthew's words, and now I understood them. Haven, that army's destination, had been equipped with windmill pumps. In his own way, Matthew had been warning me about the Lovers.

Death steepled his fingers. Such a condescending, king-of-the-castle gesture. "Before taking your head, they had intended to torment you with their ... contraptions." In a dry tone, he added, "I'm told capture by the Lovers is a fate worse than Death."

They were the ones who'd tortured Clotile, Jack's sister. I swallowed. Had she experienced their *contraptions*? Oh, God, that poor girl. Jack must never find out about this!

"Those two hunger for pain." Death rose, staring me down. "Do you really think they'll bow out of a game so rife with it?" With that, he strode away, his boots echoing through the corridor.

28

"What the hell was that?" I demanded. A hair-raising roar had just tolled over the entire compound.

After exploring the kitchen, the media room, and, yes, the pool after breakfast, Lark and I had just started touring the humongous barn, filled to the rafters with her free-roaming menagerie. Prey and predators milled together, obeying her command to ignore the food chain and play nice.

At the roar, Lark had ducked behind a stock-still lioness. Even Cyclops hunched down, his frizzy fur quivering. Seeming oblivious, a Komodo dragon waddled past, flicking its tongue.

"Tell me what's going on!"

Under her breath, Lark said, "Ogen. He's pissed about something."

"But he sounds a thousand times worse than he did before, even in battle."

She shrugged. "Look, we can take the grand tour another time. He's having a fit."

"Does he have them often?"

"There are a ton of dates that are sacred to him, annual Sabbats. And not like cool Wicca Sabbats either. These are dark. I try to keep track of them, but I haven't been with him for a full year to chart them all. Bottom line: sometimes he hankers for the occasional . . . offering."

"Will he hurt me?" I asked.

"Death ordered him not to hurt anyone."

"Does Ogen follow orders?"

In a low voice, Lark said, "There's a reason the Devil's horns keep changing lengths. Whenever Ogen disobeys him, Death lops off an inch. Once there's no more left to cut, Ogen gets beheaded. That's their deal."

How sick. "Why did Ogen agree to a deal like that?"

"Death had him at sword point. Told Ogen he'd spare his life for a time—on a couple of conditions, of course."

I heard those towering gate doors groan open, then slam shut.

With a relieved exhalation, Lark straightened her cap and stood. "He's off the grounds."

"Why would you stay in a place like this—with him? Wait a second, I know what's going on here. Death is holding these animals hostage, coercing you to work for him."

"He's not like that, at least not to me. We hooked up because my dad managed this menagerie for him. At least Dad had before he went on a surprise acquisition run and bit it in the Flash."

"So if Death isn't pulling the strings, then screwing us over is all on you?"

"I never said he didn't pull the strings. He does, often." When a peacock strutted over to her, Lark skimmed her fingers over the edge of its tail fan. "For the record, after I met you guys, I told him I couldn't go forward with the plan if you were all going to die."

This was surprising, soothing a bit of my hatred toward her. "Let me guess—he assured you that we'd be fine?"

She lifted her chin. "If you think back, I was the one who got Death to spare you in the beginning. And then to save you from drowning."

"I wouldn't have needed help if you hadn't betrayed us in the first place! I can't believe I took up for you against Selena. Unlike me and Finn, she had your number from the start!" As my voice scaled higher, more creatures eased over to Lark, surrounding her protectively.

"You're not going to make me feel guilty about what I did."

"Finn was falling for you, but now he knows what you did." The second girl to hide her true nature from him. "You broke him, Lark. There isn't a whole lot of light left in the world, but he was a bright spot. He may have survived, but you still doused him."

A hint of some emotion flitted across her face, then gone. "A small price to pay for the life I have here. Each night I watch a new movie, while my wolves doze in front of a roaring fire. At any time, I can shuffle down to the kitchen, make a grilled cheese, and have fresh milk with it. There are no cannibals or Baggers to dine on me, no militia to rape me, no slavers, no plague." She jerked her chin toward Ogen's guardhouse. "The Devil you know, baby."

"You didn't just say that? I *hate* you." I pinched the bridge of my nose. "You mention a lot of pros to living here. What about the cons? You have no free will and no future. Death will kill you eventually."

"Well, then, I'm not wasting another minute arguing with you. I'm tired of you making me feel bad." Baring her little fangs, she marched up until we were almost toe to toe. "For better or worse, we're roomies now. So you'll just have to check your baggage at the damn door."

"Or what?" I closed the remaining distance between us to stare her down—challenging, since we were about the same height. "What can you do to me? That's right, not a—*ow*." Pain flared in my leg. When I shot a glance down, I spied two puncture marks in my slacks and a cobra slithering away. "Ugh, disgusting!" I sidestepped with a shudder. "You made it bite me? Hate to tell you this, but I'm immune to poison, and likely venom too—*ow*." Another one got my other leg. "Damn it, Lark!"

She laughed. "Calm yo tits, unclean one. Those were dry bites. Nonpoisonous."

I narrowed my eyes. "I will get this cuff off me one day. Keep this up, and you'll find yourself mummified in vine."

"Noted. Now, come on, there's a ton more to see." She opened the barn door. "Admit it, this place is badass. Some steel baron built it for his wife in the twenties, but she died mysteriously. It might even be haunted! They had cold-war renovations made, so the basement is like a bunker, bigger than Warehouse 13."

"Death lived here before the Flash, prepping everything?" Must've been nice to have time to get ready. "Did he know it was coming?"

"Not the Flash necessarily. He just knew some kind of catastrophe always accompanies the beginning of a game." With pride, she said, "Boss was mega-rich and used bank to doomsday-prep for everything from snowmageddon to a great flood. My dad and I just thought he was an eccentric billionaire."

"Then Warehouse 13 is where you keep your garden?"

Lark hastily said, "No!"

I gave her a pleasant smile. "Just a matter of time. So if you've been with the Reaper this long, how come you weren't in that first battle against Joules, Gabriel, and Calanthe?"

"Death and Ogen had only planned to go on a supply run, and I had a foaling mare to tend to. Breeding is my top priority. Look, Death doesn't hold the animals over me, but I'm not stupid. Where else am I going to find hundreds of tons of hay?"

At the barn door, I gazed back. For all I knew, this might be the largest collection of animals left on earth. She was shepherding them, increasing their numbers. And despite myself, my hatred cooled another degree.

Once she'd locked the barn behind us, we meandered down a brick path past a training yard. Death was there, shirtless in the rain, practicing with his swords. I didn't think I would ever get used to seeing that kind of strength and speed. His skin was damp, those tattoos rippling as his chest muscles flexed.

What did those symbols mean? Why would he mark himself like that?

Though shot just yesterday, he'd taken no downtime, working past those stitched-up wounds, his enhanced healing clearly at work. "Did you tend to his gunshot wounds?" I asked Lark.

She shook her head. "The human servant I told you about was an EMT pre-Flash."

When Death hammered a particularly fierce blow

against a training post, she breathed, "Don't you think he's amazing to watch?"

I didn't *want* to. In a sour tone, I said, "Amazing? Maybe like a tornado is." And this was the man I was supposed to seduce?

In matters concerning boys, I'd always turned to my best friend Mel. I could imagine what she would do about this situation: ogle him thoroughly, then quip, "It's a dirty job, bitches, but somebody's gotta do him."

Lark said, "He's got that whole I-have-power-over-all-I-survey vibe. Admit it, it's sexy."

"Not when I'm one of the things he has power over. And unlike you, I don't enjoy seeing him out here *improving* his skills. How do you get past the fact that he's going to murder you?"

She readjusted her cap. "Boss said he'll let me live half a decade in safety, okay? In A.F. years, that's a lifetime."

"Never going to happen. He intends to win this game and play again in the future, right?" At her confused look, I said, "We age as long as the game spools on. *He* ages. Your half a decade would put him closing in on thirty for the next round. And this is a young man's game." The utter confidence in my words must be troubling to her. "Believe me, he'll close us out as soon as possible."

"Unless you do something, huh?"

"Bingo. You want me to forgive you? Then earn it.

You're going to give me Death's schedule, a layout of the compound, and a map of this mountain. Right after you show me the garden."

"Oh, am I?" She grinned, as if we were embarking on a new, fun pastime.

"Mark my words, Lark. You're going to do it today. . . ."

29

A week had passed and Lark had given up precisely not shit.

Whenever I demanded answers, she'd just chuckle, telling me, "Stop and smell the roses." At least she'd been leaving my cell unlocked, not that I could ever ditch my unshakable guard.

This morning I was pacing in my turret, Cyclops snoring in front of the door. Seven days wasted, and I was no closer to escaping, no closer to taking out Death.

Matthew had been of little help. In each of his daily check-ins, he'd told me how desperate Jack was to find me, how much anguish the boy felt that he couldn't save me from Death. Those check-ins made me crazed to reach Jack. I was worried sick about all of them out there.

If my only option against the Reaper was seducing him to trust me, then I was more than ready to play the up-to-a-point seductress.

Unfortunately, I was rarely around him. Most often he was either training in the yard or sequestered in his "unauthorized" rooms. The one meal Death always appeared for was breakfast, but he was usually engrossed in his newspaper.

I had asked him questions—about the weather, his home, the game, pet peeves, favorite food, anything— and he'd ignored me as if I were a pesky fly.

To my face, he showed no interest. Yet I felt his eyes on me constantly. When I took my daily walks outside to get the lay of the land, I would sometimes peer up and see him staring at me from his arched windows. And this morning, as I'd stood at the sideboard, I'd sensed his penetrating gaze on me. Stealing a glance over my shoulder, I'd caught him raising the paper— with his hands clenched into fists. . . .

I stopped pacing and sat in the turret's window seat. From here, I had a view of the entire compound, including the training yard where Death practiced every day. He never wore armor for this, usually didn't even bother with a shirt. Which made sense—clothing was going to prove harder and harder to come by.

He was down there right now, training with his horse, Thanatos, charging a moving target: a shield suspended from a swiveling post, moving in the wind. Even at full speed, Death hit it every time.

Though gusts whipped his blond hair, he seemed oblivious to the cold and rain. Mud splattered his bare chest, across those runes, as if he were fresh from the fray. Even with his new scars, Death was breathtaking.

As he practiced, I found myself lulled by his precise movements and harnessed aggression, my lids growing heavy, as if with . . . satisfaction. As if I was right where I was supposed to be. Which freaked me out. Satisfaction when in the lair of a murderer? One who planned to kill me?

Unless I got to him first.

—*Empress? You awake?*—

I'm up. Matthew, give me some good news.

—*The snow hasn't come yet.*—

Great. *Is Jack doing any better?*

—*No.*—

I squeezed my eyes shut. As much as I hated the thought of Jack suffering, I knew we couldn't be together, not until I succeeded here. *You've kept him off my trail?*

—*You're in my eyes.*— Matthew showed me a live vision. Through his gaze, I could see the interior of a run-down house, could see Jack there. God, I missed him!

His expression wild, he punched his fist through

a plaster wall, then swung around to turn over a table stacked with maps. Even through the vision, I could feel his frustration, would give anything to ease it.

He stormed up to Matthew. "You know where she is, *coo-yôn*!" he bellowed at the boy. "Doan tell me different. You'll find her, just like you did in Requiem."

Matthew turned his head to show me Selena and Finn sitting in silence, as if waiting for this to blow over.

As if used to it.

I noticed Jack wasn't drinking, and that departure from his normal behavior concerned me as much as everything else I was seeing.

He raked his hand through his hair. "Why woan you help me, boy? I told *ma fille* I'd be coming for her." My girl. When his gray eyes misted wet, my heart lurched. "What the hell is he doing to her?!"

Matthew, you haven't told him I'm safe! Do it now!

—Won't lie.—

Another worry to put on the heap of them. But for now, all I could think about was Jack.

Voice gone raw, he asked Matthew, "Is that bastard . . . is he hurting her?"

Tell him I'm fine, just passing time until the storms end! Tell him I'll meet up with you in a couple of weeks. Please, please don't make him suffer like this.

Jack looked like he would go insane if this went on for much longer. Which put an even more pressing clock on my mission to win over Death.

Matthew, please, I'm begging you to help Jack.

—He's tempted to beat your location out of me. But you asked him to keep me safe.—

I thought you couldn't read Dee-vee-oh well.

—Doesn't take a Fool to foresee this! Jack Deveaux talks with fists.—

You sound almost admiring.

—Jack is . . . unexpected.—

Unexpected? That was something for a psychic to say. Even I didn't know what Jack would do if his back was against the wall.

And it was. Which meant mine was too.

—Work on the Reaper, Empress.—

The man hates me. I can rarely even get into the same vicinity.

A couple of days ago, I'd hit my limit with everything—being a captive, missing Jack and Matthew, even Finn and Selena. And I'd been fed up with this place. It might have all kinds of luxuries, but no one laughed here, no one conversed or joked. It was like a giant tomb.

Fitting.

So I'd ignored Death's threats—and dire warnings about his privacy—and marched down to chew him out. Or seduce him. Whatever.

Before I could ever reach his off-limits rooms, Cyclops had nipped my heels and tripped me over and over until I'd given up.

Later I'd told Lark, "You've got to call off your wolf."

"So you can go snag a paring knife and cut on yourself to remove your cuff? Lemme get right on that. Besides, the wolf isn't just there as a jailor."

"Because I need protection from Ogen?" He'd had another fit midweek.

"Do you think you don't need it. . . ?"

—*Death wants Life.*— Matthew said. —*Proximity, seduction, freedom.*—

At that moment, I saw the Reaper leading his horse into the barn. He'd be in the manor in minutes. *Do as I ask, Matthew!* I sprinted down the steps and along the corridor, barreling into the great room, Cyclops padding behind me.

I was still out of breath when Death strode in, tall, pumped, gorgeous. He was swiping off rain with a towel, his torso muscles contracting in a stunning display.

He scowled to see me, then turned toward his rooms.

Undeterred, I tried to match steps with him. "Is today the day you're going to kill me?"

"Not yet, creature."

"Just so you know, boredom's already chasing me around with a scythe."

Had one corner of his lips curled? The closest Death came to a real smile? "I still gather information for my decision."

"What do you expect me to do all day?"

"Avail yourself of the library." Arching a brow, he

said, "Improve your mind. Learn to speak S.A.T."

His clever comeback was surprising. I thought this might be . . . teasing. From Death.

Then I remembered his comments about my "banal and tedious" thoughts. He genuinely found my mind lacking. "For the record, I was a straight-A student for my entire life." At least until Matthew's visions had mentally hamstrung me.

Death gave a scornful laugh. "Your entire life? And how old are you, little girl? Fifteen?"

I bit out, "Sixteen." God, he had a way of getting under my skin! "Why are you always training? It's not like you need to get better at killing."

He stopped before me. "Perhaps it keeps my mind off other things." His gaze raked over me.

Flirting?! Unused to this side of him, I asked, "And why can't you think about those things?"

"Ah. Now the seduction starts. Right on schedule. You can't even help what you are."

"What does that mean?"

He continued forward. "I'll be on my guard, which means I will retaliate if you come close to me again."

"Why do you separate yourself from me? Matthew told me you were thinking about keeping me . . . around. Maybe you've always planned it. When you got this property ready, you prepared that room in the turret with me in mind, didn't you?"

"You are not a long-term acquisition, I assure you."

Chilling. This man could steal into my bedroom anytime he wanted and behead me. Before, I'd been more concerned about Jack and Matthew. Now I feared for my own life as well. "Then why let me live for this long? Why bother with me at all?"

"Understand me, creature, I never stop playing the game. Keeping you is strategy. You are a wild card, as it were. As long as the Empress is alive, the other Arcana believe they have a chance to defeat me. They grow bolder with me." He flashed that unsettling look of his. "I like them bold."

"What does it matter?" I asked as we passed the gym. Lark peeked out, tilting her head with curiosity.

"At your demise, many would scatter across the land. They'd believe—rightly—that they have no shot against me. Which makes my job much more difficult. I enjoy the comforts of my home; I do not wish to stray far from it. Nor do I wish this game to drag on longer than it must. If fortune is with me, some Arcana might even descend on this place to rescue you, my poison princess in the tower. My alleged sole weakness."

Beware the lures. Now I was one. "Alleged?"

"I have no weaknesses. Know that when you've served your purpose, you'll be dispatched just like all the others."

Yes, chilling. "So according to that line of thinking,

you'll keep me alive as long as there are cards out there?"

"Unless you do not settle in here. As I said, I enjoy the comforts of my home. This is my sanctuary. Do anything to adversely affect that, and you'll be dead before your next breath. That is the information I gather: will you endure your time here seamlessly?"

I raised my brows. "Seamlessly?"

In a pointed tone, he said, "Such as respecting my privacy."

We'd stopped outside his study door. I'd followed him to his suite?

And now he would cloister himself in there until tomorrow, another day lost. Remembering the anguish in Jack's eyes, I reached for Death's arm, saying, "If I'm not your weakness, then why are you always avoiding me?"

Menace in every line of his body, the Reaper grabbed my wrist to block me. Yet then he gazed down at where our skin touched, his expression like that of an addict getting a quick fix. The amber in his eyes brightened to a starry gold. In a rough voice, he said, "I've warned you, Empress." Seeming to give himself a shake, he released me.

"Everyone's terrified of the Touch of Death," I murmured, "yet you seem to fear mine."

He gave me a withering look. "I don't needlessly handle vipers."

Hate him! "You just admire them from afar? Defang them?" I motioned toward my cuff.

He didn't deny it. "The only way you can let them slither around in your home. . . ."

30

Ogen is inside the manor.

At midnight, hunger had driven me—with my Cyclops shadow—from my bed. I hadn't heard from Matthew for two days, and worry had killed my appetite. But then I'd reminded myself that I needed to stay strong. Since my powers weren't.

I'd donned a robe over my nightgown, then slunk down the stairwell into the dimly lit corridor. My breath had caught when I'd spied an exterior door at the end of the east wing open, muddy prints tracked in.

Huge hoofprints.

Ogen could be anywhere, could be lying in wait behind any door. Gaze darting, I cursed my cuff yet again. Should I make a run for my room, trusting one giant wolf to keep me safe from an ogre?

I had a better idea.

I gazed down at my guard. "Find Ogen, wolf"—I

waved him forward—"go on." Cyclops narrowed his yellow eye, displaying that unnatural animal awareness. "I am not even kidding. Find Ogen!" He gave me a pissy look, but did begin sniffing the trail.

I let him get some distance away, then took off running in the opposite direction for Death's unauthorized suite. Just before Cyclops caught me, I banged on the door.

Death's door. I would've cringed at that if I weren't so freaked.

When the Reaper opened, Cyclops had a mouthful of my robe and was tugging, while I clung like an idiot to the doorframe. In other words, we looked like a slapstick duo.

But how ridiculous I looked was instantly forgotten—in the face of how gorgeous Death was.

Blond hair attractively disheveled, he wore faded jeans and an open black button-down. My gaze was riveted to the sight of his tattooed chest.

Again his scent hit me. Sandalwood and pine. Heavenly.

He didn't move from the doorway. "I've told you this area is off-limits."

Inner shake. Form words. "I need your help," I said, shuffling my leg behind me. When I connected with wolf snout, Cyclops released me at last. "Ogen's in the manor."

"Is he, then?" Death asked, staring at my body as

avidly as I had at his. His eyes began to emit that spell-binding light.

My nightgown and silk robe covered everything—but he had a way of looking at me that made me feel bare.

I snapped my fingers. "Can you concentrate? He's in here."

Death took his time raising his gaze to meet mine. "I find it amusing that you fear Ogen, so you run to the one Arcana who poses much more danger to you."

"Please?" I said, glancing past him to get a peek at this man's personal space. The room behind him was a study, with shelves of ancient-looking books and curios.

He reached to one side, producing a sword. From where, an umbrella stand? Or had he kept it at the ready—to use against me?

"You always have one of those close at hand?"

He stepped into the corridor and shut the door behind him. "Without fail." After murmuring some foreign words at the wolf, he strode away. Over his shoulder, he commanded me, "Stay there."

Alas, I did not know my commands as well as Ogen. I needed to investigate Death's study, to gain some insight into the mysterious knight. When I reached for the doorknob, Cyclops growled.

I kept turning the knob, until he wrapped his maw around my entire calf, the threat clear. "All right, all right! You are such a pain in my ass, dog." As soon as I let go of the knob, he released me.

Resigned to waiting, I crossed my arms over my chest, leaning back against the door. All along the hall hung works of art that looked priceless, definitely centuries old. I knew a little about art and thought they might be Italian.

Most were of battle scenes, with the faces of the soldiers obscured. Though the artists had depicted splintered lances and cavalry horses in mid-leap, I still found the effect static. Frozen.

Like this entire place.

The wolf had probably saved me a lot of grief, because Death returned in just a few minutes. "Evidently Ogen wanted *ham*," he said dryly. "And he wanted it badly enough to disobey me. He's gone now—you may return to your room."

"Did you dock his horns?"

At the doorway, he said, "Fauna's been talking, then? Yes, I punished him. I've been softer in this game, and he reacted, testing boundaries. He will come to heel now."

"This is you being soft?" My thoughts flickered back to Death looming at the end of that mine, more fearsome than his Grim Reaper tableau. "What would have happened if I'd stumbled on him?"

Instead of answering my question, Death said, "Ogen won't enter the manor again."

When he opened his door, I was a total Looky Lou, but he didn't invite me in. "You've got a lot of books." *Scintillating, Eves.* "Can I come in for a sec?"

With an aggrieved air, he turned and walked in. Taking that as a "sure," I followed, shutting the door in Cyclops's face.

Death sat behind his oversize desk, which was covered with weathered scrolls. From the looks of it, before I'd interrupted he'd been deep in the study of . . . something. Beside the scrolls was a bottle and a shot glass.

Like Jack, Death drank spirits. Unlike Jack, he shot vodka.

Without a word to me, Death rolled up the scrolls. When he didn't offer me a seat, I took my time exploring. He had two walls of bookshelves that stretched from floor to ceiling. I ran a finger over a line of spines, noting the age of the books. All collector's editions, no doubt. Most of the titles were in foreign languages, what looked like Greek and Latin, some in French.

Dozens of swords hung on one wall. Behind his desk, a bank of Gothic windows arched high—the ones I'd seen him gazing out of.

On either side of the windows stood display cabinets filled with unusual objects. Four kingly scepters lay on one shelf. The same number of crowns was highlighted on another.

Everything about the room screamed wealth and

taste. Yet all his possessions were mired in the past, no signs of life. The crowns had once been worn. The swords had once been wielded. Those dusty books had once been unread, untapped, filled with mystery.

Was this the existence Death wanted? The sanctuary he craved? I pictured him sitting here all alone, surveying his lifeless collections. As on the riverbank, I felt a confusing pang of pity. "So you collect swords and books and . . . crowns?"

"Among other things," he said dismissively.

"No electric lights?" The room was lit with candles. "How can you read like this?"

As if his reply had been dragged from him, he said, "For eons, I've read by candlelight. If you must know, it makes the words more . . . alive."

"Death wants the words to be alive? Cats and dogs living together, huh?" Yet his comment made me look at his room anew. Maybe he didn't prefer this cold, solitary existence. Maybe he was trapped like this.

Maybe Death wished he could dream in color.

His eyes narrowed. "What do you want?"

"To talk." Before he could kick me out, I sat in one of the plush chairs in front of his desk. I was playing with fire, irritating this man. When his gaze dipped, I drew my robe tight to my neck. Some femme fatale.

Even he frowned at my actions. "As I've told you, I will not touch you like that. You've nothing to fear from me on that score."

"But on another score, I'm not so lucky? I guess I should get this out of the way: is tonight the night you kill me?"

He sighed. "Not yet, creature."

Feeling bolder, I said, "So what are those scrolls about?"

"Chronicles from a past game," he said. "Details about . . . certain players."

"Anything you want to share?" At his annoyed expression, I said, "You have all the advantages over the rest of us, don't you? A fortress, supplies, insight into the game, and hand-picked allies who don't seem to care that you'll kill them."

"Correct on all counts." He shot his glass, refilling.

He still hadn't kicked me out. Deep down, did this man crave talking to another? "So what does vodka taste like? I've never had it." At his disbelieving look, I reminded him, "I'm sixteen. I hail from a land of bourbon and beer."

As if he couldn't help himself, he rose to collect another glass from a side table, then poured straight vodka.

I stared at the clear liquid he set down in front of me. My mission was seduction; liquor lowered inhibitions, right? When I raised my glass to sip, he shook his head slowly, demonstrating with his own shot how it was meant to be enjoyed. Bottoms up, with an immediate refill.

Giving him a pained smile, I knocked back my glass, coughing at the burn.

"Well?" He poured again.

Throat on fire, I said, "Don't know how I lived without it. I'll bet you've got bottles and bottles of this stuff—in your bunker beneath the manor."

Stony stare.

Undeterred, I asked, "How did you know when the Flash would be?"

He sank into his leather chair once more. "The icons on my hand began to fade, and I started to hear the Arcana calls. Those events usually happen just prior to the catastrophe."

"There's truly one in each game?"

"They're are all card-themed. The Black Death was a nod to me. A region-killing volcano was for the Emperor."

"That's right," I said, remembering that card's powers. The Emperor could create mountains, volcanoes, and earthquakes, his character as hard and unyielding as the Empress was supposed to be soft and lush.

"A shame that you can't remember your famine tribute."

In one of my early visions, villagers had blamed the red witch for their famine. Had they been right to? In as innocent a tone as I could manage, I asked, "Has there been a catastrophe to honor that card, the other one who's immune to my poison?" I'd tried so hard to remember which one it was. Maybe Death would spill. . . .

He gave me a thin smile. "For me to know."

"Let me guess—now it's the Sun's turn?"

He nodded. "These events have a way of pulling Arcana together and keeping us from the notice of humans. One doesn't look up to the sky to see a flying boy if bodies are writhing all around one's feet."

"The field of battle." Just as Matthew had told me. "But those other tragedies weren't apocalyptic. Why was this one?"

With raised brows, he glanced at my untouched glass. *Fair's fair.* I chugged, gasped, winced at the refill.

"I believe something about this damaged world— the planet, not the card—couldn't take the sunlight. The gods might have salvaged things, but they've gone."

"So we're champions of various gods, right? Like you were tapped by a death deity?" A curt nod. The idea made me shiver. "And what about me? You said I was more Aphrodite than Demeter. Were you being literal?"

"The gods go by countless names. What they're called is unimportant. All that matters is what powers they gifted to you."

"Your Touch-of-Death *gift* doesn't seem very fair. Is it only in your hands, or is all of your skin deadly?"

Skewering me with his gaze, he enunciated the words: "Every last inch of me."

I couldn't tell if his words held innuendo—or a threat. Moving on. "What's your call? How come I never hear it?"

"Perhaps I'm beyond one," he said, evading.

"Have you heard each of the Arcana calls?" As king of the airwaves. "Even the distant ones?" The ones I could hear only wanted to whisper about the Empress's impending gruesome death.

"I have. But for the one who awaits activation."

I cast my mind back. Wasn't there a card who remained dormant until he or she killed an Arcana?

"You are inquisitive this time around. You've asked me more questions in days than in your other lives combined."

Added to all my other faults, I'd been a conversation hog?

"You puzzle me," Death admitted. "You seem altered from how you've been in the past—at least on the surface. I want to know why."

"I can't say why I'm different. I don't remember much about any past lives."

"Based on your history, I must assume that this is all an act."

"It's not. Look, I've gotten the impression that I wasn't exactly Miss Congeniality in past games. But in this one, I'm pretty transparent."

"Then you'll answer any of my questions with honesty."

I had a feeling he was about to test me, like he'd only ask questions he already knew the answers to. "Shoot."

"Are you and the Fool engaged in a plot against me?"

Busted. "Often."

"Would you kill me right now if you had the opportunity?"

How to answer that? "Not if you joined my truce."

"Alas, I know the futility. Do you think Arcana have never tried this in the past? Leave a few cards alive, with a pact of peace among them. It works for a time. Yet then the temptation of immortal life grows too strong. The killing begins again. Fate will figure out a way to make you fight."

I hadn't believed I was the first Arcana to have these ideas. But to know a truce had been attempted—and failed—was demoralizing. *If* Death told the truth about this.

"The strongest of the Arcana couldn't make it work," he continued. "Interestingly, you entered into a pact before. And you were the first to fold."

"How? What'd I do?"

Another glance at my glass.

When I drank my shot, he emptied his own, refilling us. Again? I was starting to get buzzed.

"If you want to know, creature, then remember."

"And what if I can't?"

"Then you'll *never* know. Haven't you heard? I keep secrets like a grave."

Again, was this teasing from him? "In any case, that was before; this is now. I'm not the same person this time around. I can't even comprehend how I was so evil." The record holder.

"Your family line has always taken the game very seriously, training you to be a vicious killer."

My lips parted as I recalled my grandmother's words: *Evie, there's a viciousness in you that I must nurture.* I remembered her eyes had twinkled with affection as she'd told me, *You're going to kill them all.*

I'd been eight at the time.

If my mother hadn't sent her away, what would I be like now? What would Gran have taught me, given eight more years of my childhood? I swallowed. What would she teach me now?

Probably not how to end the game. And truces hadn't worked in the past anyway.

I'd been stubbornly holding on to the belief that my grandmother could help me. Considering all I'd learned—and remembered—that idea seemed almost laughable. Maybe I'd held on so tightly because the alternative was murdering kids I cared about. . . .

For the first time, my urge to reach her grew a little less pressing.

"What are you thinking with such solemnity?" Death asked.

"That it's no wonder I'm different." I ran my finger along the rim of my glass. "I missed my lessons. Instead of learning how to murder, I was just a regular girl." I glanced up, saw that his gaze followed the movement of my finger.

He nodded at my icons. "You've done quite well for yourself."

I dropped my hand. "After my grandmother went away"—*was committed to an asylum*—"I wasn't taught anything more. I went to school in a small town, I hung out with friends. I was boring, with banal and tedious musings."

"That really vexed you, didn't it?"

I shrugged. "Why did you want to see my thoughts anyway?"

"It's wise to know my enemy."

"I wish you could read my thoughts now. You'd know that I don't want to be your enemy."

He steepled his fingers, as arrogant as ever. His touch might be fatal, but his hands were refined. Like I imagined a surgeon's would be. "How coincidental. When I could read your mind, you were vowing to kill me, actively forming alliances to do so. Now that I can't, you say you wish for peace between us?"

"If I managed to get Matthew to restore our link, would you remove this cuff?"

"Not until I remove you from the game." His tone was matter-of-fact, all *reigning victor*.

Which reminded me that I wasn't here to make friends. "What was the deal you made with Matthew anyway? The one that forced him to give you access to my head?"

"All you need to know is that he's broken it. By doing so, he's lost honor. It will hurt him in future games."

Just as my past broken promises had hurt me in this game. "But you broke a deal with me. I went with you in the mine, but you let Ogen continue battering the mountain."

"My deal was that your friends wouldn't be killed. They live yet. Empress, *I* haven't lied to you."

"What does that mean? Who has lied to me?"

Another stony stare.

Deciding he was just winding me up, I changed the subject. "What's immortal life like?"

"Long."

"Okay." Awkward silence. Casting about for something to say, I asked, "Are the paintings in the hall Italian Renaissance?"

He appeared surprised. "They are. You know art?"

"I used to paint before the Flash." Before such pastimes had become impossible. Things I'd enjoyed like dance, art, and reading had faded to distant memories when I was desperately sourcing for food and shelter each and every day. "I was fascinated by the Italian painters."

When I'd taken an art history elective in school, I'd read and reread their chapter in my textbook, imagining the excitement of the era, the revelry and passion.

My favorite painting had been del Cossa's *Triumph of Venus*, but I doubted Death would appreciate that.

"It was a time of great advancement," he said, as if with pride.

I gasped. "You were there, weren't you?" When he inclined his head, I asked, "Were you in Florence? Or maybe Venice?" I sighed to remember how beautiful those cities had looked.

He gazed away. "I preferred more rural locales."

Realization. He would have avoided densely populated areas, fearing he might touch others. He never would have enjoyed revelry or passion, because he wouldn't have had friends or lovers. He must always have been on guard. "Sometimes I forget that you can't touch others. Well, anyone but me."

His upper arm strained, like he was clenching his fist beneath the desk. "I *never* forget."

Whenever Jack was angry or frustrated, a muscle would tick in his jaw. Was a clenched fist Death's tell? "So you lived out in the country, away from all the excitement?"

"I had everything I needed."

I imagined him secluded in some echoing villa, all by himself, reading his books. "Any friends?"

"Mortals die so readily. I make an effort not to grow attached to anyone. Just as I never keep pets."

"Except for your horse. How'd you find one with red eyes? Is he immortal too?"

Death shook his head. "Any steed I claim as my own grows red-eyed."

"And you named him Thanatos? It's catchy. Really."

"It's the name of a death deity. Do avail yourself of the library. Improve your mind."

I ground my teeth. Though I wanted to point out how useless studying would be if he planned to kill me soon, I said, "Great idea." I rose, crossing to his bookshelves. "I'll start with your favorite book." Then I'd have to return it to him here.

"I meant from the other library."

Over my shoulder, I said, "I want to read what you like."

"You have an entire collection at your disposal, but you desire a title from my personal one? Do you comprehend how valuable these books are? How much care I've taken over centuries to keep them pristine?"

I faced him. "Because they're first editions."

"Because they're *mine*. I've spent fortunes to keep them safe in all my different homes, in all my wanderings. Through wars and catastrophes, I protected them."

I frowned. "They sound like your children."

He raised his glass. "The closest I'll ever come to having them." He said this in an unemotional tone, but the comment still struck me as sad.

After all this time, he hadn't—and could never—start

a family. He had no one. I remembered how alone I'd felt those two days I'd spent by myself on the way to Requiem. Two days.

Death might have felt that way for *seven hundred thousand days*.

The idea that someone like him might be lonely made me think of him as, I don't know, more human. As if he were a normal guy in his early twenties, maybe a former college student just trying to get by.

When he was anything but. He was the Endless Knight, an immortal killer. He probably preferred being alone, lacking the need for companionship that I had.

"You won't cough up a single book?" I said. "Are you scared I'll get clues about your personality from reading the same things you do?"

With a put-out demeanor, he rose, joining me, but not too close. Reaching high, he took down a slim tome and handed it to me.

The Prince?

"It's in English. Almost as old as the original Italian." With a touch more enthusiasm, he said, "You don't lose as much in the translation as you'd think."

"What's it about? Is it an adventure? Maybe a love story?"

"It's a political treatise, or possibly a satire. . . ." He trailed off, seeming to remember who he was talking to. His expression grew shuttered again, and he returned to his chair. I got the sense that he felt more comfortable with that desk between us.

Because of what I might do to him—or because of what he might do to me?

"You speak and read Italian?"

"I speak and read many languages. A benefit of being immortal. I have much time for study." He waved a hand, indicating those scrolls. "And I wish to continue with my research. Now."

Leaving me to return to my solitary turret. Just the thought of that made my three shots of vodka churn in my gut. At least being with Death was interesting. "I could start this book here, while you research. We could read together."

Was he wavering?

"I'll be quiet as a mouse."

He narrowed his eyes. "You think I can't see what you're doing? What your plan is? Leave me, creature. Do not come back here."

With a touch of cockiness, I said, "But I have to return this book once I'm done." I wagged it in front of him. "It's only etiquette."

In a tone ringing with finality, he said, "Consider it an early parting gift."

31

—Hunts and campaigns.—

I woke, rubbing my eyes. *Matthew, is that you?* I scowled to find Cyclops beside me again. He licked his massive chops, then dozed once more. *What time is it?*

—Dunno. Always dark.—

Yesterday the sun had risen for only an hour or so. Endless night in the lair of the Endless Knight? I tried to block that out of my mind. I'd wanted to foil the game, which wouldn't matter if the entire planet failed. *Where have you been? You haven't checked in for five days.*

—Busy.—

Tell me Jack's doing better. We'd now been separated for three weeks, and I'd grown more and more frightened for him. I couldn't concentrate, couldn't think beyond escaping to reach him.

Or finishing my job here.

I wished I had some kind of update for Matthew, but my life seemed to be stuck on pause, Groundhog Days repeating themselves. I'd gotten no closer to the arrogant Reaper. My only development was that I'd grown accustomed to the cilice. This wasn't a good thing; I'd planned to rid myself of it before I ever got used to it.

—*Better? Jack's doing different. We go on hunts and campaigns!*— Matthew sounded like a sixteen-year-old who'd just scored his first car.

What does that mean?

He showed me a vision of Jack. Instead of the frenzy he'd demonstrated before, Jack was coldly cleaning a rifle, focused with a deadly intent. Still not drinking.

What happened?

—*Others know your location. Beware the lures.*—

As Death had spoken of. *Yes, and?*

—*I won't tell Jack how to reach you. So he plans to learn your location from others.*—

As I sputtered mentally, Matthew continued. —*We go on hunts for Arcana. Planning a new campaign!*—

What are you thinking?? This was the most furious I'd ever been with Matthew. *Jack doesn't HAVE POWERS.*

—*Selena and Finn help too.*— His tone was surly now.

Please lead them all away from danger! Promise me, Matthew.

—*Proximity. Seduction. Freedom. Hunts! And campaigns!*—

Then he was gone, as good as hanging up on me. Leaving me even more frantic to return to them all.

How? How? How?

Proximity? Death had a marked aversion to me. I'd ambushed him twice, but only felt farther away from my goal. My next move would be standing in the rain while he trained, looking like an even bigger idiot.

What did I know about seduction? I was sixteen going on seventeen. I'd had sex once. I'd always gotten advice from the worldly Mel.

She would know what to do about this. I remembered one time when we'd had a car wash fund-raiser for our cheer squad. She'd shown up in a tissue-thin white T-shirt and a black bra.

Her line of cars had stretched around the school.

But there were no cars around here to wash. In what situation could I be expected to wear a wet T-shirt?

It dawned on me. I turned to Cyclops. "Boy, you *stink*."

Drizzling rain? Check. Wolf? Check. Thin white shirt and black bra? Check, check.

I'd just set up buckets of warmed water and my wolf prop in the courtyard—in full view of Death.

Though he hadn't even glanced over at us, my mind had briefly blanked to see him. Today he wore a chain-mail shirt—like a long-sleeved T-shirt made of woven metal—that left little to the imagination. The mesh hung lovingly over the ridges and planes of his swollen muscles, teasing across the runes on his skin.

Focus! I grabbed the dishwashing liquid I'd filched from the kitchen. Assuming that Death's lair had all the soap in the world, I squirted a good portion onto Cyclops.

Earlier, I'd found Lark in the gym, telling her, "I'm giving Cyclops a bath."

Her response: "Your funeral."

Strangely, the wolf cooperated, even when I began working the liquid into his frizzy fur. But he cast me a one-eyed look of such bafflement that I knew Lark had never washed him before. So I gave him a *whatcha gonna do?* look in turn and scrubbed.

Like washing a scarred, mangy Wookiee.

Sudsy water began running down the courtyard to where Death practiced. Whenever he stepped through it, bubbles splashed up around his boots. He must have noticed that. For a moment he stilled, then continued on with a determined look on his face.

Okay, now he was just ignoring me. Not acceptable.

I dumped the entire bottle on Cyclops, lathering his fur until he was covered in bubbles, a foam blanket. "My wolf in sheep's clothing, huh, boy?"

A thick river of suds floated down to Death. *Ignore us now, Reap.*

Even when bubbles clung to his pant legs, the man wouldn't glance over, just battered his target with punishing hits.

Damn it, this had seemed like such a good plan. I peered down at the wolf. "Might as well get you washed up for real." Imagining how much better my turret would smell, I dug in to my task.

It was kind of soothing to take care of him, and when I realized he was liking it too, I smiled.

Without warning, he gave a great shake, sending foam all over me. I shrieked and jumped back, but he sidled up to me at once, wanting more attention. "You're like a big feline!"

I squatted to work out some tangles on his neck. He snuffled, and bubbles formed over his nostrils, floating into the air. I couldn't help laughing. It felt great to laugh. I hadn't since that night in the cabin with Jack—

I caught sight of Death striding over, looking like he was about to annihilate something. "You interrupt my training?"

"Hmm?" *Here goes nothing.* I stood.

His head immediately dipped, eyes focused on my chest. I followed his gaze. My headlights were on, high beams engaged. Oops. "Just wanted to wash my roommate. Is the yard off-limits to me?"

Death's blond brows drew tight, and he rubbed his gauntleted hand over his mouth.

"You have no other motive to brave this rain?" he said absently, still staring. "This *cold* rain." Had his accent thickened? A change in accent was always an indicator of Jack's heightened emotions.

I walked around Cyclops to stand in front of Death. "The wolf has taken to sleeping in my bed. I'd rather he smelled like zesty lemon than wet dog."

Death's hand moved just a fraction, as if to reach for me. Then his arm fell back, his fist clenching.

His tell. Born from lifetimes of craving contact? Only to remember that he killed with it?

It was so strange to think that this immortal could only have sex with one woman in the whole world. And that he thought about touching me all the time. Would he fantasize about it tonight?

At the thought, I shivered; he bit out a foreign curse. *Remember the mission.* "Um, thank you for lending me *The Prince.*" It was a weird book, all about unscrupulous acts in war and ruling. Plots, scheming, and ruthlessness were to be applauded. "I'll finish it this afternoon. I was thinking I could drop by your study tonight and return it."

Still staring at my chest, he cleared his throat before he could speak. "You wish to come to my room this evening?" Then he raised his gaze, seeming determined not to look down.

"Yes. You loaned me a book. That means we're supposed to discuss it together. Sharing makes the book new for you all over again." When I smiled, his eyes locked on my lips, his irises going from amber to starry.

Was he imagining kissing me right now? I detested him so much I'd figured the mere idea would make me sick—yet I felt no aversion when I imagined Death's lips on mine.

Which left me guilt-ridden. I was in love with Jack; how could I be thinking about this man's kiss?

My cheeks heated, and I think Death noticed.

I reminded myself that the Reaper might be attractive to, like, a glorious degree—but he was arrogant and cruel and merciless. He wanted to murder me. With that in mind, I made my tone flirtatious. "Did you choose *The Prince* to show me how you play the game, big guy?"

As if cut off with a switch, the light in his eyes dimmed. "I gave you that book to illustrate how *you* play."

Oh. The spell was broken.

"Creature, I know what you plan. You intend to win my trust so I'll remove the cilice. Once I've unleashed your powers, you'll bide your time until I've let down my guard, then strike."

"Death, wait." I took a step forward.

He took one back. "And all the while, you're intending to return to *him*. I wonder what your precious mortal would think about your actions today." His fists clenched.

With jealousy.

There was no longer any denying it. This was more than an opposites-attract interest on his part, more than his need to touch. I recalled how he'd reacted the night

I'd been with Jack, the rage in Death's tone. Something deeper was at work here.

How far had things gone between us in my past lives? Needing to know the truth, I said, "I dreamed that you wanted to take me to bed. Long ago. Did you succeed?"

"If you want to know, then *remember*." With a forbidding look, he said, "You will not seduce me, Empress. Cease trying." He strode away.

Didn't matter. I would still go to his study tonight.

32

There was no answer when I knocked on his door. Death was gone.

I sought out Lark, finding her in the den watching a movie. "Where is he?"

She pushed pause on the remote. "Away on business. He said he'd be back before dinner in two nights."

"He left to go make a kill?"

"Maybe not. He travels a lot to source things for us." She popped a handful of popcorn in her mouth, chewing loudly. "Hell, he could've been trying to get away—from you. For gods' sakes, Evie, you wet-T-shirted him. I've never seen him so rattled."

I felt a little thrill at the idea that I'd managed to rattle an ancient immortal, but it was immediately doused. Death would be gone for two days. Which meant more nights separated from Jack and my friends.

Jack, who could be out right now, risking his life to hunt Arcana.

How much longer could I remain here? Despite having more time on my hands than I'd ever had in my life, the days seemed to fly by, as if on fast-forward.

As if I were trapped in the Castle of Lost Time.

Feeling the pressure, I said, "Where's the garden, Lark?" I knew she was loyal to Death, but to what degree? I'd have to risk it. "Help me get my powers back, and we could take this freaking manor from Death and Ogen. Your animals would be safe. You'd have all the comforts here, and you'd get to live past your teens."

If she was tempted, she didn't show it.

"I could send for my friends to help us. You could see Finn. We'd be an alliance again."

"Nah, I'm good here."

Squeezing my temples, I sank down on the couch opposite her. "Why this loyalty to Death?"

She set her popcorn bowl to the side. "He's not like you think he is."

"So you're saying he's not a stone-cold killer?"

With reluctance, she admitted, "No, he is. But he's not like the Lovers, or the Hierophant."

"We use them for comparison now?"

She shrugged. "Try to put yourself in his shoes. The only girl in the world he can touch has vowed to kill him."

I almost yelled, *He started it!* Even before the Flash, he'd threatened me. "I just wanted to live on my farm and mind my own business. He was the one who terrorized me, telling me he'd drink my blood from his sword and such. How was I supposed to react?"

"Have you asked yourself why he'd do that?"

"Oh, I have. And I've asked Matthew. And even Death himself! Do *you* know?"

"If I did, I wouldn't tell you."

"Speaking of fauna—you're being *pig*headed. You are stubbornly sticking to a path that leads to one outcome, and it's the worst possible."

"I'd say that's debatable. You forget, I've seen the inside of a cannibal pantry."

"Have you and Death worked out a system for your execution? Will he tell you when you've got a year left? A week? It's sick what he's doing to you. Why would you tolerate it?"

She shrugged again, tinkering with the remote.

"I wonder what will happen to your pets once you're buried. Or do you think Death will let Ogen feast on your bones?" Out of patience, I stood. "When the Reaper's sword is at your neck, I want you to remember this night. Remember that you could've changed your future. . . ." I trailed off when the mountain rumbled. A quake? We'd had them at Haven, an additional A.F. perk.

Outside in the wet night, Ogen responded with a bloodcurdling roar.

Lark met my gaze, suddenly looking very young. "The Devil you know."

Done with her, I made my way back to my room, flagging with each step up. Groundhog Days were exhausting.

When I reached my bed, I fell back, passing out.

Later that night, I shot awake with a strangled cry.

I'd dreamed of Death again, but this time it was no memory of a past life. This was my mind betraying me, because I'd dreamed he'd taken me into his arms, kissing me out in the rain—and I'd *loved* it.

In the chill downpour, his lips had been hot on mine, as hot as they'd been when he'd breathed air into my lungs, bringing me back from the dead.

As he'd claimed my mouth over and over, his grip had been crushing, but I'd nearly cried with pleasure.

On the very night that he'd ridden out, likely to reap some unsuspecting kid, I'd experienced the most erotic dream in my life—of *Death*?

Dear God, what was happening to me?

33

Death was expected back tonight, and I had my excuse for going to his study: returning his book. I simply chose to ignore his "parting gift" jab.

With the memory of that kissing dream firmly buried, I readied myself to see him. I took care with my clothes, wearing a fawn-colored skirt and a scoop-neck navy blouse. The neckline plunged lower than any I'd worn since the apocalypse. I left my hair loose.

I had an agenda for tonight, one made even more important in light of Matthew's curt check-in last night: —*We got away. We all lived.*— It was as if he'd been overridden by other calls, the Arcana abuzz for some reason. Something about the Arcane Navigator?

My friends were out there in a dangerous world, doing God only knew what. And I couldn't help them from here.

I exited the bathroom, crossing to the bed, where

Cyclops was sprawled. "How do I look. . . ." I couldn't manage another word, too stunned even to shriek.

Part of Death's book was still lodged between the wolf's mighty jaws; the rest was an array of slobbery bits scattered over my bed, like a crime scene. Cyclops belched wetly around his new four-hundred-year-old chew toy.

"Oh my God." I had to tell Death that one of his precious books—his favorite—was no more. Under my care, his "child" had been eaten.

When Thanatos's hooves charged onto the property, heralding Death's arrival, I trudged down the stairs with leaden feet.

Death strode through the front doors not long after, removing his helmet. He looked exhausted, his eyes dim, blond stubble highlighting his defined jawline. His armor was splashed with mud.

Once he saw me, I could have sworn his eyes lightened a fraction, as if he was happy I was here. He looked approving of my appearance.

Then his eyes went dark once more. "Ah, my lady awaiting her knight's return," he said in a derisive tone. "I am far too tired for your intrigues tonight, Empress."

He looked so whipped that I actually felt sorry for him. How could I be softening toward someone who had me in the crosshairs?

This was probably not the best time to tell him about the book, but I could still shoot for proximity.

"Where did you go? Lark said you might be sourcing." Nothing. I fiddled with my blouse. "Won't you talk to me?"

"Leave me, creature. I'm in no mood."

"It doesn't have to be this way between us."

"So says the girl who wants me dead."

I exhaled with disappointment. "I only wanted you dead because you kept terrorizing me, and I knew you'd force the issue until only one of us survived."

He gave a harsh laugh as he removed his spiked gauntlets. "You believe that's changed?"

"I believe it could. Wouldn't you rather have me as a friend than an enemy? Maybe you've forgotten what it's like to have friends. Maybe you never knew."

His expression said I'd hit the nail on the head.

How awful. "But you could have them now," I said quietly.

"I hold your life in my hands—and you dare to pity me? Your eyes are filled with it. You think I *want* friends? Perhaps some like yours?" he scoffed. "Then I wouldn't need enemies."

"What does that mean?" My question was forgotten when I spied a new icon on his right hand, a simple white star. "You made a kill."

Death gave me that unsettling sneer. "The Star was *very* bold."

So that's what the buzz was about. The Star, the Arcane Navigator, was no more.

Feeling sick, I turned away. What if Death truly craved killing? Like Ogen, who hungered for offerings?

In past games, Arcana had said Death preferred to kill with his touch. Perhaps, like Finn, he was *compelled* to use his power?

Death grabbed my arm, yanking me around. "You, of all people, are giving me a repulsed look? You've nearly as many markings as I have!" He released me, splaying his fingers as if he'd just handled a live grenade.

"I took mine in self-defense."

"And you assume I didn't? The Star neared much too close to my sanctuary. He sought me." Death ran his palm over his jaw. "I will protect my home and anyone in it. Even you."

In a faint voice, I said, "How did you do it?"

"Without my customary ease. Long nights had strengthened the Star, making for ideal conditions for him to use his powers."

"Like what?" I couldn't remember.

"Echolocation, heightened senses, the ability to create a light blast from his skin, like a supernova. In a black night, he detonated himself, paralyzing my senses, my body." Was that the quake we'd felt? The one that had made Ogen roar? "Then he used his night sight to attack."

"But you got the upper hand? How'd you end him?"

Death closed in on me, armored, terrifying, staring

down at me until I started to tremble. He lifted one glove to my face. "These spikes"—he lightly skimmed them down my cheek—"through his temple."

Death had battered some teenager with his gauntleted fist.

When I realized this man was trying to stoke my hatred for him, I yanked my head back. "Is that how you'll do it to me? Before you take my head, of course. Is that what you'll do to Lark?"

He said only, "Our play toils on. It's kill or be killed."

This game will make murderers of us all. No, I refused to accept that. "It doesn't have to be that way! What if I vowed on my mother's soul never to hurt you?"

"How easily those beautiful lips spill lies. Empress, you never keep your vows."

So I kept hearing. "I'd never break that one."

He exhaled, seeming like he regretted revealing too much of himself. "It is late, and I'm weary. I take my leave." He turned toward his rooms.

Another wasted day in the Castle of Lost Time? I needed proximity! I squared my shoulders and followed him into his study. "I've figured out why you avoid me. If you get to know me better, it'll be harder to kill me."

"You enter here?" He laid his helmet and gloves on his desk. "I've warned you. And still you test me." In a voice vibrating with rage, he said, "But you'd risk anything, would *do* anything to get back to your mortal. Anything to be in his arms once more. Even endeavoring to get closer to the man you hate above all others."

"Just wait—"

"Deny that you want to be with him right now."

I couldn't make myself deny it. Death was right. I would do anything to return to Jack.

When I didn't answer, Death looked like something snapped inside, his iron control shattering. "How can you possibly want *him*? The mortal thinks of your powers as a curse, a problem. You're a god among humans, but he's too blind to see that!"

"*I* look at this as a curse, as a problem. If I weren't the Empress, then you and I wouldn't have to be enemies. I'd never have to worry about your sword at my throat."

"Do you believe yourself *in love* with Deveaux?" He snarled the words.

As far as my mission to seduce went, it probably wasn't the best idea to be honest about that.

Between gritted teeth, he said, "It's emblazoned on your pretty face. But you wouldn't love him if you truly knew him. Your feelings would wither and die."

"What are you talking about?"

He headed for his vodka bottle, pouring a shot for himself only. "He's lied to you repeatedly." He tossed off his glass, running the back of his marked hand over his lips, then refilled.

I crossed my arms over my chest. "Uh-huh. I'll just take your word for it?"

"No, I received my information from the Fool. He was quite worried about his Empress's safety when you were in Deveaux's keeping."

This was coming from Matthew? No, no, Death was just trying to keep me on edge, to rattle me as I had him. "You know I'll fact-check."

"I expect you to."

I swallowed. "And why would you two be discussing my safety?"

"We had a shared interest."

"That's right!" I snapped my fingers. "You wanted to keep me alive, so I could be your wild card. At least before you off me yourself. Now it makes sense why you intervened with the Hierophant. And with the other Arcana, warning them away."

"I've been up-front about my intentions with you, unlike Deveaux. Did you never wonder about his instant infatuation with you?"

"Maybe he had a thing for cheerleaders." Jack had told me he'd wanted me from the first time he'd seen me. I would never forget that morning. I'd been riding in Brand's Porsche, leaning over to kiss him, when I'd seen a motorcyclist pull up alongside us. Jack.

Death shook his head. "No, he targeted you before he ever saw you."

"That doesn't make sense."

"You were possessed by someone he hated." He downed another shot.

"Jack despised Brand. That was no secret."

"You never asked yourself why?"

"Because Brand was rich and seemed to have everything so easy."

"I'm sure that had something to do with it. However, the main reason he hated Brandon Radcliffe"—Death's eyes had never looked so flat and dark—"was that they shared a father. A father who adored one son and spurned the other."

Dizziness swept over me. "You're saying Brand and Jackson were . . . half brothers?"

This made a certain sick sense. What was it Jack had told me about his biological father? *He was too busy spoiling his legitimate son to spend time with me—or to send a single dime to ma mère.*

Mr. Radcliffe had been a lawyer; Jack had said his father hadn't wanted to admit *culpability.* Something an attorney might say. I pictured the two boys, both so tall and built, detecting a resemblance I hadn't noticed before. I remembered how Brand, a well-liked guy, had been baffled about why the Cajun had acted so aggressive toward him.

Only one son had known of their connection.

Was this why Jack's eyes had darted when I'd asked him if he had any secrets? I folded my hands behind me, because they shook.

Death was relishing this. "Deveaux coveted all his brother had: the perfect family, the house, the car. The *girl*. He could never have any of the others—but he could have you. And he did."

"You're lying." *You can trust me alone, Evie.* "Matthew would've told me about this."

Death tsked. "Such trust you have in the Fool. How do you think I learned what my armor would do to your powers?"

I tottered on my feet. "H-he wouldn't!"

"It's nothing personal with him, just strategy and scheming."

I'd thought Matthew an innocent, wide-eyed boy.

"The Fool knew that I'd kill you if I had no means to control you. In essence, he's saved your life. So far, at least."

Not all bad is bad, Matthew had said. *Endgame, endgame.*

While I digested this gut-wrenching information, Death continued, "Deveaux didn't even like you, but he pursued you."

"You don't know anything!" I cried, though I could hear Jack's words: *Even when I hated you, I wanted you.*

"One benefit of my endless life? I have quite a grasp on human behavior. How triumphant the mortal must have felt to claim you, to *steal* you from his dead brother."

Though everything Death had told me hurt, I

refused to let him undermine what I'd found with Jack. "Maybe he did target me. But his feelings grew from that. You'll have to do better than this."

"Do better? As you wish, creature." With an evil grin, he said, "Deveaux killed your mother."

34

MATTHEW! Answer me this minute!

I'd just reached my tower, was nearly hyperventilating from Death's reveal.

In his mocking tone, the Reaper had explained that not only had Jack ended Mom's life so I'd run away with him, but that Matthew—my supposed best friend and ally—had known all along and decided not to tell me.

I'd stormed out, calling Death a liar and much worse. But I feared deep down that the bastard had spoken the truth.

—Empress?—

Death told me things about my mother. About Jack. Did the Reaper lie to me?

—No.—

I squeezed my eyes shut. *Matthew, why didn't you tell me? Why let me be with Jack?* I replayed his behavior the morning Mom had passed away. He'd been shaken, almost stunned. Though the Army of the Southeast had been closing in on us, he'd tried so hard to give Mom a decent burial—I'd thought as a kindness to her, or even to me. Now I realized it might have been guilt that had driven him.

I'd slept with that boy, had given him my heart. And all the while he'd known what he'd done. He'd berated *me* for keeping things from him? Then he'd looked me in the eyes and said, "I got no secrets, *peekôn*."

Other than escorting my mother to the other side? He was worse than Death!

When I'd explained to Jack that nothing was more important than trust, he'd assured me that I could trust him alone. No wonder Matthew had called him Dee-vee-oh. Devious!

Maybe you could've given me a heads-up, telling me not to fall in love with him?

—*Whenever he helps, he hurts.*—

How many times had Matthew told me that?

—*Your mother wanted you gone before army descended. End was near.*—

Unless I could've gotten her help! Yes, she'd been in dire straits, but surely there had to have been a better way. *So Jack assisted her suicide while I was asleep in my bed? And he did it so I'd leave with him?*

Silence.

Because he'd been hard-up for me since learning I

was his brother's girl! So how'd he do it? Suffocated Mom with a pillow? I stifled a sob. *Helped her OD?*

—*I looked away.*—

Fury blazed inside me. Even with the cuff, my hair began turning red, my claws struggling to bud. *Looked away as she died?* It was like he'd . . . he'd deserted her. *You bastard! Why didn't you foresee what would happen to her, before she'd even gotten hurt? Maybe warned me not to let her go out?*

—*Matthew knows best.*—

His tone was eerie, his words a disturbing echo of his mother's—"Mother knows best"—when she'd been about to drown him. *This is unforgivable. What else have you kept from me? I trusted you!*

—*The Empress is my friend.*—

No longer! Don't ever contact me again!

—*I won't talk so loud.*— Then his presence in my head vanished.

I had never felt so betrayed and alone.

Since my mother's passing, Jack and Matthew had been the only constants in all this terror and misery; now those anchors were gone.

I was completely adrift, trapped in the Castle of Lost Time.

Tears pricked my eyes, and I let them fall.

35

Nearly a month had passed since that night of revelations, and I remained a wreck.

Hair tangled, face puffy, I sat on my bed in a nightgown, staring out the turret window into the dark. I absently petted Cyclops, who was sprawled beside me, and reflected on the days that kept passing.

The first week after, I'd tried to block out everything. The next week, I'd replayed Jack's behavior countless times. Since then, I'd been spiraling even lower, imagining how he might have done it. . . .

Walking in a fog, I'd wandered the halls of the manor. I hadn't felt the pouring rain as I scuffed across the grounds, shadowed at every second by Cyclops. I'd never cried again, but only because I sensed Death was always watching me, or Lark through the wolf.

The few times I'd seen Death outside, he'd been

sharpening his swords with those rhythmic movements, the ones that seemed to soothe him.

What the hell would he need soothing for? I was the one in a spiral—because of him.

I hadn't belonged in a nuthouse before. Now? I might. My grief over my mother's death had been reopened. After her passing, I'd been on the run for my life, mayhem around every corner; I'd had little time to think about how much I missed her.

Currently I had all the time in the world, and it was killing me.

At night, I dreamed of my life with Mom at Haven. I'd had reveries of sugarcane harvests and horseback riding. Of shelling pecans for pie and picking blackberries along the river. Mom and I had been happy before Matthew's disturbing visions had begun.

I remembered how she'd looked that last morning, pale, her chest still. She'd been clutching a photo of me, her, and Gran, taken during a time when life had been so good. . . .

This week, I'd climbed up to my tower and never come down. Lark kept leaving food at the door, but I rarely touched it, giving the spoils to the wolf.

Whenever Matthew called to me, I shut him down.

—*The Army grinds on, a windmill spins.*—

Tell that to one of your allies. I'm not among them.

Though tempted to demand from him how Jack had

hurt Mom, I decided that knowledge might send me over the edge.

I would've thought I'd miss communicating with Matthew more, but I found the absence of decoder-ring talk a profound relief—

My door suddenly opened.

Death. He was dressed in black jeans and a black cashmere V-neck that molded over his chest muscles, looking as impeccable as ever. But his eyes were dim.

"You ever hear of knocking?"

He rested his shoulder against the doorframe, arching a brow at finding Cyclops on the bed.

That wolf was about the only living thing I didn't want to strangle. I'd gotten used to having him around. Petting his frizzy fur was soothing.

Death studied my face.

"Come to gloat?" I asked. "Isn't this what you wanted? I recall you telling Lark that you like seeing me suffer."

"If you're going to languish up here, then I might as well end you."

"How did you expect me to react?"

"As you would have in the past—with a vengeance that would have made the earth tremble. You'd have sharpened your claws and bayed for the mortal's blood."

"Baying for blood? What will it take to convince you that I'm not that person?" I asked, even as my conscience whispered, *You wanted this man's blood when you attacked him, and Lark, and Ogen.*

"Nothing," he said firmly. "There is nothing you can do to convince me."

"Why are you here?"

"Determining if you plan to starve yourself. Our game is no fun if you're weak."

"Plan?" As if I had one.

"Before I was exiled from your thoughts, I understood your missions to be: kill me, and find your grandmother."

What was the point of either? I longed to see my last living relative, and I'd promised my mom I'd find her. But the more I remembered of Gran, the more I comprehended that she would expect me not only to play—but to win.

Could being with her tip me over the edge? What if I went full-on Empress, and never turned back to Evie?

"Even if you escaped this place, which is impossible," Death said, "you would never reach her. With your healing powers, you might be safe passing through the plague colonies, but there are still cannibals out there, including others unrelated to the Hierophant. Militias, Bagmen, and slavers swarm the roads and countryside. I know this; I ride those roads often. Wouldn't she be angry that you took such risks?"

I glanced up at Death. "So my plan should be to

wait here, docile, until you murder me? Along with the rest of your lackeys?"

Saying these words out loud was like a corner turned, a line crossed. One answer rang through me.

Never.

After my mother's sacrifice for me, I'd be damned if I rolled over now. I owed it to her to fight.

I had a new mission: self-preservation. I had to get this cuff off, so I could protect myself from Death. Sooner or later the novelty of having me here, his princess in the tower, would wear off.

I needed to be ready.

"Ah, and there's the conniving glint I'm used to seeing in my Empress's eyes." He appeared relieved, as if he'd just found more comfortable footing. "You've destroyed armies; it should take more than one mortal to bring about your downfall."

"Why didn't you tell me about Jack earlier? And Matthew? Why not just torpedo me from the beginning?" Jack and grief had grown intertwined in my mind. I couldn't separate them, could scarcely think about him without going down a rabbit hole.

"My reasons are my own. But I did warn you not to give Deveaux your innocence."

I rolled my eyes at his terminology. "Really, Father Time? And what business is it of yours anyway?"

He didn't deign to answer.

"At least tell me why you hate me so deeply. What

happened between the time you were raring to take me to your bed and when you began raring to take my head?" Had Death and I slept together? I had to know! "What did I do to you?"

"To know, you must remember." I thought he would leave at that, but he remained. He opened his mouth, then closed it. Was he casting about for something to say? Maybe a reason to stay?

After finding myself utterly alone in the world this last month, without friends or family, I'd garnered some insights into Death.

I'd known he lived a solitary existence. I'd known he trusted no one. But I'd questioned whether he preferred his life like that.

My misery had made me hypersensitive to his own, and now I had my answer.

No. No, he did not prefer this.

As I'd wandered down those hallways lined with his lifeless art, I'd realized that Lark was right—the house was haunted. By him. By his loneliness.

He acquired these grand collections because there was nothing else for him. I'd told him the game was all he'd ever really have; I saw the evidence of that in every room.

I tilted my head at him. "You'd rather be up here trading insults with me than sitting in your study all alone, wouldn't you?"

He stiffened. Bingo.

When I was young, Gran had often caught me staring at Death's Tarot card. She'd asked me if that card frightened me or made me really angry. I'd shaken my head firmly and told her it made me sad.

In other words, I'd felt sorry for him.

Gran had sputtered, "Why would you feel that way, Evie? He's a villain!"

My answer: *His horse looks sick, and he has no friends.* Maybe that had been my eight-year-old way of saying his life seemed like it'd be hell.

He camouflaged his bone-deep loneliness with arrogance. But there was no hiding it from me now. I told him, "You probably wish I was still trying to get on your good side, because at least then I'd ask you questions over breakfast. I'll bet you've gone an entire decade without being asked a single one."

Had his face paled? "You think you know me, yet you are as mistaken as ever," he said smoothly, but his shoulder muscles were bunched with tension. Without another word, he turned to go.

Lark appeared at the door, nearly running into him.

"Watch yourself, Fauna," he grated, rubbing his thumbs over his fingertips. "There is no greater pain or doom than touching my skin."

For everyone except me.

Wide-eyed, Lark backed away from him. "Sorry, boss. I-I forget."

"Maybe your visit with the Empress will be worth

the climb. Mine was tiresome." Then he was gone.

"I see you and my wolf are hitting it off." Lark sniffed, "He was always my least favorite. No depth perception in that one."

I buried my fingers in Cyclops's scruff. *She didn't mean it, boy.* "I suppose Death told you everything?"

"All he'd say is that you'd 'discovered some allies were enemies.' Judging by your brokenhearted reaction, I knew it had to be the Cajun."

And Matthew.

From behind her back, Lark produced a box, tossing it on my bed.

"What's that?"

"Not a Jack-in-the-box, if that's what you're wondering."

"I really hate you."

She grinned. "Open it, asshole."

With a glare, I did. "Workout gear?" Sports bras, athletic shorts, leggings. Even a little tennis skirt.

"I go to the gym every afternoon," Lark said. "Join me later. You were a cheerleader, right? A dancer?"

I nodded. I'd been a better gymnast, but I'd enjoyed ballet more, had taken classes through my sophomore year.

"You could show me some routines."

I set the garments away. "You're doing this out of the kindness of your heart?"

"I'm doing it because I didn't get to make fun of

cheerleaders enough before the Flash hit. You're my only hope to meet quota."

"And?" I could all but see the strings attached.

"Hold on." Her eyes flashed red. Checking via some animal if the coast was clear?

In a lower voice, she said, "Because if you dance, he won't be able to stay away."

"Why would you think I might care about that?"

"Again, not stupid here. This is your only play, the one way you can survive. Look, we've both got approaching expiration dates, and we've both got end-games. Maybe our paths can intersect every now and then."

Yes, Lark's card had once been associated with single-minded purpose. Had she been working toward her end-game all along?

My own agenda was self-preservation, but how could I trust her? When I remained unconvinced, she said, "I'm not all bad."

Which reminded me of the first time we'd met Lark, when I'd asked Matthew about her. *Good. Bad. Good* . . . Decoder-ring talk. She'd briefly been my ally, then my enemy. Was she to be my ally once more?

She headed toward the door. "I'll see you later."

Alone, I recalled a time before the Flash when my mom's invitation to an old-boys'-network meeting had gotten "lost in the mail." As the sole female farmer in our parish, she'd been spitting mad. I'd tried to tell her it was their loss, that they didn't matter. She'd held up her hand and said, "Sometimes you just need to be mad or sad, Evie. Sometimes you just need to let it happen. But put a cap on it, then get back to happy."

Could I claw my way out of this depression, getting back to happy? Or at least in the realm of . . . ?

The first step was blocking out painful thoughts. Just as I'd done in school, I would refuse to think about hurtful things. Basically anything to do with Jack. He was in my past and needed to stay there. Matthew as well.

The two of them equaled pain.

That afternoon, I pulled on a red sports bra and the tennis skirt, combing my hair into a ponytail. I grabbed a towel, opened the door wide for Cyclops, then set out.

I found Lark in the spacious gym with her other wolves, music going. She trained in front of the mirrors, punching dummies. "Hey, look who's joining the land of the living," she said.

"So says the girl who lives in Death's house."

Cyclops trotted past me, sniffing his comrades' butts in greeting.

"Wanna get started?" In a fake bubbly tone, she said, "Ready, set, go, team!"

"Yeah." I tossed down my towel. "It was just like that."

"Show me some moves."

The floor had a thin layer of padding, so I did an easy roundoff. Another. I worked up to a back handspring. Lark laughed when I did a series of exaggerated pirouettes. God, I'd missed this. I could hardly believe I was using my muscles for something other than fleeing or fighting.

The barbed cuff wasn't fun as my bicep moved, but I'd grown so used to that pain, I wouldn't let it get in the way of my enjoyment.

As I danced, I realized I *could* claw my way out of this despair. All I had to do was keep my mind off the ally who'd betrayed me, and the boy who'd broken my heart.

I began sweating, pleased that I hadn't lost much flexibility. To test myself, I lifted my leg behind me, grabbing my ankle for a standing split.

Death chose that moment to stride by, doing a jaw-slackened double take before moving on. Yet then he eased back to lean against the doorframe—with his eyes full of . . . undisguised lust.

In my bra and skirt, I had everything covered; but as usual, I felt bare as he looked at me. I hadn't even felt this naked with Jack, who'd actually seen me without clothes. *Don't think about him!*

I kept stretching, refusing to let Death ruin this. "Never seen a girl warming up before?"

"Not one I wouldn't kill with my touch," he said in that raspy voice.

"Oh. Speaking of which, is today the day you're going to gank me?"

"Not yet, creature." When his starry eyes glowed, I barely stifled a gasp at my reaction. Just from his look, my glyphs had begun stirring.

Which made him scrub a shaking palm over his mouth.

"My Gawd"—Lark fanned herself—"sexual tension, much? Get a manor, kids."

Death shot Lark a scornful look, then strode away.

In a lower tone, she said, "What'd I tell you, Evie? You're a lock for the next Mrs. Death. You planned to wreck the entire game? Bet that'd do it."

I wanted to roll my eyes, but I couldn't quite take them off that doorway.

"Don't worry. He'll be back. And when he is," Lark continued, all excited, "I'm gonna get scarce and let nature take over. . . ."

Well into the night, I awoke, panting for breath, my glyphs illuminating the room. I'd had another sensual dream of Death, felt like I was aching for him.

I could all but feel his lips on mine, could all but feel *my* lips—on his body.

I didn't understand it. He still wanted me dead, still hated me.

How could I dream of kissing him, when he dreamed of killing me?

36

"I might be immortal, but I'm still a red-blooded male," Death had told me out on the road. Every day for the last week, he'd proved it.

The first couple of days, he'd made sure he passed the gym whenever I was down there, poking his head in for a look. The third day, he'd entered, taken a seat on a bench, then pretended to read from a fading newspaper. Now he came every day—while Lark remained as scarce as promised.

He always acted so reluctant, so grudging, as if he'd been dragged by his spurs into the same space as me. But his lustful looks followed my every move, tension emanating from him.

Lark was right. The attraction between us sparked like electricity.

While my emotions had been leveling out, his seemed to be approaching some kind of troubling fever-pitch. In the training yard, his practice had intensified to a brutal degree. No longer was I seeing precise movements and harnessed aggression. No longer did that weird feeling of satisfaction slip up on me.

Watching him now was like watching a berserker.

I played with fire. I was tempting Death, possibly getting closer to a cuff removal, but at what cost?

Today when he strode through the door, I knew something was different. As I warmed up, he abandoned any pretense of reading, sinking back on a couch that I didn't remember seeing yesterday. His expression seemed to say, "To hell with it, done fighting."

"No paper today, Death?"

"Here solely as a spectator." An avid one. When I stretched, he leaned forward, elbows on his knees.

"I've been a spectator for you too," I said. "Your workouts have gotten really . . . energetic?"

"I often train harder when my thoughts are . . ."

"In turmoil?" I supplied, stretching my hamstrings.

"In transition," he said, tilting his head to keep his gaze on my ass.

Whenever his eyes raked over me like that, I had to admit I experienced a toe-curling rush. Still, I cleared my throat; he gave me an unapologetic look.

"So, Death, is today the day you're going to kill me?"

For the first time, his answer was different: "There's all the time in the world for that, is there not? For now, I'll watch you dance."

Deeming this a good moment to strike, I crossed over to him. "You can take this cuff off me, you know." Standing before him, I gazed down at his perfect face. "I won't ever hurt you."

"I could never give you free run of my home without it."

This close, his sandalwood scent swept me up. "I'm not like I used to be. You have to sense that." I eased my legs between his knees.

At once, his eyes flared brighter. "I trust no one fully in the game. Keep your distance." There was enough steel in his tone for me to back away.

I simply didn't know him well enough not to find him intimidating at times. I managed an indifferent shrug, then began to dance, soon losing myself in my thoughts.

Which turned straight toward last night's dream, the one that had starred the man before me. He was my Arcana enemy. So why could I still taste him on my tongue?

As I bent and swayed, working up a sweat, I replayed each second of that dream. I'd run my lips over all the runes on his chest, tracing them with my tongue before descending—

At that moment, I caught him staring at my chest, gaze focused on the peaks of my breasts beneath my sweat-dampened bra. My glyphs stirred, and there was nothing I could do to disguise them.

"What are you thinking about, creature?" His words were husky.

Licking your runes? Thank God he couldn't read my thoughts anymore. Face flushing, I grasped for something to say. "I bet you were expecting a taller Empress this time around." Lame.

"I would change *nothing* about your appearance."

When we locked eyes in the mirror, his burning gaze made even more heat cascade through my body.

Death rose with that lethal grace and strode toward me. I swallowed. Would he try to kiss me? And what would I do if he did?

He stopped short a slight distance away. "Come to my study this evening."

"Wow, actual permission to enter?"

"There is a game from long ago. Join me in a hand. If you win, I'll give you a boon. Lose, and you'll give me one."

A boon? Maybe I could finally get him to tell me about our past interactions! "I'll be there. What's the game?"

"You'll see. . . ."

Plagued with curiosity, I'd showered, then peered into the closet. What to wear? My gaze was immediately drawn to anything red, my favorite color.

I settled on jeans and a poppy-red cashmere shell with a matching sweater. On the scale from whoresome

366 -+- KRESLEY COLE

to wholesome, my twin set was definitely skewing toward the latter. At least I could remove the sweater, baring my arms.

He seemed to prefer my hair loose, so I left it down.

It was like getting ready for a date. In a way, this *was* a date. A date with Death? *Cringe.*

If my thoughts drifted toward another boy, I shut them down ruthlessly.

In fact, as I made my way downstairs, I felt excitement for the first time in ages. I knew I'd learn more from Death tonight, and I wouldn't be spending hours alone up in my turret.

When I knocked at the Reaper's study, Cyclops plunked down onto the floor in the hallway.

Instead of calling for me to enter, Death came to open the door. His eyes lightened when looking at me, and I felt myself smiling in response. A good start to the evening.

He ushered me to a seat, all polished manners. I guessed since he'd invited me here, he was going to act the gentleman. He'd certainly dressed up more, in an expensive-looking black button-down and slacks. His belt and shoes looked like they'd cost more than an entire sugarcane crop.

Outside, the rain came down in torrents. Inside this room, we were warm, the space lit only by a fire and candles. I removed my sweater as I sat.

Then I caught sight of a tome on his desk, recalling that my pet/guard had eaten one of Death's kids. *The Prince.*

"What is it, Empress? You just went pale."

So observant. "I, um, have to come clean with you about something. The book you loaned me . . . is totaled."

He placed a glass of vodka in front of me. "Pardon?"

"It's gone." I ran my hand over my nape. It felt like all his other books were glaring at me accusingly.

"How did this come to pass?" he asked, returning to his seat. His expression was impassive. I couldn't gauge his anger level.

"I'm so sorry, but it's never going to be returned."

He steepled his fingers. Before I'd seen that as an arrogant gesture, but now it struck me as a more thoughtful one. "Strange that you do not wish to implicate anyone else."

"You already know what happened, don't you?"

"You could have blamed the wolf—or Fauna, for that matter."

"Both of them are kind of growing on me, okay?" I couldn't believe I'd made this connection, but at times Lark's attitude reminded me a little of . . . Mel's. "If it makes you feel better, I was sick with guilt over this."

"Why?"

I frowned. "Because I took responsibility for

something that belongs to you, that you treasure, and it was destroyed in my care." When I thought of all his efforts to safeguard these books, my face heated. "And it was"—I squirmed—"your favorite one of all."

"I would gladly have forfeited the book to see this."

Huh? "My discomfort?"

"The evidence of your empathy. And your honesty." He tilted his head at me, like he was seeing something new.

"You're not mad?"

"Fortunately for you, the *Italian* edition is my favorite."

Was he teasing me? I found myself smiling again, relaxing. "So, what are we going to play?"

"Tarocchi." From his drawer, he took out a deck of cards, old-fashioned looking ones that were longer than regular playing cards.

He handed the deck to me. They were . . . Tarot cards. "What's this? Are you going to read my future? That wouldn't be very fair, since it's already in your hands."

He arched his brows. "The cards have been used for fortune-telling—and for play. Tarocchi is a trick-taking game."

"Like bridge?"

"A little more cutthroat."

"Figures."

As I familiarized myself with the deck, he explained the rules. The twenty-two Major Arcana were numbered trump cards that overruled all of the fifty-six Minor Arcana. Those cards were divided into four suits: wands, swords, pentacles, and cups.

"Do Minor Arcana exist in real life? Like we do?" Several of the images on the minor cards were as frightful as the major ones. The ten of swords depicted a bloody corpse stabbed through with ten blades.

"Some games I see evidence of them everywhere; others I see nothing."

Interesting. "Wait, my card has less trump value than yours does?"

"In this, the game makers were wise." He continued recounting the rules—describing bids, kitties, discards—concluding with, "If you are my wild card in real life, *il Matto*, the Fool, is the one for this game."

Matto. Matthew. Wouldn't think about him.

"Until you get the hang of this, I'll assist you with your bids."

Though there were a lot of rules to remember, I tried to boil it down. "Lead low, follow suit, and play trump cards only when necessary." I handed him back the deck.

"That'll do for now." Death expertly shuffled the cards with those refined and deadly hands. He dealt, then motioned for me to lead.

I played a two of cups, he a four. We went on from there. I won the first trick, stacking the cards into my new pile. "Beginner's luck?"

"Indeed."

When I grew more comfortable with the rules, enough to play and talk at the same time, I asked, "So what do you do in your off seasons? The centuries between these contests?"

He cast me a suspicious look. "Why do you want to know that?"

"Because I'm curious. You act like no one has ever asked you about yourself."

He downed his vodka, motioning me to join him. *And always with the refills.* "Of course they've asked. When probing for weaknesses."

"Weaknesses? I'd be happy just to know your name. Or even where you were originally from. Let me guess: Russia?"

"Are you finished?"

"How could me knowing these things hurt your game?" I asked, though I couldn't blame him for his evasiveness. From what I'd heard—and seen in visions of the past—the Empress hadn't been one to trust.

Was she now?

"We'll speak of something else," he said shortly, "or nothing at all."

"Fine. Let's talk about your place. How long have you lived here? And what made you choose such an isolated spot in . . . Virginia?" Okay, maybe I was prob-ing a bit.

"Are we in Virginia? Regardless, I've lived here for thirty years. I chose the property because it met all my strategic requirements: altitude above sea level, stone exterior, remote, defensible." With a pointed look at me, he added, "Little vegetation." The polar opposite of Haven.

How sad that he'd spent decades preparing for some mysterious future catastrophe. What kind of life was that, just thinking about what could possibly go wrong?

Determined to stay off hot-button subjects—the game, his past, his nationality, my former crew—I said, "Do you know how to drive a car?" Or was he like those anachronistic knights in movies, afraid of all technology?

That corner of his lips curled. A Death grin. "Yes, creature. I own several."

I relaxed, already halfway buzzed from the vodka. "That's right—you were crazy rich before the Flash. How'd you make so much money?"

"I started my career early." At my raised brows, he said, "Assassin. My deadly gift made me well suited for the job. A single handshake could bring down a mon-archy. The money grew over the centuries."

His tone was blank; I couldn't tell how he felt about his past deeds.

"So that's where you got those crowns." Trying to keep things light, I said, "Admit it—you wear them when no one's around. Play air tennis with the scepters?"

"No, Empress. I do not."

"Can I, can I?"

On the verge of grinning, he said, "No, Empress, you may not."

After that we talked more freely, the ice broken. I asked him which of the languages he spoke were hardest to learn ("Arabic, or possibly Hungarian") and whether he watched TV ("Not if I can help it").

He too steered clear of sensitive subjects when he asked me how old I was when I'd started dancing ("Three—and even you would've gone *awww* if you'd seen me in a tutu") and what was my favorite medium for art ("Oil paint, for wall murals").

The game was brisk. I'd win a trick, then Death would. All the while, our conversation was lively. As we repeatedly one-upped each other's cards, we bandied back and forth, an ebb and flow as natural as tides. It felt so familiar.

Which confused me. I could swear I was attuned to this man in a way that I hadn't been with Jack.

The Cajun and I had never conversed like this. Was that because we'd never had the opportunity? Or because we'd never been on the same page? Jack had even said, "We do best when we doan talk." *Stop thinking about him!*

During a particularly point-rich round, Death said, "This game is close." Both our piles of taken cards looked equal, but I had no idea how many points were in each.

He played the Empress card. "I've had this beauty in my keeping," he said, voice raspy.

The double meaning made my toes curl. Not to be outdone, I played my own trump, one I'd been saving. Death. "I've been holding on to him for dear life," I said, suggestively tracing my finger over the length of the card.

His lips parted in surprise. Score one for Evie.

When I collected the pile, I gazed down at his image. "You never use your scythe. Why do you carry it with you?"

In that dry tone, he answered, "I'm a traditionalist."

I laughed. Was I really having this conversation with the Grim Reaper? My chuckles got worse and worse, until my eyes were watering.

Both corners of his lips curled, almost a real smile.

My laughter died. I was starstruck. "You should smile more often."

I looked at him, really looked at him, in a way I hadn't allowed myself to before.

Of course, I'd acknowledged that Death was a gorgeous, educated, sophisticated knight who was rich in luxuries. Like me, he was an Arcana.

But on occasion, I spied hints of the man behind the knight. Such as right now, when he appeared uncomfortable under my scrutiny and a flush spread over his chiseled cheekbones. I smiled when he pulled at his collar.

I could finally admit that these hints were devastatingly attractive to me. With my feelings for Jack blunted by lies and betrayal, would this attraction grow? Especially since Death had stopped threatening to murder me all the time?

Matthew had told me to beware the Touch of Death. Since contact with the Reaper's skin didn't harm me, maybe Matthew had meant something deeper—like involvement with Death, as a man, would prove dangerous. What if Death's power over me was my budding infatuation with him?

Clearing his throat, Death led another round. I found myself paying more attention to him, playing by rote. I put my elbow on his desk, propping my chin on the back of my hand as I noted new details about him.

The blond tips of his eyelashes. The way the end of a rune peeked from his open collar. The faint line in the center of his fuller bottom lip.

Maybe I was just buzzed, but I didn't think he'd ever looked more handsome than right at that moment. My glyphs began to wind along my arms.

At the end of the round, he collected the remaining cards, sifting through his pile. "I've won the night then." He gave my arms a quizzical look. "You can't expect to defeat another Arcana if you allow yourself to get distracted, Empress."

Yet another double meaning. "Maybe the Empress would rather get distracted than play at all."

He inclined his head, as if to say, "Touché."

But I'd spoken the truth. I still had no interest in this Arcana contest and continued to believe that securing allies was key. Why couldn't Death be mine?

My mission to take down this knight was evolving. What if I could win him over as my ally, as a friend, as—

"Tell me your thoughts, creature."

"Hmm? I was wondering what boon you'd want from me?"

His gaze fell to my lips, eyes alight. "There is one . . ."

I held my breath.

Yet then he stood abruptly, shutting himself down, that light dimming. "I believe I'll save it for another time. The hour grows late."

"Late? So?" This was A.F. Did time really matter? Today the sun had risen for scant minutes, merely hovering on the horizon. "Do you have to be on Ash Campus early tomorrow? At the University of Nothing Matters?"

He crossed to the study door, opening it for me. Booting me out?

I rose, tying my sweater around my waist, wondering what to say. *Had a blast, Reap. We'll do this at my place next time.*

I'd just frowned to find Cyclops missing when Death joined me in the hallway. "I'll escort you back."

"I do know my way."

"Indulge me."

I teased, "Chivalry never died for you, huh?"

"I *am* a knight," he replied, making me grin.

On the way up the stairs, I remained at his side. If he was bothered to be pressed together in the narrow stairwell, he didn't show it. His shirtsleeve brushed my bare arm, and again—

My breath hitched when skin touched skin. Death had furtively shoved up his sleeve? Was that his cuff button pinging on a step?

With each contact, his lids seemed to grow heavier, his eyes gone starry once more.

Now that I was hyper-aware of the loneliness inside Death, I'd begun having this overriding urge to ease it. To be fair, what woman wouldn't?

Yet at the door to my room, we stood in awkward silence. It was as if he were dropping me off at the porch of Haven after a date.

The spacious landing felt small to me. "Can we have a rematch tomorrow night?"

He leaned his shoulder against the wall. "Perhaps."

"If I'd won tonight, I was going to ask you to tell me about our past."

"You wouldn't have asked me for longer to live?"

I shook my head. "You're not going to hurt me."

In the muted light of the landing, his gaze was so brilliant as he said, "Will I not?"

"I know you enjoyed tonight. Why deprive yourself of me?"

With a perplexed expression, he turned toward the stairs. But I thought I heard him murmur, "Why indeed?"

I couldn't tell if he was being sarcastic, or asking himself a genuine question.

Once he'd gone, I floated into my room, pleasantly buzzed, marveling at how much fun I'd had. Cyclops was already on the bed. As I changed into a nightgown, Matthew tentatively called for me. —*Empress?*—

I was in such a good mood, I felt bulletproof. I allowed him in. *What is it?*

—*The Empress is my friend. I miss Evie.*—

The pang in my chest shocked me with its intensity. I missed him too. Even after everything. Didn't mean I could forgive him.

—*Don't be angry.*—

You hurt me, Matthew. And I wonder if you even care. Maybe he was scheming right now.

—*We need you. We fall to ruin.*—

Fall to ruin. *J'tombe en botte.* Jack had told me that the night at Finn's place when he'd bared his soul to me.

Or at least, select, edited parts of it.

Jack and Matthew weren't my responsibility anymore. The two of them equaled pain. Still, I couldn't stop myself from asking, *Did you tell Jack what I learned?* That I knew he'd helped my mother kill herself, then lied to me repeatedly?

Now that I was in a somewhat better state of mind, I could see things more clearly, accepting that Jack would never have hurt my mom on his own. His motives might not have been pure, but my fierce mother could be . . . persuasive.

If she'd decided her suicide was the only way to save my life, then Jack had never stood a chance. I could only imagine the toll that night had taken on him, a boy who despised violence against women.

When he'd worked so hard on that dinner for us the last night at Haven, making it as nice as he could, they both must have known it would be her last. Which made me realize that Jack *was* devious. By his behavior, I never could have guessed what he was on the cusp of doing.

Jack had said he didn't have secrets. Another lie. And I sensed I'd only scratched the surface of them. At least Death had been up-front about his continual impulses to kill me.

—I told Jack.—

And?

Matthew sighed. *—And.—*

What does that mean?

—You're in my eyes.—

A vision began, and I saw a blur of Jack. He was frenzied, tearing at his hair as he yelled—

NO, Matthew! I shook my head hard. *No, I don't want that!* I'd only recently gotten my emotions under control. I wasn't *that* bulletproof.

It faded. *—Empress?—*

I don't want to see him. I can't. I couldn't handle any more rabbit holes!

—I feel your heart; it actually aches.— The same words he'd told me on the night Jack had confessed his feelings to me.

You need to get him far from the game, Matthew. It's not his war to fight, and what he hopes for isn't going to happen anyway. I couldn't be with someone who reminded me of grief, someone I couldn't trust. *You need to make him go.* It was for the best, anyway.

Over these weeks, I'd come to accept that I didn't belong with a non-Arcana, which Matthew had told me again and again. Jack, for all his faults, deserved a long life. He wouldn't get it if he continued to wade into our deadly contest.

For the best . . .

—*You're not ready, Empress. The machines won't end without Death.*—

Yet another decoder-ring statement. My head started hurting as I tried to make sense of his words. *I'm almost afraid to ask.*

—*You sail on weeks of lull, then the storm. The game begins in earnest. You must be ready to strike. . . .*—

37

"I want to show you something," Death said as he escorted me back to my turret. He'd done this for each of the three nights we'd played cards this week—would've been four but for another one of his excursions.

When he'd returned that next night after, he'd caught me checking his hand, telling me, "Relax. I'm still only one ahead of you."

Now I asked him, "Show me what?"

He ushered me toward the gym. "A surprise."

It was as if he knew I needed cheering. The sun had never risen today. Endless night.

Would I grow even weaker? All day, I'd been filled with disquiet. Lark had as well. Even her animals had seemed anxious. Ogen had howled like a maniac. . . .

When Death turned on the gym lights, I spied an unbelievable new addition. In one corner, in front of the wall of mirrors, a ballet barre had been installed. A pair of ballet shoes were tied by the laces over the barre.

A shocked sound left my lips.

Somehow Death had found a barre and toe shoes. Had made the effort to. That's where he'd been?

"I believe the shoes are in your size."

As I stared, I imagined him using those refined fingers of his to tie those laces just so. The idea was so sensual to me that I shivered.

He was doing a much better job at seduction than I ever had. I gazed up at him. "How?"

"I source things. It's a talent of mine."

He did have a power-over-everything-I-survey vibe. And it was sexy. "You seem to have a lot of talents." Was there anything he couldn't do?

Well, except for trust me. Each time we had really seemed to be getting somewhere this week, breaking down the barriers between us, he would shut down.

"Are you pleased?" he asked.

Pleased didn't even begin to describe my feelings. Ballet. After the apocalypse.

I'd believed that part of my life had been burned away along with everything else. Now I had all the time in the world, toe shoes, and a studio. Despite the rain, I still had enough energy to dance because I ate well, and I slept in a lush, warm bed.

All because of the man before me.

The gift of this opportunity was mind-boggling.

Before I thought better of it, I'd stood on tiptoe to press a kiss on his cheek.

He stepped back with his unnatural speed. "Ah-ah, creature."

"Why do you shut me out? You know any plans I had against you are done."

His fists were clenched so hard, I thought he'd break the bones in his hands. But not with anger. He seemed to be thrumming with the need to touch me. "Then what is your plan now?"

"I'm getting back to happy." I explained what my mom had said. "That's all I want to do."

"That involves kissing me?"

In a softer voice, I admitted, "Yes, you. I've enjoyed being with you this week. We get along well. And you were right before—I don't believe you've ever lied to me. That means a lot." There was also one other thing.

After months here, I finally admitted to myself that I desired . . . Death. Not just attraction, but a full-out physical need for him.

He gave a sharp shake of his head. "There's still a game, with immortality at stake."

I frowned. "I don't want to be an immortal."

"Would you not? Never to grow old, to sicken, or die?"

"If there's one thing I know about myself, it's that I don't do well being alone. I'm not built that way.

Besides, winning would mean hurting you. I have no intention of doing that."

"Then you don't mind wearing the cilice? If what you say is true, then you'll never ask me to remove it?"

I nibbled my bottom lip. "I worry about Ogen. And it hurts when I overuse this arm."

Death exhaled. "Even if I wished things could be different, they cannot."

"It's like you've vowed never to let me get close. Whatever I did to you in the past must've been terrible."

He gave a noncommittal shrug, but I sensed emotions churning in him.

Deciding not to press, I crossed to the barre and collected the shoes. They were too precious to let out of my sight. When I untied the laces, I shivered again to think of his fingers brushing this silk. "Thank you . . ." I trailed off, wishing I knew his given name.

He appeared uncomfortable with my gratitude. "You think I did this for you? In case you haven't noticed, I enjoy watching you."

I quirked a brow. "*Enjoy* is a bit mild for what you do, huh?"

He hiked those muscular shoulders. "It's late. To your room, then."

On the landing, I noticed he kept his distance. With a sigh, I asked him, "If I'm the weakest of Arcana, why this continued caution around me?"

"Perhaps because you're the most tempting of Arcana."

I smiled. "I'll wear you down."

With his eyes emotionless and dark, he said, "You cannot."

Oh, we'll see. Death didn't know this about me, but I liked the occasional battle of wills.

Alone in my room, I lay in bed, lovingly tracing the ballet-shoe laces with my fingers. I couldn't seem to stop smiling. Amazing. The more I was around Death, the more I liked him.

For the last eleven months, I'd been terrified of him. Now I couldn't wait to wake up so I could see him again.

That night I fell asleep with my fingers threaded through the laces and a smile on my face.

When my dreams of Death arose, I welcomed them.

38

Today, I went almost an entire hour without thinking about Jack....

39

"Do the dance you performed yesterday," Death commanded with the authority of a man who was never denied. He had an arm stretched over the back of the sofa, so at home with himself, with his world.

"You liked that one, huh?" It'd been one of my more daring pieces. Over the last few weeks, I'd pushed myself hard, reclaiming most of the skills I'd lost. And Death had been there almost every day, watching each trickle of sweat.

As I started to dance, I reflected on my new life. Compared to the outside world, Death's lair was proving to be a paradise. Here, I could dance, read, and even paint.

Courtesy of this man, I now had the supplies for that pastime as well. I'd started painting the walls of my room—because I had a room, a place where I could rest my head every night.

Scenes of sugarcane fields and verdant forests had begun taking shape, much like my mural at Haven. There, in the sunny days pre-Flash, I'd depicted dark clouds over fields. Here, in this shadowy apocalypse, I painted sun-dappled landscapes.

Just as Lark had told me, I could pad down to the kitchen, and there was always delicious food. Apocalyptic delicacies like fresh bread and butter.

In the afternoons (hard to call them that, since they were still dark), she and I would watch movies with dozing wolves, a fire crackling, and steaming popcorn. Sometimes we went "shopping," combing the attic, which was filled with vintage clothes.

I regularly found myself laughing at her humor. Today she'd given me a broad wink about all the time I'd been spending alone with Death, then said, "I feel like a teapot who's about to sing 'Tale as Old as Time.'"

Maybe I was bonding with her because she reminded me of Mel, who'd been like a sister to me. Maybe it was because Lark was the only other girl here.

Or maybe I was learning that nothing was black and white.

Bad and good were getting blurred in my head. We were players in a game that would make killers of us all; and the man who'd been my standard of Ultimate Evil . . . had sourced ballet shoes for me.

Up was down. Down was up.

As the storms of the late summer raged, Death and

I met each night. In his warm study, we would talk into the early hours or sit on his couch before the fire, quietly reading from his collection.

I'd started *The Odyssey*, had just gotten to the part where Odysseus and his men landed on the island of the lotus-eaters. Those who ate of the lotus didn't mind their isolation, never wanting to continue their voyage.

Death had read the story in the original Greek. Naturally.

He and I were meshing more and more. There was no one else in the world that he could touch, and no one I knew who could discuss history and literature and art with me.

Being with him felt . . . inevitable. But in a good way.

He'd complimented me on how quickly I learned, seeming delighted to teach me more. If Jack had awakened my desire, Death was enlivening my mind, attracting me in a way I'd never experienced before.

I knew he enjoyed my company as well. Oftentimes I'd glance up from my page and find his gaze on me, eyes brimming with satisfaction.

Much as they were right at this minute, as he watched me dance.

My dreams of him continued, escalating into even more erotic territory. Last night, I'd dreamed he'd peeled off my workout clothes, lifting me atop the barre so he could lick my damp skin, wedging his hips between my thighs. . . .

Yet if I ever admitted to him how much fun I had with him, he'd grow distant. If he ever came close to laughing, he'd close himself off.

It was a constant push/pull with him.

Occasionally, he left the compound. I'd figured he must be out hunting, at least some of the time, but he hadn't returned with a new icon, and I'd heard nothing on Arcana Radio. Plus, Lark's laminated player list— the little twit actually did keep it on the fridge door— had had no updates since the Star.

Well, other than her scratching my title out and scribbling in "The Unclean One." Har.

Whenever Death left, I was out of sorts. Missing him? I'd admitted to myself that I desired him, but could I be feeling something deeper for a man like him?

He was so often on my mind, I had little time to regret and pine for things that might have been. Though I'd reestablished contact with Matthew—sparingly—I still felt betrayed by him for looking away.

And by Jack.

Whenever Matthew popped into my head, he'd predicted more doom and gloom. At least, I thought he had. He was making less and less sense. Once it was —*The lightning hides the monster.*— And another time —*You must slice yourself when the altar is empty.*—

I'd asked him about my history with Death. His reply? —*Better worry about your future. Devil is in details.*— No explanation for that had been given.

Again, I'd instructed Matthew to get Jack somewhere safe, but the boy responded with gibberish. Though I'd tried to listen better, I'd grown increasingly exasperated, my head pounding. . . .

The days had been flying by. The summer-that-wasn't waned, my seventeenth birthday nearing. The only drawback to this sanctuary was Ogen. I rarely saw him, and then only when he was tearing across the compound. I could have sworn one of his horns was even shorter.

Despite my continued uneasiness over the Devil's fits, I felt this bleak manor was becoming—

"What are you musing about behind those pretty eyes?" Death asked in a low tone.

Without thinking, I said, "That your home is becoming mine."

Looking like I'd slapped him, he rose, striding toward the door.

While I wondered why he was reacting like this, he grated over his shoulder, "You make me think dangerous thoughts, creature."

Dangerous thoughts. In transition, or in turmoil? Would he now go train in the storm, burning off aggression in a frenzy?

I didn't know how much longer we could continue like this before something gave.

40

"Why did you not dance today?" Death asked.

I'd just taken a seat on his study couch, curling my feet up under me. "I didn't sleep very well." Yes, I'd had dreams of him almost every night, but last night I'd been bombarded by scenes so lifelike, I'd awakened confused to find myself alone.

When he sat beside me, though not too close, I swallowed hard. I wondered what he'd do if I kissed him.

He was studying my expression. Could he see my cheeks heating?

"You looked flushed. Are you ill? The mortal here worked in medicine before the Flash."

"No, I'm fine."

"Very well," he said, looking unconvinced. "I wanted to tell you that I leave tonight for another trip."

My spirits sank. "How long will you be gone?"

"Two or three days. Will you miss me, Empress?"

Not to talk with him into the night? "Yes," I admitted.

"And I'll worry about you. I wish you wouldn't go."

My answer seemed to rattle him worse than my wet T-shirt had. He moved to sit behind his desk, clearing his throat before saying, "Fauna tells me you both fear Ogen when I'm away."

"You've had to dock his horns again, haven't you?"

Curt nod.

"I wouldn't fear him as much if you removed my cuff."

His expression darkened. "You know I can't do that. Would it make you feel better if I locked him out of the compound?"

Best I was going to get. "Yes, thank you."

As ever, he seemed uncomfortable with my gratitude, changing the subject. "Fauna also tells me tomorrow is your birthday."

"I suppose it's not a big deal for you, since you've had thousands of them."

"If you ask me for a boon, perhaps I'll provide it."

I rose with excitement. "Like a birthday present?" I sauntered behind his desk, trespassing into his comfort zone. I hopped up on the desktop beside his chair, my thigh inches from his hand.

He clenched his fist. "I've warned you. I won't be seduced."

I said softly, "If we weren't competitors, perhaps you could be? Why do you insist on playing this game?"

"Because it is what we were born to do."

A non-answer. "You don't strike me as the type who would blindly follow the dictates of some long-ago gods."

"It is so much a part of me I wouldn't know how to extricate myself."

"You called me willfully naïve, but you're stubbornly stuck in the past. Won't you even *imagine* a different future?" My temper was getting the better of me.

So was his. "I play—because there is no choice! You think I haven't tried to upend the game?"

"You? You were one of the ones to make a truce?" My surprise appeared to infuriate him.

He shot to his feet, beginning to pace the study. "Talk of ending the game is a blasphemy—I was twice a blasphemer!"

"Don't you, well, live for this?"

He raked a hand through his blond hair. "I wanted to change my existence so much, my bloody Tarot card is associated with change to this day." Voice rising with each word, he said, "This game is a hell we've all been damned into. It's designed to madden us. The most intelligent Arcana ever to play is called the Fool. The one who least wanted to kill was named Death. And you, Empress, rule over nothing!"

"You don't *need* to kill?"

He turned to his vodka, drank. "Need. Want. Doesn't matter. I do it." When he refilled, the bottle clattered against the glass. "If any of these Arcana knew what awaited the winner, they would not be so keen to snatch a victory from me. They would thank me for reaping their lives."

"I had no idea you felt this way." Understatement. He wasn't merely weary of killing, he despised it.

Another glass down. "You have no idea about me at all."

"You're right. And now that I'm thinking about it, I do want a boon. I want to ask you questions about your life and past, and have you answer them honestly." Still atop his desk, I reached over and took the bottle from him to refill his glass.

"And so I am snared?" With an exhalation, he sank into his chair once more. "Then ask."

"What do those runes on your skin mean?" The runes I'd dreamed of . . .

"As much as you watch me training, I'm surprised you haven't deciphered them."

I gave him a helpless shrug.

"They tell a story, one I can never forget—even if I die in this game. Each morning I look at them in the mirror to remind myself. And I'll never reveal it to you, so don't bother asking."

I pursed my lips. "Will you tell me what you do between games? Please?"

Leaning forward aggressively, he said, "I wander the earth and see men age before my eyes. I read any book or paper I can get my hands on. I watch the stars in the sky; over my lifetime some dim, some brighten. I sleep for weeks at a time and chase the dragon." When I frowned, he explained, "Opium."

Made from poppy, one of the Empress's symbolic plants. Their red blooms adorned my card.

"I take it any way I can ingest it." He seemed to be daring me to say something about that, which I would never do.

I couldn't imagine how harrowing his existence must be, thanking God—or the gods—that it hadn't been my fate. Was that why I'd pitied him when I was younger? When I'd gazed at his card with fascination, I must have sensed something about this man. *His horse looks sick, and he has no friends.*

"On the cusp of a new game," he continued, "the anticipation is like fire in my veins. I endeavor to locate other cards. To shepherd them, or mark them for elimination. I prepare for all different catastrophes. This is what I've done for millennia."

"I see. If you're looking for judgment, you won't find it here," I said. "All I want is to learn more about you. Will you tell me about growing up?" Maybe he had happy memories like I did. "Where are you from?"

He gave me an accusing look. "Why should I tell you? You won't remember it anyway."

"That really bugs you, that I can't recall the previous games."

Instead of answering, he stood and crossed to

a wall safe. Withdrawing something glittering, he handed a jeweled piece to me, his forefinger briefly brushing my wrist. "Perhaps this will assist you."

My gaze narrowed on the stunning emerald necklace. "You gave this to me once." He must have taken it off my corpse. After he'd killed me last time. "I'm surprised you were able to get my blood off it."

He scowled, turning toward the window. Lightning forked down in the distance.

"Why show me this?" I set it away on the desk, not wanting to touch it any longer. Though I was amazed that he'd kept it this long, the piece reminded me of a bloody and violent death. "Why not just tell me what you want me to remember?"

"Because relating our past won't have the same impact. Because you won't trust what I say."

"Fair enough. In the meantime, you can at least tell me about yourself. I know you were born three games before this one. What was your boyhood like? Will you finally tell me your name?"

"My name?" Staring out into the night, he murmured, "I was called Aric. It means *a ruler, forever alone*." Harsh laugh. "How prophetic of my parents."

Aric. At last, he'd told me. When I'd first arrived here, he'd said, "Death is all I'll ever be to you."

No longer. "Go on."

"When I was a boy, I was well aware that I'd been blessed with fortune. My father was a warlord who ruled a fortified settlement, a great trading center in what's now Latvia."

So that was his accent.

He returned to his seat. "We were the wealthiest family in the land, and my parents loved each other very deeply. Wanting what they had, I agreed when my father urged me to marry. I'd just turned sixteen, and it was time for me to start a family of my own."

Had Death—or rather, Aric—been married? I'd never imagined it was even possible. I felt a surprising flare of jealousy. "But your touch . . ."

"I wasn't born with my curse." Shot, refill. "My father held a dance for me to choose a wife. I danced with many. The next day, they were all plagued with illness—just from holding my hand. Yet at the time, no one had reason to believe I was the cause. It wasn't until my curse grew in strength, until my touch killed in seconds, that I knew I was responsible. Two of my last accidental victims were my parents."

Even after all this time, the guilt in his expression was raw.

"Crazed with grief, I left my home, stumbling blindly into the game. In time, I began to comprehend what I was. I was damned to win, to be immortal for all time, to be alone." He exhaled a weary breath. "And then I met you."

Was he finally going to reveal what had happened between us?

"I'd gone more than a year without contact by this time. It doesn't sound like much, but imagine that long without a single handshake or a relative's embrace. Without so much as a brush of skin as coin changes hands."

Even here, I'd had contact. I roughhoused with Lark, and I'd had those fleeting contacts with Death. His existence must've been a living nightmare.

"I stroked your face, intending to end you. Yet you never fell ill. I can still remember how shockingly soft your skin was. How warm." He seemed to get lost in the memory. Voice gone hoarse, he said, "I shuddered to feel it against mine." He glanced up sharply, clearing his throat. "You were as stunned as I was."

"Did we . . . ?"

He gave a curt shake of his head, eyes beginning to glow—this time with fury.

Heedless of his anger, I pressed on. "Then if we haven't slept together, have you ever?" I wasn't a virgin, but he might be.

His glass shattered in his fist.

"I-I guess not. But you'd intended to with me?" *To my bed, Empress.*

"Until you betrayed me."

"How?" When he gave a pointed glance at the necklace, I said, "What if I never can remember? I need to know!"

He grated, "I told you, creature. You folded first."

"The two of us had called a truce before?"

He rose with a disgusted expression—but I didn't think it was directed toward me. He looked disgusted with himself, as if this encounter had just gone sideways.

"I'm ready for my departure," he said dismissively, striding toward an adjoining door.

I scrambled to follow. He muttered a curse when I barreled through the doorway behind him.

I gaped at his firelit room. The ceiling and walls were solid black, the floor veined black marble. His jet-black armor hung on a stand, as if another man were in the room with us. The sole piece of furniture was a carved sleigh bed. His sheets were twisted.

Did he suffer from wicked dreams as well?

He scowled around his room, clearly regretting that I'd seen his most personal space.

"Do you know what I think, Death?" When I perched on the edge of his bed, he turned away with a sharp inhalation. "I think you missed me this morning in the gym."

Jaw clenched, he crossed to his armor.

"And I think you're going to miss me when you leave. Whenever you're out there by yourself, does that gut-wrenching loneliness come creeping back?"

He stiffened.

"You hate this existence, and I think you secretly hope I can help you find another one."

"It doesn't matter what I hope. Because I can't trust you."

"If you could, would you want more with me? Would you want to be with me?"

"This was a mistake. You need to leave." With hasty movements, he buckled a layer of metal over his right leg, another over his left. "You are forbidden from this part of the manor from now on."

I gasped. "You *do* want to be with me." As soon as I said the words, I accepted that I might want my life to be here with him as well. "Please don't go yet. Just talk to me, Aric."

He tensed at the use of his name, as if I'd struck him. "Leave now. If I recollect your betrayal, I might kill you. If I recollect how you've betrayed me already in this life . . ."

I shot to my feet. "What have I done to you?" He'd captured me, imprisoned me. When I'd attacked him and his alliance, I'd only been defending myself.

"I am warning you—leave me." Turning away, he yanked off his shirt to don his breastplate. Even in the midst of this discord, I gazed longingly at his back flexing.

He shoved on his gauntlets and turned, seeming surprised to see that I was still there. Did no one else disobey him?

"Any woman with sense would've heeded my warning." He strapped on his sword belt.

Yes, he had warned me, but I'd already learned more about him than ever before, and I sensed he was on the verge of confiding even more. Or, well, killing me. I squared my shoulders. "I'm staying."

He reached for his helmet, tucking it under one arm, then stalked up to me, a fearsome sight. At that moment, I completely believed some death god had chosen this man to be his knight. When we were toe to toe, I craned my head up.

Emotions sped over his face, too many to latch on to just one. "Then I'm *going*." He stalked around me and left the room.

I trailed him down the corridor to the outer doors. "Damn it, Aric, can your trip not wait?"

Without another word, he charged out into a blustery storm. From the doorway, I watched, feeling like I'd just missed my one opportunity for . . . something.

Keeping him here suddenly felt crucial.

When he rode from the stable at a blistering speed, I ran out into the rain to intercept him. His mount reared, red eyes wild as its sharpened hooves pawed the air.

"You've lost your mind!" He yanked off his helmet, revealing his anguished glowing eyes. "What are you thinking?"

I hurried to the side of his horse, yelling over the downpour, "How have I betrayed you in this life?" When I rested my hand on his armored leg, he flinched. "I have to know."

He dismounted, his movements deliberate, almost

sinister. My heart raced as I backed up a few steps. Had he reached his limit with me?

Once he stood just before me, I had the impulse to run away. Too close, too much, too intense. But I had to know. . . .

He reached down to clamp my nape in his punishing grip. Between clenched teeth, he grated, "You weren't meant for him." Rain spiked his lashes. "That you allowed the mortal to have you—it makes me crazed! You gave him everything."

"You've hated me for two thousand years. Tell me why you care who I was with."

His hand shook. "I care."

"Why?!"

He tenderly grasped my face with his lethal gauntlet. His touch might be tender, but his expression . . .

Filled with lust and longing and other feelings too seething for me to read.

This had been building inside me for weeks; it might have been building inside him for centuries.

Then his lips were on mine, scalding in the rain, covering, claiming. His tongue swept in, demanding more, more. For someone so out of practice, his kiss was perfection—but savage too, as if it was the last one he would ever have. Surrendering to it, I threw my arms around his neck. Just like in my dream.

Better than.

Incredibly hotter.

Over the rain, I could hear my moans, his groans. He looped his free arm around my torso, squeezing me so tightly against his armor, but I loved it.

As he slanted his lips over mine again and again, I dimly noticed my feet weren't touching the ground. I clung to him as if I'd never let go, fingers clutching at his hair.

I wanted this kiss to last forever.

Yet he drew back, leaving me dazed, breathless. "Aric?" My lips were bruised, cold without his against them.

Between heaving breaths, he rasped, "I care because . . . because you were my wife. You still are."

My legs went weak with shock.

"You took vows, then tried to kill me on our wedding night." Voice gone raw, he said, "You forced me to murder my bride." The pain in his starry eyes . . .

He released me to mount his horse. With a last burning look, he rode away, leaving me to collapse to my knees.

41

I lay in Death's bed, staring at the black ceiling, clutching the emerald necklace he'd once given me.

For the last two days, I'd avoided Lark, stealing into this room and spending the nighttime hours here. My guard wolf waited outside the door.

I hadn't slept since Aric had ridden away, hadn't eaten. I both wanted and feared the dream of him I sensed was coming. Somehow I knew I would relive the past the next time I slept.

I believed everything Aric had told me—what he'd said *felt* true. I'd been married to Death. This explained why I'd always felt a connection to him, some kind of soul-deep bond—why I'd stared at his card when I was little, as if gazing at a picture of a loved one.

When I'd fallen for Jack, it'd been sizzling and combustible. The blazing inferno. What I felt for Aric was like a wave pounding against a shore for all time. He had two thousand years of longing, lifetimes of it, and now I'd tapped into that well forever.

I knew I would never be the same. My relationship with Jackson had felt fated. Whatever I had with Aric felt . . . endless.

Why hadn't he returned? What if he never did?

Lying on his bed, surrounded by his addictive scent, I longed for him, longed to take away the pain I'd delivered.

If he could survive whatever I'd done to him, I could at least witness it.

I stopped fighting sleep. . . .

"Now that we're wed, perhaps you will call me by my given name," Death says as he escorts me to our extravagant lodgings—only the best for my highborn knight.

As soon as we cross the threshold, he releases me to yank off his hated gloves.

"But I will always know you as Death, my love," I say, my voice all sweetness.

No matter how he's treated me over these past weeks, I will never forget the menace in his eyes when he stabbed me. I will never forgive his arrogance when he assumed I would accept him just because he spared me.

He never asked for my hand, merely informed me that I was to marry him, that we would bow out of the game. In his mind, he is death, and I am life; therefore we belong together.

All throughout the planning of this ceremony, I kept hidden my true motivations. He might have quit the game, but I continue to play. And I know I cannot defeat him until he lowers his guard with me. He will, now that he's my husband.

Today, I became his wife. Tonight I will become his doom.

"'My love' will do for now," he says, his lips curling, all confidence. He reaches for me, eager for our skin to touch. "As lovely as you are in this dress, I crave to see you without it."

My bridal gown was a gift from him, cut from the most exquisite emerald green silk. Upon seeing the finery, I'd felt a disturbing amount of girlish glee. Then I'd remembered I'm the Empress, a killer of the first order.

"Of course, my love. If you'll assist me, you'll soon have what you crave." *What you deserve.* I turn, presenting my back to him.

As he begins to unlace my stays, I fight the tension building in my muscles. He draws the silk from my shoulders, brushing searing kisses across my skin.

He's been impatient for this day to come, and even more so about our first night as man and wife. Yet Death will never know me this way.

Throughout my childhood, I was taught that he is my enemy. That his inevitable desire for the Empress would prove to be one of my strengths—and weaknesses.

Because a lesser Empress would desire him back.

The woman in me feels attraction toward him. He is charming when he wants to be, and he's beautifully formed. Never have I seen his equal. I admit my breaths shallowed when I joined him in the temple earlier today—he was stunning in his impeccable attire.

But this union is doomed because the Empress in me sees him only as a kill to be made. A predator viewing prey.

He has no idea, confident I am now his. Earlier, as we toasted our wedding vows, he whispered in my ear, "You belong to me. Forever."

When my dress slips down my body, pooling at my feet, he turns me, the better to survey his new belonging.

The possessive gleam in his eyes makes me bristle. The thinly veiled hunger. His appetites are so marked, I've barely been able to hold him off thus far. He is too intense, too carnal, too desirous.

The boy called Death is so full of . . . life.

He lays me upon our bed, then disrobes himself. Yes, he is beautifully formed—everywhere. My body helplessly responds. But I have control over my own appetites.

Once he joins me, he grasps my hand to kiss my palm. "Empress, I will make you happy, for all our days."

Our limited days. If we exit the game, we will age. Though immortality beckons?

His hand is covered with icons, there for the taking. I disguise my greed as I count them.

With a proud mien, he twirls my new ring on my

finger. A symbol of ownership? I can view it no other way since men of his culture do not require one, just as livestock do not brand their masters.

To me, the ring is as detestable as a collar, and that I cannot abide! When I taste bile, my path becomes clearer: I crave his icons more than I do his breathtaking body.

As he leans down to kiss my neck, I ask, "Will you fetch me wine for my nerves, my love?" I muster a teasing smile. "In this, I'm an anxious innocent."

He inhales, quelling his eagerness, though it roils from him. His manly needs, his lusts. "As you wish."

He turns his back to the Empress. How trusting. How foolish. The heat of battle rises, taking me over. Without a whisper of hesitation, I slip soundlessly from the bed.

Before he can react, I shove my poisonous claws into him, hissing in his ear, "Till Death do us part."

I woke with tears streaming down my face.

Husband. He was my husband. And I had betrayed him.

Somehow he'd survived my poison. Somehow he'd gotten the upper hand and ended me.

"Forced me to kill my bride," he'd said with such pain in his starry gaze. No wonder he hated me—he had every right to! How could I have been so evil?

It was one thing to battle an enemy, to fight and prevail; quite another to exchange sacred vows with someone you had every intention of murdering that very night.

No wonder I'd had no chance of seducing him. *I don't handle vipers.* He'd learned not to trust, he'd learned so young.

All his hardness, his ruthlessness, had been honed by me.

That Empress had seen only his hungers. She'd ignored the tenderness in his expressions, the warmth in his eyes as he'd beheld her. He had intended to make her happy.

To make *me* happy.

Yet even when blind to all he offered, that woman had fallen for him. She'd just refused to admit it.

Could I?

Suddenly my feelings for him were clamoring, too big for my chest. I *felt* like his wife. I needed to explain to him that I would never betray him. But he remained away. Leaving me alone in his bed.

Return to me, Aric.

Silence. Too much silence. I didn't want to be alone right now. Dashing my sleeve over my face, I hurried from the room, startling Cyclops. Together we climbed up one flight of stairs to Lark's bedroom.

A light knock. I had no idea what time it was.

Lark opened the door, rubbing her eyes. "What's up, girl?" She wore a football jersey and leggings. A baby squirrel peeked its sleepy eyes from her mane of black hair.

"C-can I come in?"

When she swung her door wide, I entered. In all this time, I'd never been to her room. It was just as I might've pictured it—posters of animals plastered the walls, cages and aquariums lining shelves. Her falcon rested on a wooden perch next to her bed like an alarm clock. She had a tiger lamp, kangaroo sheets, and a thick smattering of live butterflies coating the high ceiling.

I knew there were no monarchs. Months ago, Matthew had told me that the last two were thousands of miles apart and flying *away* from each other. Again, I felt gratitude that Lark was caretaking these treasures. Still, I couldn't let her think I'd softened toward her too much. "Kangaroo sheets, Lark?"

"Dude. Don't judge me," she said without anger.

My presence had agitated some of her menagerie, but a single wave of her hand quieted mewls and caws. "So you wanna talk about it?" She climbed back in bed, scooting a snoring hedgehog from her pillow.

Did I? Where to even begin? As I sorted through my thoughts, I crossed to her bay window, staring out into the stormy night.

Somewhere out there both Aric and Jack roamed the world. Jack had broken my heart, and I'd broken Aric's. "Did you know Death and I were involved in a previous game? Married?"

"Um, some cards speculated."

"I just dreamed about it. About how he used to be."

"I tried to tell you he's not all bad," Lark said. "From

what I understand, you kinda put him to shame on the evil front. Like judges' scores of ten."

"I did. Nothing could be worse than what I did," I murmured.

"Once he gets back, you two kids can work things out. I'm confident about that. You've seen the way he looks at you when you dance, right? Well, you can't imagine how he looks at you when you aren't aware. You're still a lock."

I sighed, not convinced. There was so much in our past to be overcome. When lightning flashed, I said over my shoulder, "I never see lightning without thinking of Joules."

"I know, right? At least he doesn't want to off you."

"For now." I turned back to the window just as another bolt struck. Lightning forked out over black. Greenish-yellow forked out over red?

My breath caught. Slitted black eyes stared back at me.

Ogen.

42

"FEAST! OFFERING!"

"Lark!" I screamed. "Run—"

"SABBAT!" Ogen's mighty fist burst through the window. Glass shattered, riddling me as his fist connected with my entire torso.

Lark was shrieking when I slammed into the far wall. Bones fractured. Skull? Ribs? Shoulder blade? Shards jutted from my skin. Unable to rise, I watched Ogen snatch at Lark as the wolves defended, tearing at his arms. This far across the room, she and I were out of his reach.

Though I expected her to flee, following the exodus of creatures tromping and flying to safety, she darted over to me, helping me stand. She'd caught a lot of glass too.

Ogen twisted his great bulk, wedging himself through the window opening. "ALTAR EMPTY!" he boomed. "FRESH ENTRAILS."

Recognition hit my panicked mind. In his own way, Matthew had warned me of this. *The lightning hides the monster.* I'd just glimpsed Ogen by the light of a bolt. And Matthew had given me instructions: *You must slice yourself when the altar is empty.* Ogen's altar was empty; it was time to lose my cuff.

I whispered to Lark, "T-take me to the basement. To the sunlamps."

"Shit, shit! Boss'll kill me." But she did start out the doorway, whistling for her wolves to follow. She yelled to Ogen, "Hey, dickwad, meet me in the kitchen!"

"MEAT YOU!" he yowled, withdrawing from the window so quickly the building shook.

With my arm stretched across her shoulders, we scrambled away, heading in the direction opposite to the kitchen, a trio of wolves at our heels. As we fled upstairs, I gasped out, "What's happening?"

"It's some Sabbat that I'm not aware of," she murmured. "Could be some big annual one."

We lurched up more stairs, a flight that I didn't remember seeing before.

"I've never seen him so big, Evie. I've called for reinforcements from the barn, but it might take them a while to follow my instructions to pick the lock." We careened along a corridor until she stopped in front of a wall.

She pressed her hand against the wainscoting, and a panel swung open. Just before it hissed closed behind our troupe, her falcon gave a piercing cry and dove inside.

In total darkness, I was again forced to rely on Lark's night vision as we hastened down flight after flight of stairs. Had we gone up, just to go down into the belly of this building?

The air grew humid, our surroundings quieter. I couldn't hear the rain, only paws padding behind us, wings flapping, and my bones grinding as they began to reset themselves.

I called for Aric. *We're in trouble—you have to return!* No answer. I even called for Matthew. Nothing.

"Just hold on, Evie. We're here." She propped me against a wall.

I heard a key jangling in a lock, then the sound of a wheel turning, like with a bank vault. With a click, a door groaned open, and light spilled into the landing where we stood.

Warm light.

I was dumbfounded by the sight in front of me. As big as Warehouse 13, and filled with table after table of growing plants. Sunlamps covered every inch of soaring ceiling, cascading light onto my thirsty skin.

Lark locked us and her creatures inside. "This door might not keep Ogen out when he's in this form." Leaning back against it, she pulled a shard from her hip. She was bleeding from the glass almost as badly as I was. "I'll leave the falcon here to listen for him. Let's get to the back."

As Lark and I set off across the bunker, wolves in

tow, I soaked up the light, feeling my brain starting to fire again. I plucked shards from my own skin, my regeneration accelerating.

We passed rows of plants, like orderly battalions. There were potted vines and even saplings. They wouldn't be as strong as giant oaks or as stealthy as my weapon of choice: roses. Still, this was a decent army—if I could reclaim my powers.

Ogen would find us down here eventually; I only hoped I could lay a trap before then. "Lark, I need a really sharp knife." Or, depending on time . . . "Maybe an ax?" *It'll grow back.*

"Gee, forgot both of mine in the rush." She peered around the garden. "I can get you a spade. Or a trowel."

I gazed down at her claws, dreading what I knew must happen. "You've cut through skin before, right? With your claws?"

"Oh, hell, no. Don't even think about this, Evie."

"Believe me, I'm open to alternatives."

"Boss is supposed to be back today. Maybe he'll get here in time?"

"Willing to bet your life on that?" I snatched her hand. "You help me get this cuff off, or we die."

She gazed at me as if awed. "You are stone-cold, aren't you?"

"No. Not at all. But I'll still get you to cut on me."

By the time we'd reached a back corner, I'd gotten her to give in.

"Fine!" She flared her claws. "Tell me what you want."

I explained how she needed to slice the skin above and below the cuff, along the edges, like she was tracing around a Solo cup. The barbs were in too deep for the metal piece to be slipped down my arm, so I figured we'd just work that circle of skin down too. Easy, peasy. Oh, and we'd do this while excising my bicep. So a couple more slices on each side of the muscle, please.

I yanked off my sweater, twisting the sleeve for something to bite down on, because I'd seen that before in a movie.

When I stuffed the material between my teeth, she raised her scalpel-sharp foreclaw. "This is so messed up." With her pupils the size of saucers, she began to cut around the cuff.

The pain made my eyes water, but I nodded for her to keep going.

Once she'd made all the cuts to my skin, blood was streaming, making everything slippery. I was growing so delirious that I thought I saw a flicker of enjoyment in her eyes. *Red of tooth and claw.*

But when I looked closer at her face, all I saw was queasy paleness.

I drew the material from my mouth. "You have t-to hurry," I choked out. "With this much green and light . . . I'll heal right up. When I pull the cuff higher, you slip beneath and"—my voice quavered—"yank on the muscle. Quick." Back in went the sweater sleeve.

With an unsteady nod, she used her claws to get a good pincer hold of the slick muscle, then began her gruesome task.

Through gushing tears, I stared up at the ceiling, feeling pressure, pain, pressure, *pain*! I shrieked against my sweater. As if he'd heard even that muted sound, Ogen bellowed from somewhere above, bounding through the manor.

"We're done with that part." Why was she swaying so much? Or was that me? Delirious. *Stay conscious, stay conscious.* She started pulling down on the cuff.

Oh, God, the barbs! I vomited in my mouth, choking it back. My legs tottered as I tried to give her a counterforce.

Almost to my elbow, almost . . .

The metal came free in a rush of blood, hitting the floor with a bounce. Done! Shuddering, I spat out my sweater, then rested my good arm on a plant shelf. As I leaned over, I narrowed my eyes at the grisly sight of the cuff. The barbs looked like roots growing into my former skin.

Lark tore the hem of her jersey, using the material to tie a bandage around my mutilated, limp arm.

Good. Didn't want to see it.

"I can't believe we did that! Now don't mummify me in vine, 'kay?"

Freed, I commanded everything to grow. Despite my injuries, I was brimming with power.

Conserve? I had for months.

My army obeyed so quickly, I could hear their skittering spurts. As stalks, stems, and leaves sprang to life, Lark's eyes darted. "This is so disturbing."

"So were your cobras."

"What's the game plan?" she asked.

"We'll have to behead Ogen, right?" At her nod, I said, "To reach us back here, he'll have to fight his way through a jungle, getting weaker and weaker. I'll hold him in place while your wolves tear at his softer belly. After we force him to the ground, we'll use their fangs to sever his neck."

"Okay. They know the program."

Somewhere above us, he roared, "I smell pretty MEAT."

"He's coming, Lark. Use my blood. Get it on any leaves you can. It'll make them even stronger. I'll create a last barrier to defend us."

She dropped down to flatten her palms in the puddle at my feet. Patty-cake. Delirious.

"Our blood is mixing like crazy." She rose to flick her coated fingers. Crimson on green. "Like we're blood sisters. Think that'll give me an extra life in this battle?"

"I have no idea." While my barricade thickened, I spied something along the back wall . . .

A rosebush. My lips curved. *Oh, Aric, you shouldn't have.*

As Lark lined up her wolves in front of the barricade, I grew the rose until the thorns were as big as blades, the stalks like chains. Recalling another Arcana's tactic, I positioned the stalks just so for Ogen. A last backup.

Finished, I turned to Lark. "You could leave the wolves and go hide." When she hesitated, I said, "Weirdly, I care if you live or die. I'll be more concerned with saving your bony ass than taking him out. You can't help me against him."

"That doesn't feel right. I'll stick around—"

Rock and rubble exploded down from the ceiling; not fifty feet from us, Ogen had punched his way through the floor of the manor!

He lowered his head through the new hole, sharpening his horns on the jagged side of the opening. "Smell BLOOD!" When he dropped down into the warehouse, tremors rippled beneath our feet.

Lark's face paled even more. "Oh. Shit."

Ogen wouldn't have to negotiate a jungle before he got to us, wouldn't be weakened.

When the wolves hunched down, snarling to fight, I snapped out of my shock. With a wave of my hand, vines shot out to lasso him. They bound his wrists and ankles, coiling around his horns.

Once he was caught, the wolves attacked as one, going for his belly. He roared with pain as the three snatched chunks out of his hide. Greenish-yellow goo seeped from his wounds.

The falcon dove into the battle, hovering above Ogen's head, scratching and pecking at his eyes.

"It's working!" Lark cried.

I'd just nodded at her when Ogen thrashed, ripping free from all my vines. He whipped his head around, jabbing one horn into the falcon's breast. A bloody bundle of feathers thudded to the ground.

Eyes wide, I threw everything I had at him, unending vines. The wolves took turns snapping at any exposed hide.

Despite this all-out assault, he began to advance, shuffling past a minefield of plants. If I could restrain his right arm, he used his left to peel off the bindings. If I managed to snag one leg, he'd drag it behind him until it pulled free.

Where was he getting this strength from? Was he growing even larger?

"NO boss." He grinned, dripping saliva. "Now FEAST!"

When he reached the barricade, the wolves redoubled their attack—

He scooped one up, twisting its body like a blood-soaked rag. I cried out when he broke Cyclops over his knee. He trampled the third under his hoof.

Through each attack, Lark jerked and gasped for breath. Turning watering eyes toward me, she sputtered, "Wh-what do we do now?"

We were trapped in the back corner, with only one barricade to keep Ogen out.

With a slobbery grin, he squeezed his right hand into a fist. I braced myself, knowing what was coming. He launched that fist at my barrier, punching a hole through it, sending agony all over my body. Though I fought to seal the rift, he'd already gotten one leg in.

He yelled, "ALTAR!" and busted through. Lark scurried out of the way, but he was too quick. With the back of one hand, he swatted her. She flew into the wall—and didn't move.

My fear gave way to the heat of battle. "You're going to die for that." Needing to get him into position, I skirted closer to my trap. "Come, Devil. Touch." In our Arcana battle at the riverside, Gabriel had surprised Death with a net. I had one of my own at the ready.

When Ogen lunged for me, a net of rose stalks cascaded over him, giant thorns sharper than barbed wire.

"But you'll pay a price."

He roared as I tightened the stalks around him, their blades razoring his hide. Tighter, tighter, cutting to the bone. "Don't you remember your commands, Ogen? I'm telling you to stay . . ." My words trailed off.

Ogen was morphing again. As I watched in horror,

he grew even larger, his height stretching toward the lofty ceiling.

That sly brute had been sandbagging all this time. He'd hidden the true magnitude of his power. Did Death even know?

When his horns speared the sunlamps above, raining glass down, I knew I couldn't hold him.

Ogen flailed against his bonds. They disintegrated, pain scoring me. The giant had freed himself.

Hunching over, he stomped closer to me. I backed away from him, throwing vines between us.

My back met the wall. Nowhere to run.

He snatched at me, seizing me in one of his enormous hands. "Pretty meat!" He inched me closer to his face.

I slashed at him with my claws, but he didn't seem to feel them.

His slitted pupils expanded as he sniffed me, his foul breath hitting my face. "DEAD meat." He slammed me to the ground, wrenching a scream from my lungs.

He began strangling me as he had once before. Only this time he took my neck between his thumb and forefinger, savoring, making it last.

The pressure was excruciating. Did he mean to pop my head off, like a doll's?

Did this doll no longer have teeth?

As consciousness wavered, I thought I heard Aric bellowing for me to hold on. Delirious. I'd never see him again, would never get a chance to convince him how different I was. Would he pass another seven centuries of misery?

Ogen's drool pinged my cheek. This would be my last sight?

Almost a relief when my lids slid shut and scenes flashed through my mind. I beheld Jack's face as he'd gazed down at me in that suspended moment of time. So perfectly, I saw him. Heard him. *I am home, Evangeline. Finally found the place I'm supposed to be.* With my death, would Matthew tell him to stop hunting, to stop searching?

Dimly I perceived a yell. Aric? I managed to crack open my eyes in time to see him speeding into view. Behind his helmet grille, a menacing light burned. I never thought I'd be so happy to see Death charging toward me with both swords drawn.

"You disobey me, Devil? I warned you never to hurt her again." He had?

Ogen leapt up, releasing me. "Not my boss. I sit upon Lucifer's knee!"

I sucked in breaths, struggling to rise. This wasn't over. The battle still called.

When Ogen barreled toward him, Aric feinted right, then struck with his left sword. Ambidextrous. The blade cut deep into the Devil's flank.

Ogen howled with fury, shattering more lamps. Beating the ground, he charged once more.

Aric leapt over a table, but Ogen caught him with a long sweep of his giant arm, flinging him into the wall not far from Lark. His head snapped against it so hard his helmet was knocked off.

"Aric, no!" I choked out. I threw another wave of vines at the Devil. Connected to so many plants and soaking up the light, I was swiftly regenerating. But even at full power, I could only buy Aric so much time.

Somehow he'd kept hold of his swords. Somehow he rose to a crouch. He gave a shake of his head, as if to clear his vision. "Ah, Ogen, all brawn and no brains. No skill—no style. Don't you know that quality will always win over quantity?"

Ogen roared so loud it pained my ears. He charged once more.

At the last instant, Aric rolled out of the way, dodging an anvil fist, driving one sword up into the Devil's guts. Rancid goo oozed.

"B-boss?" Ogen whimpered. He began to shrink as if he'd been deflated.

Twisting that sword, Aric planted his second one.

Ogen's body dwindled until he was not much taller than Aric. Only then did Death remove his swords—to scissor them at Ogen's neck.

As Ogen tottered dumbly on cloven feet, Aric said, "Until next time, Devil." Slice.

The Devil Card was no more. . . .

With an exhausted rise and fall of his shoulders,

Aric stared down at the still-shrinking body of his one-time ally.

The battle was done.

Aric's back was to me. No more cuff on my arm. No helmet for him, leaving his neck vulnerable. An impulse seized me.

The heat of battle? *More than.*

"I heard you calling for me, Empress," he said as he began turning toward me—

I'd already bounded up and struck, planting five claws into Death's neck.

43

All his muscles tightened, but Aric didn't try to defend himself. Just hung his head and let me stab him—surrendering, allowing me time enough to pump poison into him.

When I released him, he faced me with an agonized look. "Well-played, creature." He dropped one sword, grasping the blade of the other to hand me the hilt. "Finish me, then. I won't fight back."

Reeling with confusion, I took the blade, but made no move to strike. I'd meant to explain my actions, but his expression robbed me of breath. "Y-you want to die?"

With a bitter laugh, he said, "Why would I want to live on for centuries more when I would despise myself at every second?"

"Despise?"

"For coveting you yet again. Over and over, I fall for

this. The first time you attacked me, I defended myself, disbelieving it was you. I struck you down before you could deliver a full dose of your poison. You died in the next game before I could find you, but in the third, I watched you and waited."

I remembered when the red witch had destroyed those galleons. He'd been on the shore, an observer. She'd remarked that Death had always been "fascinated with her Empress gifts."

"Eventually I revealed to you that we'd been wed— and what you'd done to me," he said. "You acted so horrified that you convinced me you'd never hurt me again. One night you told me I'd possess you fully. At last, I thought, I'd know a woman's flesh, *my* woman. Instead, you gave me your poison kiss."

I gasped at the unbearable pain in his eyes. The hopelessness.

He wanted to die, in order to . . . forget. To start over.

"Your lips were so sweet that even after I'd comprehended what you were doing to me, I kept taking your mouth. Only at the last second could I break away. It took me months to recover." He reached behind him to touch the wounds on his neck. "And now this."

"Aric, wait."

"I've waited long enough." He yanked off his breastplate, bowing his tattooed chest, offering his vulnerable skin. "What is that saying about being fooled? If shame comes to those fooled twice, then it's only right that defeat comes to those fooled thrice." He positioned the end of his sword, forcing me to raise it against him. "You wanted to know what the runes across my chest mean? It's our story, Empress, a reminder never to give you my trust—and certainly not my heart. Yet I did this time." Eyes glinting, he rasped, "I desired you before, but I never loved you until this life."

My own heart beat faster than it had in the battle. He loved me!

"Come now, plunge this sword. I'm worth five icons to you." He raised his right hand, displaying his markings, Ogen's among them: a pair of horns.

Before I could react, Aric had leaned into the blade, planting the tip above his heart. Blood trickled from one of his runes. As if it wept. "You won't even spare me the agony of your poison? Or perhaps you could deliver one last kiss? Now bitten, I can touch the viper."

I dropped the sword hilt, and the weapon fell between us. "Speaking of vipers, I gave you a dry bite." At his confused look, I explained, "I didn't use my poison on you—but I could have. Those puncture marks will be healed by tomorrow. Maybe now you'll trust me when I tell you I'll never try to kill you again."

His expression said he didn't dare believe.

"While you were gone, I dreamed the memory of our wedding night. And this time, I am truly horrified by what I did to you. I won't ever hurt you again, Aric."

His jaw slackened, and his brows drew tight. "*Sievā*."

He'd called me that before. "What is that word?"

"It means *wife*." He reached for me. "Because that's what I'm going to make you tonight."

I was limping to him when Lark murmured groggily, "What's going on?"

My head swung around. "Oh, God, Lark!" She looked really busted up.

Her mauled wolves had crawled toward her, their fur leaving mop trails of blood. *Oh, Cyclops.* Despite looking like road kill, they'd positioned themselves around her, still needing to protect. Even the falcon had hobbled over to her.

They would heal, just as long as Lark did. "Are you okay?" I asked her. Aric had said he had a medic in the compound. I really hoped that Ogen hadn't eaten him. "Can you stand?"

With effort, Lark said, "Is the Devil dead?"

Gazing back at Aric, I answered, "Lots of things died down here tonight."

The Arcana were buzzing.

—*Death turned on his own.*—

—*Devil no more!*—

—*Empress next.*—

I sat in my darkened room, lit only by fire. Aric was going to come for me tonight. Again, I wondered what I would do.

I'd left Lark and the animals in the care of Aric and the medic, a nondescript human who'd been hiding from Ogen in the coal cellar. The young man had wanted to bandage me, but once he'd pronounced his other patients stabilized, I'd left to go scour off the layers of gore.

Aric had said nothing more to me, but he'd been thrumming with tension whenever I was near. . . .

By the time I'd finished my steaming shower, my arm was almost regenerated. Puny-looking, but healing. If only I could shore up mentally. I was nervous. In essence, this was my wedding night.

I'd braided and unbraided my hair, debating clothing choices. I'd settled on a royal-blue silk nightgown and robe.

Why was I so nervous about the prospect of sex with him? I was hitched to the man, for God's sake, and I'd already done this once.

With Jack. In that moment of time. *I'm all in, peekôn.*

It seemed that as soon as I'd decided to sleep with Aric, my feelings for Jack had surged to the fore, memories of him invading my mind: *Evangeline, I've got to feel you with my every step. Or I go a little crazy, me.*

When I'd been sure I was dying, it had been Jack's

face I'd seen most clearly. Why? He was non-Arcana, I reminded myself. He'd lied to me in the worst possible way. These were obstacles that simply couldn't be overcome—

The door burst open. I shot to my feet.

Eyes aglow, Aric stood in the doorway, seeming to take up the entire space. "I've waited"—his voice broke lower—"so long for you to be like this." His accent was thicker than I'd ever heard it.

Then he was striding toward me. His mesmerizing gaze pinned me in place as he cupped my face. When his lips covered mine, I gasped. He took the opportunity to deepen the kiss, groaning into the contact. His hands tightened on my face. His sexy groans made my toes curl, muddling my thoughts.

Though he hadn't undressed a woman in centuries, before I knew it all my clothes had melted off me, his shirt and boots vanishing as well. He broke the kiss to scoop me up, carrying me to bed.

Like Jack had. *Don't think of him.*

Aric gazed down at me unclothed in his arms and hissed, "Great gods." He laid me back on my bed, climbing in beside me. He still had on pants, but for some reason I wasn't shy with him as he surveyed my every curve.

Probably because I'd felt naked in front of him for months.

His hunger was undisguised, yet when he dipped his head down to my body, he kissed . . . my healing arm. "My fierce Empress. I could not be prouder." He bestowed a real smile on me, not a mocking sneer, not a grudging half-grin.

Glorious man.

His lips were flawlessly shaped, his teeth even and white. Though his eyes were starry, I could see their golden color. They were filled with warmth, with . . . love.

If he'd been gorgeous before, now he was devastating. My glyphs flared in response, drawing his gaze. "These used to fill me with confusion. I find them so beautiful, but whenever I saw them, you were usually about to strike."

Jack had found them beautiful too.

Block that out! I was Aric's wife. I'd wronged him in the past, had consigned him to misery for hundreds—no, thousands—of years. I needed to make this right. Like penance.

He rubbed his thumb over my bottom lip with a hand that had begun to shake. I got the sense that he was losing his polished control, his desire stoking hotter and hotter. "You could not be lovelier." He looked like he was about to devour me, giving me both shivers—and chills. "I am a patient man, *sievā*, but tonight . . ."

There was something vaguely threatening about his words. Misgivings about this arose. *Too fast.*

Yet then he leaned down to kiss me, taking my mouth until my thoughts had blanked again. When he trailed his lips to my neck, flicking his tongue over my skin, his mouth was so hot, it was dizzying.

He'd always been polished and sophisticated. Now the raw force of his need staggered me. Between kisses, he murmured in Latvian.

"What are you saying?"

He drew back, curling his finger under my chin. "That you taste like life. You *are* my life now."

His words felt so final. If he'd looked possessive in that far-distant past, now he looked as if he'd lost himself.

In *me.*

I was about to ask if we could take this more slowly, when he lowered his head to my breasts, kissing me there. The pleasure was so intense, I had difficulty recalling my misgivings, could only sigh his name.

When I arched my back for him, he groaned around one tip, then the other, pulling with his lips, flicking with his clever tongue.

Had penance ever felt so right?

Against my damp skin, he rasped, "Better than millennia of imaginings." When I squirmed with need, he lifted his head. Eyes smoldering, he said, "I've imagined other things as well."

His grazed his lips past my breasts, down my belly, his warm breaths ghosting over my skin. He nuzzled my navel, then continued his path lower. Lower.

"Uh, Aric?"

With a desperate groan, Death . . . kissed.

44

I stared up at the ceiling, limbs sprawled, mind dazed from the pleasure he'd just given me. "I . . . you . . . where did you learn *that*?" Was there anything he couldn't do?

Quaking with eagerness, he gave a pained laugh. Eyes brighter than I'd ever seen them, he said, "You've never wondered what I think about as you dance for me? I pretended things were different and you craved my touch, my kiss. I fantasized a thousand things I wanted to do to your beautiful little body."

Mouth back at my breasts, he snatched off his pants. I caught glimpses of him naked—and the mere sight of him made me weak with need.

As he moved over me, between my legs, he shuddered out three words: "At last, *sievā*."

Wait, something was wrong . . . what was missing? My eyes widened. "Do you have, um, protection?"

He tensed. "At this particular moment, are you truly asking me to go *fetch* something for you? Perhaps you'd like a glass of wine as well?"

"No, it's not like that. What if I got pregnant?" Jack had been so careful. *Stop torturing yourself, Eves.* For the best . . .

"It might not even be possible for me to help create a life," Aric said. "But we've nothing to lose by trying. If you want to end the game, this is one move that's never been tried. How could we ever harm each other if we started a dynasty between us?"

"Aric, I'm too young!"

He rested his forehead against mine. "You are not. Now that we are together, the game will lag on. We will continue to age as long as more than one Arcana lives. Already seventeen of your brief mortal years have passed. Twenty-three of mine."

He was talking about starting a family? When I wasn't even sure the sun would ever rise again? This was too intense. *He* was.

Too carnal, desirous. His manly needs.

No, don't think of the witch! "I can't do this tonight."

"Are you jesting?"

"Things are moving too fast." Spinning, flying, like the days here. Maybe I needed to get back out into the world, stop eating the lotus, and *then* find my footing with this man?

Aric raised himself on straightened arms, his gaze

narrowing down at me. "Your hesitation stems from another cause, does it not?"

Did it? I'd accepted that there were serious obstacles between me and Jack. But he'd said the two of us could get past anything—and at the time, I'd believed him. He'd asked me to give him a chance just to *get* to me.

If I did this tonight, I wasn't giving Jack the chance I'd promised him. Didn't I at least owe him the opportunity to tell me his side of the story?

I knew this thinking was naïve, ridiculous even. It could never work out between us, not after what he'd done. Hell, I was probably too far gone in my feelings for Aric.

Then a simple truth struck me: by sleeping with Aric, I was making a decision about my life—but I didn't yet have enough information to make that decision.

And no one could make me choose anything before I was ready.

No one.

"It *is* because of him." Aric twisted around to sit on the edge of the bed, squeezing his brow so hard his arm bulged.

I sat up and touched his shoulder, but he flinched. "Aric, please. For whatever reason, can we take this more slowly?"

"Do you deny it?" Jealousy emanated from him in waves.

"I'm not saying that I don't want something with you. But I made a promise to him. You said I didn't keep them in the past, but I do now. I owe him at least one conversation about all this, before I decide to take things further with you."

"I told you how he wronged you, and still you want him!"

"I could say the same about your feelings for me."

With a brusque sound of annoyance, he rose to dress. "I thought you were past this. Past him."

So had I. My life flashing before my eyes seemed to have jarred something loose. "Do you want me to always wonder about him? Don't you want to start things clean with me?"

He yanked on his pants. "Damn you, Empress, you will choose *me*! You must. He can move on. I cannot!"

I thought back over Jack's behavior, not certain at all that he could move on. *À moi, Evangeline!*

Pacing the room, Aric said, "You never gave your heart before. I was convinced you didn't have one."

I pulled the sheet over my chest. "I do, and right now it's breaking in two."

"Why is it that the first time I've vowed retribution against you, it's the one time you were born like this? With honor and empathy? The sole time you are perfect for me—and you're in love with another man!"

I whispered, "I'm so sorry."

"After the Flash, if I'd gone to Haven and protected

you and your mother, would you have chosen me to love?"

Before being on the road with Jack? Before learning what a complicated boy he was? Before he'd saved my life? I had to answer honestly. "Yes."

Aric yelled with frustration, launching his fist into the stone wall. The entire turret rocked. Between heaving breaths, he grated, "I should have gone to you! I should have looked past my hatred and protected you."

He didn't say *instead of terrorizing you*, but I knew we were both thinking it.

"We can't change that now."

"No, we can't. I've been patient with you. I've stretched the limits of even *my* eternal patience. I see now that the mortal must be taken out of the equation."

As Matthew had said. In a tone like ice, I said, "If you hurt Jack, whatever this is between us will end. Do you want us to be enemies once more?" My claws began to turn.

He noticed, scowling. "No, I do not."

"You should feel grateful toward him. If it weren't for Jack, I would've been captured by the Lovers, tortured and killed." Saying this out loud only cemented my decision to go to him. He'd saved my life; I owed him a conversation.

"If you have feelings for him, *fight* them," Aric commanded me. "By going to him, you'd be stoking them once more. Don't you understand? He can find another woman—I cannot. If you choose him, you'll be consigning me to a hellish fate. As you've done again and again. No, this will be even worse, because I've had a greater glimpse of what I'll be missing."

"I just want to talk to him. I'm leaving this weekend," I said in an unwavering voice.

"No, you will not." His arrogant demeanor back in place, he said, "Understand me, I'm not surrendering the one woman who was born for me alone. Not to a human, not to anyone."

"You can't keep me here against my will any longer. What are you going to do? Put that cuff back on me?"

"I regret that—"

I held up my hand to stop him. "I understand why you did it. But I won't be a prisoner anymore."

He snatched up his shirt, threading his arms into the sleeves. "You say you keep your promises now? You made a vow before gods to be my wife. In this life, you will keep your promises to me—before you ever honor one to him!"

"You can't stop me from leaving. I have my powers back. I *earned* my powers back."

With a cruel curve of his lips, he said, "You promised never to harm me, Empress. Know that you'll have to kill me before I would ever let you go."

As he strode out the door, I said, "And know that you'll have to put that cilice on me to keep me prisoner again."

Alone, I called for Matthew.

—*Empress lived today.*—

Was there doubt on that score?

—*A battle that fraught. So many tree limbs. Eddies.*—

His way of saying he couldn't always see the thousands of ways a fate could unfold. *You still sound upset, Matthew.* Confused. Too much so? *I need to talk to Jack. If I leave this place, can you get me back to you?*

—*The Fool guides your way. . . .*—

45

Lark was asleep in her new room, looking so young, with her mammal sleep pile dozing in the bed all around her.

Two days ago, the medic had given her an air cast for her broken forearm, another for her snapped ankle, and a sling for her busted collarbone. Then he'd confined her to bed rest.

The wolves healed apace with her, presently laid out in front of the room's fireplace. Since Cyclops couldn't yet manage the stairs, he remained down here with his pack. Her on-the-mend falcon nested in a nearby laundry basket.

I was worried about leaving Lark behind when I departed. Somehow that little punk had become my friend.

Good, bad, good.

Weren't we all? Jack, me, Aric.

He'd been avoiding me, as if it pained him to look at me. He didn't even share meals with me. Despite my driving need to talk to Jack, I pined for Aric.

On my way back from yesterday's visit with Lark, I'd run into him.

"How does Fauna fare?"

"She's getting better."

With a nod, he'd turned to walk away.

"That's it?" I'd called. "How much longer are we going to do this? We have to talk about what happened."

With a harsh laugh, he'd turned to me. "It's very simple. I want you, you want another, and I'm owed a wife." Struggling to regain his composure, he said in a rougher voice, "If our situation were reversed, you would never let me go either."

I'd fallen silent, unable to deny that. Then I'd stared after him as he left me.

The strain in the manor was almost worse than when Ogen had been jonesing for offerings. Aric's thoughts must be in utter turmoil, because his training had intensified more than ever before. The last time he'd been like this, I'd felt like I was watching a berserker. Now?

A bomb sequence ticking down.

—*Empress!*— Matthew called.

I'm here. I pulled Lark's comforter up to her chin,

then crossed to the fireplace to add a log for her and the animals. The temperatures continued to drop, the winds whipping. My turret would sway in the worst of them. *But now's not a good time, Matthew. Have a lot on my mind.* Too much, and most of it centered on Aric.

—Please, Empress! PLEASE!—

I stilled at his panicked tone. *What is it?*

—They've taken him. Set a trap. Can't see his future! Didn't know. They have him.—

Slow down. Who has who?

—Duke and Duchess Most Perverse. JACK.—

My heart thudded with dread. The Lovers had Jack? A fate worse than Death.

—Cajun set traps against the army. Vincent was out scouting a new encampment, surprised him. Violet will join her brother. Once the Lovers reunite, Jack will be . . . hurt.—

How long do I have?

—Before they kill him, or before they break him beyond repair?—

I tasted vomit in my mouth. *Can I reach him in time?!*

—They camp within days of Death's.—

Anything could delay me. Storms, militia, Bagmen. *What about Selena? Can we send her in?*

—She risked her life for him. Left for dead. Finn too.—

Send another Arcana to save him, promise anything!
I will give ANYTHING!

—The Tower pledged his alliance to Empress. Rescue
your mortal if you bring him Death's head.—

What? Joules will free Jack, like a mercenary?

—Mercenary Tower!—

I'm not going to pay what he wants. Try to negotiate
something else. Anything except that! I'll let you know
what I plan.

—Hurry, Empress!—

I wanted to think about this coolly, rationally. But
fear for Jack had me shaking.

I stumbled down the stairs toward Aric's rooms. As
far as I could see, fate had left me two paths. Ask for
Aric's help, or . . . the impossible.

Why would Death ever help the boy who'd made
love to his wife? I had no hope of getting him to assist
me, but I had to try.

Without knocking, I slipped into his study. I found
him lost in thought, lying on the couch. He was shirtless, wearing only low-slung leather pants. Staring at the
ceiling, he had one arm behind his head, using his free
hand to run his fingers over his chest. He traced different runes, as if he'd memorized their exact placement.

What was he thinking about as he touched those
shapes?

"Aric, I need to speak with you."

He rose with his unnatural speed, striding to me. "What's happened?" He pinched my chin, turning my face side to side. "Why are you so pale?"

Trying for a steady tone, I said, "Jack has been captured by the Lovers."

He dropped his hand. "Then right now he's wishing I'd ended him in the mine."

Struggling not to cry, I said, "I need your help to free him."

"Take on an army for him? And why would I do that? I hate him more than I've ever hated anyone. Even you." He turned away, heading straight for the vodka. He poured but didn't drink. "Accept this: your mortal is doomed."

"Please, Aric. I'm begging you!"

He whirled around, fury in his expression. "You refused—twice—to beg me for your own life, but you'd beg for his?"

I whispered, "Yes."

With a calculating gleam in his eyes, he said, "This isn't an impossible task you ask of me. I could call in ancient favors, contact old allies. They could be here in mere hours. We'd ride out as one."

"T-truly?"

"On one condition: you'll become my wife in truth, mine in every way. Beginning tonight. Comply, and I'll take on an army for you."

My lips parted with shock. "How can you do this to me?"

"Deveaux is lost to you in one way or another. He'll either be slaughtered by the Lovers—or saved by *my* female, by her sacrifice." He offered his hand. "Come with me, and begin this."

"Don't, Aric! Don't destroy what I do feel for you."

"I'll take"—he seized my hand, yanking me close—"what I can get."

Despite myself, I shivered from the contact, from his husky voice.

His hold on me was firm, proprietary. Because he believed I was about to become his. The red witch in me whispered, *Death thinks he has you at his mercy. But the Empress doesn't get collared or caged—or con*trolled. *Take his head and pay the Tower.*

Shut up! "Please, Aric. I'll grow to hate you for this. I don't want to feel that way about you. Never again. Don't force me to do this."

"Force?" Unmoved, he led me toward his bedroom. "I'm not forcing you to do anything. Just as you can't force me to save your lover's life. We each make sacrifices to get what we want."

With my heart pounding, I crossed the threshold into his dark world. Black walls, black ceiling, black night beyond his windows. Yet outside I thought I saw . . . a single fluttering snowflake.

Like a sign.

"Come, *sievā*. I'll wait no longer."

As Death led me to his bed, to the promise of pleasure, I felt the rising heat of desire—and of . . .

Battle.

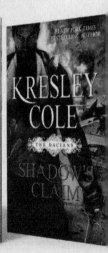